SHADOWS
— of —
Nyn'Dira

Also by H.C. Newell

FALLEN LIGHT

MAIN SERIES

Curse of the Fallen
The Forbidden Realms
Shadows of Nyn'Dira
A Storm of Sorrows*
The Child of Skye*
Ashes of the Fallen*

ADDITIONAL SHORT STORIES

The Banished
The Brave*
The Broken*

*Forthcoming

H. C. NEWELL

SHADOWS *of* NYN'DIRA

Book three in the Fallen Light series
To be read *after* The Forbidden Realms

Laeroth

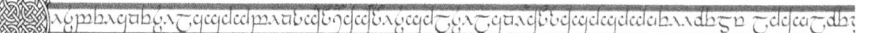

Iziazan

Nik'va Erasiin

Trelan Leirin

Tildra'dira

Peaks of Draak

Aragoth

Fru'skogmir

Sandir

Trelan Aeniwyn

Zaos

Reinwald Gorge

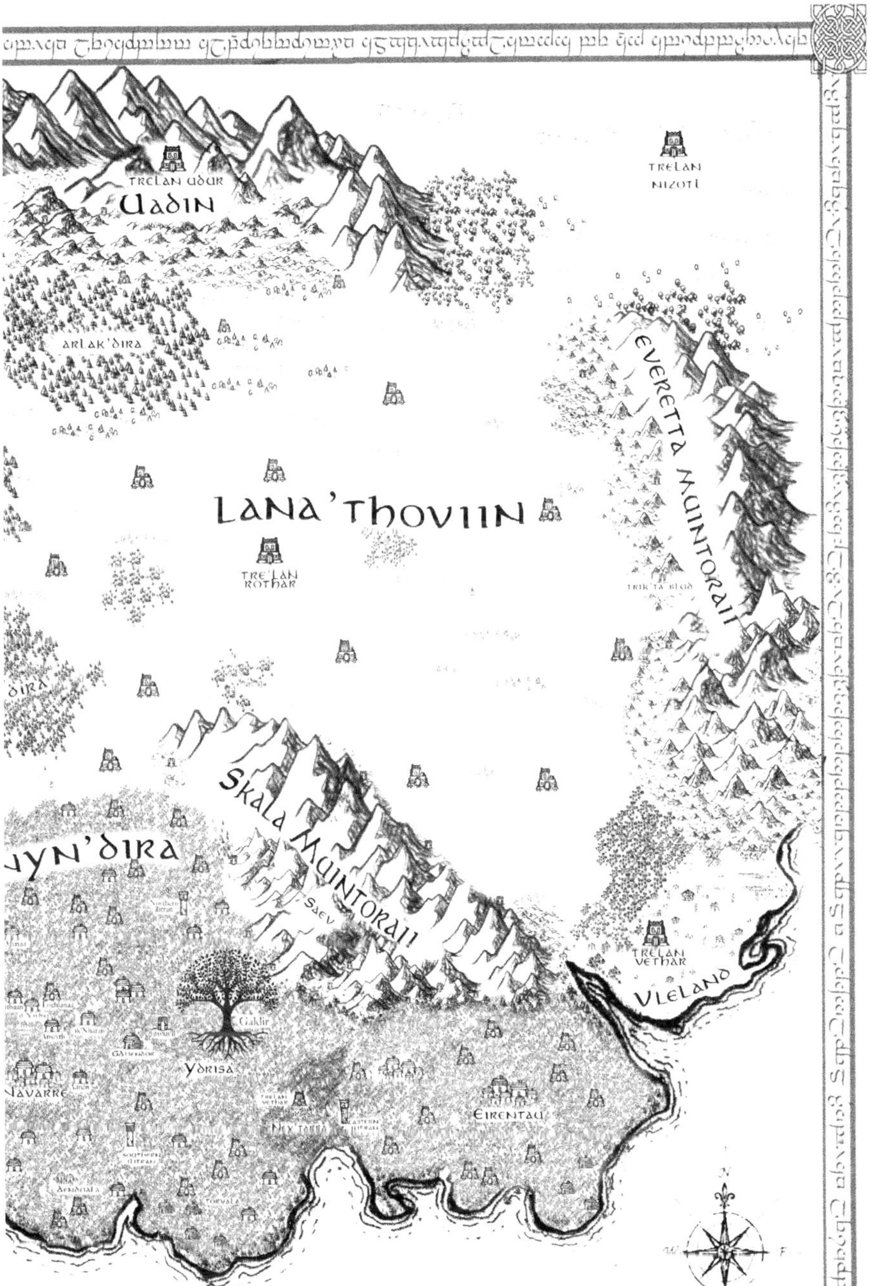

TRELAN UDUR
UADIN
TRELAN
NIZOTL
ARLAK'DIRA
EVERETTA MUINTORAII
LANA'THOVIIN
TRE'LAN
ROTHAR
SKALA MUINTORAII
SAEV
YN'DIRA
DIRA
TRELAN
VETHAR
VLELAND
YDRISA
NAVARRE
EIRENTAU

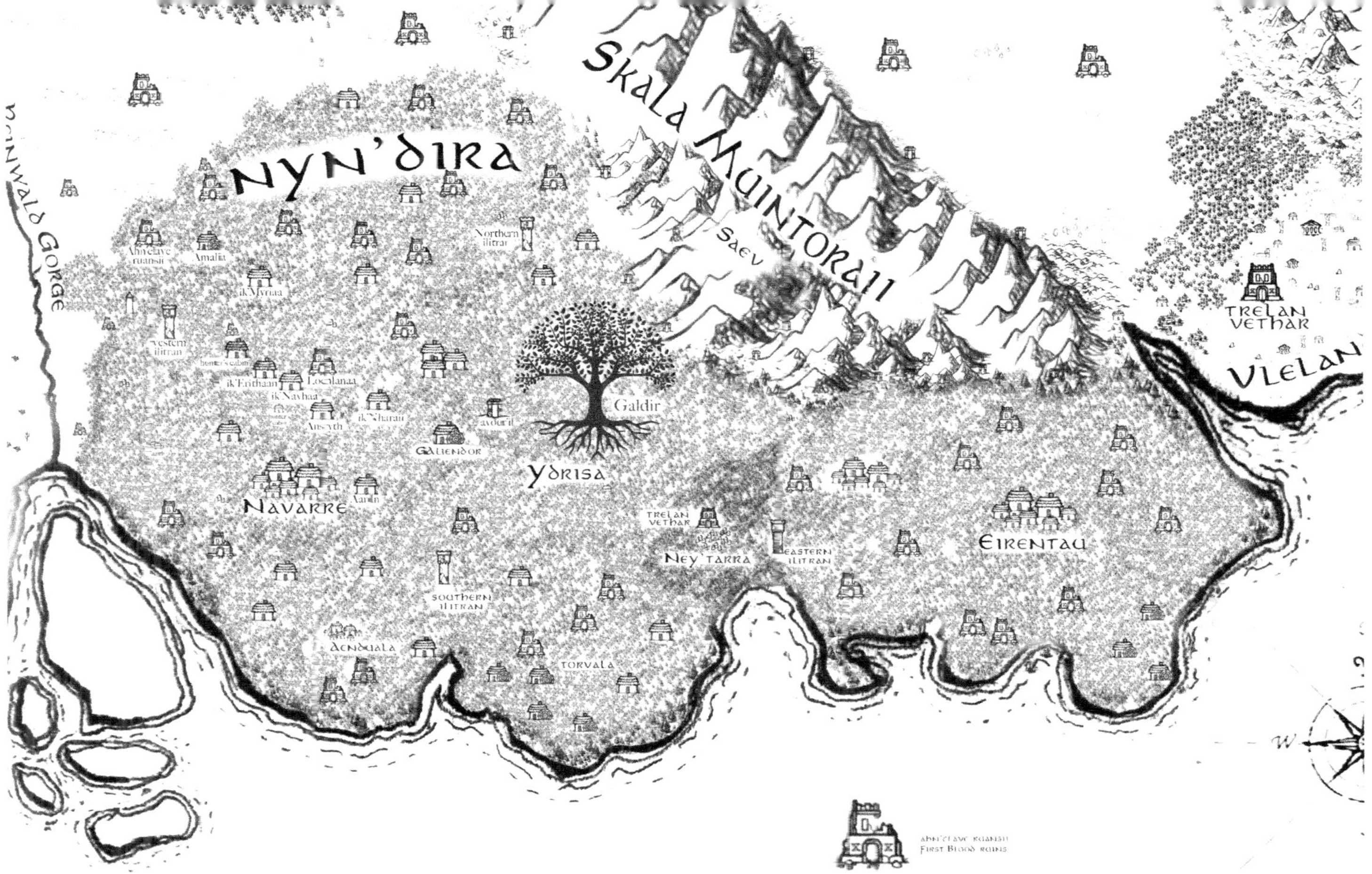
Skala Muintorah
Saev
Nyn'dira
Vlelan
Trelan Vethar
Northern ilitran
Amalia
ik'Myriaa
Western ilitran
ik'Erithaan
ik'Navhaa
Locilanaa
ik'Nharan
Anscyth
avourl
Galiendor
Galdir
Ydrisa
Navarre
Aarin
Trelan Vethar
Ney'tarra
Eastern ilitran
Eirentau
Southern ilitran
Acnduala
Torvala
Rainwald Gorge
ahn'clave ruansh
First Blood ruins

Shadows of Nyn'Dira
Copyright © 2023 by H.C. Newell

All rights reserved. Printed in the United States of America. No part of this book may be used or reproduced in any manner whatsoever without written permission except in the case of brief quotations embodied in critical articles or reviews.

This book is a work of fiction. Names, characters, businesses, organizations, places, events and incidents either are the product of the author's imagination or are used fictitiously. Any resemblance to actual persons, living or dead, events, or locales is entirely coincidental.

> For information contact:
> info@hcnewell.com
>
> Cover design: Thea Magerand
> Map design: H.C. Newell
> Art designs: H.C. Newell
> Editing: Horrorsmith Editing

ISBN: 9798857900055

First Edition: September 2023

10 9 8 7 6 5 4 3 2 1

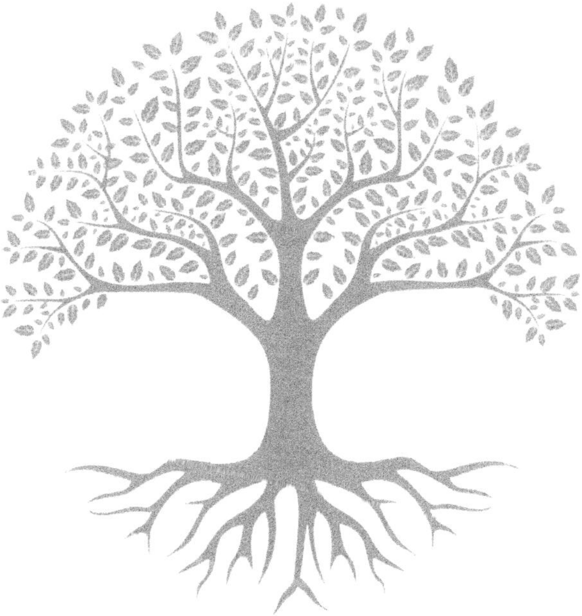

A special thank you to the following people who have made this journey possible:

My alpha and beta readers:
Ann, Dee, Kelly, Katie, Kris, Michelle, Amalia, Krina, Jas, Jules, Beki, and Cristian (who didn't actually read it, but he made me add his name. The nerve.)

Thank you also to the following for helping take my writing career to the next level:
Ross, Max, Kris, Jord, Boe, Sadir, Esmay, Rosalyne, Indie Fantasy Fund, John and Grimdark Magazine, Escapist Book Co,
The Fantasy Review

For Ann
I know you don't want the credit, but I like annoying you.
Your endless help has been so invaluable.
Thank you for not giving up on me and my noisiness.

Note from the Author

Thank you for making it this far into my series. You have no idea what it means to me.

For further immersion, please visit hcnewell.com for an interactive map, downloadable guides, and more information about the world.

I've always considered Curse and Realms to be more like "prequels" meant to acquaint you with the world, the characters, and the conflicting goals of Nerana and Aélla. As such, I like to consider Shadows the unofficial start to the story, with a slower pace, more character and world depth, and more downtime between fights for a deeper, richer reading experience.

Along with the personae dramatis, I have created an evaesh translation guide that you will find at the end of the book. Do not confuse this with the glossary, which defines all words or phrases and is to be read *after* completion of the novel.

You may download the translation guide at the website mentioned above. This is meant to help you understand the world and language of the evae as you dive into their lands and immerse yourself into the enchanting forests of Nyn'Dira.

As always, I hope you enjoy the journey.

This is only the beginning.

Your friend,
H.C.

Contents

Prologue	*Aragoth*	1
Chapter One	*Stranger in the Wood*	4
Chapter Two	*Of lies and men*	11
Chapter Three	*The Chiming of Bells*	21
Chapter Four	*Creature of the Night*	29
Chapter Five	*The Hills of Aardn*	41
Chapter Six	*The Eirean*	50
Chapter Seven	*Fade to Black*	57
Chapter Eight	*Mercy and Vengeance*	66
Chapter Nine	*A Long Rest*	78
Chapter Ten	*The Way of Fate*	87
Chapter Eleven	*The Afahél*	94
Chapter Twelve	*Haunted*	99
Chapter Thirteen	*Hunted*	107
Chapter Fourteen	*The Ilitran*	116
Chapter Fifteen	*Wayfarers and Wolves*	124
Chapter Sixteen	*Blood of the Lanathess*	134
Chapter Seventeen	*Forgiveness*	142
Chapter Eighteen	*Lost*	148
Chapter Nineteen	*The Path of Salvation*	159
Chapter Twenty	*Reflections of Pain*	169

Chapter Twenty-One	*Ik'Erithaan*	183
Chapter Twenty-Two	*Free Us*	193
Chapter Twenty-Three	*Tek'Brenavath*	208
Chapter Twenty-Four	*Trials of War*	222
Chapter Twenty-Five	*The Rightful Respite*	231
Chapter Twenty-Six	*Taken*	246
Chapter Twenty-Seven	*A Fleeting Dream*	255
Chapter Twenty-Eight	*Vale of Shadows*	265
Chapter Twenty-Nine	*Light of the Seven*	279
Chapter Thirty	*Home*	289
Chapter Thirty-One	*Fractured Faith*	301
Chapter Thirty-Two	*Of Axe and Flame*	312
Chapter Thirty-Three	*A Father's Love*	323
Chapter Thirty-Four	*Purpose and Prayers*	334
Chapter Thirty-Five	*Galiendör*	343
Chapter Thirty-Six	*All Shall Fade*	358
Chapter Thirty-Seven	*Echo in the Void*	369
Chapter Thirty-Eight	*First Breath*	381
Chapter Thirty-Nine	*Blood and Fear*	389
Chapter Forty	*Desperation*	401
Chapter Forty-One	*Unforgiven*	409
Chapter Forty-Two	*Last Breath*	420
Chapter Forty-Three	*Fading Light*	430
Chapter Forty-Four	*Survival*	447
Chapter Forty-Five	*A Shift of Fate*	457
Chapter Forty-Six	*The Power of Rage*	465
Epilogue	*The Drums of War*	474

SHADOWS of NYN'DIRA
PRONUNCIATION GUIDE

Broken Order Brotherhood
Nerana (Neer) – NEER-ahna
Y'ven – YEV-in
Druindarvenia (Dru) – DROO
Reiman – RIY-man
Gilbrich – Gill-brick
Coryn – COR-in
Morganis (Mor) – MOR-gone-iss

Evae
Aélla – AYLA
Avelloch – AV-uh-LOCK
Klaud – Cloud
Thallon – TALON
Thurandír – THUR-an-deer
Elidyr – EL-ah-deer
Aen'mysvaral – ANE-miss-verr-ALL
N'iossea – NEE-oh-SAY
Nasir – Nah-SEER
Ithronél – EE-thro-nell

Order of Saro
Beinon – BAY-nin
Eiden – EE-den
Nizotl – Nih-ZOLT
Rothar – ROW-THAR

SHADOWS of NYN'DIRA
PRONUNCIATION GUIDE

Races
Dreled – DREHL-ed
Evae – EE-vay
Klaet'il – klee-uh-TIL
Rhyl – RILL
Ydris – EE-driss
E'liaa – EE-lee-ah

Territories and Place
Navarre – Nah-vair
Aardn – ARR-din
Ik'Nharaii – EEK-nah-riy
Ik'Navhaa – EEK-nah-vah
Galdir – GALL-deer

Evaesh Words or Phrases
Kanavin – KAHN-ah-veen
Evaesh – Ay-vish
Lanathess – LAHN-ah-THESS
Drimil – DREM-EL
Brenavae – BREE-nah-VAY
Senavae – SEE-nah-VAY
Travaran – TRAV-are-ahn
Naik'avel – NYE-kah-vell
Kila – kee-lah
Stia'dyr – stee-ah-deer

DRAMATIS PERSONAE

Guardians of Drimil'Rothar

Aélla Líadrinel	Drimil'Rothar
Nerana Leithor	Sorceress
Avelloch Líadrinel	Shadow master
Klaud Alwinör	Eólin warrior
Thallon Galadúr	Scholar
Y'ven Úmragul	Warrior
Druindarvenia	Fire mage

The Order of Saro

High Priest Beinon	High Priest of the Order
The Child of Skye	Pseudonym for Nerana Leithor
Eiden	Priest of the Old Ways, former
Ealdir	Priest of Kirena, former

The Broken Order Brotherhood

Reiman Leithor	Founding member, active leader
Nerana Leithor	Adopted daughter of Reiman, sorceress
Gilbrich Willby	Advisor
Coryn Wainwright	Apothecary
Morganis Euri	Spymaster
Y'ven Úmragul	Warrior
Druindarvenia	Warrior
Wallace Marge	Warrior
Loryk Vaughan	Emissary, former

Forest races and clans

Evae	Humanoid race
Klaet'il	Evaesh clan
Rhyl	Evaesh clan
Saevrala	Evaesh clan
Ydris	Half evae-half deer race
Gorn	Goblin-like race

Eirean Council

Glisseríel Jaravel	Clan Rhyl
Falavar Tahilyth	Clan Rhyl
Naisannis Tormaris	Clan Klaet'il
Aelwyn Sehefil	Clean Saevrala
Calasiem'Nym	Ydris
Rahd'Nuitharis	Gorn
Torvála	Keeper of Aardn

Evaesh titles or factions

Eirean	High ranking official of any race or clan
Avel	Esteemed warriors of Clan Rhyl
Tóavel	Esteemed warriors of Clan Klaet'il
E'liaa	Half-human half-evae race
Stia'dyr	Evae with the ability to see through the eyes of an animal
Drimil	Magic user, typically with the power of all the magical realms
Eólin	Magic user with the power of one magical realm
Nes'seil	Healer
First Blood	Evaesh race who vanished long ago

Clan Rhyl

Glisseríel Jaravel	Eirean leader
Falavar Tahilyth	Eirean leader
Klaud Alwinör	Eirean advisor
Torvála	Keeper of Aardn
Elidyr Galadúr	Commanding Officer
N'iossea Galadúr	Avel warrior, former
Thallon Galadúr	Scholar of the First Blood
Thurandír Yarris	Bow master
Évara Ryy	Swordsman
Aegrandir Líadrinel	Commanding Officer, former
Avelloch Líadrinel	Exiled
Aélla Líadrinel	Drimil'Rothar
Elias Cain	E'liaan villager
Morganis Cain	E'liaan villager, former
Altvára	Companion
Blaid	Companion

Clan Klaet'il

Naisannis Tormaris	Eirean leader
The Nasir	Prominent figure
Ithronél Eólin	Elemental sorceress
lat'Runa	Warrior

Ydris

Lady Calasiem	Eirean leader
Maeve'Nym	Daughter of Calasiem
T'kyrus	Commanding officer

Others

Elashor Eólin	Necro sorcerer
Aen'mysvaral	Sitria of Elidyr Galadúr
The Zaeril	Sitria of unknown warrior
Galdir	Largest Ko'ehlaeu'at tree

Summary of Book Two

Six months after Loryk's death, Nerana is on her way to the colleges of Styyr to continue her training with the scholars. Her travels carry her through Ravinshire, where she plans to gift Loryk's family with his book of poems and stories.

She encounters a Priest who has sentenced an innocent family to death, and plunges her sword through his chest, saving them. In her attempt to flee, she winds up in the desert wastelands of Aragoth, where she meets a member of the Brotherhood, Y'ven, who is escorting another sorceress through the treacherous lands.

Neer joins in on this journey, choosing to follow in the path of fate as she was given a prophecy by a Divine in Mange (book one) who told her to seek out *four trials* in order to gain the strength to defeat High Priest Beinon.

Their journey through the desert sees them chased by a Hunter named Thorne, who has been contracted by the Order of Saro. In addition to Thorne, the Nasir has entered the desert in search of a powerful weapon called the *clavia muinsii*—a ring that can turn any living being into a creature of darkness.

Thallon, an evaesh scholar and long-time friend of Drimil'Rothar, is also in the desert searching for this ring, which he hopes to find before the Nasir can locate it. Neer and Aélla find him chained to the ground in one of the many vaxros prison graveyards and save him. He joins the crew soon after, knowing he can't survive on his own.

In their efforts to enter the Realm of Elements, which will grant them the full capabilities and strength of their elemental energy, Aélla and Neer must enter each of the hidden elemental realms to gain their energies and unlock the doors of the final Realm of Elements.

Aélla enters the Realm of Wind and the Realm of Water. Neer enters the Realm of Fire and Realm of Rock. During her time in the realm of fire, she is given the *clavia muinsii* by a vision of herself. Thallon soon takes it, claiming its too dangerous for anyone else to wield.

During her time in the Realm of Fire, Neer must also make a life-changing sacrifice. In order to save herself from the realm and obtain the elemental energy, she relinquishes the last memories of her father, Zeke Vindagraav. This, in turn, causes her to be entirely absent of his existence.

Throughout their journey, they encounter Reiman, who has been in the desert searching for his daughter, Neer. He knew that her magic had taken her to the desert, and eventually joins them on their quest.

Once all four elements have been collected from each of their hidden realms, Aélla returns to Elandorr with the others. She and Neer enter the Realm of Elements. While Aélla is taken to a peaceful place of meditation, Neer must sacrifice something she loves that's worth more than gold. She struggles over which item to let go of: Loryk's note or Avelloch's sword. She eventually makes her choice and is released from the realm.

Outside, Thorne ambushes the group. He strikes Thallon through the shoulder with a bolt, and Reiman heals him with a painful ointment called travaran. This causes Thallon to pass out for the duration of the battle.

The Nasir and Klaet'il soon arrive, and a large-scale battle takes place. The Nasir steps through Aélla's magical barrier, proving that magic holds no force against him, and he steps on Thallon's throat. He steals the ring and uses it to turn Thorne into a gaelthral.

Aélla is thrust against the wall by Ithronél, cracking her ribs. Y'ven is lying on the ground, unconscious with several bleeding wounds to his chest and abdomen.

Reiman retrieves a transporting stone and tells Neer to flee with the others. While he sees himself out of the desert, Neer rejoins with the others as the gaelthral attacks. Aélla wraps Thallon in her arms and tells Neer to go to the forest and find her brother, Avelloch, and then she vanishes.

As the gaelthral closes in, Neer pulls Y'ven and Dru into her arms, and they disappear.

WANTED

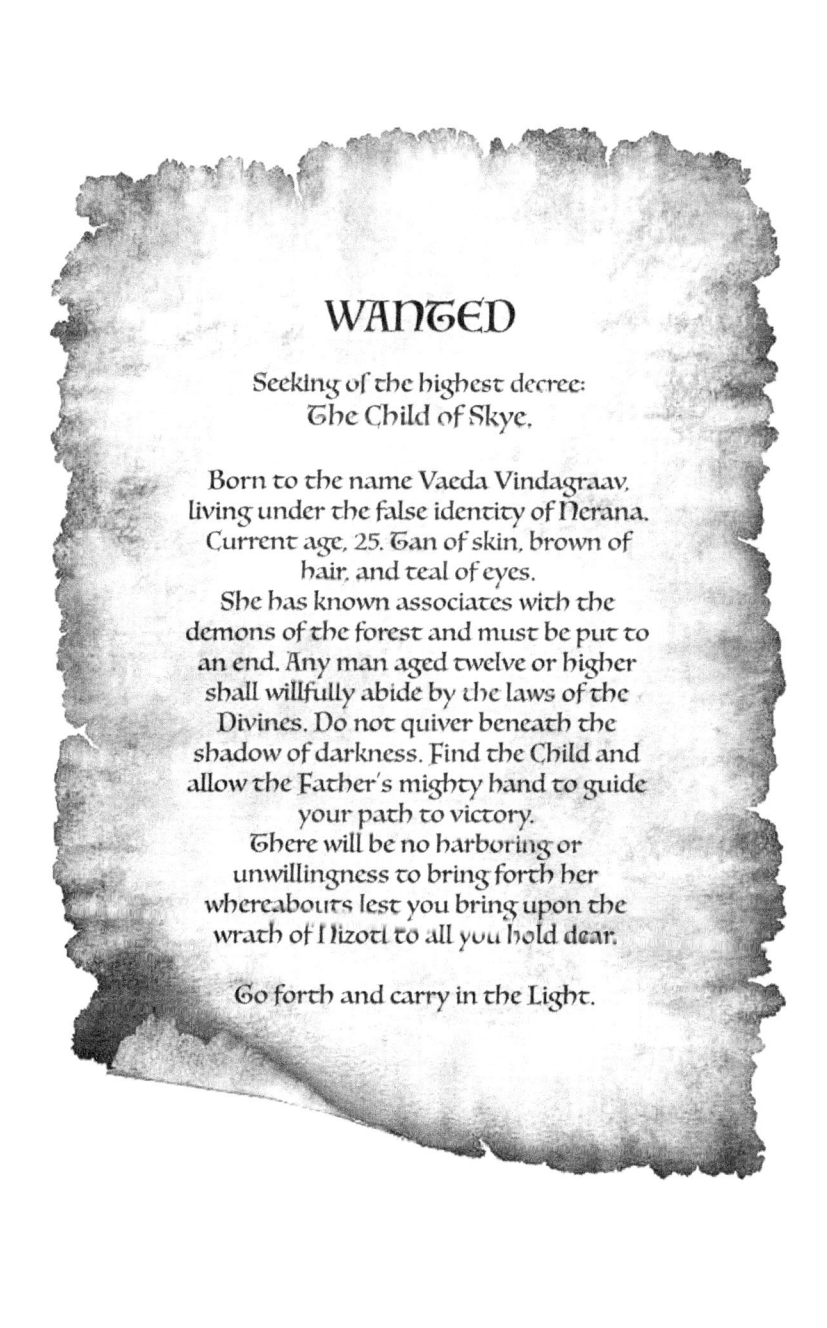

Seeking of the highest decree:
The Child of Skye.

Born to the name Vaeda Vindagraav, living under the false identity of Nerana. Current age, 25. Tan of skin, brown of hair, and teal of eyes.
She has known associates with the demons of the forest and must be put to an end. Any man aged twelve or higher shall willfully abide by the laws of the Divines. Do not quiver beneath the shadow of darkness. Find the Child and allow the Father's mighty hand to guide your path to victory.
There will be no harboring or unwillingness to bring forth her whereabouts lest you bring upon the wrath of Hizoti to all you hold dear.

Go forth and carry in the Light.

Prologue

Path of Vengeance
Temple of Elandorr

"Do not fear the night, for the darkest of creatures rise with the sun."

- Udur, *The Book of Wisdom and Verity*

MEN IN CHAINS PISSED THEMSELVES before the blade struck their throats.

Blood gurgled from their lips, draining down their necks and washing them in red. Vengeful eyes cast hatred upon their leader. A man they trusted, who once stood for something far greater, now slayed his own men.

Dust billowed from the arid desert ground when they collapsed to the dirt. Pools of crimson spilled over rocks, carrying away from their lifeless bodies. A dagger, coated in fresh blood, was wiped clean on a victim's shoulder and then shoved into its scabbard.

The man stared down at the warriors he'd slain, moonlight veiling his face. Emotionless, he turned away, gazing at the carnage of his attack. Bodies lay amidst the desert, mutilated and torn. Flesh had been shredded, exposing bones and pulsing organs waiting to die. Light blue eyes flashed to a woman crawling across the ground. Her choked groans filled the empty air.

There were no marks on her body other than the deep gash that opened her calf. Dancing aurora shimmered from above, casting against a bone hiding beneath layers of her torn muscle and flesh. She could survive, and there was a *nes'seil* ready to aid her. But as the healer stepped forward, the man in charge raised his hand, and the nes'seil halted.

The injured woman turned to her leader, her scowled face filthy and bruised. He glanced at Ithronél, who stood by his side. Her thin lips pressed into a tight line, and she gave a stiff nod. A thick bandage wrapped her left hand—a wound from the battle they had faced. An injury that would leave lasting effects to her abilities, but none she couldn't overcome. She was strong, a true warrior.

The crawling woman who whimpered in the dirt shed no tears, not as her blood left a trail of red across the cold desert floor. But she was weak, unable to withstand the agony of war, and thus, she was no longer needed. Weakness of any kind must be snuffed out. That was their way.

The leader stood tall with pride, watching Ithronél hold an open palm ignited with flames above the injured woman. A wave of heat engulfed the woman in fire, panic forever engrained on her face.

Within an instant, it was over.

There was no scream. Her body had been incinerated to a pile of ash before she could muster a sound. Ithronél stepped back to her leader's side and crossed her arms. Together, they surveyed the destruction before them. Blood painted the ancient courtyard in patterns of red. Deep claw marks had been scratched into the surface of the stairs leading up to the bodies lying at the threshold of Elandorr.

"We failed," Ithronél said, fury sliding from her tongue.

"No," the man replied, his cold eyes scanning the scene before them.

Several soldiers stood by their winged beasts, awaiting orders. The gaelthral roared, catching their attention as it paced at the top of the stairs, waiting. But it couldn't act without proper command.

The man absently twisted the ring between his fingers, relishing in its power.

"They got away," Ithronél argued.

He turned to her with a flash of deadly anger. Wordlessly, she cowered, though it was hardly noticeable.

Turning away, he retrieved a *n'aeth* from his cloak. The transporting stone was smooth against his calloused fingers. "They'll be in the forest," he said.

Her eyes flicked to the stone, and she timidly asked, "What about the gaelthral?"

Staring at Thorne's new form, he said, "Set it loose in the forest."

She stiffened. "What about us? What is *our* goal?"

Cunning eyes shifted to hers, and as the stone began to glow, ready to transport him away, he said, "To wage war."

Chapter One

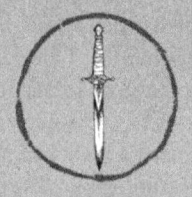

Stranger in the Wood
Nerana

"Take comfort in the divinity and grace of the one true Father and know that his watchful hands will guide you to the path of serenity and peace."

— Rotharion, *the Book of Light*

The Gods have no place here.

Deep in the forest, beneath the swaying limbs and streams of moonlight, Neer lay alone, broken and defeated. Her skin was covered in bruises and dried blood, and her hair was singed from her time beneath the surface, fighting against flame and terror. Burned holes and tears in her clothes exposed the deep wounds across her body that leaked pus and blood.

Shadows swayed across her body as branches rustled above, shrouding the faint purple shimmer of the moons. Glowing plants kept the underbrush illuminated in colors of orange, pink, green, and blue. Thick vines clung to tree trunks, winding like serpents into the limbs.

Neer was immobile, unable to fully breathe from the agony tethering her to the soil. The teleportation had left her depleted, and her spirit was drained.

Her mind went to Reiman and how she had left him in the desert. Surely, the transporting stone had allowed him to flee to safety. But she couldn't push away the possibility that maybe it hadn't. Then she thought of the great beast

SHADOWS OF NYN'DIRA

Thorne had been transformed into. The darkness and power needed to create such a monster...

She closed her tired eyes. Too exhausted to think. Too exhausted to feel. All she wanted was to rest. To drift into a never-ending slumber and embrace the peace of nothingness. It was so close. Too close. She could feel the icy sting of death lulling her to sleep.

Moonlight crept across the forest as she lay alone, willing that darkness to pull her asunder, wishing for the Divines to grant her one last request. But it never came. Her breathing never halted. Her mind never stopped, and she knew death was far from reach.

With a slow exhale, she opened her eyes. Her arms buckled and ribs ached when she sat up, observing her surroundings through half-opened eyes.

The forest was beautiful. Storytellers and scribes could never hold a candle to the breathtaking lands of Nyn'Dira. Her shoulders slumped forward, and eyes closed.

She had made it.

Somehow—beyond her own understanding—fate had led her here. To the place she had meant to go. Her previous endeavors with long-range teleportation had proven her inexperience, bringing her far from her intended destinations. Aside from the forest, Aragoth was the most recent and dangerous place her magic had taken her.

She sat straighter and winced at the pain in her back. Her face was tight with blood, and she grazed her dirty fingers over the painful healing scar across her cheek. Searching the area, she looked for any signs of Y'ven or Dru, and her heart sank when she found she was alone.

"Y'ven—"

Her cracked voice faded into a deep, painful cough. She leaned forward, clutching her chest and struggling to calm the itch in her throat. Heat rose in her face, and she slowed her breathing. She reached for her canteen but found herself without her belongings. They had been left at the campfire during the ambush.

But she didn't care about her dry throat or missing items. Not when Y'ven and Dru were out there, injured and alone. They wouldn't survive in the darkness of the forest. She had to find them.

Pain coursed through her bones, and Neer withheld a shriek as she pushed herself up and rose to her feet. Her weak legs trembled, and she stumbled into a tree. Landing hard against the trunk, she braced herself with her arms, breathing heavily. Her teal eyes scanned the forest. Not a soul was in sight. But she knew this place was dangerous. Avelloch had warned her of it. Should the evae find her, they would kill her, and with weakened magic and no supplies, she would surely see her end.

And she couldn't allow that to happen. Not until she knew the others were safe. She had to keep going for them.

Her feet dragged across the ground as she stalked through the desolate trees. Deep breaths escaped her lungs, and her eyes struggled to stay open. Neer searched the surrounding area, finding not a drop of blood or impression in the grass that could lead to their whereabouts.

She closed her eyes, dreading the worst. When she had teleported to Vleland, before her journey to the Trials of Blood, Loryk and Gil wound up miles away from where she had appeared. Gil's severed arm had hung from his shoulder by thin strands of muscle and flesh. She couldn't imagine the horrors Y'ven or Dru might have faced at the hands of her power.

Her mind rattled as she shook her head, ridding herself of the horrific thoughts. They were here. They had survived. Neer knew it. She had to believe they were alive.

Wandering further through the darkness, her legs grew weaker with every step, and she collapsed to the ground. On her hands and knees, she trembled with agony and regret. Tears burned her eyes, and her throat tightened.

When a light whisper sang through the air, Neer lifted her head, searching for the noise. Her eyes settled on the soft flicker of firelight drifting through the shadows. Slowly, she stood and trailed toward its luminance.

She crossed her arms over her chest. Sweat dripped from her face, and chills covered her body. The night was mild, yet she was cold. Freezing, as illness crept its way through her, burning her forehead and setting a tremor to her limbs.

With every step, the song became clearer, and she found they weren't evaesh words that hummed a soft melody—they were human. A beautiful, human voice rung elegantly through the silence, like a ghost in the night. Neer swallowed through a dry throat, fearing who could be out there. Wondering why a human would have found himself in the forbidden evaesh woodlands.

"I sing my praise, my gods o' to thee
How loved you are, how loved you are...
I sing my praise, my gods o' to thee
How loved you are, how loved you are..."

Neer stepped closer, her dragging feet creating a low shuffle in the grass. The man's head shot up, and he cautiously reached for the dagger on his belt, peering through the darkness.

"I'm not your enemy!" he called. His accent was smooth and calm, as if he had been trained to speak in such a way. "I come with good intent!"

Neer stopped. Tucked into the shadows, she was hidden from view, watching the man curiously, realizing that his words weren't spoken in their native tongue. They were spoken in evaesh.

Perfect, unbroken evaesh.

"I know you're out there!" the man called, with not a quiver of fear or anger to his perfectly trained tenor. "I have stew. Come join me if you'd like."

Neer stared at the small black cauldron hanging above the fire. Her stomach grumbled, and she clutched it with weak arms, hoping to muffle its noise. The man merely smiled and then turned back to his meal. She didn't want to approach him. Didn't want to put herself in that kind of danger. But she wouldn't make it far on her own. She could either risk dying by this stranger's hands or by the infections coursing through her opened wounds.

Her stomach ached when the aroma of perfectly seasoned venison stew brushed past in the slight breeze. She inhaled its scent and followed in its path.

Neer approached the man, who was no older than forty, with short brown hair and bright blue eyes. He turned to her with a pleasant smile, but his grin faded when he took in her battered appearance. She hadn't known entirely what she looked like, but she knew from his expression it wasn't good.

His brows pulled together, and his jaw dropped. "Are you…Are you all right?"

Neer's eyes flashed to the cauldron of bubbling brown stew. The man rose to his feet and guided her carefully to an empty space by the fire.

"Come, come," he said, ushering her to the grass. "Sit. There you go."

He dug through his belongings before wrapping a thick cloak around her shoulders. Neer curled into the soft fur, ignoring his intent, concerned stare. Without speaking, he took his place across the fire, collected an empty bowl from his belongings, and filled it with steaming stew.

Neer quickly accepted the meal when he passed it to her. Its warmth was intoxicating as she blew on every spoonful before taking a bite.

The man watched her curiously while she devoured her meal, but she purposefully avoided his gaze.

"By the Seven," he said, refilling his own bowl, "the Divines have surely blessed you tonight."

Neer turned away, still slurping her soup.

"What's your name, young one?"

The question was one she had expected, but still, she froze. His words were laced with poise and precision. He spoke too kindly—too *strategically*—to be any normal human. Neer could hear the guile in his voice. The hint of authority and influence. It had been spoken by the leaders of her country. By those who led the faithless into mass graves and conquered nations by the words of their tongues.

She licked her lips and inhaled a shallow breath. Still avoiding his gaze, she said, "Lynn."

It was better to use an alias, even out here in the forest. She never knew who could be watching, and if what Reiman had told her in the desert were true, then the humans had invaded, and they'd burn every village in her pursuit.

For a moment, this fact made her consider telling the truth, and revealing her identity, but she couldn't. Not yet. Reiman had warned her against such impulsiveness. She couldn't save everyone, and there were bigger goals in mind.

The man tapped his iron ladle against the edge of the cauldron before placing it onto a wooden plate by his side. He blew away the heat of his spoonful before eating another bite. "My name is Eiden. I have to say, I'm surprised to see a young human woman out here. We're pretty deep into the forest." He eyed her torn clothes and bloody injuries. "Gods be good, it's surprising you are alive at all. The Divines have certainly had their eyes on you."

Neer repressed the scoff threatening to escape her throat. Instead, she stared at her food, not speaking. Not wanting to give this man any reason to suspect she was anything but ordinary.

But he watched her for too long, inspecting her clothes, her cuts, and her singed hair.

"I came with the man I loved," she lied, realizing she needed an alibi. "He was from Ravinshire, in a village called Rhys."

The man nodded, seeming to believe her tale. "He let you come to the forest with the raiders?"

Anger struck her, and she nearly cut a glance at him. "He did not *let* me do anything," she said. "I make my own choices, and I chose to come here. To fight."

He smiled. "You're lucky the Divines saw to keep you alive. It was Rothar's gentle hand which guided you to me." She didn't speak, but he didn't seem to mind as he said, "I came here of my own choice too. I'm a priest, you see. But not a priest of the Order. No, I'm…I follow in the Old Ways."

"The Old Ways?" she asked, curious. "They've been outlawed for decades.°"

"Yes, but there are still few of us who are devoted enough to the Seven to seek their truth, no matter the consequences or obstacles of the Order."

Neer stared into her bowl, suddenly lost for appetite. "What are you doing out here?"

He wiped his lips with a white cloth and cleared his throat behind his half-clenched fist. "I'm here to do what everyone else is doing." His words were like ice, freezing her lungs and halting her breath as he said, "I'm looking for *you*."

˙ The Old Ways are a belief in the original teachings of the Order of Saro.

Before the reign of High Priest Beinon, who set forth the New Ways, the Order believed highly in the Circle of Seven, who are the seven divines of unity and peace that oversee and retain balance of the mortal plane.

Soon after his inauguration, the High Priest bestowed a system of belief that abolished one of the seven Divines and cast another as the purveyor of darkness and evil.

Chapter Two

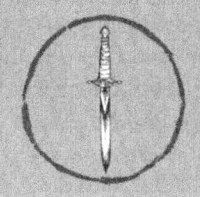

Of Lies and Men
Nerana

"Should untruth be told from a devoted man's tongue, take heed of his disservice to the gods and slice it from his jaws. Let the blood drain unto the flames and wash away his sin."

— Udur, *the Book of Wisdom and Verity*

A COLD SWEAT FORMED ACROSS Neer's temple, and she stared at her food, immobile. Unable to breathe or think under the shadow of his stare. His words weren't spoken with malice or contempt. They were soft. Curious, even, to be in the presence of the very soul he sought to find. A soul who would fetch a nice bounty should he return her to the Order.

"I don't know—"

He interrupted her lie with a lift of his palm. "Please," he said, his voice still displaying the calmness and comfort all priests were taught to carry. A voice that could move mountains and convert the hearts of the wicked.

The voice of a liar.

"I'm not here to hurt you," he continued, taking another bite of his meal. "The Divines have led me here. They've woven our paths to meet at this very moment. And do you know why?" She was silent, refusing to meet his gaze. "Because they want me to save you."

Neer exhaled a shaky breath.

"Have you heard of the story of Ateus? It's quite the tale, but one I'll keep short. Ateus was a man born of magical energy, much like you. Only, Ateus was considered a god because of this power—not a demon. No, Ateus is still revered in the legends as a fierce and noble patron of the saints. A descendant of Rothar and savior of our peoples.

"Some say he soared the skies with fearsome draak, laid waste to lands that sought slavery and oppression, and worked to bridge the divide separating man and elf. He was a hero who was loved by many."

"Ateus was evil," Neer stated, reciting the teachings of the Order. "He was mad with power and conquered civilizations in his thirst for control."

"So the Order has *made* you believe. History is always told in favor of the victor. It's something many scholars and priests are hesitant to admit, and Ateus was slain by those who considered him a false prophet. He was cast into the Realm of Darkness, where his soul will remain for eternity."

Neer gulped through a dry throat. She had never heard of the Realm of Darkness, but after witnessing the terrors of the elemental realm, she was certain whatever lay within its depths was unimaginable and full of pain.

"The Order has convinced the world that you are a descendant of Nizotl, just as they had convinced everyone the same of Ateus. They have dispatched every man, aged twelve and older, to Nyn'Dira. Your posters are nailed to every tree they can get their hands on. If the humans find you…well, they'll inject you with their serums and keep you as indisposed as possible. And the elves"—he exhaled a scoffed laugh—"they'll grind your bones to dust and leather your flesh into armor."

Neer's stomach churned. She set the bowl aside and wrapped further into the cloak. "The elves haven't done so much to you," she challenged, still avoiding eye contact. Still speaking too weakly to pose any real threat.

"The Divines' grace keeps me alive. Just as it has kept *you* alive. Do you think yourself lucky to have survived for this long? Losing your family at such a young age—surviving on the streets and being found by the Brotherhood?"

SHADOWS OF NYN'DIRA

He paused, watching her expression, which never changed from its dreary, tired state. "Vethar[*] has big plans for you, young one. Plans that even the Order and High Priest cannot prevail."

"And what plan is that?" The venom in her tone was diluted by fatigue. It sounded more like genuine intrigue than a spiteful remark.

He smiled and pointed to the sky. "Only *they* know the answer to that."

Neer shook her head. "I'm not who you think I am."

He studied her for a moment and then softly nodded. "Being cautious will keep you alive. I admire that courage. But your falsities and fables are wasted on a poor wandering soul such as mine. I'm not here to turn you over to the Order or the elves. The Divines have other plans for me." He dug through his large travel sack, pulling out black books, worn leather strips, an extra pair of shoes, and several of Neer's wanted posters—crumbled and torn, as if they had been ripped from the trees and shoved into his pack. Finally, he retrieved a small vial of clear liquid and gently tossed it to the grass beside her. "Tears of Numera," he explained of the potion. "Enjoy the comforts of warmth and health. I'll be getting some rest."

She carefully took the potion, inspecting it to find it was the same elixir she had used in Mange, the one that healed her wounds and saved Loryk's life. "Am I your prisoner?" she asked.

Eiden straightened his bed roll.

"I have no desire to steal your freedom, Vaeda."

She was stricken by his use of her given name.

"Come morning, I will be out of your company and on my way to spread the words that Kirena has blessed upon my tongue. She will heal the hearts of the wicked. She will end this era of madness."

---

[*] Vethar was the Divine of history and prophecy. Upon High Priest Beinon's inauguration, Vethar was removed from the teachings. The High Priest claimed the Divine spoke falsities against the Order and Divines. His temple was destroyed, and any mention of his name is met with the harshest of punishments.

While most of the human country follows in the New Ways, there are few who cling to the Old Ways, which includes Vethar's teachings and prophecies.

"So…you aren't here to capture me?"

"No, young one. I do not desire your death, nor do the Divines. And I'll make sure the others know that your place is not in the hands of the Order."

Neer curled her fingers around the vial. Tears burned in her eyes. "Thank you."

He nodded in silent response.

"You said that you're searching for me?" Their eyes met. "Why?"

"Be wary of the path laid out for you. It will corrupt your soul and be filled with sin." His eyes bore into hers. "Seek only to gain wisdom within yourself. Trust no one, and you will be free."

Her heart stopped. Trust no one. Those were the words uttered by Avelloch when they had first met in Vleland, after she saved him.

Eiden rolled over with his back to Neer. His dagger lay in the grass beside him, leaving him defenseless.

Neer considered all he had said, but in her growing delirium, she had no energy to truly ponder or make sense of their conversations. Instead, she twisted the potion in her hand, studying its verity and hoping it wasn't a trick. With a glance at Eiden, to be sure he was still turned over, Neer slipped off the cloak and carefully removed her blood-soaked top.

Purple bruises blossomed across her arms and torso, lying beneath thin lines of red. She splashed the potion first over the infected, pus-filled cuts, wincing when they sizzled and hissed. Moving over her arms and legs, she dripped the elixir across her wounds, thankful to be relieved of their minor pain.

Chills covered her skin when she slid back into the dirty top, wrapped into the blanket, and finished her bowl of stew. She stared through the forest, worried about Y'ven and Dru, and made a silent vow to find them. Though she knew trekking through the forest alone, ill-equipped and weak, would find her a victim to whatever crawled through the night, she was still riddled with the guilt of knowing they were out there.

Knowing there was nothing she could do to help until morning, she lay on the grass, wrapped in the thick furs, and forced herself to sleep.

SHADOWS OF NYN'DIRA

Birds sang when dawn rose across the slumbering land. Animals scurried through the grass and trees, searching for their morning meals. Leaves broke away from limbs, falling gracefully through the crisp autumn air.

Embers burned atop blackened logs where a cauldron once hovered over the flames. Sunlight gleamed across her face, gently waking Neer with its warm kiss.

She groaned.

Turning over, she attempted to sleep, but images of Y'ven's face—his mangled and bloody body—tore her from rest. Her eyes opened, heavy with exhaustion, and she pushed herself up, looking around. The forest was quiet and peaceful. Large trees with spiraled trunks surrounded her in every direction. Thick grass lay beneath her, and she ran her fingers through its softness, wondering how such foliage came to be beneath such a thick canopy of leaves.

A light breeze brought the subtle sting of magic. She lifted her hands, mesmerized by the surge of energy. Her body didn't ache quite as bad as it had the night before, and her wounds had healed entirely, some leaving thin scars.

Neer eyed the camp, noticing a folded parchment with the name "Vaeda" written in beautiful calligraphy. She grabbed the note and slowly unfolded it—her wanted poster with an updated image, description, and increased bounty.

"Imbeciles," she remarked at the human writing on the page, knowing the evae couldn't understand such markings. Turning the page over, she saw a note written in the same beautiful font as her name:

> *Have faith in the Light, young one.*
> *There is a village north, Myriaa, that will accept both human and evae.*
> *Rothar's hand guide you.*
>
> *Your friend,*
> *Eiden*

Neer crumpled the note in her hand, took another glance around, and then headed north.

"Y'ven!" she called, her voice echoing far through the trees. "Dru!"

She wrapped further in the cloak, still shivering beneath its warmth. Her throat became raw as she continued shouting. But there was no response. Not a flicker of flame to signal Dru's presence or a rustle in the shadow of a vaxros.

They were gone. Sent far from where she had been. Dread settled deep into her bones, compressing her chest, making each breath harder than the last. She leaned against a tree and closed her eyes, overcome with grief.

"Come on," she said. "You can find them. They're alive."

With a hard sniff, she shoved away her sorrow and pressed onward, determined to find them. Wallowing wouldn't bring them back. There was no time for such grief.

"Y'ven!" she screamed, her voice cracking. "Dru!"

Two steps forward and the sound of quiet footsteps caused her to freeze. They weren't the heavy steps of a vaxros. Instead, they were nimble and quiet, almost too silent for her to hear, and her heart thundered in her chest at the sound of rustling grass coming from every direction.

Neer reached for her sword, and her heart stopped. It wasn't there. Avelloch's sword was gone, thrown somewhere during her escape from Aragoth. She knew she had it when she fled—yet it was no longer there. Her mind spun as she wondered where it could be and if she'd ever find it. Eiden's face appeared in her mind. Had he taken her weapon? Surely, he didn't—

"Lanathess," a voice growled from behind, and Neer stiffened. Chills ran down her spin when five shadows emerged from the trees, encircling her with their bows and swords drawn. The man behind her spoke again, his voice low and angry. "A fool to wander so deep into our territory. Alone."

"She is near death," a woman hissed. "We should just end her right here."

A dark-skinned evae, much younger than the rest, looked at Neer with curious eyes. She stared at him, addled by his dark complexion. Many of the humans had varying skin tones, but the evae were all believed to be fair complected. *Pale-faced.*

The woman drew back her arrow, and Neer tightened her fists, collecting her energy to defend herself. Fury emanated from their eyes as they challenged one another. Before the arrow was released, the younger evae jumped between them with his hands raised.

"Wait!" he cried.

The woman turned to him with bewilderment and anger.

"She is the one they search for!" he said. "The one on the parchments!"

Neer glanced between them, her eyes wide with rage and fear. The younger evae turned to Neer with a hint of fear in his eyes. But not fear of her. It was something else. Fear of her fate. Fear of what his companions might do to her.

His eyes flashed to the man behind Neer, and she followed his eyes. The stranger was tall, with wavy hair pulled back into a messy bun. A deep scar stretched across his left brow and cheek, leaving his eye blinded and white. His features reminded her much of Thallon, though he had more prominent bone structure, giving him an older, war-torn appearance.

Parchment crinkled as he dug through his satchel to collect her wanted poster, and Neer's heart raced. She had no time to think. Glancing at the strangers, Neer inhaled a deep breath, conjured a faint swell of magic in her chest, and then pushed her arms outward, releasing her energy in a hard gust that flung the evae back.

Though weak from such exertion, Neer ran, ignoring the pain in her chest. She tripped over her feet, fleeing faster than her legs allowed, weaving through the trees in no particular direction. Her throat burned and lungs heaved.

Focused on her escape, she didn't notice when an enormous elk with wide antlers stood in her path. The animal turned to her, and she came to a halt, startled by its sudden approach. She lurched to the left, and the elk followed her movement. Neer halted, realizing it was intentionally blocking her.

She staggered back when the elk raised its head and released a call that rose into a high-pitched squeal. Before she could react, a jolt hit her arm from behind, and she collapsed to the ground. Grass and dirt filled her mouth when she slammed into the soil. Pain throbbed deep in her flesh. She attempted to push herself up but was stricken by agony tearing through her arm. Shifting her eyes aside, she saw an arrow penetrating her limb. The sight of her injury exacerbated the pain, and she unleashed a raw groan.

The female evae approached, her arrow nocked and eyes fuming. "Stupid lanathess," she sneered. "You come here, thinking you can outsmart us. Thinking we are *inferior* because we aren't like *you*." Neer cried when the woman stepped on her injured arm, causing the arrow's shaft to further tear her muscle and skin. "You are *weak*. Even with your magic."

The woman twisted her boot against Neer's arm, causing her to shriek.

"Évara," the scarred man's voice called.

Évara removed her foot, and Neer exhaled a deep, shaky breath.

"She is the one, Aen'mysvaral!°" Évara hissed. "She has brought this upon us!"

Aen'mysvaral stood silently, staring down at the human at his feet. The elk came to his side, and he glanced

---

° Pronunciation: ane-MISS-varr-all

Aen'mysvaral is a rare, unofficial title known as a sitria, or nickname. It is given by the people to warriors who are widely known for their triumphs or bravery.

While many warriors are famed for their sitria, there are two who possess the title, yet their true identities remain completely unknown: the Nasir and Zaeril.

Aen'mysvaral's sitria translates roughly to 'one with a mark upon his face.'

at it with an approving nod. The animal stepped away without a sound, disappearing into the forest.

Neer trembled in agony, her body too weak to fight. Too weak to feign bravery or attempt to flee.

"We'll take her to the Eirean," Aen'mysvaral said, and then he turned aside as someone approached. His brows lowered in disdain when he eyed the younger evae. "Thurandír," he started, "your compassion is admirable, but I saw the sympathy in your eyes. Do not show their kind any sign of weakness. They will not hesitate to end your life if given the chance."

Aen'mysvaral placed his hand on Thurandír's shoulder.

"I know where your heart lies. But these people are not like the e'liaa. They will not show the same kindness as the lanathess of your village. Remember this. It will keep you alive."

Thurandír nodded. He glanced at Neer, eyes burning with guilt.

"Tie her up," Aen'mysvaral stated coldly. "We're taking her to Navarre."

He stepped away, leaving Évara and Thurandír alone with Neer. The evae shared a glance before Évara tilted her head toward Neer in a sour demand for Thurandír to deal with her.

His sad eyes fell to the human writhing in the grass. He wiped his hands on his trousers and knelt by her side. "I'm sorry," he whispered.

Their eyes met, and she was taken aback by his kindness. He appeared to be truly remorseful for his actions.

"They would have killed you."

Neer didn't speak or resist when Thurandír placed a hand on her back and guided her to her feet. Évara watched with angry eyes as he gently pulled Neer's arms back and tied her wrists together with twine. She winced at the pain in her arm where the arrow was still struck through her flesh.

Thurandír secured her hands together, palms flat and facing each other, rendering much of her magic useless unless she sought to harm herself while using it. He then wrapped the twine around her ankles, leaving enough slack for her to walk. The bonds tying her wrists and ankles were connected with a final piece of twine, making her arms completely immobile.

Thurandír turned to Évara, and she gave a stiff nod of approval.

Then Neer was led away, toward the heart of Rhyl territory.

Toward the fate of the Eirean.

Chapter Three

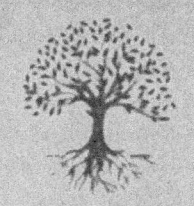

The Chiming of Bells
Aélla

"Do not fool yourself into believing victory lies with the living, for we walk among the ashes of the fallen, engulfed by the pain they've left behind."

— Aegrandir Líadrinel, Avel Warrior

NIGHT SWEPT OVER THE LAND, and the forest was silent. A rift tore through the air, sending a rush of heat and rippling light through the cool darkness. Aélla fell from its height with Thallon in her arms. She gasped in pain when they landed atop roots and dirt. Thallon rolled aside, unconscious. Bruises covered his throat, and orange veins displayed across his arm beneath thick travaran.[*]

She crawled to his side, huffing as her broken ribs sent shockwaves of pain through her chest. Blood leaked from the cuts across her skin, and her platinum hair stuck to her face in uneven patches, filthy with dust and blood. A purple bruise swelled her right eye, blurring her vision and throbbing with every heartbeat.

"Thallon..." She shook his shoulders, begging him to wake. Through clenched teeth, she fought against her affliction and pressed her hands to his chest. Hot energy radiated through her, breaching her core and ascending into her palms, where it transferred into Thallon.

---

[*] A magical potion meant for healing. This thick paste quickly heals various types of wounds, though many avoid its usage as its fleeting affliction carries more pain than the injury itself.

The swell of magic increased as their energies melded. But it wasn't enough to help him. She was too weak, and if she were to use more of her energy, she could find herself too depleted to recover. Exhausted, she slumped into the grass and closed her eyes.

Golden rays of a setting sun warmed Aélla's skin as the sun rose and fell during her slumber. She sat up with a groan, wincing at the agony in her chest. Her eyes shifted to Thallon, watching as he slept. She examined her surroundings and found they were deep in the forest. Far from civilization. The overgrown grasses and untouched berry bushes were a clear indication of their isolation. She had meant to take them close to her home of Navarre, but her magic was weakened, and carrying two people through teleportation was draining.

Her thoughts were broken when Thallon began to stir. Slowly, he opened his eyes and blinked them into focus. For a moment, he was silent, staring at their surroundings in confusion. "Aélla?" he asked hoarsely through a dry throat. "What—"

His voice faded into a fit of coughing. He leaned aside, fighting for breath as he hacked and gasped. Aélla watched him sadly, unable to aid him without further injuring herself.

The waving lights of a stream illuminated against a gathering of trees nearby, and Aélla exhaled a relieved sigh. As Thallon breathed slowly through a raw throat, Aélla took his hand and guided him toward the water.

Thallon broke from her grasp and approached the edge of the bank, dropping to his knees. He drank several handfuls, water splashing onto his face and armor. Aélla sat by his side, gently placing her hands beneath the water and wincing at the pain in her bones.

Her hands shook when she struggled to lean forward and drink. Liquid spilled from her fingers as she whimpered.

"Here." Thallon washed his skin before cupping a handful of water into his palms and lifting them to her lips.

She slowly drank from his hands, wetness spilling down her chin. After another handful, she nodded, and he leaned back, examining her injuries.

"Are you all right?" he asked.

She clutched her side. "I think my ribs are broken."

"Kila!" He helped remove her chest piece and lifted her blood-soaked top. "Aélla…"

Trembling, she glanced at her side where deep bruises patched her chest. She groaned and turned away, feeling sick, and Thallon pulled her hair back as she vomited into the grass. He gently rubbed her back and cupped water into his hands for her to drink.

Thallon then looked around, scanning the darkness. "Where are the others? Did they…"

His voice trailed away, and Aélla closed her eyes in sorrow. "Nerana is alive…She fled with Y'ven and Dru."

"Kila…they're in the forest? Fuck!" He smacked the ground in his frustration. "They're going to be killed! We have to find them!"

Aélla leaned forward, tears spilling from her eyes. She whimpered and sobbed, clutching her aching chest as emotions consumed her, filling her with agony and regret.

"Aélla?" Thallon's voice was soft, like a father with his child. He moved closer and gently pulled her into his arms.

She collapsed into his embrace, her face wet with tears while she released the pain she'd been taught to withhold for so long. Pain from causing her friends so much agony, from her journey and the things she had to face.

Pain from knowing where this road would lead and how unfair fate had been. She didn't have to take this path. Aélla could still turn back and try to find another way to break this cycle and put an end to naik'avel.

But those paths had been sought by souls long dead, and each of them had fallen.

Each of them had failed.

"Come on," Thallon said. "We need to go somewhere safe."

"There is nowhere...," she cried.

He gently pulled away and wiped her tears. "You are Drimil'Rothar. The strongest person I know. You can't let this get you down. The Nasir won't get away with this. We won't let him." He pulled her bloodstained hair from her face. "We will go to the Eirean and tell them what happened. They won't stand for this. Our people won't stand for it."

"It's too late..."

He sighed. "Come on, where is that bravery? Don't tell me you are turning into that *nesiat*. Always wallowing and stuck in his emotions." Thallon gave her a playful glare, while she glowered.

With a sniff, she wiped her face and looked around. The world was peaceful and calm. It could be peaceful again...She was their only hope. "You are right," she said. "Thank you, Thallon."

"Ah," he said with a smile. "What are friends for? Now let's get somewhere safe. I think Amália is nearby."

"Amália?" she asked as he helped her to her feet.

"It's a small settlement along the foothills of the mountains. I've been there once, for research."

"It's a First Blood village?"

He shook his head. "No, but it's near some of their ruins."

They walked slowly through the forest, with Aélla stopping several times to quell the pain in her side. Wind hummed through the air, and she could feel the tinge of magic pulsing through the trees, giving the forest life. It was a subtle sting that pricked her skin, enough for her to feel the essence of the forest. Its life and tranquility.

But the forest was not tranquil. The winds did not whisper of calmness and ease.

Instead, there was panic, dread, and pain. Insurmountable pain. Aélla could feel it with every slight shift in the wind. With every touch of her skin against the bark of the trees. She was connected to the forest, as all evae were. The glowing Ko'ehlaeu'at trees[°] were the sources of great power and energy, and Nyn'Dira was the only place left where they held any influence on the land.

"There is pain here," she said, her eyes shifting through the forest.

Thallon could feel it too, she could see the worry in his eyes. Stepping to a tree, Aélla placed her palm to its surface and melded their energies, feeling the distress and sorrow moving through her like a dying heartbeat.

"It's coming from the north," she explained.

Thallon's face paled. "That's where Amália is."

They shared a fearful glance.

"Just a little farther." Thallon led her onward.

She clenched her teeth and fought through the pain as they trekked through thick grass and glowing mushrooms. With every step, the smell of blood seeped into her nose. She lurched forward, grasping her chest. Emotions that weren't her own raged inside, and her growing fear was quickly diluted by a strong sense of agony and terror.

"Aélla?" Thallon asked in a panic.

She grunted through the pain, which was made worse by her own agony. "We have to keep going," she said with a wince.

They stepped through the underbrush and halted at the edge of the tree line. Pain ripped through her, and she stumbled, gazing at the village ahead. Nestled deep in the woods was the village of Amália.

Twelve small homes once full of promise and life had been reduced to ash—a tomb for those who once called this place their home. Blood spattered the trees and grass, painting a scene of the terror the innocent had faced at the hands of another. Trails of red passed through entryways of missing or broken doors left half-hanging on shattered hinges.

[°] Known as "Tree" in human terms. Being evaesh, Aélla can commune with nature, holding deeper bonds with animals and a spiritual connection to the land. Her First Blood lineage offers her the ability to better sense the magic flowing through the trees.

Aélla stiffened, staring through misty eyes at the scene before her. She gazed at each of the homes, then set her eyes on the bodies lying in the dirt. They were scattered across the village—fleeing from their homes before being struck down. In the midst of the evaesh corpses were the remains of five human men. Rotten and bloated, their skin had been slashed and torn apart by animals.

Aélla clutched her chest. The evaesh screams and pleas echoed through her mind like a dying wind. She heard the laughter of the humans who cut them down. The wailing of mothers and fathers...the last breaths of their terrified children.

A strike of pain flashed through her, and she lurched with a gasp.

"Aélla?" Thallon asked, placing his hand on her arm.

"Something's here...," she said through clenched teeth.

He glanced around and then took her arm, ready to lead her away, when the faint chime of a bell tinkled in the distance. And Aélla's blood ran cold. The forest was still, and the world, for a moment, was silent to the sound sweeping through the air, quiet as a whisper.

Thallon slowly, carefully, retrieved a dagger from the sheath on his belt. His wide eyes peered into the darkness ahead. Aélla stood taller, withholding the cry pressing against her lips as her ribs ached.

The silhouette of a misshapen woman caressed by a veil of moonlight appeared through the trees. Twisted sticks and vines made into runic symbols were woven through its short, red hair. Dark crimson designs lay across its body, which was a mess of different limbs and pieces patched together from several races and victims.

Realizing this creature was a skrata, Thallon stepped forward, his boots making hardly a sound as he guarded Aélla from their intruder.

It stepped closer, its unmatching feet crunching quietly through the grass. The golden bell hanging in its hair, twisted with the sticks and vines, was still chiming, still warning of its arrival.

"Silently, she lays asleep…
Dreaming of things she cannot see…"

The beautiful, angelic voice of a woman whispered through the air as the skrata sang. Its hypnotic tune lulled Aélla into a calming trance. Her body was numb, and her mind was heavy as the voice wove through every fiber of Aélla's soul, slowly untethering her consciousness. She knew she had to fight. Knew she had to get away before the skrata entranced her completely. But she couldn't. She didn't want to—not while its beautiful voice embraced her.

"For when she wakes, they will find…
A scattered, broken, empty mind…"

The skrata's dark figure leaned over a fallen human. Its long, crooked fingers hovered over the man's body, twirling through the air while the creature examined his corpse.

"For the feast will last 'til the dawn…"

Its beautiful voice never broke as it clutched the man's wrist and, one by one, ripped off his fingers, flinging drops of thick blood through the air.

"No one hereafter sees the morn…"

It tossed the rotten fingers into its mouth, humming as it crunched into bone and flesh. Blood dripped down its chin, and the runes on its body glowed. Low growls and hungry grunts escaped its throat.

With its voice silent, the clouds diluting Aélla's mind cleared, and she clawed through the haze, fighting to regain her thoughts. Soon, her body became weighted, and she reclaimed her ability to move.

Thallon stood with his head in his hands, fighting against the skrata's power. Aélla touched his shoulder, and he whipped his head aside. Their eyes met, and she was stricken by his terror. She gave him a reassuring nod, and he forced his own.

A vibrating, hellish screech that broke the silence as the skrata's soprano chiseled through the cold night air. It turned toward the sky with its wide jaw stretched open. The runes along its body brightened, and its black, boney fingers started to bubble, like water simmering in a cauldron.

Aélla and Thallon sank to their knees when its shriek pierced their minds. Their thoughts scrambled and ears bled as it fell silent. Its arms dropped to its sides with human fingers now replacing its once long, decrepit digits.

Thallon reached out to Aélla, and she carefully rose to her feet. His fingers grazed against her filthy robes, unable to grasp her as she stood. Her dark blue eyes were set on the skrata, which stood across the village with its back toward them. Aélla stepped closer, her boot drawing the faintest sound, and the skrata's head twitched in her direction.

She froze, staring into the hollows of its eyes. Its face was gaunt, with a lipless mouth stretching from ear to ear. Empty sockets made up its eyes and nose. It had no discernable gender, though Aélla knew it would once it consumed different parts from its victims. Judging by this skrata's half-filled appearance, it was a newborn, freshly risen from the energy of the departed.

And during infancy, the skrata were the most dangerous. They were erratic and uncontrollable. Their hunger and instincts made them mad with rage. And while this skrata could not see, its ears were equine, giving it a keener sense of hearing.

Aélla didn't breathe, focusing on the grotesque creature of darkness. Its wide mouth had two rows of razor-sharp teeth. Its skin was plump and white, as if bubbling with infection.

The skrata stood taller, still staring in her direction, as if gazing into her very soul.

And then it vanished.

Before Aélla could draw a breath, the skrata reappeared behind and pulled her into its arms.

CHAPTER FOUR

CREATURE OF THE NIGHT
Thallon

THICK, CALLUSED HANDS GRIPPED AÉLLA'S arms with bone crushing force, and she whimpered as it leaned close, exposing slime coated fangs. Thallon lunged forward, but before he could sink his dagger into its spine, the skrata sank its teeth into Aélla's skin, piercing into her neck, collar, and back.

She screamed, and her magic unleashed in a shockwave that tore through the air, stripping leaves from the trees. Thallon groaned as he and the skrata were flung back.

He rolled across the dirt before coming to a slow stop, aching from the impact to his deep bruises and still-broken ribs. The skrata scratched and clawed across the ground, sending dirt and grass raining from the sky before regaining its balance. On its feet, it charged at Aélla, who knelt motionless on the ground, gripping her chest.

Thallon leapt to his feet, chasing after the bloodthirsty kanavin as it towered over Aélla like a growing shadow. With its mouth open, the skrata lunged. Its human fingers reached for the crouched evae who had yet to move, and when callused hands brushed against her filthy platinum hair, Aélla disappeared.

The skrata fell through the empty air, landing hard against the ground, and Thallon halted. It knelt in the grass, ready to crawl, twitching its ears in search of any sound. A light sniffing came from its nasal cavity, and it turned its head from side to side.

Thallon stood several paces behind, his shoulders rising and falling with every deep breath. He stared at the skrata, lifted his arm to aim down his sights, and then hurled his dagger at its skull.

The weapon flipped through the air, moving closer to the back of its head, when suddenly, the skrata turned around, too quickly to see. It released a gasped wheeze when the blade sank deep into its forehead, between its empty eye sockets.

It collapsed, fading into a pile of ash before its head touched the ground. Thallon's dagger lay in its remains. He glanced around, searching for intruders, and carefully approached the ash, snatching his weapon.

"Aélla!" he called, peering through the shadow. "Aélla?"

"Thallon…"

Her voice was hardly a whisper. He turned toward the noise and quickly followed its direction. Moving away from the village, he found her lying on the ground, fighting for consciousness.

"Come on," he said, gathering her into his arms and wincing from the ache in his muscles and injuries. The pain was crushing, but he had to push through. They couldn't stay here. He had to get them to safety. Aélla was motionless when he lifted her from the ground. "Kila…," Thallon complained with another wince. "What the hell is happening?"

He ran until his legs collapsed, and he tumbled to the ground.

"Shit…," he griped and quickly looked at Aélla. Her breathing was shallow, and her face had gone pale. "Come on, A…don't do this! Stay with me…Come on!"

Tears burned his eyes, and he scanned the forest. His lungs ached with every deep breath, but he had to keep going. He couldn't let her die. But they were lost. Completely, undeniably lost. And he knew that any noise or movement would alert the kanavin[*] of his presence. He was lucky to have made it this far without detection.

"Kila!" he snapped, quickly wiping the wetness from his eyes. Aélla was heavy in his arms as he pulled her close and struggled to his feet. His legs trembled with weakness, and

---

[*] Pronunciation: kah-nah-veen

In the language of the evae, kanavin is a term that loosely translates to *creature of darkness*.

he took two forced steps before collapsing to his knees. "Dammit...*fuck*!"
With a loud sniff, he reluctantly lay Aélla on the grass and then leaned forward with his hands on his knees. Breathing heavily, he shook his head. His fingers curled inward, scratching along his trousers.
A breeze swept across the land, bringing with it a sense of calmness and peace. He looked around, hopeful for a savior, but that wish slowly died when he realized they were alone, at the mercy of the creatures stalking the land.
"Help me!" he begged, hoping the trees would listen. But they only gave another calm breeze, and Thallon exhaled a deep breath. The forest was at peace. It would warn him if danger was near, and he knew he had to rest. Stealing a glance at Aélla, who lay unconscious by his side, he collected his dagger and leaned against a tree, waiting to regain his strength.

Dawn crept along the horizon, drawing mist from the grass and leaves. Thallon's head bobbed aside as he crept in and out of sleep. Dreary eyes opened, and he inhaled a sharp breath, glancing around for the hundredth time. When light hit his eyes, he jolted awake and rushed to Aélla's side.
"Aélla," he said. "Aélla. Wake up. Please!"
She stirred before opening her eyes and then slowly closing them again. Thallon glanced around, noticing the trees were sparse, with moss crawling up their thin trunks. Dirt and leaves covered the grass. He had never been to this area of the forest and worried they were still days away from civilization.
He turned to Aélla and carefully pulled back the collar of her robes, revealing the deep, pus-filled bite marks across her skin. Dark bruises blossomed across her shoulder, painting her fair skin in shades of purple and blue. Thallon exhaled a defeated sigh and bowed his head. With another look around the desolate forest, he gathered Aélla in his arms and continued south, in the direction of Navarre.

He walked for hours, taking several breaks to rest or rehydrate. Aélla's face was growing pale, and deep circles formed around her eyes. The sun rose higher, pulling at Thallon's frustration, time quickly passing them by.

"Klaud's going to kill me if you die," he said, speaking weakly through exhausted delirium. "Is that what you want? Both of us dead?" Beads of sweat dripped down his red face, and he exhaled a tired huff. "Kila...where are the villages? Where is *anyone*!"

The sun edged closer to the horizon, and his spirit started to wane. Aélla lay in his arms, her breathing shallow.

"We're getting close," Thallon said, lying to himself, hoping beyond hope that his words could somehow bring truth and they'd find refuge. His thighs burned and feet ached with every step. The winds rushed ahead, pressing him forward, guiding him southeast.

He followed, trusting the forest to guide them to safety. Soon, the soft murmuring of voices chimed through the air, and he exhaled a breath of relief. Trudging through the forest, forcing his legs further, he came to the edge of a small settlement. Wooden fences outlined the sprawling community of nearly one hundred homes. An overgrown cobble path wove through the grasses, connecting each house to various shops, inns, and bakeries. Villagers, dressed in modest clothing of natural tones, wandered through the settlement with pleasant smiles and soft voices.

Some carried baskets of wares and vegetables picked fresh from the gardens, while others wore aprons covered in flour or soot. A blacksmith worked with his apprentice at the edge of the territory. The hard clink of their mallets against forging steel resounded through the quiet woods. Six hunters emerged from the trees, carrying handfuls of rabbits, birds, and rodents.

Thallon trudged through town on dragging feet, and the hushed voices of the residents fell silent. He looked around, realizing this village wasn't like any ordinary evaesh community. It was an e'liaan[*] settlement, made up of humans

---

[*] Pronunciation: E-lee-ah

SHADOWS OF NYN'DIRA

and evae, who each looked upon him with shocked expressions. Several women brought their fingers to their parted lips, while men stood with their weapons drawn.

"It's Drimil'Rothar!"

"What's happened?"

"Is she alive?"

Thallon held Aélla closer, his tired eyes peering through the village as people gathered outside. His arms trembled, and he forced himself to hold her steady. Many of the residents reached out to touch her.

"We need a nes'seil!" Thallon said. "Hurry!"

Several villagers rushed away, and Thallon came to a stop. The others crowded around him, weeping while touching Aélla's hair and face. He was silent, watching them sink to their knees in deep, respectful bows. After all this time, he was still unfamiliar with Aélla's respected and praised position as Drimil'Rothar. During their lives, he had always viewed her as his friend's little sister. An annoying kid who would follow them around like a defenseless *dren'seol.*˙ As they grew older, Thallon and his friends drifted apart, as most did with time and age. He saw little of Aélla after that, but when he learned she had taken the vow of Drimil'Rothar, he was humbled to find that sweet, rambunctious child was now titled a savior.

Still, he couldn't see her as anything more than a kid. Someone to tease and share stories with.

Though Thallon didn't believe Aélla had ever been to this village, the residents recognized her platinum hair. It was a unique and telling feature all First Blood carried. Only two evae were known to have such bright locks, and the thought of the other made Thallon's blood boil.

E'liaa is a term which loosely translates to mean *half-blood*. This race of evae and human lives peacefully throughout Nyn'Dira, making up nearly 1/8 of the total population. While not every person within the settlement is of mixed blood, any who live among the human/evaesh villages are considered o'liaa

˙ Pronunciation: Dren-see-ole

Dren'seol roughly translates to *one with my soul*. It's a term used to describe the bond between an evae and their animal companion.

"Drimil." A human man rushed to her side, his eyes wide with panic. "What's happened to her?"

Two women pulled Aélla from Thallon's arms and placed her on a stretcher. He watched as she was carried away to a nearby home. Without her in his arms, Thallon felt weightless and sank to his knees, unable to stand. The human knelt to his side.

"Are you okay?" he asked. "What's happened?"

His green eyes were bright, studying the war-torn scholar, whose skin was etched in blood and dirt. Thallon exhaled several deep breaths, his throat dry and lungs tired. The human took his arm and helped Thallon to his feet. He then brushed through the crowd, leading the scholar to the home where Aélla had been taken.

They stepped through a wooden gate and into the large two-story dwelling. Thick, leafy vines encased its eastern wall, while weeping limbs from surrounding trees scratched against its gabled roof.

Inside, the air was warm and the home was inviting. The human closed the door and waved Thallon ahead. They stepped through a small living space with a large, cushioned bench, a chair, bookshelves, and a roaring hearth. Toward the back of the home, they entered a bedroom, where woven dolls and dried flowers were displayed across the shelves.

Aélla rested on the bed, her eyes remaining closed. The two nes'seil* tended to her wounds. Her white hair was coated in dirt and blood, and her face was masked in bruises. Linen rags saturated with red and yellow stains were tossed into a bucket at her side. The odor of infection filled the room, and Thallon turned away, unable to witness her in such a state.

The human pulled out a chair and motioned for Thallon to sit. He did so without argument, eager to get off his feet. Thallon was handed a cup of water and quickly drank its contents, spilling half of it down his chin. The stranger stood nearby, patiently waiting for Thallon to speak.

---

* Pronunciation: Ness-EE-ell

Evaesh term for apothecary or healer.

But words were far from his mind. He had been unconscious for the fight and knew from their injuries that things were bad. Very bad. Neer, Y'ven, and Dru were all missing. Reiman, as well. He wondered what had become of them or if they had survived at all. He shook his head and wiped his eyes, not willing to give in to the emotions simmering just beneath the surface, begging for release.

Thallon sat with his head in his hands, wishing to be alone. The nes'seil spoke quietly to one another before shuffling through the room. Thallon lifted his eyes, watching as they gathered their things and left. Aélla lay asleep on the bed. Thick bandages now wrapped her shoulder and chest.

"My name is Elias," the stranger said, and Thallon's eyes shifted to him. Light wrinkles creased his eyes when he smiled. "You are welcome to anything in my home. Master Drimil should make a full recovery. Are there any injuries of yours we should tend to?"

Thallon shook his head, setting his gaze on Aélla again. Elias tilted his head in a light bow and then quietly left the room.

* * *

The sun rose for the third time since Thallon's arrival to the village, gifting the world with a new beginning. After sharing breakfast with his host, Thallon made his way into Aélla's room. He sat next to her, elated to find the coloring had returned to her face. She breathed evenly, no longer whimpering in her sleep with every slow, agonized draw.

He sat for hours, watching through the window as villagers wandered the small community. Children with half-evaesh features chased each other with sticks and sparring weapons. A sad smile lingered on Thallon's lips while he watched them, remembering his own childhood with his brothers and friends.

The thoughts of a time long past quickly faded when Aélla began to stir in her sleep. Thallon stood, watching as face twitched before her eyes slowly opened. Relief washed through him, and he exhaled a deep breath.

"Aélla…," he said, lightly clutching her arm. "You're awake."

He passed her a cup of water and helped her sit up. She looked around with lazy eyes. Her hair was unkempt from days of rest.

"Thallon?" she asked, her voice groggy with exhaustion. "Where are we?"

"Ik'Myriaa," he said. "Still days away from Navarre."

She sighed, closing her eyes.

Thallon rubbed her arm. "You should get washed up," he said. "Eat something. Once you're ready, we can keep going."

"Wait." She weakly clutched his arm when he moved to help her up. "I can't…I need a moment."

"Are you all right?"

"I don't know. Something feels wrong. Dark."

"Yeah…I feel it too." Their eyes met, and he pressed his lips into a thin line. "Looks like you'd better get a move on, Drimil. Wispers and khiut and skrata…" He scoffed in disgust. "This world is falling to shit."

"It's getting worse. The darkness. The imbalance…" She crossed her arms tightly over her chest, as if to quell the sense of dread spewing from her eyes. "I don't know if I have what it takes."

"Don't start with that again," he said with a bit of ease and humor to his voice, though it was still drier than he intended. "Once we find the others, everything will work itself out. Just stay strong, all right?"

She nodded, keeping her eyes low. "That ring…the one that Nerana found…the Nasir used it on that human. He…" Aélla gulped down her sorrow and fear. "He turned him into a gaelthral."

Thallon's blood ran cold. He'd heard of the gaelthral during his studies. They were vicious, hostile creatures, hunting and killing for food and sport. Monstrous in size, they were nearly impossible to take down.

He turned away, nausea rising in his throat, and beads of sweat formed across his temple. His fingers clenched into a tight fist, imagined such a beast existing and, worse, being in the command of the Nasir.

"Did you know?" Aélla asked.

She wasn't asking about the fight, but about the ring's power. He looked away. Couldn't bring himself to look at her. Not now. Not after he had kept such a dangerous secret.

"Thallon," she pressed.

He closed his eyes. Through gritted teeth, he nodded. "Yes."

Her eyes burned through his flesh like a hot branding iron. But he couldn't turn to her, though she quietly beckoned him to do so. Instead, he sat with his eyes closed, wondering if things could have been different. If fate would have changed had he made other choices.

If he had chosen to trust in his comrades rather than view them as potential enemies.

"Why didn't you tell me?" Aélla demanded. "Thallon!"

"Because I didn't trust them!"

"You didn't trust Y'ven and Nerana?"

"No." He turned to her, finally peering into her eyes. "They are nice. I like them. But I do not know them, and I certainly couldn't trust them with something like that!"

Her lips pursed together in anger. "If I had known, then we could've taken measures to prevent what happened! I could've taken the ring straight to the Eirean and returned to Aragoth!"

"The Eirean entrusted this to *me*, Aélla. This was *my* responsibility. Not yours."

She exhaled a deep breath, the anger slowly leaving her eyes, though it still lingered deep inside. "Now the Nasir has it...It doesn't matter what we could have done. It's done now." She paused, forcing her anger to subside. "What can it do?"

"It's called the *clavia muinsii*. In Alveryan, it means *shadow and night*. We don't understand its power—the Eirean weren't even sure it existed."

He paused, collecting his thoughts.

"It can turn any living being into a kanavin," Thallon continued. "The victim's energy determines which type of creature they'll become." Another pause. "Whoever wears the ring has control of them. *All* of them. The Nasir could create an entire army—one that doesn't eat or sleep or breathe, and they will do whatever he says."

"What if he takes it off?"

Thallon sighed. "I don't know. Some texts say that the ring fuses to its bearer. Others say it'll consume and eventually transform *them* into a kanavin. There was a reason it was hidden. No one is meant to wield power that great."

Aélla swallowed. Her eyes shifted to her twisting hands. "It was given to Nerana…Is…*she* meant to have it?"

Fear sank into his gut, churning with uncertainty as her words repeated in his mind. Surely, Neer wasn't meant to wield a power so destructive. But she was Drimil'Nizotl. Her very existence was an improbability, yet she was alive and fighting against the very forces that lured her further into madness. Into a cycle of devastation that could never be stopped.

Thallon shook his head, ridding himself of the thoughts. "No," he said, though he didn't fully believe it, "I think it would have been given to anyone who survived the fall into the tre'lan.˚ Had Neer never gone to Sandir…had she never fallen through the ground…it wouldn't have been found at all."

They didn't look at each other. Didn't speak. The silence was dark and heavy as they fell into a state of despair. Thallon was riddled with guilt and unease.

"We have to stop him," he said, the words spilling from his mouth. "The Eirean can stop him."

"We're a long way from home, Thallon. I'm not strong enough to take us across the forest right now."

"I know. So, let's just stop bickering and get you strong again."

Aélla nodded, and they became silent once again. Clouds parted the sky, and sunlight brightened the room. Gold and red leaves broke away from their branches outside and drifted through the air, creating shadows that danced through the room.

˚ Pronunciation: tray-lahn

Evaesh term meaning *magical realm*

"Where do you think they are?" Aélla asked, her voice quiet as she peered out the window.

"I don't know." Thallon looked around, pondering her question. "Come on, we should get you cleaned. There's a bathhouse nearby."

He helped her out of bed, and carefully, they walked outside. Aélla closed her eyes and accepted the warmth of a new day. She exhaled a slow breath, allowing the tension in her shoulders to soften.

"How long have we been here?" she asked.

"Three days."

She sighed. "We need to find them. I can't—"

"Master Drimil!"

A woman's elated shriek filled the air, and soon, a crowd formed around them. People gathered, touching her face and robes, begging to be healed or weeping with praise. Thallon clenched his jaw, angered by their selfishness.

"Please, Master Drimil," a woman begged, falling to her knees and clutching Aélla's robes. "My son was wounded by the lanathess. Please, help him! Before it's too late!"

Thallon argued, but Aélla lifted her hand to quiet him. She winced while leaning over and touching the woman's head. "Where is he?"

The woman sniffed. "The *nes'rávei*! Please! Help him, Drimil!"

Aélla stood tall, her jaw clenched and eyes hard as she withheld her agony. She stepped forward, following the woman. Thallon was at her side, fuming.

"You need to take care of yourself, Aélla," he said. "You haven't eaten in days! Your injuries—"

"Can wait." Her voice was sweet yet still rang with authority. "His may not."

Thallon gritted his teeth, wanting to argue but knowing it was futile. Instead, he bit his tongue and followed his respected leader as she approached a longhouse with a covered porch. Flowered vines clung to the posts, masking the odor of blood with the sweet aroma of daffodils and roses.

The door creaked when the grieving mother stepped inside, and the others followed. They entered a large room lined with half a dozen beds on either wall. Bloody sheets were tossed into a bucket by the door. Chamber pots, crusted in brown and crimson, lay between every other bed. The odor was pungent, burning their eyes and catching in their throats.

Eight of the twelve beds were occupied. Two of the patients had sheets covering their faces—one of them caved in at their nose. Nes'seil wandered from bed to bed, checking on the groaning, crying victims, while the others rested.

Thallon held his breath, and Aélla covered her mouth. Many of the wounded had severed limbs, slashed faces, or growing infections.

"What happened?" Aélla's voice was a whisper.

Before Thallon could find the words, the mother pulled Aélla away, dragging her to a nearby bed where a young boy lay whimpering. Bandages, stained with a thick line of blood traveling from his nose to jaw, wrapped his right-side face. Aélla gently touched his face and sealed his wound.

The mother rushed to her son's side, wailing with relief. Thallon's attention was torn from the boy when Aélla inhaled a sharp gasp. He turned to her and then followed her gaze across the room. Misery crushed his soul when he spied a soft glowing light, like the spark of a dying flame, resting on a blood-soaked bed. Beneath the glow was the silhouette of a large, blood-coated vaxros.

A thin sheet shrouded his face.

Chapter Five

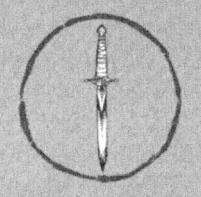

The Hills of Aardn
Nerana

> *"There is no mercy in the land of the forsaken, where the heathens will rip and claw and tear until you're nothing more than bloody, terrified screams."*
>
> — Human propaganda against the non-human lands

SEVERAL DAYS AFTER HER CAPTURE, Neer walked alongside Thurandír. Her back ached and wrists were raw. Tired eyes scanned the forest as they trekked through a thicket of wide trees with spiraled trunks. Sunlight beamed through the leaves, gifting her with a kiss of warmth when she stepped through each golden column.

Neer kept her eyes focused on the ground, listening to the group of evae who spoke, yet again, about her fate. They walked several paces ahead, leaving Neer behind with her younger escort.

"We should end her now," Évara sneered, breaking the hours-long silence that caressed the morning. "Send a message to her people with blood."

A man agreed. Stealing a glance at Neer, he said, "We can place her arms and legs at every corner of the forest. Let them know we won't take these threats."

Évara nodded. "And send her head back to their precious leaders."

"Enough," Aen'mysvaral said, though his voice was calm. He needed no further argument as the others fell silent.

Neer closed her eyes, thankful they hadn't gone through with any of their awful plans.

"I'm sorry about my friends," Thurandír, her escort, said. "They don't like your kind much. I guess they don't really understand you." He peered at the others, who were too far ahead to hear his quiet words. "We aren't bad people."

Neer glanced at him, noticing the distant look in his eyes. He was kind, gifting her water and small comforts over the last few days while the others weren't looking. Keeping her company and telling her stories.

"My mother is human," he said. "There are some of us who coexist here. The others look down on us, but Aen'mysvaral accepted me as a warrior. I have a lot to prove, but maybe I can show them that the e'liaa aren't as ignorant as they believe us to be. Just because we are human and evae doesn't mean we're inferior." He turned to Neer, and she averted her gaze. "Hopefully you will prove the same. Everyone here thinks you're a monster...but you don't seem evil to me."

Neer didn't respond. She didn't want to give him any reason to suspect she could understand his language. All she needed to do was find a way to escape. Her energy had strengthened since her capture, but she was quickly warned that if she attempted to flee, Thurandír's life would be on the line. Though she didn't want to believe these warriors would sacrifice their own companion, she also couldn't take that risk. Thurandír was young. He was innocent and kind. Neer wouldn't be responsible for his death. So, she stayed, biding her time until she could think of a way to escape without risking his life.

"I think there were others who were looking for you," Thurandír stated, his voice low as he carefully thought of each word.

Neer's heart stopped when he mumbled the name, trying to remember it.

"Ava...Aver-lack..." He struggled for a moment before finally saying, "Avelloch. I think that was his name."

Her eyes widened in disbelief. She stared at him, teal eyes glowing in the morning light. The others continued onward, passing by weathered and broken ruins while she and Thurandír halted. Their eyes connected, and he stared at her, curiously.

"You know him?" he asked. His eyes narrowed. "Can you...*understand* me?"

Her jaw clenched and eyes hardened. She turned away, trying desperately to find a way out of this. But he knew.

"How..." He stepped closer. "Are you e'liaa?"

Their eyes met, and she breathed heavily, unwilling to reveal what he knew was truth, that she could speak and understand their language. That she had heard everything his companions had said over the last several days: how they desired to torture her for bringing war to their lands and the hatred they had for humankind. She had heard all of it, every angry, vengeful, gory word that slipped from their tongues.

Thankfully, no one had touched her since her capture, though their glares cut through her like glass. Aen'mysvaral, their leader, warned them several times to keep their distance. Even with their weapons and strength and numbers, they were afraid of her. Afraid of what she could do. So, they avoided any confrontation but kept Thurandír as her guard—a kid no older than seventeen who would stand little chance against a sorceress, but maybe that was their goal. They assumed she wouldn't use her power to hurt him. It was a dangerous game, one that filled her with rage as they gambled with his life.

"Hey." Thurandír's sharp voice broke through her thoughts.

She blinked them away before meeting his gaze.

"Are you—"

"Thurandír!" Aen'mysvaral called, his voice strong and commanding.

Thurandír exhaled a deep breath. He turned to Neer and said, "Don't keep this from the Eirean. If you're good, then you should tell them." He glanced at Aen'mysvaral, who waited impatiently by a large stone pillar. "The others surely won't."

He stepped toward his leader, and Neer trailed behind, contemplating his words.

They wove through eroded limestone walls and pillars, many of them cracked and encased in vines and moss. Aen'mysvaral gave Thurandír a disapproving glare, and the younger warrior stepped past without a glance in his direction. The leader eyed Neer as she followed Thurandír, her mind riddled with everything she had been through and seen.

Over the last few days, she had learned little of the Eirean, only bits from the conversations she overheard. They were the leaders of the evae, most likely from each clan, and two of them resided in Navarre, the main settlement of Clan Rhyl. Neer didn't know what to expect from them, but she judged by the fearful way the others spoke, they were dangerous and unforgiving. She had done everything she could to protect Thurandír while they traveled, but she wouldn't allow the Eirean to hand her over to the Order.

She wouldn't allow them to end her life.

The group of evaesh warriors waited for their leader and captive to arrive. Three of the warriors, including Thurandír, followed behind Neer when she walked past, while the other two, along with Aen'mysvaral, walked ahead, putting her directly in their center.

The forest was alive with rustling leaves that painted the world with colors of brown, red, gold, and green as they fell from the limbs. Waterfalls broke across the hillsides, trickling over large rocks and filling the many streams with glistening light. Tall trees stood like sentries guarding the full and bustling village.

Homes, varying in size from one-room to three-story residences, were sprinkled throughout the grass-covered hills. Stone bridges extended over a wide waterfall cascading through the apex of the village. Beautifully manicured dirt paths trailed through the grasses leading to each home, shop, and garden.

Several residents walked by, pausing to view the filthy, blood-covered human walking amidst their band of warriors. Each person held the same features, with long faces, high cheekbones, slender noses, and slanted dark-blue eyes. Their skin tones, however, weren't all as pale and porcelain as the stories had told, ranging from dark to fair complexions. They each had intricate braids woven across their heads, giving them fierce, intimidating looks.

Neer kept her head down, still contemplating her escape. She could teleport, but her wrists and ankles would still be bound, leaving her defenseless. Casting fire could melt the metal binds on her wrists, though this theory could prove more dangerous than helpful if she wound up melting off her skin.

They trekked further into the village, following the paths up winding hills and through gardens and trees. The homes were denser and the paths more congested as they entered a more populated area. Woodworkers, glassblowers, bakers, blacksmiths, and armorers had shops sprawled throughout the wide meadow.

"Thurandír!"

A young woman with tan skin and long hair broke through the crowd. Thurandír halted as she rushed to his side and wrapped her arms around him.

"You're back!" she cried.

"Aeraviin," he started, holding her close.

She looked into his eyes and then averted her gaze to the warriors at his side. Her jaw dropped at the sight of Neer, who kept her focus on the ground.

"Go home," he said, tucking the woman's hair behind her ear. "I'll be there soon."

The warriors nudged Neer ahead as they continued on their journey. Aeraviin staggered back, her worried eyes darting between Thurandír and his companions as he regretfully stepped back into the formation.

Thurandír was quiet while they marched through the bustling village. The citizens parted when they walked by. Aen'mysvaral kept his head high, nodding slightly at each of the villagers who bowed in respect.

The aroma of tree bark, grass, and dirt replaced the scent of burnt wood, molten steel, and fresh baked pies as they climbed higher up the hill, with loose rocks and grass overtaking the pristine pathway. Large boulders, denser trees, and far less grass covered the wooded area.

At the top of the hill, where the rugged path led, was an enormous building. White walls, encased with vines and flowers, stood proudly against the surrounding greenery. Glowing willows, bright flowers, and trickling waterfalls spread across the hills leading to the beautiful meadow.

Neer slipped on a loose rock, and Thurandír grabbed her arm when she lurched forward. They shared a glance, and the hardness of his eyes shook her. He didn't look at her with anger but with worry. Fear.

She turned away, hating his kindness, for it bound her to these evae and their leaders. Had he been as vicious as the others, Neer would have already fled. Unwilling to meet his gaze a second time, Neer shifted her eyes, where a bright glow rested within the forest.

All thought of Thurandír escaped her as she gaped at the mystical light. She thought, for a moment, it must be a Pillar of the Divines, towering above the surrounding trees ten times over. But as she looked further, she came to realize it wasn't a pillar or gift from the gods at all.

It was a Tree.[*]

Neer's jaw dropped at its enormity, which could be seen from where she stood nearly halfway across the forest.

Thurandír approached her side. Staring at the tree, he said, "That's Galdir. The Mother of all Ko'ehlaeu'at trees. They—"

"Come on!" a warrior with dark, shoulder-length hair hissed, shoving Thurandír forward.

The younger evae snarled at him. He then straightened his back and turned to Neer. She stole another glance at the Tree and then followed Thurandír up the hillside. They trailed behind the others, keeping a measured distance as they approached the lonesome building.

"This is Aardn," Thurandír explained of the longhouse ahead. "The seat of the Eirean. We only have two council members here, but the others gathered when the lanathess started their invasion." Their eyes met. "Do not try to fool them. Do not try to fight them. That friend of yours—

---

[*] Tree is a term used for the large, glowing trees that are found throughout the continent of Laeroth.

The origin of the Trees are unknown, though they are believed to hold powerful magical energy, and even in the harshest of climates, they never lose their glowing flowers or leaves.

Avelloch—he's a *nesiat*. Banished. If you want to come out of here alive, then don't tell them you know him."

Neer glanced at the building. It was tall, with large arched windows outlined in dark wood. The roof had a steep pitch, with a large chimney protruding along the left side of its apex.

"Don't pretend you can't speak our language," he said, trailing behind his companions. "You can't convince them of your innocence if you're a mute."

She stared at the ground, still unwilling to speak to him. Unable to get close to the person she might wind up killing, should she choose to flee. It all depended on the Eirean and their judgement. It all depended on her chance of survival once she entered those immaculate double doors.

Neer's shoulders rose and fell as she breathed in deep, heavy breaths. She peered at her surroundings, realizing they were far from civilization. Even from the top of the hill, she could see nothing but trees and dirt.

Find Avelloch. That's what Aélla had told her. She had to find him. She had to bring everyone together again. Her mind shifted back to Thurandír and his warning to keep her friendship with Avelloch a secret. He was banished. The thought sent chills down her spine. Her binds tugged when she instinctively reached for his sword on her hip, searching for its comfort, but her blood ran cold when she remembered it wasn't there.

"Hey!" Aen'mysvaral's voice caused her to flinch when he called out from the top of the hill. Everyone turned when he pointed at Neer, who stood alone on the hillside. Two warriors made angry remarks at Thurandír, shoving past him and marching to Neer's side.

She didn't fight when they grabbed her arms and forced her up the path.

They gathered at the hilltop and removed their weapons.

"Check her," Aen'mysvaral stated, placing his bow onto a long wooden table.

The two men holding Neer captive quickly patted her down. She fought against them, unable to break free, when they stole a dagger from her belt loop and tossed it onto the table.

"She's clean."

The leader nodded without a glance in their direction. Neer huffed as they released her and then placed their own weaponry atop the table with the others. Six bows and nearly two dozen daggers and swords lay side by side. Each of them held beautiful, swirled designs etched into the blades or wood.

The silence lifted when the double doors slowly opened, and everyone watched as a woman stepped outside. Two thin antlers stood atop her head, attached to the woven hooded shawl hanging to her mid-back and over her eyes. Red runic designs were drawn over the white tempera covering her face, while blackness coated her lips in a jagged, uneven pattern.

Her robes were made of thick white canvas laden with black.

"You have come with another," she said, her voice pure as a sunrise.

"We have the one the lanathess seek," Aen'mysvaral stated.

The woman turned to him, though she could not see through the material shrouding her eyes. "Elidyr Galadúr," she greeted, and Neer wondered if this was another name he carried. "Son of Kyo'Dorith and Uthaarin."

"Torvála," Aen'mysvaral greeted the woman, taking her hand and kissing her fingers. "It is an honor to be in your presence."

"Bring her forward."

Aen'mysvaral turned to his companions, and Neer struggled against the two warriors leading her to the mysterious woman. They thrust her forward, and she stumbled to her knees at the woman's feet.

"Stand," the woman stated, her voice emotionless and pure.

Neer stared at the ground, frustrated and afraid. She closed her eyes, ready to harness her energy and flee, but the woman whispered a chant, and Neer felt suddenly absent of her magic. Emptiness and ice filled her chest where it had once gathered. She exhaled a pained breath, unable to quell the ache in her lungs.

"Stand," she said again.

Neer choked, her face turning red as she struggled to ease the burning in her chest. Her wrists bled as she fought against her restraints, and beads of sweat formed across her brow.

Thurandír stepped closer, and his leader lifted an arm, silently commanding him to stay put.

Neer breathed quickly. "What..." She strained to speak, using her native language in her panic. "What did you do to me?"

The woman was still as a statue, the veil blanketing her eyes. "Stand."

Neer sat on the ground, heaving, and then rose to her feet, dirt coating her knees. She stood with a slouch, unable to find strength now that her magic was blocked.

"The council awaits within," the woman said before turning to Aen'mysvaral. "You may enter with the *valaforael*."

He bowed and then turned to Neer. She stared at the ground when he took her arm and led her through the doors, into the chambers of the Eirean council.

Chapter Six

The Eirean
Nerana

"Trust your instincts. They are all that will keep you alive."

— Zeke Vindagraav to his daughter, Vaeda

The room was spacious and open. Large wooden beams arched across the ceiling, creating a natural pathway to the large firepit near the back of the room.

Hanging from above by various lengths of ropes were bird, elk, and wolf skulls—wind chimes made of animal bones—and woven trinkets matching the one Avelloch had gifted Neer. Weathered swords and bows, both ancient and new, hung on the walls, showcasing their scars and stains.

Golden sunlight filtered into the wide, open room through the skylights and windows. The scent of jasmine and blood filled the air as they stepped closer to the smoldering firepit.

Sitting in a half-circle around the heat were six strangers, each of them unique in appearance. The man on the far left, who was more elegant than the rest, with longer limbs and a narrower face, raised his hand. Aen'mysvaral and Neer stopped at his silent command.

His skin was olive-complected, and his dark green, upturned eyes gave him an air of power the others didn't hold. He wore a grey fur shawl over his shoulders, and ebony hair flowed to his mid-back.

"*Oot velok midory?*" he said in a deep voice that rumbled through the air.

The man sitting next to him, with an appearance better matching the people of Clan Rhyl, translated, "Who is this outsider?"

Aen'mysvaral stood straighter. His shoulders broadened, and he explained, "This is the one the lanathess seek."

Parchment crinkled as he removed Neer's wanted poster from his pocket and passed it to a young woman standing against the wall. A beige sack dress hung loosely from her frail shoulders. She was one of many—both men and women—who stood behind each of the wooden posts upholding the ceiling.

The woman handed the note to the man in the shawl, and he dismissed her with a lazy wave of his hand. She obediently returned to her place, standing like the others with her back pressed against the wall and her hands tucked together at her waist.

Neer's poster was handed to each person in the semicircle. They studied the image for a moment before shifting their eyes to her. She glanced at each of them, showing no distress beneath their harrowing gazes. Without a weapon or magic, she was defenseless, but she couldn't let them see the fear swelling inside. The fear that could be her downfall should they see how deep it festered.

A woman—who Neer could immediately identify as Klaet'il from her pointed chin, scowled expression, and dark tattoos—leaned forward in her chair. The wooden furniture creaked beneath her weight. Her language was harsh and direct, sending chills down Neer's spine as she spoke with the same intimidating tone as the others of her clan. Much like all the other klaet'il warriors, her skin was tan, eyes were light blue, and her head was shaven on the right side, revealing the angled and intense markings etched across her scalp.

Her angry voice cut through the air, and Aen'mysvaral was silent. She leaned back with a hateful sneer, rubbing her finger and thumb together while she glared at Neer.

"Master Eirean," Aen'mysvaral stated. "I request that you speak *lana'igrit*, the common tongue of the lanathess, so that she may—"

The woman scoffed with a loud laugh. "Speak the common tongue?" Her words spewed from her lips like venom. "What does this matter to you, *warrior*? Do you wish to bed this *dro'fahmel*? Has she laid some claim to you that we are not aware of—"

"No," he said, a hint of hesitation in his strong voice. "She doesn't understand our languages."

"No?" the woman asked with harsh curiosity. Her chair squealed as she rose to her feet and marched to Neer's side. She stood a hand taller, with eyes that cut like daggers. The woman walked in slow circles around Neer, a thin finger trailing along her jaw, examining every inch of her battered, broken body. "She has survived this far into the forest, yet she does not speak our tongue?"

Aen'mysvaral inhaled a deep breath. "Not that I'm aware."

"Hmm…" Her footsteps tapped against the wooden floor as she rounded Neer, taking in a slow sniff of her singed hair. "What is her name?"

The man from Clan Rhyl glanced at the wanted poster and then announced, "Vaeda."

The woman scoffed. "Disgusting creatures." She stood in front of Neer and took half a step forward, bridging the gap between them.

Neer narrowed her eyes and clenched her jaw when the woman spoke in the common tongue of the Klaet'il.

She paused and then spoke in the language of the Rhyl. "I will start with her tongue," she said, and Neer inhaled a deep breath, preparing for the pain. The woman smiled a sinister grin and then turned back to the others. "She can understand us."

They inhaled quiet gasps. Aen'mysvaral glanced at Neer, who avoided his gaze and stared at the Klaet'il leader.

"Naisannis," the Eirean from Rhyl started, "how can you be sure—"

"*Speak*," Naisannis growled, her eyes burning into Neer's.

A thousand shards of broken thoughts spun through Neer's mind, unsure of what to do or how to survive.

Naisannis stepped closer, pulling a bone dagger from its sheath. She pressed it against Neer's stomach. "*Speak.* Like the dog you are."

Neer inhaled a deep breath and said in perfect Evaesh, "I understand you."

Aen'mysvaral's eyes widened with shock and fury. The Eirean council remained silent, staring at Neer with the same stunned expressions.

Naisannis's lips twisted into a furious scowl. "Why are you here?"

Neer straightened when the tip of the dagger pressed against her abdomen. "I was running."

"From what?"

Her eyes narrowed. "The Nasir."

The room was deathly silent. Naisannis displayed a look somewhere between madness and humor. Her eyes flashed to Neer's hair and then to the scorch marks on her clothes. "You were in the desert. You've brought war upon us!" She turned sharply, eyeing each of her comrades. "There is talk of a revolution in Aragoth! Look at her clothes! Her hair is singed!" She yanked a fistful of Neer's hair, causing her to wince. "She must be executed! This treachery, this...*abomination* cannot stand!"

"Naisannis," the man sitting to the right of the Rhyl Eirean spoke. He, too, resembled the people of Clan Rhyl. "Please. Let us discuss this with civility and—"

"*Civility?*" she snapped. "This is a *drimil'lana*! She has torn her country apart, waged war against the vaxros, and seeks to destroy our very home! Her people are massacring ours each day! Do you—"

"*I* am not responsible for the war with the vaxros," Neer said, her voice strong with resolve.

Naisannis whirled around, glaring at her with eyes of hatred.

"And I didn't call my people into your lands."

Naisannis trembled with fury. Her eyes widened and lips pursed together.

Sitting at the far right of the Eirean assembly was a small humanoid creature with wrinkled green skin, a robust stomach, and solid yellow eyes. He was no taller than a child, with stocky arms and legs. A loin cloth covered his waistline, and a necklace of thick bones hung over his chest.

His mouth was wide, stretching nearly from ear to ear, and full of sharp fangs. Dark green scars lay intentional patterns across his skin. When he spoke, his voice was thick and raspy. The language was harsh, sounding more like a hacked cough than words.

Naisannis nodded when he fell silent, and then she returned her gaze to the Eirean. "Her intent doesn't matter," she said, translating the green man's words. "This *dro'fahmel* must be executed at once! Her body should be torn and placed at every corner of the forest as a warning to all those who seek entry into our lands!"

Sitting between the Rhyl Eirean and Naisannis's empty chair was an evaesh woman with large antlers growing from her head. Her ears were like that of a deer, and her legs were animalistic at her shins, with hooves instead of feet. She wore nothing but a thick scapular of furs and tails, and a bone mask, adorned with swirled vines, covered her upper face.

She was more muscular than the others, with thick arms and legs. Her eyes were on Neer as she asked, "Must we condemn her to death for the crimes of her people?"

Naisannis hissed. "She brings war and death to us all! Her very existence will be our doom!"

"The Klaet'il have always seen the world through distorted colors," the half-deer, half-evae said, leaning back in her chair. "We should allow her to speak. The spirits of the land have brought her this far."

"No. It was not the spirits or forest that led her to our doorstep. It was your *warriors*." Naisannis glared at the Rhyl leaders, who sat without expression, as if they expected her condemnation. "Had *my* people found her, they'd have torn her apart before she had time to think. What have you done, Falavar? Glisseríel?" She spoke to the Rhyl leaders. "She's a powerful drimil, and you've not only allowed your esteemed warriors to guide her through our lands, protecting and feeding her, but she's been invited into our sacred chambers! How long ago did you find her, Elidyr? One moon? Two? How long have you given this meena'keen time to plan her escape or revenge?"

"Enough!" Glisseríel, the second man in the formation, called. "I concur with Calasiem. Let this lanathess state her intentions. Allow her the chance to prove her innocence." Falavar, the man to his left, nodded and raised his hand. The shawled evae repeated his gesture, casting their votes in favor of Neer. The green man never raised his hand, though he didn't need to—the consensus was four to two.

Glisseríel clasped his hands together at his waist. "Take your seat, Naisannis. Allow Vaeda to speak on her own behalf."

Naissanis's lip twitched and fists balled. She marched across the pit and sat in her chair with one leg crossed over the other, still clutching the bone dagger in her right hand.

Glisseríel waved his hand and said, "Speak."

Neer exhaled a shaky breath and twisted her aching shoulders. Eyeing each of the Eirean, she said, "My name is Nerana. I was born to Ria Vindagraav. I'm a human...and I'm a sorceress."

Glisseríel translated as the shawled evae spoke. "How do you speak our language?"

"My magic."

Calasiem, the half-evae, half-deer, asked, "What are you doing here?"

"Running from the Nasir."

Naisannis scoffed with a disgusted laugh. The others glanced at her before returning their attention to Neer.

"Why are your people invading?" Calasiem asked. Her voice was soft and kind.

Neer licked her lips before gulping through the dryness in her throat. "They're here because I killed one of my leaders. I stopped him from massacring an innocent family."

The second Rhyl Eirean asked, "So they invade the forest?"

Neer stared at the ground, wishing she could cross her arms. "The evae started an invasion of their own. Through Vleland, they entered our borders and killed many innocent people...The Order is using my attack as an excuse to invade."

Naisannis barked with laughter. "This is ridiculous! You can't possibly believe that—"

"It's true," Aen'mysvaral stated. He stood tall with his arms behind his back. "I spoke with your advisor, and he confirmed these claims. The Klaet'il were attacking nyx and lanathess territories. We're still investigating the depth of this incursion, but it seems that since the lanathess invasion, they've pulled back."

"You!" Naisannis shouted, her face red and eyes wide. "How dare you! I should have your tongue sliced from your throat for speaking such heresy!"

An argument simmered on Aen'mysvaral's tongue, but before he could speak, the door behind opened, and a wave of sunlight swept across the room. A long shadow disrupted its warmth when a man stepped inside.

Glisseríel scowled at the man who had disturbed their meeting. Aen'mysvaral turned to him, while Neer stared at the floor, hoping to find a way out of this. The footsteps of the stranger echoed from behind as he slowly entered the room.

"You were meant to be here at the start of the meeting," Glisseríel warned, and the footsteps halted.

When the leader continued, Neer's heart stopped, and a fire brewed deep within.

"Where have you been, Klaud?"

Chapter Seven

Fade to Black
Aélla

"Until the sun fades to ash, shall my oath remain."

— Vow of the Al'Yavan warrior

Aélla stood motionless, her heart wrenching and eyes burning with tears. She didn't want to believe it. Couldn't face the reality of what she saw.

"No...," she whimpered. Her hand curled over her heart, and she stepped forward, staring at Y'ven's body.

Aélla raced across the room, tears dripping down her cheeks as she approached his side. Dru lay on his chest with her knees pulled inward. Her leafy skin was paler than usual, appearing more yellow than red. She opened her tired eyes and attempted to lift her head but collapsed onto Y'ven, weak.

"Dru...," Aélla cried. She lifted her gaze to the nes'seil mixing herbs at a table on the back wall. "Why haven't you healed them?" The nes'seil turned to Aélla, who marched closer. "Why are you allowing them to die!"

"Aélla!" Thallon rushed to her side and took her arm to keep her from further approaching the healer.

The human nes'seil, dressed in dark robes, glanced at Y'ven. His head bowed in sorrow. "We do not know the way. Our herbs did nothing for them."

Aélla trembled and her lip quivered. She yanked herself from Thallon's grasp and moved to Y'ven's side. Her fingers hovered over his body, and she struggled over what to do. Her mind went back to a battle they had faced before allying themselves with Neer, when Aélla had attempted to heal him. Back then, he had informed her that the best means of healing for a vaxros was not by magic or herbs…It was by fire.

Energy sparked within her, radiating from her eyes as she sprang forward and cupped her hands together. A ball of flames ignited between her palms, sending flickering tendrils of heat that cast light across her skin. She held her hands out toward Dru, who lay motionless on Y'ven's chest.

"Come on, Dru…," she begged, but the faeth never budged. "Thallon!" she called, her voice cracking in her agony. "Put her in the flames."

"What?"

"Do it!"

He hesitated before carefully lifting Dru into his hands and placing her on the edge of Aélla's palm, avoiding the blaze. Dru rolled into the flames, and they burned hotter. Aélla breathed heavily, watching as the faeth was engulfed in heat.

Firelight glistened in Aélla's eyes as she stared, unblinking, at Dru. She sniffed and choked on her breath. "Come on…"

"Aélla…" Thallon placed his hand on her shoulder. She closed her eyes, releasing a quiet whimper.

She lost hope, and the flames receded, reducing to a simmering glow around the unmoving faeth. Aélla shook her head, overcome with grief.

Her heart skipped when a flicker of light sparked in her palms. Through misty eyes, she watched Dru's wings twitch. With a gasp, Aélla strengthened the flames, and Dru slowly opened her tired eyes.

The faeth pushed herself up on weak arms and looked around through half-opened eyes. Her gaze paused on Aélla before she turned aside, scanning the room. Sorrow replaced her exhaustion when she noticed Y'ven. Three times she glanced between Aélla and Y'ven, before her brows pulled inward into a deep, angry scowl.

Her aura returned when the flames erupted, sending waves of heat high into the air. Aélla leapt back, stumbling onto the empty bed behind her. Dru darted to Y'ven's side, clutched the sheet, and then flew to his chest, dragging the linen away from his face. Bruises darkened his cheeks and forehead, painting his yellowed skin in shades of deeper red.

Dru knelt atop his exposed chest, pushing flames into his skin. Aélla followed, stumbling forward and pressed her palms against his stomach. Hot magic scorched through her as heat blazed beneath her palms. White energy burned the air around her hands, rippling with heat waves that drifted into the air. She pushed harder, forcing her energy into him. Energy that drained her strength.

Slowly, his chest rose, and Y'ven inhaled a ragged breath. Dru flinched. She turned to him with wide eyes, watching as his face twitched.

Aélla slowed her magic and turned to face him. Tears stained her cheeks, blurring her vision. She sniffed and stepped to the head of the cot. Her searing hands touched his face, and he opened his dreary eyes.

A low cry, like the tinkling of bells, escaped from Dru, and she collapsed to her knees in tears.

"Drimil...," Y'ven stated in his native language. His voice was gruff with exhaustion.

"Rest, Y'ven," Aélla said with a hand on his shoulder. "You're okay."

He groaned and clenched his teeth.

Thallon moved to his side. "Hey, big guy. Didn't expect to find you here in our lands."

Y'ven blinked his dull yellow eyes into focus and scanned the room.

"You're in the forest," Aélla explained. "Nerana brought you here. Were you together? Did you—"

"I don't..." He clutched his side with a groan. "I don't know."

Dru stepped across his chest. Her hands twirled together as she approached his face. Tears welled in her eyes. Y'ven shifted his attention to her, and he lifted his arm, ready to touch her, when his breath caught in his throat.

Wide eyes stared at his right arm, which was covered in black, necrotic skin. His bones displayed beneath layers of rotten flesh. Dry blood stained the edges of his opened wounds. He breathed heavily, staring at his severely injured limb.

"Shit...," Thallon said breathlessly.

Aélla covered her lips with her hand. Her breathing halted as she eyed his injury.

The nes'seil approached Y'ven's side. Gazing at his arm, the human explained, "We must remove his arm. Once he's strong enough we can—"

"No," Y'ven said. He breathed heavily, overcome with rage, and suddenly struck the healer with his left fist.

The nes'seil crashed into the wall before collapsing to the floor.

"Y'ven!" Aélla exclaimed.

A woman rushed to the healer's side. She inspected his face with a gentle touch. "I think your jaw is broken," she said.

The healer kindly pulled away and gripped his face. "I'm fine, Nicolette," he said.

A deep growl vibrated from Y'ven's throat. He sat up and gripped his forehead, overcome with vertigo. Aélla gripped his left arm to steady him, while Dru hovered at his face. Her big eyes were full of concern.

"How long?" Y'ven said with a slight growl.

Aélla stepped away to give him space. "I don't know. Thallon and I woke days ago. We escaped together, and Nerana brought you here."

Y'ven stared at his arm as Dru spoke to him. He inhaled a deep breath, and his broad shoulders rose. His face hardened and lips pressed into a thin line. When she fell silent, he closed his eyes and exhaled. Exhausted, he spoke in his native language when he said, "Druindarvenia woke alone. It took her a full cycle[*] to find me."

---

[*] A cycle, or sun cycle, is a vax term meaning day.

SHADOWS OF NYN'DIRA

Aélla translated, and then Thallon asked, "Did she see Neer?"

Y'ven shook his head, and the room fell deathly silent. Aélla crossed her arms over her chest to quell the dread festering inside. She couldn't believe that Neer would have run away after leaving Y'ven in the forest like this. She wouldn't have abandoned them.

"A?" Thallon asked.

Aélla lifted her gaze to meet with his and then swiftly turned away. "We must speak with the villagers. See if they've seen her."

"Magic is unpredictable," he said. "Neer isn't strong like you. She could have been torn apart or wound up across the world."

"Y'ven is here. That means Nerana is too." She paused. "We just have to find her."

Thallon placed his hands on his hips. "I'll go speak to the leaders. You three stay here."

Aélla nodded as he left the room. Her teeth clenched when pain struck her ribs, and she leaned forward with her palms against the edge of Y'ven's cot. Dru fluttered to her side, staring at her with a tilted head. Aélla breathed heavily, overcoming the agony.

Her fingers clutched the sheets, and she fell into her thoughts, becoming lost in her worry. Visions moved through her mind like dreary clouds, fading from one to the next, reminding her of the fate she faced.

Of the fate they all faced.

When Neer entered her mind, she held her breath. It was the face of a broken, defeated warrior. The face of darkness and despair. Neer needed saving, but there was no one to find her. No one who could understand the depth of her pain or rage. Aélla could see it swelling inside her, but in all her power, she couldn't heal the fractures of Neer's worn and battered soul.

And now she was in the forest—a place Aélla had told her to be...but she was lost, unable to be found in a land teeming with war and rage. Should the evae find her, she'd have to fight or face her end. They'd never

---

Each cycle is one day on Erolith

allow her to go. They'd never give passage to someone like her. A "monster" and "demon."

Aélla shuddered at the thoughts, pushing them far from her mind. She couldn't allow herself to be consumed with grief or worry. Not now, when everyone needed her strength. But she was tired and wished that she had never taken the vow. Life would be simple, and she could've had all that she wanted.

She shook her head, not allowing herself to fall into a state of longing or despair. This was her path. It was her choice, and she would see it to the end.

"Drimil...," Y'ven started, still speaking in his native tongue.

Aélla blinked away her thoughts before focusing on him.

"I am sorry. I have failed you."

Her heart ached at his sorrowful words. She stepped closer, gripping his arm and staring into his eyes. "No," she said. "You kept us alive, Y'ven. If you wish to return to Aragoth, then I will take you...but...but I would be honored if you would see this through with me."

His eyes shifted to his infected arm. "I am no longer a warrior. I cannot fight."

She focused her magic, sending tendrils of heat through her palms that absorbed into his skin. His doubt lifted and misery faded when she touched the deepest parts of his soul, shifting his emotions from sorrow to peace. "So long as you are alive, you can fight," she said. Their eyes met, and she held his gaze. "Do not let this define your worth, Y'ven. There are many who prevail against the worst odds."

He closed his eyes, allowing her words to sink into his mind. "Thank you, Master Drimil. I would be honored to fight by your side. Honored to follow you."

Aélla smiled. "We stand together. You can do this."

He nodded and gripped his injured arm. Aélla watched him with deep concern, noticing the paleness of his skin and tiredness in his eyes. Her eyes fell to his wounded limb. The poison eating his flesh would continue to spread, and she knew if they didn't act soon, he would lose his entire arm.

Possibly his life.

But he had refused the idea of amputating his limb, resorting to violence in his panic. Aélla understood his belief—any warrior who was maimed or crippled was considered unworthy and disgraced. It was a brutal stance that all vaxros warriors upheld. But no matter his views, Aélla wouldn't allow him to die, and should he continue to refuse aid, she would force it upon him. Whatever was necessary to save his life.

For now, she gave him the honor of making that decision himself. Though, it wouldn't be long before the choice would have to be made, regardless of his pride.

Aélla turned away, realizing now how long she had been staring, when Y'ven said, "I need sunlight or flame."

She nodded. "Of course."

Aélla led him outside. Through the threshold, they stepped into warm sunlight. Y'ven raised his head to the sun, basking in the golden rays shining from above. He inhaled a deep breath that expanded his chest and broadened his shoulders. When pain struck his arm, he winced and clutched above his elbow, where the necrosis faded into healthy skin.

He and Aélla turned their attention to Thallon when he approached from behind. A look of sorrow pulled his expression, and with a glance at Aélla, he softly shook his head, wordlessly answering what he knew she would ask. Neer wasn't there, nor had anyone seen her.

"Taken," Y'ven suggested in evaesh. "Captured."

"Maybe," Aélla said, the words weighing heavily on her mind as he spoke such devastation into existence. If Neer had been captured, she might not be alive. The thoughts were unspeakable. Aélla clenched her teeth, hoping it wasn't true.

"They did find this," Thallon said, revealing Avelloch's sword.

Aélla's eyes widened, and she stepped closer. Her hands lingered above the enchanted steel.

"But there is no sign of her."

"Where was this?" Aélla asked.

"Just south, where they found Y'ven. They assumed he was attacked by the Zaeril." Their eyes met when he spoke Avelloch's *sitria*,° or nickname.

Aélla carefully wrapped her hands around the sword and collected it from Thallon's grasp. Red dirt from the desert clung to the blood staining the blade. It filled the cracks of the leather-wrapped hilt. "This was hers," Aélla said. "She's here."

Thallon asked, "Where would she have gone? Why isn't she with Y'ven?"

"I don't know." She scanned the village. "But something is happening in the forest...The magic here is weakening." She paused. "I'll seek guidance from the ilitran. It could also help us find Nerana."

"Are you sure?"

She pulled the sword closer, as if protecting it would somehow keep Neer safe. "There is no other choice." Her gaze set to her companions, who looked to her for guidance.

This was her duty. Her vow. She had to keep her strength, even in times of desperation or sorrow.

With forced resolve, she straightened her posture and said, "Thallon, once I've healed, I will take you to Navarre. You need to speak to the Eirean and let them know of the ring. Let them know what happened in the desert." She paused. "If Nerana was captured by our people, they'll take her there. Be her voice. She'll need an ally."

He nodded.

° A sitria is bestowed upon warriors who are known throughout the forest as remarkably gifted. Most warriors with a sitria are respected and revered members of the avel, but some are mysterious. Their true identity unknown.

Avelloch gained his nickname long ago after fighting against human and Klaet'il invaders. Those who saw the lone fighter quickly took note and proclaimed him as the Zaeril, or wolf.

"Y'ven," she continued, "I will have the nes'seil start a fire for you and Dru. I will return here after bringing Thallon to the Eirean, and then the three of us will go to the ilitran together."

He gave a stiff nod and then grimaced, clutching his arm.

"We will rest here," she stated, her voice resounding with promise. "Tomorrow, our journey begins."

Chapter Eight

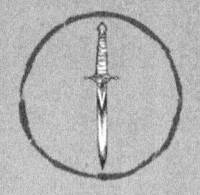

Mercy and Vengeance
Nerana

"Forgiveness brings peace to the mind. Vengeance brings power to the soul."

— Nizotl, the Book of Darkness

NEER'S DARK EYES SET ON KLAUD, burning with hatred and rage. If she could use her energy, he'd have been dead before taking his next breath. But she was powerless in her chains, forced to endure the torment of his presence in utter silence while the Eirean studied her furious expression.

Steady footsteps tapped against the floor as Klaud brought himself closer. His head was held high, and his eyes were emotionless. He was as she remembered—full of confidence and poise, emitting a tone of calmness and power, though not in the threatening or arrogant way that many carried. His was elegant and peaceful.

Neer seethed as he moved closer. His hooded evergreen robes were layered and refined, splitting at his waist where a thick leather belt held buckled pouches and an empty sheath for his dagger.

"My apologies," Klaud said, his voice sending fire through Neer, scorching her soul.

She glared, wishing she could vaporize him.

He never glanced in her direction. Instead, his eyes remained focused on the leaders, though he stood near her, so close she could reach out and touch him had her arms not been bound so tightly.

"I came as soon as I received the call," he said.

"Are these claims true?" Falavar, a Rhyl Eirean, asked. "Were the Klaet'il invading lanathess territory while you were in pursuit of the Trials of Blood?"

He inhaled a deep breath and stood taller, bolstering with confidence. "Yes."

Naisannis spit on the floor. Her light blue eyes narrowed as she simmered, glaring at Klaud. "Lies!"

"What reason would I have to lie, Naisannis?"

"You were in their lands! You traveled with that *nesiat*!"

Klaud's jaw tightened at her mention of Avelloch. Neer breathed heavily, never averting her gaze from his face.

"You have been influenced by these mongrels!"

Their attention turned to Aen'mysvaral when he stated, "The Klaet'il's invasion is not why we are here." He pointed at Neer. "*She* is! This meena'keen has scourged our lands with war and violence. Why is she given the chance to speak? Are you to trust the words of a lanathess? Of *Drimil'Nizotl*?"

Klaud's eyes narrowed with disdain. "If this lanathess is so dangerous and vile, then why are you still alive, Elidyr? If she were truly as mad and powerful as you all fear her to be, she wouldn't have allowed herself to be captured."

Aen'mysvaral's lip twitched with fury. He turned away with balled fists but said no more.

The Eirean with the grey shawl and green eyes spoke in his native language. Klaud tensed when the leader flung an arm in his direction. Glisseríel, the second Rhyl Eirean, exhaled a deep breath and lightly nodded.

"Klaud," he started, averting his attention to the drimil. "You traveled through their lands and told us of your time in *Lana'Thoviin*.° During that time, did you ever come across a warning such as this?" He offered Neer's poster, and a servant stepped forward, passing it from the Eirean to Klaud.

° In the language of the evae, Lana'Thoviin translates to mean *human territories*

Klaud's hard eyes were on the Eirean when he accepted the note and then reluctantly set upon its image. His jaw tightened. "No," he said, turning away from the parchment.

Naisannis marched to Neer's side, her eyes blazing. "You're saying that you've *never* heard of this woman?"

Neer winced as the leader grabbed her hair and forced her to face Klaud. Their eyes met, and his hollow, regretful eyes averted from her gaze.

"We've all heard of Drimil'Nizotl," he explained. "That doesn't mean the rumors are true."

Her eyes narrowed with suspicion. "You're hiding something."

Klaud tensed.

"What do you know?"

Klaud was frozen. His jaw clenched and his breathing was heavy as he became silent. Neer watched him, studying his hardened expression. She had never seen such turmoil or unrest in his eyes. It made her sick. Before she had the chance to say it—to reveal that they did in fact know each other, a low voice rumbled from outside. The tension was split when the doors burst open and someone scurried into the hall.

"It's important!" a man said to the woman in white.

Neer's breath caught in her throat when Thallon's voice rang through the air. His steps were quick as he eyed the Eirean, stepping past Neer without a glance in her direction, as if he hadn't noticed her at all. "I'm sorry to interrupt!" he called. "But the Nasir—"

The fur-shawled Eirean stood, his deep voice resounding through the room in the native tongue of the Rhyl. "What is the meaning of this?" His thin lips pursed together, and wrinkles formed lines around his upturned eyes. "The Rhyl have truly lost their way to allow such disrespect and indiscipline!"

"Thallon," Glisseríel hissed. "Why have you interrupted this meeting?"

Thallon bowed. "I apologize, Master Eirean. Drimil'Rothar brought me here. I was instructed to bring you news of the Nasir's actions in Aragoth!"

"His actions?"

"Yes!" He gulped and took a deep breath. "He has the ring!"

Their fury deepened. The shawled Eirean shook his head. "This is an outrage!" he said before speaking quickly in his native language, mentioning Neer more than once.

Thallon's face paled. He turned back, and his jaw dropped at the sight of her, bound and bruised. "Shit…"

"Thallon," Klaud started, catching the scholar's attention with his pained voice. "Where is she?"

"She's, uh…" He wiped his palms against his trousers. "*Kila*…what are you two doing here?"

"Where. Is. She?"

"She's at the ilitran. Shit! Shit! *Shit!*" His eyes shifted to Neer and then back to Klaud. He breathed heavily, overcome with panic as they stood in the presence of their leaders.

Their attention returned to the Eirean when Falavar called Thallon's name. He stood tall, the fear in his eyes betraying his forced sense of confidence.

"You were tasked with retrieving the *clavia muinsii*[*] undetected and without suspicion. How could it have wound up in the hands of the Nasir?"

"Preposterous!" Naisannis snapped. "The Nasir has never stepped foot in the desert! This entire debate is futile and full of lies!"

Glisseríel shot her a glare and then returned his focus to Thallon.

The scholar inhaled a deep breath. "I was captured by the vaxros and saved by Drimil'Rothar," Thallon explained. "It is how we came into alliance with one another, but they never knew what I was searching for."

"Then how did you find it?"

"He didn't."

Everyone turned to Neer, who spoke with raw fury. Her eyes cut through them. She could end each of their pathetic lives if she had her magic. They were weak, inferior, and she could tell by their silence that they knew it too. But her best chance of survival wasn't in killing this

---

[*] A weapon with the power to transform living beings into creatures of darkness

council. She had enough to run from without putting an evaesh target on her back.

"I did."

"Excuse me?" Glisseríel stated. "How dare you—"

"Let her speak," the Eirean with antlers said, her voice soft and pure. "Go on."

Neer eyed each of them. "The ring was given to me in the Realm of Elements, beneath the dirt that pulled me under and trapped me in a pit of fire." She paused with purpose, studying their expressions. "The Nasir ambushed us when Aélla and I returned from Elandorr.°"

"Lies!" Naisannis snapped.

Fury exploded from Neer in a shockwave that rumbled through the air, cracking the walls and causing everyone to stagger back. She glared at Naisannis, who held an equally hateful gaze. "He came with several others. Riding on the backs of large, winged beasts." Her eyes moved to the Eirean resting in their semi-circle. "There was an elemental with him. A woman."

"Ithronél," Falavar explained, causing Naisannis to tense.

The Eirean with antlers asked, "Who gave you the ring?"

Neer's jaw tightened as she relived the harrowing moments beneath the ground. Without further explanation, she said, "I did."

Glisseríel grumbled. "Did you offer it to the Nasir?"

"No. Thallon took it and said that no one was to touch it. He said it was too dangerous to be handled by anyone else." Her eyes met with his, and she could sense the easement in his expression. "When the Nasir ambushed us, he nearly killed Thallon and stole it from him."

"Do you know what this ring can do?"

Her arms tightened and lip twitched. "Yes. He used it on a human…turned him into a gaelthral."

The Eirean exhaled a whispered gasp.

"We were defeated, so we escaped using our magic and came to the forest."

° A vast, ancient temple in the deserts of Aragoth. Elandorr holds the entrance to Tre'lan Aenwyn, or the realm of elements.

Falavar asked, "Why did you come here? Why not go back to your lands? Turn yourself over to your leaders and put an end to this massacre you've brought upon us!"

She exhaled a deep breath, tired of being blamed for the actions of others. Tired of being viewed as a monster. "Aélla told me to come here."

"And we're supposed to believe this? The words of a lanathess who doesn't hold the decency to call Drimil'Rothar by her rightful title?"

"It's true," Thallon stated. "She was there when Aélla—*Master Drimil*, saved me from the vaxros imprisonment. They are allies! She can be trusted."

Naisannis barked a laugh. "You're all *f'yet* if you believe this pitiful blather! This *dro'fahmel* will be the death of us all!"

"Do not call her that!" Thallon argued. "Neer is not one of them! She has proven herself worthy!"

A sinister grin pulled Naisannis's lips. "Oh, the sweet taste of love."

Thallon lowered his chin as he glared.

"Tell me, Master Scholar, did you start to see her as a trusted ally *before* or *after* she took you to bed?"

Klaud's jaw dropped as she said this, and he glanced between Neer and Thallon, a heavy pain lingering in his eyes.

Thallon's eyes narrowed with fury. "What would you know about love, Naisannis? Your people kill without mercy and condemn those you view as weak!"

She clicked her tongue. "You are clever, Scholar. I will assume the answer is *after*."

"Enough," Glisseríel said. "You can take your lover's quarrel elsewhere. We have heard from the lanathess and Thallon...Klaud"—their eyes met—"what is your opinion of this meena'keen?"

Neer held her breath, ready to fight should she have to. Slowly, he turned to her, and the sight of his sorrow—his guilt—sickened her. She tugged against her restraints, wanting nothing more than to end his miserable life. All she saw when she looked at him was a liar. A murderer. A man who put his own desires above all else and had chosen without mercy to end Loryk's life.

"Nerana…," he started, turning back to his leaders with confidence, "is not our enemy."

Naisannis scoffed with disgust. "He's hiding something! Why would you advise to trust this stranger who has brought death and destruction to our doorstep?"

Klaud turned to her, his eyes blazing with darkness and anger. "Because my friends trust her."

"Your friends?" She laughed. "Do you mean the innocent, *naïve* Drimil? This *madman* from the caves who has fallen for her tricks…" She stepped closer, eyes peering deep into his soul. "Or that *nesiat* you've been roaming the forests with?"

Klaud's jaw clenched at her mention of Avelloch.

She turned to the others. "This is an advisor of our council, yet he associates with a known murderer and enemy of our people! If he's willing to trust *Avelloch*"—the word cut through the air like sharp glass—"then how can we trust *him*?"

She set her attention back to Klaud, her thin lips pressed so tightly they were invisible.

"You never answered my question, *eólin*. Do you know this lanathess?" A long finger was pointed at Neer.

The silence was deafening as he struggled to speak. Struggled to appease his leaders or tell the truth. Klaud folded his hands into tight fists, his knuckles turning white. His arms were tense and eyes were red as he stood unblinking in his thoughts. "No."

Anger erupted through Neer. Her eyes darkened and soul fractured with rage. "Liar!" she proclaimed.

The building trembled as her suppressed magic ripped through the air. Klaud lowered his head, staring at the floor.

Thallon's fearful eyes set on Neer, his complexion matching Klaud's natural white tone. "Neer…," he said in a voice trembling with uncertainty and terror.

Naisannis set her eyes to Neer. "You know him?"

Neer's lip twitched. If she had control of her magic, if it wasn't empty and forced to be unleashed through her rage alone, she'd end his life. Anger swelled inside, and she willed her magic to return, forcing energy that was numbed to strike him down and make right the injustice he had caused.

"We traveled together," she said, and his head fell lower, eyes closed. "We went through the Trials *together*. He survived because of *me*. Aélla is alive because of *me*!"

Her anger rose, seeping through her pores with a dark glow that vibrated the air. The teal of her eyes darkened, and the light tremors of her magic shook the air, rattling the walls and windchimes.

"He betrayed me. He killed my best friend and left me to die!"

Glisseríel exhaled an angry breath. His condemning eyes were set on Klaud, whose gaze never veered from the floor. "Klaud," he said, forcing the drimil to look him in the eye. "Is this true?"

Klaud's jaw tensed. He breathed heavily, overcome with grief. His eyes fell to the floor, hesitant to reveal the truth. Neer glared at him, and the swell of emotions boiling within her set her chest ablaze. Her throat was tight with fury, and she knew just one wrong syllable would send her over the edge.

"Klaud...," Thallon pressed, the worry still evident in his voice.

"Silence!" Glisseríel snapped.

Klaud licked his lips and gave a stiff, reluctant nod. It was his only response.

Thallon's shoulders dropped at this revelation. He turned to Neer, seeping with remorse, but her eyes were set on Klaud, watching as he admitted to the lie he had so brazenly spoken to his leaders.

With a glance at the others, who gave subtle nods, Glisseríel rose to his feet. "It is decided," he said. "Because of her ties to Drimil'Rothar and our trusted scholar, this Ianathess will not be sentenced to death. She will instead be returned immediately to her people, as an offering of peace in hopes they cease the war and return to their lands."

"No!" Thallon argued. "Please, you can't do this!"

"Silence!"

Thallon clenched his jaw, worry bleeding through his eyes while his expression held on to its anger.

Glisseríel continued, "Klaud. You have greatly disappointed this council and proven disloyal to your people. We have overlooked your relationship with a known nesiat—a crime punishable by death. But you have forsaken your vow of trust in this sacred chamber by lying to this council." Anger and disappointment rose in his voice. "You have attended many meetings since the lanathess invasion, yet you have failed to mention your close alliance with Drimil'Nizotl. Had you been forthcoming with this information, the forest may not see the peril that has been cast upon us!" He paused, collecting his rage. Speaking through clenched teeth, he said, "These acts of treason cannot go unpunished."

Klaud stared at the floor, unblinking.

"It is the decision of this council to hereby banish you from Clan Rhyl. We will bestow upon your flesh the *fil'veraal* to signify your punishment."

Thallon stepped forward. "Wa-wait a second!"

They ignored his cries, waving a servant forward who placed a branding iron into the fire.

"Klaud is loyal!" Thallon continued. "He should be pardoned! And Neer is an ally of Drimil'Rothar! You cannot break the treaty! She can't be given to her people!"

"Quiet!" Naisannis growled. "You come here with false accusations and forbidden alliances! You should be banished with the others!"

"She was there—in the desert! We traveled together! Do not condemn her to death! Do not condemn him to a life of seclusion!"

"Thallon!" Aen'mysvaral hissed.

"Please, listen to me!" His voice echoed through the wide chamber. Everyone shifted their eyes to Thallon, who stood before the council, glistening with sweat. "Naik'avel has come! The forest is dying—we can *all* feel it!" His jaw was tight, and he peered into the eyes of his leaders. "If she is not set on the right path, we *will* fall."

A chair creaked when the Eirean with antlers stood. She was nearly a head taller than the average human man, with a long, muscular body.

"The ydris stand with Drimil'Rothar. If what this scholar says is true, then we must do what is best for the fate of our world." Her eyes met with Thallon's. "If Master Drimil seeks to tame this lanathess...then we will put our faith in her."

Naisannis scoffed. "This is absurd! He's clearly been deluded by this demon's magic! Look at her! There is fury in her eyes and darkness in her heart."

"And there isn't in yours?" Thallon rebuked.

Naisannis's eyes widened, and her rage simmered. He ignored her, returning his attention to the council.

"If Neer isn't with *us*, she is with *them*...Would you truly pass her to our enemies on the brink of war? Whatever plans they have, they aren't in the best interest of the world. The lanathess don't give a shit about the rest of us! But Aélla does! And she believes the best thing for everyone is to keep Neer close." He paused, gauging each of their troubled expressions. "Please...allow her to return to Drimil'Rothar. She is the only one who can make this right."

Naisannis scoffed with a sharp laugh. "You're more deluded than I thought if you believe Naik'avel is anything more than a children's tale."

The first Eirean spoke, and the Rhyl next to him translated, stating, "We will keep her here until Drimil'Rothar—"

"There's no time!" Thallon called. "Allow me to escort Neer to the ilitian. Aélla will be there, and we'll continue to the Realms. Toward tre'lan Rothar and our salvation."

The Eirean deliberated for several minutes, and Neer listened while they spoke of her fate. She didn't expect them to allow her freedom and knew she'd have to fight. But doing so would make her an enemy of both the evae and the humans. Right now, they viewed her as a pawn—a way to find peace and end the war. If she attacked or fled, they'd have every warrior scouting the forest in her pursuit.

Her thoughts were broken when Glisseríel said, "Thallon Galadür. You have been a trusted member of this clan and an invaluable asset to our society. We trusted you to collect the clavía muínsii from Aragoth, a most dangerous feat, and while you have failed, we will put our faith in you once more." He paused with intent. "You will escort this lanathess to Drimil'Rothar. Have her in Aélla's care within the fortnight, or you will face the consequences most dire."

Thallon gulped down his emotions and gave a timid nod of agreement.

The Eirean continued, "We will allow a member of Aen'mysvaral's company join you on this endeavor, and we will be watching from afar."

Aen'mysvaral's eyes narrowed, and his arms tightened. He stood by Thallon, unwavering in his silent rage. "I will escort her alongside my brother."

"As noble and respected as you are, Aen'mysvaral, we would request another in your stead. The war against the lanathess is rising, and we must prepare for their attack."

He forced a bow. "I understand."

Glisseríel waved his hand, and two servants stepped away from the wall to approach Neer. She exhaled a deep breath when her binds were cut. A low grunt vibrated in her throat when she stumbled forward, her shoulders aching and back stiff.

Klaud was silent and still as six servants surrounded him, tugging his arms and forcing him to his knees. A tear slid down his cheek as he knelt with closed eyes, accepting his fate.

Glisseríel and Falavar stepped around the fire, towering over their advisor. A young servant passed Glisseríel the hot branding iron. Its head, which was in the shape of the Sigil of the Order, glowed bright orange.

Falavar lifted Klaud's right arm, placing his hand onto the pedestal brought over by a servant. He straightened Klaud's fingers and pressed his palm firmly against the flat surface.

"Klaud," Glisseríel stated. "You have committed unforgivable acts against your council and people. For this, your crimes cannot go unpunished. You are henceforth banished from Rhyl territories. Any homes, properties, titles, or belongings will be stripped of your name immediately. You shall not speak to anyone of our Clan. You shall not have their children. You shall not enter our borders or do business of any kind lest you face the punishment of death.

"This judgement will last until your dying breath."

Neer closed her eyes when the branding iron was pressed against his skin. The Eirean held Klaud in place as he grunted and shook in agony. The odor of burnt flesh filled the air, causing Neer's stomach to turn. Tears filled her eyes as she was brought back to her childhood, and she fell to her knees, unable to break herself from the visions plaguing her mind.

Thallon watched with misty eyes. His jaw was clenched so hard his muscles could be seen beneath his skin. But he held his composure, not showing a sign of weakness when Klaud was forever labeled as a traitor.

The Eirean stepped back when the iron was removed from Klaud's hand. He pulled back his arm and gripped his wrist, trembling with agony.

"This meeting has served its purpose," Glisseríel stated. "You are all dismissed."

Klaud curled inward, holding his breath, and then disappeared.

Chapter Nine

A Long Rest
Nerana

"Come to thee with your worries and woes, and the Light shall cast them asunder."

– Blessing of Kirena, Divine of purity, compassion, and health.

Neer walked through the streets of Navarre, the clan Rhyl city tucked deep within the forest. Large trees towered above the homes, casting deep shadows that danced across the forest floor with every light breeze. Wide streams cut through the grass and dirt, winding beneath bridges and cascading over small hills with rocks and moss.

Thallon walked alongside her, keeping a close distance as they passed several natives who glanced at Neer, speaking harshly of her arrival and mentioning death and torture. She kept her eyes on the ground, hoping to avoid confrontation. Though she had been given temporary passage into their village—so long as she stayed within reach of Thallon—she knew she wasn't welcome.

A white cape hung over her shoulders, covering her torso and back. It was a symbol of peace from the Eirean and a physical depiction telling the locals of her acceptance.

"This way," Thallon said, leading her down a path to the left.

The narrow dirt trail was outlined with beautiful trees, creating a natural tunnel of colorful leaves. Far less people traveled this path, and Neer was happy to be out of their presence.

SHADOWS OF NYN'DIRA

She crossed her arms. "Thanks for getting me out of there," she said. "You didn't have to do that...I know how dangerous it is to know me."

"What are friends for?" He offered her a pleasant smile.

She turned away, clutching tighter to her aching stomach.

"How did you wind up here?" he asked. "You're lucky it was Elidyr[°] who found you instead of someone else."

"I woke up alone. I was looking for Y'ven and Dru when they found me..." She gulped through a tight throat, and tears filled her eyes. "I still don't know where they are or if they're alive..."

Thallon shoved his hands into his pockets. He watched her through the corner of his eye. "They're alive," he said, and her heart skipped.

She turned to him, waiting for answers.

"Aélla and I found them in a village north of here. They're okay. He's nearly missing a few pieces, but...he'll survive."

Overwhelmed with relief, she pulled him into a tight embrace. Tears slid down her face, and she sniffed. "Thank you."

He touched her back. "Sure."

With another sniff, she realized what she had done and quickly backed away. But his hands lingered on her waist. Soft eyes gazed at her with affection and kindness.

"Are you all right?" he asked.

She stepped out of his grasp, putting much needed distance between them. "I'm sorry. I didn't—"

"It's fine. We've been through enough. I suppose you're allowed a hug or two."

She choked out a laugh. Though it hadn't been long since they met, she felt as if they'd known each other for far longer. It could be the familiarity she felt when looking at him, though the thought of Loryk receded from her mind with every glance in his direction. Now, when she thought

---

[°] Elidyr Galdúr, better known as Aen'Mysvaral, is Thallon's brother. Older by nearly ten years, they and their middle brother, N'iossea, grew up very close, despite their age differences.

of her old friend, it was Thallon's face she pictured, and it made her sick.

Neer turned away, eyeing the path once again. "Where are you taking me?"

"My home is at the end of the trail. I figured you'd want a comfortable bed before we started on our journey again. And a bath wouldn't kill you either."

She shook her head with a smile. "Can't smell worse than you did in the desert."

"We were all in need of a bath."

"Yeah. Some more than others."

Thallon chuckled, and a comfortable silence settled between them. Neer basked in its serenity. She noticed him staring at her from the corner of his eye, but she avoided conversation. For now, she just wanted to rest her mind. With every step down the lonesome trail, she found herself growing more exhausted. The sleepless nights and long days had finally caught up with her, and now that she was in the company of a friend, she could relax.

They walked past a woman and child who smiled pleasantly at Thallon, before setting their eyes on Neer and her white cape. The woman placed a hand on her child's back, urging him quickly past.

Further down the path, the trees became sparse, allowing more sunlight to touch the soil where the pathway opened into a wide meadow. Wooden planks creaked when they stepped across a flat bridge hovering over a slow-moving river. Several canoes rested along the bank of the water with paddles, ropes, and buckets.

The small community was made of six one-room cottages circling a cobblestone courtyard. A breeze blew past, sending the aroma of fresh water and grass into the air. Neer inhaled a deep breath. Not a sound came from any of the homes, only the gentle hum of the wind brushing against limbs and rocking the canoes.

"This is your home?" she asked.

"Nice, isn't it? This is where the scholars live. Well, some of us, anyway. The libraries are nearby, so we built this place to stay together."

He stepped past the first two homes, which were decorated with flowers and hanging ornaments.

"Nyhelia and Joruun live there. They are herbalists." He pointed at each of the homes, going over the residents and their professions. "And then you have Siothi," he said of the fifth home. "She studies humans."

Their eyes met, and Neer raised her brow, pressing him for more.

"She is fascinated with your kind. Loves the simplicity of your minds and values."

His eyes veered from one thing to the next.

"She says she enjoys how easily you can be manipulated. Something about how your kind is 'born to belong.' You don't question many things…just allow the masses to determine your thoughts."

Neer was offended but soon realized there might be truth to her claims. "And this house?" She pointed at the last home, with potted plants and overlapping vines decorating its entry.

A bashful smile pulled his lips. "Some scholar of the First Blood lives there. You probably don't want to meet him. They say he's gone mad from all the excavating and solitude."

"I've met him. The stories have proven true so far."

They shared a smile, and he chuckled while shaking his head.

"Come on, *lunathess*. Before you burn the place down with your stench."

Thallon opened the unlocked door and stepped inside. Neer followed, standing in the doorway and examining the small room. It was cozy, with light wooden floors, several windows, and a stone hearth built into the corner of the room. Bookshelves and plants filled the space with color and life. A cushioned bench rested beneath a large window, while a small table with two chairs were across the room.

Thallon stepped to the back of the home, carefully removed his tattered shirt, and then tossed it onto the floor. "You can bathe in the river," he explained, rifling through his dresser. "I don't have much that can fit you, but we can find some clothes in town tomorrow."

He gathered a bundle of folded clothes before returning to her side. Her eyes shifted to the healing scar on his chest, where his skin was once peeled back to expose his ribs.

"Thank you," she said, accepting his offering.

"I'll get dinner started. You should go wash up before it gets dark."

Neer excused herself from the home and walked to a secluded area beneath the hanging branches of a willow. She removed her clothes and moved to the center of the shallow river. Through a thicket of trees, she watched Thallon walk to a nearby garden.

Neer turned away and scrubbed herself clean. Water glistening against her skin as she stood alone in the middle of the woods, surrounded by nature and peace. There hadn't been many times where she felt entirely safe, and she inhaled a slow breath, basking in the forest's serenity.

Animals wandered through the underbrush, and a light smile tugged Neer's lip when several birds took flight, soaring together in moving patterns of darkness. Turning aside, admiring her surroundings, she caught sight of a shadowy figure lurking nearby.

The bushes quivered, and Neer stilled. Her heart stopped when an enormous wolf, black as night, stepped closer to the bank. Their eyes connected, and her worry was washed by a wave of calmness. Somehow, she felt safe. As if this beast could see into the very depths of her soul.

The feeling vanished when the animal receded back into the forest, becoming invisible as it swept through the trees. Neer gripped her head, overcome with confusion.

When the bridge behind creaked, she gasped and turned around. Her eyes fell to Thurandír marching over the pathway toward the settlement.

"Hello?" he called. "Is anyone here?"

Neer hurriedly stepped from the water and threw on Thallon's ill-fitted clothes. Her bare feet scrambled over sticks and grass as she approached the village.

"Thurandír?" she called.

He turned to her with wide eyes, his dark skin becoming a shade lighter. "You...," he started, breathless. "You *do* speak our language."

A door creaked when Thallon stepped out of his home, his brows knitted together. "Who are you?" he asked.

Thurandír ripped his attention from Neer. "I'm Thurandír," he said, the heavy hint of shock still trembling on his tongue. "The Eirean said that one of our warriors must accompany you to Drimil'Rothar. I volunteered."

Thallon gave him a suspicious look and crossed his arms. "They want a *child* escorting us?"

"I'm no child!" he argued. "I'm a warrior with the Avel, stationed under *your* brother."

A smirk eased Thallon's brooding expression. "Why did you volunteer to help us?"

"Because...I don't think she's a monster."

"Why not? She's Drimil'Nizotl. A human sorceress. The *definition* of madness and chaos."

"No. If she were truly mad and evil, then she would have killed us all." He looked at Neer with eyes of compassion and sympathy. "She's good. I can tell."

Thallon shifted his stance and shoved his hands into his pockets. "That's a huge risk you're taking, trusting a lanathess."

"And you aren't?" Their eyes met. "People have judged me my entire life because I'm e'liaa.[*] I won't do the same to others."

Thallon glanced at Neer with a raised brow. "What do you say, *Drimil*?"

She focused on Thurandír. "Traveling with me will put a target on your back. Are you sure you want to do this?"

Thurandír stood taller with pride. He gave her a stiff nod. "I'm an Avel warrior. It's my duty to protect the innocent."

---

[*] As mentioned previously, e'liaa is an evaesh term meaning *mixed blood*.

Thallon chuckled. "You're certainly my brother's prodigy. Meet us in the markets tomorrow. We'll gather supplies before heading out."

Thurandír gave another nod, took one last glance at Neer, and then left the village.

Thallon's home was warm with firelight as he and Neer sat inside, eating vegetable stew. The sun had set, leaving the world at the mercy of shadows and darkness. Thallon glanced at her each time he lifted his spoon. She wasn't bothered by his silent stares, though, as her mind flashed between all the worry and confusion brewing inside.

Avelloch, Y'ven, Dru, Reiman. Neer couldn't stop herself from wondering where they were and if their paths would ever cross again. She thought of the war and if the humans had truly begun invading. Klaud's banishment and his reasons for refusing to acknowledge they knew one another. The Priest, Eiden's words, and if the Old Gods were truly on her side.

Chills ran down her arms when she pictured the shadowy wolf that stalked the forest, glaring at her from across the river. As quickly as it had appeared, it was gone, and she couldn't settle the fear swelling in her chest.

Her stomach twisted in knots. She pushed her bowl away and leaned against the table.

Thallon's chair creaked when he leaned back, wiping his mouth with a cloth and staining it with brown broth from his lips. He crumpled the dirty linen in his fist. "Are you all right?" he asked.

She sighed. "What you said in that meeting...that I have to be controlled or everything will fall...Did you mean it?"

"That's true of both of you." His eyes flashed to hers, and she could feel the depth of his words. "Energy keeps us in balance, and you and Aélla have the strongest of anyone else alive. If either of you lose your way, it would be bad for everyone."

Neer crossed her arms. "You really stuck your neck out for me in there. You could've been branded a traitor...like *him*."

Thallon's face twisted in confusion and slight offense. "I don't know what happened between you and Klaud, but I've known him my entire life. He is like a brother to me. He didn't deserve to be banished like that—"

"He deserved *worse* than what he was given!" She glared at him.

Thallon's face twisted with anger. "Had he not defended you, they'd have sentenced you to death, Neer."

"Handing me over to the Order is just the same! They either wield the blade or pass it to someone else, but in the end, I would've been dead."

"He got himself banished to keep you from being executed. He could've said you were lying, but he didn't."

"So I'm supposed to view him as a hero now? Is that what you're getting at?"

"Feel about him however you want. Hate him. Don't. But you can't change the truth. Klaud sacrificed his home to keep you alive, and you don't give a shit."

Neer shook her head. A strike of anger surged through her, and she slammed her fist against the table, attempting to quell the madness swirling inside. Wishing it was Klaud instead of the wooden surface beneath her hand. Thallon jumped at the sudden noise. He turned away, considering her outburst.

Her face twisted with rage. "He cost me *everything!*"

"And you've cost him the same." Her anger dwarfed his when their eyes met. "You two have to get along, Neer. Chances are we'll have to travel with him. If he and Aélla—"

His voice fell silent as the home began to tremble. Objects rattled before falling off shelves. The flames popped and whirred when logs split, sending embers into the air.

Thallon glanced around before setting his attention on Neer. Her teal eyes were solid black, staring into the void as she was consumed with fury. The roof creaked, and Thallon lurched forward with his arms above his head.

"Neer." He shook her shoulders. "Neer—!"

His voice squeaked when she clutched his throat. He stared into her dark eyes.

Emotionless. Unhinged.

Enraged.

He tried to speak, but her grip tightened. The house shook. Walls cracked and the floor splintered. "Neer…," he wheezed, clawing her hands bloody.

Her clutch tightened before being released. Thallon sank to the floor, coughing.

Neer breathed heavily, her mind muddled and memory unclear. She eyed the home, wondering how it had become so disheveled and worn. Her jaw ached from being clenched. She examined the puncture wounds from her fingernails on her palms.

"What happened?" she asked. "Thallon?"

Neer gasped at the sight of his red face and bloodshot eyes. The chair toppled over when she backed away. Her chest heaved as she breathed quickly, feeling faint.

"What the fuck?" he snapped. The table shifted when he stumbled into it. "What the fuck!"

She shook her head. "I'm sorry…I don't know what happened. I…"

Neer was lost for words. Tears welled in her eyes. Gazing at the home, she was overcome with fear and grief. This had happened once before in the village of Valde, when she attacked the drunkards in the alley. Her magic took control, and she lost herself to its will.

To its rage.

"Neer," Thallon said, still clutching his neck.

Their gazes met, and she could see the fear in his eyes. It was the same as all the others, those who viewed her as the Child…a demon.

She turned away, gulping through a dry throat and shaking her head. Without speaking, she fled the home, choosing to spend her night alone.

Chapter Ten

The Way of Fate
Aélla

"I will not forsake the path of my ancestors, who have kept the world alight through magic reborn."

– Vows of Drimil'Rothar

AÉLLA WANDERED THE WOODS WITH Y'ven and Dru, keeping her eyes open for any kanavin. But the creatures of night weren't her only enemy, and the thought of being spotted by the Klaet'il or humans made her skin crawl. There had been whispers of a human invasion. She had witnessed their wrath in Amália but hoped the rumors weren't true.

But she knew they were. She felt a shift in the balance. A cold, dark rift that left her aching as icy tendrils gripped her soul, beckoning her toward an endless void. Forever shackled to the darkness, consumed by torture and wrath.

As the thoughts plagued her mind, Aélla found herself spiraling into an abyss of doubt and dread, thinking of all the terrible possibilities should she fail. And worse, if the balance was causing her so much pain, she wondered how it could be affecting Neer. It wasn't an easy thing to ward off such a strong pull of madness and rage. Any step in its direction would lead her further down its path. Aélla struggled against its will every day, and she found herself growing tired.

"Drimil," Y'ven said, pulling her from her thoughts. "Should we rest?"

With a deep inhale, Aélla lifted her head high. "No. We need to keep moving. The ilitran isn't far."

"What is…ick-tree-oh?"

She smiled at his mispronunciation. "They're places of great power and energy. The First Blood created them long ago as a way for magic bearers to commune directly with the energy of former drimil. The culmination of their magic heals us, and we're able to receive visions of the past or future. It's a very sacred place."

"Vaxros and faeth enter?"

"No. The ilitran may only be opened with my blood, or my brother's." She gulped nervously. "Once I'm inside…we'll need to wait for him to come and reopen it."

"What if he does not? You will be trapped. There is no other way?"

"No. But he'll come." A smile brightened her eyes, and she turned to him with newfound purpose. "Avelloch has never let me down. I don't expect he'll start now."

Dru lay asleep on Y'ven's head with her mouth open wide. He walked at a slow pace, gripping his bandaged arm with a deep groan. Blood stained the beige linen wrap with patches of light and dark red.

After Aélla had taken Thallon to the Eirean's chambers, she returned to Ik'Myriaa and tended to Y'ven's wound, smearing it with ointment and wrapping it tightly in a thick bandage. Though she knew it wouldn't help, he refused to have it amputated.

"Are you feeling well?" Aélla asked.

He gave a light nod, being careful not to move his head and disturb Dru. Unsure of what to say, Aélla fell silent, and they walked together without a word. It was an uncomfortable silence filled with concern. If she had to, she would put him to sleep and remove it herself. Whatever would keep him alive.

Her thoughts shattered when a loud shriek sounded overhead. Aélla glanced to the sky and then pulled Y'ven aside, ducking beneath a thicket of trees. They crouched into the shadows, watching in silence as the Klaet'il flew overhead on the backs of powerful glynfir.

SHADOWS OF NYN'DIRA

Their wings were liquid black against the night sky, casting large shadows across the forest floor. Aélla struggled to see through the dim moonlight, searching for the Nasir. But they moved too quickly for her to see, heading east, in the direction of Klaet'il territory.

The Nasir and his followers hadn't made it home. She still had time. All wasn't lost, not yet.

Dru stood atop Y'ven's shoulder, hiding in his hair. She peeked through as the last glynfir disappeared. Aélla exhaled a deep breath and closed her eyes. Leaves rustled when she stepped out of their hiding place. Her eyes scanned the heavens, dread washing her soul with unshakable fear.

"Klaet'il?" Y'ven asked, coming to her side.

She nodded. Her fists were clenched and eyes seeped with worry. "Come on," she said. "We have to keep moving."

Y'ven was silent as Aélla pressed on, paying no mind to the vaxros she left behind. He and Dru shared a worried glance. They took one last look at the sky before following in Aélla's path.

The moons rose higher as they stalked through the woods. Aélla closed her eyes, feeling a swell of energy the closer they moved toward the ilitran. Its pulsing sting thrummed with her heartbeat, throbbing against every vein—filling her with power and peace.

"We're close," she said.

Y'ven's tired eyes struggled to stay open. It had been too long since he was in the sun or near a flame. The magic grew stronger, and Aélla knew they were close. Several paces ahead, they came to the edge of a large meadow. In its center, standing tall and proud, was the ilitran—an enormous construct made of stone towering above the trees. Beneath the ilitran was a wide, circular courtyard made of stone, sun-bleached and cracked with age. Sprinkled throughout the meadow were ancient ruins, half buried in the dirt.

Aélla gazed upon its height, humbled to once again be in the presence of her ancestors. She had visited this very monolith long ago, before she embarked on her journey as

Drimil'Rothar, and again after Avelloch and Klaud had woken her from her cursed slumber.

"We are here?" Y'ven asked, his voice slurred with exhaustion.

"Yes. I'll help you create a fire, and then I'll enter."

"Go, Drimil. I am good. Strong."

"Y'ven, you can't—"

"Go." His large hand pressed against her shoulder, and their eyes met. "Protect."

Her jaw clenched and back straightened. She eyed the ilitran once more, now filled with doubt.

"What kind of savior would I be," she started, turning back to face him, "if I can't protect the ones I care about?"

Without argument, they gathered large armfuls of tinder and returned to the edge of the tree line. Aélla set it ablaze with her magic and sat beside Y'ven as they warmed themselves.

"I don't know how long I'll be in there," she explained. "When Avelloch comes, you'll know him by his hair. It's the same color as mine."

Firelight transformed her white locks into shades of orange and yellow.

"Klaud may come too," she continued. "He has golden eyes. You can't mistake him." She paused with consideration. "They may think you're a threat, but please…do not attack them."

Y'ven's eyes flashed to Dru, who was hovering within the flames. He gave her a knowing look, one a father would give his unruly child. The faeth stuck out her tongue and crossed her arms.

"We will respect Drimil's kin," he said to Aélla, reassuring her of their promise.

"Thank you, Y'ven. If I'm there for too long and your arm worsens, there are potions in my pack to numb the pain…if you decide to take care of it yourself."

He rubbed his arm and gave a gruff nod. She forced a smile and then rose to her feet. Staring at the ilitran, ready to face her fate, Aélla inhaled a deep breath and stepped into the meadow.

SHADOWS OF NYN'DIRA

Energy stung her skin, sinking like sharp talons through her flesh. She winced, fighting against the pain that had stricken her. Passing the uneven cobbles and weathered ruins, she came to the base of the ilitran. Rocks and soft dirt were gathered along its base in a steep, uneven mound. Aélla climbed up, losing her footing several times before reaching the ancient relic.

Her heart thundered in her chest. The ilitran was a place of immense power, and the few times she had been, it was a horrific experience. Gulping down her fear, she retrieved a vial of blood from her pocket. In preparation for her journey, she had it taken from her veins in Ik'Myriaa, the e'liaan village where she had reunited with Y'ven. They had filled several vials, which were all secured in her pack.

She and Klaud had attempted to use her vialed blood to reopen the ilitran once before, but it wouldn't work. Aélla was sealed inside its narrow prison for days while Klaud feverishly searched for Avelloch, who couldn't be located.

Staring at the vials in her hand, she worried he wouldn't be found again—or worse, that he might not be alive. With the war, she knew he would be hunting the lanathess down.

Aélla shook her head. There was no time to second-guess. The Nasir had returned to Nyn'Dira, and without the guidance of her ancestors, Aélla had no clear direction. She was lost, unsure of which path to take.

Holding her breath, she closed her eyes. "Please...," she begged. "Let this be the right choice."

She placed the vial on the ground and smashed it with a rock. Her blood soaked into the soil, and the ilitran began to glow. Red light shone through every crack and crevice, glowing brighter with each pulsing shockwave that rolled through the air. The trees swayed and danced with its rhythmic beating.

A blast of energy emitted from its center, and Aélla shielded her face, anticipating the harsh flow of magic. The hidden stone door slid open, and bright light crept across the ground, traveling upward across Aélla's body until she was engulfed in its radiant warmth.

She gulped down the knot in her throat and forced herself to stand on shaking legs. With a step closer, she hesitated and took one last glance at the forest before stepping inside.

The door slid closed, and the light that once brightened her skin dwindled, concealing her in darkness. Magic sweltered inside, burning her skin. She removed several layers of clothes, leaving only her strapless undertunic to cover her sweat-laden body.

Within the ilitran was a confined cavity big enough for one person to sit and meditate. Aélla shuffled her piles of clothing aside and rested on her knees. She pressed her fists together and exhaled a deep breath.

Hot energy tore through her, reaching the depths of her soul, converging her essence with the power of the ilitran. She felt the lives of each person who had sat before her, their faces flashing through her mind faster than she could see them. Their voices overlapped in a haunting song of ancient proverbs. Only the most esteemed scholars and magic users were meant to use the ilitran.

Only the most powerful drimil were meant to carry the mantle of Drimil'Rothar.

Aélla meditated amongst the lingering energy of the greatest drimil who ever existed. Some spoke with long forgotten accents and dialects she couldn't understand. But others were clearer, and she fought to grasp them. Fought to weave her consciousness with spirits long passed, hoping to find answers.

Energy swirled around her, bouncing through her body and mind like ribbons in the wind. Along with the voices were images, flashes that held no meaning. They were quick as lightning and left a lingering feeling of confusion and dread, which called upon more voices. More stories and prophecies and warnings.

More flashes. More screams.

Bloody hooves. Ancient bones. Forged steel. Glowing runes.

"Someone please…," a faint voice spoke over the visions.

SHADOWS OF NYN'DIRA

Branded flesh. Ash. Empty tombs. A broken lute. Crimson flames. Light blue eyes. Enchanted steel. A mother's wail.

Quiet weeps…A fading light…
"Save me…"
Darkness.

Chapter Eleven

The Afahél
Nerana

> "Sleep with the moon, sweet child of mine; Sleep with the moon and dream. For the night is dark, but don't worry my sweet; For always my baby you'll be…"
> — Human lullaby

THE FOREST WAS SILENT AS Neer spent the next several hours fighting through restless, terrifying dreams. Her body quivered as she faced the demons of her nightmares. Each night they worsened, shifting from memories of her burning village to horrific creatures of darkness, covered in blood.

She imagined herself lying in the forest, alone, shrouded in darkness. Mist rose from the ground. Clouds overlapped in the sky, leaving the world dark and cold.

Creatures skittered across the land. Their bones creaked with every step. A cold wind replaced the warmth of dawn. It prickled her skin with an icy touch, and then a shadow, cold as night, shrouded her in darkness.

Neer woke with a gasp and clutched her chest, her heart pounding against her ribs. The world was quiet and dark. Branches danced above, chiming with soft, haunting melodies.

"Come on!" a boy called. "They're this way!"

"Wait up!" another exclaimed. "Wait for me!"

Neer scanned the darkness surrounding her. Dangerous creatures lurked at night, and these boys would be easy prey. She had to find them—had to get them to safety.

"Guys!" the second boy cried, panting for breath.

The first boy huffed, and their footfalls ceased. "What's the hold up?" he remarked. "You got rocks in your shoes or something?"

Neer moved quickly, following the voices until she spotted three young children, no older than ten, standing together amidst the trees. One of them had solid white hair and stood shorter than the others. His face twisted with annoyance. The boy next to him was tall and skinny, with deathly-pale skin and long black hair. He stood with his head down and shoulders slumped.

The other boy, who was panting and unable to keep up, approached his friends with heavy footsteps. He was skinny, with shaggy brown hair and bright eyes. "*No...!*" he cried, responding to his friend's playful remark. "You're going too fast!"

"Kila...," the white-haired boy griped. He draped an arm around his slower friend's shoulders. "Maybe the lanathess will crawl their way through the forest"—he wriggled his fingers in a walking motion before them—"and you'll be able to catch up to them!"

The tired boy's face twisted with anger. He balled his fists and smacked his friend in the jaw. They fell to the ground, fighting. The black-haired boy inched closer, trying to break them up. His voice was fragile, urging them to stop.

"Hey!" Neer called, bursting through the trees. "Hey! What are you doing out here?"

But the boys paid her no attention. It was as if they hadn't heard her at all. She clenched her jaw and marched closer, but the sound of clattering weapons and chainmail filled the air. The brawling kids stilled at the sound. They peered through the darkness, searching for the source of the noise, and Neer reached for a sword that wasn't there.

"W-we should go..." The tall boy took a cautious step back.

"Come on!" his white-haired friend proclaimed, dashing through the trees. "Before they get away!"

"Wait!" the tall one cried. "Avelloch!"

Neer froze. The cool night air became frost against her skin, sinking deeper into her flesh and stilling her heart. She stood in a daze, staring at the boys as they ran into the darkness.

"No!"

Her heart skipped when a boy shrieked. Footsteps drew nearer, but Neer couldn't move. Quick, shallow breaths kept her heart pulsing. Her fear heightened. Closer now, the footsteps grew louder—faster. Someone was running toward her. The steps pounded hard against the ground. Her body tensed, waiting for the stranger to burst through the darkness and cut steel through her flesh.

But the panting sound of a child broke through the crunching of grass, and the slower boy sprang from the shadows. He stumbled over his feet, taking three sloppy strides before catching himself and continuing on.

His eyes were wide with terror, and Neer took half a step back. This boy wasn't a stranger...He was Thallon. His long face was rounder in its youth, but it was undeniably him.

Thallon glanced backward and then cut his gaze ahead. He quickly approached Neer, running as if she weren't there at all. They collided, and she inhaled a deep gasp as the icy wind of his body moved through her.

His footfalls continued, but she remained still, paralyzed by the visions she was trapped inside. Haunted by the memories of her friends.

Suddenly, the forest faded into a translucent haze. The ground was replaced by packed dirt. Stone houses with square cut windows appeared all around, their outer walls nearly swallowed by enormous trees. Broken archways created a perimeter around the forgotten city. Pillars were left half standing and crumbled, devoured by vines and roots.

Neer stepped forward, and a voice, ancient and powerful, shook through her mind, speaking from within. She collapsed to her knees in agony.

SHADOWS OF NYN'DIRA

*Long awaited a presence has been
Tortured and shackled, broken within.*

Black mist coiled up Neer's legs like a slithering serpent, stinging her skin with frost and ice. The world brightened as morning light drifted across the horizon. Neer clawed at the mist tightening around her calves and thighs, fighting to free herself.
She winced when the voice spoke again, trembling her mind and fracturing her thoughts with its power.

*Darkness unchained brings terror and rot,
Lost and unspoken; all is forgot.*

Blood dripped from her ears, and she groaned, clutching her compressed skull.

*Power too great leaves the wounded alone.
Give forth that right, unshackle, atone.*

The tendrils wrapping Neer's legs evaporated beneath the sun's gentle glow. Ice no longer etched her bones with its chill. She collapsed forward when the visions faded, and Neer sat in the forest alone.

Chapter Twelve

Haunted
Avelloch

"Any man aged twelve or higher shall willfully abide by the laws of the Divines. Do not quiver beneath the shadow of darkness. Find the Child and allow the Father's mighty hand to guide your path to victory."

— Proclamation to the residents of Ravinshire

VOICES RANG THROUGH THE AIR as shadows marched through the lonesome wood. Dusk was nearing, and the world would soon fall into a state of tormenting darkness. Kanavin would rise, stalking the void and consuming all in their path.

Avelloch trekked the quiet forest, following the call of the wind, hoping it would lead him to Neer before the others found her trail. He leapt over a fallen log and splashed across shallow streams. Up ahead, nestled deep within the woods, were the bones of an ancient temple.

Dying sunlight sprayed through a broken window at the top of the back wall. Ivy clung to its cobbled surface, covering most of the aged stone in vibrant green. The left and right walls were crumbled and broken with age. Surrounding the disjointed walls were the scattered remnants of a civilization long dead. Trees had swallowed many of the broken pillars, and statues of faceless scholars or drimil were half sunken in the dirt.

Avelloch approached the mystical ruins, water splashing beneath his boots. The magic was heavy, still guarding the temple. A slight surge of heat burned his hand, and he winced, clutching his wrist. Beneath his glove, burned atop his right hand, was the *fil'veraal*, a branded symbol of the lost or wicked. He had received it long ago, and with it, he was banished from entering any sacred places or Rhyl territories.

Strong magic warded these relics and prevented his arrival, sending pangs of heat and agony through his limb when he passed its threshold. But after the events of Nhamashel, when Neer had nearly drained his life in her grief, he found the power of the fil'veraal was weakened. The branding once displayed as an old scar atop his flesh had been stripped away by her magic, and he was no longer bound by the curse segregating him from his people.

Water lapped when he continued forward. Along the left-side wall, hidden beneath the overgrowth, was a stairwell leading deep underground. Avelloch stood at the top of the stairs, gazing at the darkness before him. He felt the sweltering heat of energy pulling him closer, beckoning him toward its depth.

But he resisted the urge, knowing the ancient First Blood were deceptive and cunning with their traps. Even after all this time, their magic still lingered, and he wouldn't become a victim of their games.

Avelloch stepped away, and voices whispered through the winds, speaking a language he didn't know. He looked around, staring at the trees, when suddenly, an arrow grazed his arm, splitting the fibers of his sleeve.

Grabbing his sword, he whipped around. The light of dusk faded into thin columns, brightening the faces of the humans who stood before him. Three men glared at him. They were the same as all the others: large, with muscular arms built for labor or hauling. Their clothing was tattered and filthy with blood, and dirt coated their arms and faces, revealing their deprivation and inexperience in the wild.

Avelloch was surprised they had survived so long. The border was nearly fifteen days from their location. Many of the humans had used their wits when entering the forest, choosing to stay in small groups and attacking at night while the villagers were asleep. This had proven a useful tactic, as many of the smaller settlements and homesteads were destroyed with minimal casualties to the human invaders. And the fires kept the kanavin away, giving them security in its glow while they camped at the smoldering villages until sunrise.

Two more men trailed behind the others. They were smaller, with one holding the features of an adolescent.

Avelloch waited, matching their glares, and the largest man stepped closer. The human reached into his pocket and retrieved a crumpled parchment. On it was Neer's face. Avelloch's eyes narrowed as he stared at her portrait.

"*Oy!*" the man called, though Avelloch couldn't understand his words. "*You seen this'n runnin' around?*"

Another human shook his head with disdain. "*All these pale-faces 're the same, David! Just chop 'im up and let's keep movin'!*"

"*Aye,*" another added. "*The Order's wantin' us to cleanse this place pure, and these 'etheans don't understand a word, any'ow. Just end 'im before those creatures rise up from the shadows and tear us apart, like they did Lenny!*"

Avelloch's eyes narrowed at the mention of the familiar human word, *pale-face*. The leather of his hilt creaked when he clutched the handle tighter.

David, the leader, spat. His tired eyes displayed a sense of confidence and power. He had survived this deep into the forest, and that made him feel invincible. But even if he was built for war, these men were too tired to fight. Too fat and weak to keep up with a true warrior's skill.

As the human spoke, no doubt warning Avelloch to surrender Neer, the evae was studying them. Taking in the feeble grips on cracked axes and iron swords. The heavy lean in the archer's posture. The fear in the boy's eyes.

"*Last chance, elf!*" David demanded.

Avelloch's lip twitched, and jaw clenched. David stepped back to his men and nodded at the archer.

Avelloch lunged forward as an arrow flew too far overhead. He came to the first human, slicing upward against his gut. The water turned red as he collapsed to his knees, sealing his wound with blood-coated fingers. Avelloch spun, and the man's screams were silenced when his head rolled from his shoulders.

Before it fell to the ground, Avelloch was at his next victim. Stuck in a daze, the man was immobile as the evae plunged his sword deep into his side. Blood spurted from his chapped lips, and he gasped when the blade was ripped from his flesh.

Another arrow flew past Avelloch, cracking against the wall behind. Water splashed as the humans trudged forward. Avelloch ducked beneath the sloppy swing of an axe. He shoved his dagger upward, plunging deep between his attacker's legs. The man released a squealed shriek, and Avelloch ripped the blade from his flesh. He turned and hurled his dagger at the archer, who stood far behind the others.

The man attempted to nock his arrow, but it fumbled to the ground in his haste.

"*Jeeves!*" David exclaimed.

The archer lifted his eyes just as the blade struck his forehead. He collapsed to the ground.

Avelloch turned when the youngest of the group shouted in sorrow. His voice was raw with pain. The adolescent was thickly built like the others, with large hands, frizzy auburn hair, and freckled skin. His dirty fingers coiled around the hilt of a polished longsword. No chips or stains told of its time in battle. The leather of its handle was fresh, still holding its tautness and sheen.

His hands weren't properly positioned. His posture wasn't strong.

The young man unleashed a rageful cry. He lunged, swinging at Avelloch's chest. The evae twirled aside, easily evading the slow, predictable movement. The lad stumbled forward, and his blade sliced through empty air. He whipped around, red-faced and full of hatred. His chest heaved, and he stared at Avelloch, who stood nearly a head taller and appeared twice his age.

Avelloch glanced at David, who remained behind the boy with a proud smirk. He spoke to the youngster and placed a hand on his shoulder. Their vengeful eyes were on Avelloch, who was still as a statue. Unblinking. Unwavering beneath the weight of their anger.

But Avelloch's fury was stronger. It stoked the fires of his soul, simmering deep within, fueling his rage. Despite his hatred, he wouldn't kill a child. He couldn't. Even if this boy was nearly a man in height and strength, Avelloch couldn't end his life. But leaving him here alone would prove equally as fatal. He considered allowing both of them to live, but another glance at their eyes told him they wouldn't back down.

They would fight to the death, and so too would he.

Fate was cruel and merciless. How many children had been sacrificed at the hands of these humans? How many more would be slain and tortured while they slept at night? Avelloch couldn't risk his people for the sake of these humans. These *murderers*.

He would fight. He had to fight.

When the boy lunged, Avelloch raised his sword. Weak iron collided with alveryan steel. He kicked the boy in the stomach, causing him to stumble back. Avelloch twisted his sword, keeping himself agile and ready. He swiftly paced in front of the humans, not allowing them to predict his movements.

David yanked the boy back and stole his sword. His eyes were set on Avelloch, and vile words spewed from his lips.

"You'll be feastin' with Nizotl tonight, demon," the human said with a growl. "*The Divines'll 'ave no mercy on your twisted soul!*"

When the man charged, Avelloch stepped aside. He slashed his blade across the man's back. His leather armor split, exposing the line of red across his skin.

The man turned, swinging his sword in a fit of rage. His movements were predictable and sloppy. Avelloch danced around him like water, redirecting most of his strikes with his glowing sword. Sweat dripped down David's red, bearded face. He halted, glaring with deadly eyes at the evae before him.

"*Come on, you swine!*" Spit flung from David's wet lips as he growled. "*Fight like a man!*"

Avelloch didn't react to his fierce, roaring voice, and David's anger erupted. With a vengeful shout, the human lunged. Avelloch twisted aside. Pain sliced his shoulder where David's blade struck his skin.

He hissed but never lost his stride. In the same motion that evaded the attack, Avelloch turned, bringing the edge of his sword to the human's neck.

"No!" the boy's raw, shaky voice pleaded.

Avelloch halted with his blade against the man's neck, eyes unflinching.

David spoke to the boy, though his eyes were fixed on Avelloch. "*Say the prayer, boy!*"

"*What?*"

"*Say the blessed prayer!*°"

The boy trembled. He whimpered and stepped back. Tears filled his eyes, and his trousers became wet with the stench of urine.

Anger no longer darkened Avelloch's eyes as he watched the quivering boy. David whispered a solemn chant, and his sword dropped to the ground. He turned his empty hands toward the sky.

The world was still as Avelloch waited, watching the trees and listening to the wind. He expected something to happen. For the magic to gather and strike him down, or these *Divines* to take form and rip him apart.

But there was nothing. Not a shift in the wind or otherworldly presence. The world was calm as the man whispered to himself, speaking words Avelloch didn't know. He slowly removed the sword from the man's neck. With a glance at the boy, who stood motionless nearby, Avelloch sheathed his weapon and stepped to his side.

° The Prayer of Pleading, recited just before death, is said to Kirena, who graces her beloved with compassion peace.

The prayer is a sacred ritual performed by those who wish to be forgiven for their sins and allowed entry into the eternal lands of Arcae.

The prayer is spoken to each of the six Divines, and is recited as followed:

"*Father, bless me and carry me home. Numera's strength devour my bones. Kirena cleanse my aching my soul. Udur guide me to a place untold. Zynther reach out your deathly hand. Nizotl has led me to the end.*"

He placed a gentle hand on the boy's shoulder, and when their eyes met, the lad became calm. But the peace was disturbed when water splashed from behind.

Avelloch turned around and then dove aside when the man lunged at him with his sword.

A gurgled gasp froze the world. Avelloch and the man were still, their gazes set to the boy. He choked on his breath, tear-filled eyes staring at the man before him.

"Rory?" David cried. He released his grip on his sword, which was plunged through the boy's stomach. The man inhaled a sharp breath when Rory reached out to him and then collapsed to the ground.

Avelloch stared at the boy, guilt and dread washing through him. He was young. Too young to be a victim of war. The water became dark red, and the boy's twitching body stilled.

The man knelt to the ground, sobbing. He hadn't meant to kill him, but his foolishness and anger had taken yet another life. Avelloch wanted to kill him. He needed to pay for what he had done.

Low chitters and howls rose from the forest. Moonlight kept the forest aglow as the world faded to darkness. Glowing plants illuminated the shadows as day faded to night. Avelloch scanned his surroundings, knowing the kanavin would soon appear to feast on the dead.

The leaves rustled above, and Avelloch lifted his sword. Glancing from left to right, his eyes fell upon a raven perched in the limbs. The fear melted from his shoulders, and he stared up at Altvára, wondering why the raven had tracked him down.

Altvára's feathers ruffled, and he cocked his head aside. A light caw echoed from his throat, and he soared from the trees, landing atop the crumbled temple wall. Altvára looked into Avelloch's eyes and then pecked at the note tied to his leg.

Avelloch glanced at the human, who was too lost in his misery to pay the evae any mind. Stepping aside, Avelloch quickly untied the string and struggled to read the note through the darkness of night. Leaning aside, he hovered the paper over a brightly glowing cluster of mushrooms clinging to the wall.

A has returned. Altvára will guide you. N is alive. Safe for now. Make haste, brenavae. The nights grow longer.

Avelloch scanned over the words half a dozen times. Neer was alive and safe. A deep breath escaped his lungs, carrying with it his dread and fear. His eyes veered to Altvára, who was perched on the wall, awaiting Avelloch's orders.

When the sound of cracking bones and chittering calls echoed through the wood, Avelloch inhaled a sharp breath. They were coming. His eyes veered to the human, who was too weak and ill-equipped to fight against the onslaught of kanavin racing closer.

But his hatred ran deep, and without a word, Avelloch marched past the weeping man, leaving him to his fate.

"Let's go," he said, and Altvára soared into the air. Avelloch snatched his dagger from the archer's face and fled the ruins. He followed Altvára without a backward glance as the kanavin approached the humans and tore into their remains.

Chapter Thirteen

Hunted
Nerana

"Vas neemo dren'seol. Tu'naka dösframehl."
I see into your soul, a bond we carry until the end.

— Sayings of the evae

NEER SLUMPED FORWARD WITH HER fists in the dirt. Her mind spun too quickly to form any coherent thoughts. She gripped her forehead, reliving all she had witnessed. With a glance around, she realized she was nowhere near the village. Somehow, she'd wound up deep in the forest, far from where she had fallen asleep by the river.

The leaves rustled, sending a gentle wave of magic through the air. She closed her eyes, listening to the sound of nature, feeling it call her south.

The amber haze of morning became bright as the sun crept across the sky. Following the call of the wind, Neer walked alongside the riverbank, and her ears perked at the sound of shifting rowboats. Relief washed over her when the familiar cluster of cabins came into view. The wind had led her back to Thallon's village...exactly where she needed to go.

She glanced from left to right, examining the leaves. Wondering, for a moment, if it was the forest that had guided her path, or something more. Something divine. Whatever it was, maybe it had led the priest, Eiden, to her that night too.

Maybe it would lead her back to the others. To Y'ven and Reiman and Avelloch.

Her fingers reached for his weapon, searching for its comfort, and she pulled her hand away, feeling as empty as the scabbard on her hip.

"Neer?"

Thallon's voice ripped through her thoughts. He marched forward with a look of worry and contempt. "Where have you been?"

Her eyes fell to the bruises on his neck, and guilt swelled through her.

"I...," she started, trying to find the words.

If he knew she had these visions, he might think her madder than he already did. After last night, she couldn't take that chance, not with the hint of terror and uncertainty lingering in his eyes.

"I'm sorry," she said. "I just got turned around."

"Kila!" he exclaimed through a raw voice. "Well, come on. I've been searching all morning."

He walked back toward his home, and Neer stayed her feet, watching him stride away. Her eyes moved back to the forest, and she touched her empty scabbard, wishing the wind would have led her down a different path. Thallon turned around, and Neer blinked her thoughts away.

"Well?" he pressed. "Are you coming?"

She followed behind and entered his cracked, half-destroyed home. Inside, he leaned against the door and raked his fingers through his hair. Objects lay on the floor, and sunlight beamed through cracks in the walls.

"You can't just go wandering around," Thallon said. "You could get yourself captured or killed! What were you thinking?"

She turned away, too uncomfortable and ashamed to meet his gaze. "I was by the river. I...I don't know what happened last night."

"Your magic," he stated flatly. "This is what happens when humans wield power...Your emotions are too unstable. We need to get you to Aélla. She's the only one that can keep you in control."

Neer's face pulled inward, not so much as a scowl, but with pain. "No one *controls* me."

"Stop!" He rushed to her side and gripped her arms. "Neer, you have to stop. Your impulsiveness and emotions are going to get you or someone else killed. You *have* to control yourself."

Neer inhaled a deep breath, realizing he was right. She was unstable and reactive. A disaster waiting to happen. "I don't...know how."

"Well, figure it out." Their eyes met. "What you did last night...you could have killed me. Just for mentioning someone else's name!" He paused, waiting for a response.

When she had none to give, he continued.

"You aren't like the rest of us. You don't get to act on your emotions like we do. And you can be mad and pout and blame everyone else, but it won't change the truth."

His words sank into her mind like acid.

"You. Are. Dangerous, Neer...*Very*. Dangerous. So, figure it out, or someone else will do it for you."

His footsteps receded to the back of the home, and Neer stood alone. She understood her magic had grown since Nhamashel, festering and boiling, like the anger she carried. Anger she couldn't release.

Thallon returned, dressed in clothes more suitable for leaving the home, and said, "I'm heading to the markets to get supplies. You should stay here. The last thing we need is another incident causing chaos."

Neer crossed her arms, hating his condemnation but knowing she had no argument to hold. Unable to speak beneath the weight of his anger, she simply nodded in response.

His look softened into what she thought was sympathy, and then he left the home without another word.

Morning faded to midday, and Neer waited in Thallon's home for him to return. Her thoughts were gripping, settling in her gut where they swirled and twisted, causing her stomach to groan in protest. She leaned forward on the cushioned bench, willing the discomfort away.

Her eyes flashed to the door when Thallon's familiar tenor perked her ears. She sat straighter, staring intently at the entry as his footfalls drew closer. Seconds later, sunlight streamed across the room as the door opened and two shadows stepped inside. Thallon carried a sackful of supplies in his arms, and behind him, dressed in light armor and equipped with a bow, was Thurandír.

His eyes moved to the streams of light entering through the splintered roof and walls. "What happened?" he asked.

"Guess I'm a bad builder," Thallon remarked.

Thurandír's brows pulled together. As he gaped at the room, his eyes fell to Neer.

"Hi, Neer," he said with a smile. "It's good to finally know your name."

The pleasantries of a greeting had evaded her, but she enjoyed Thurandír's company and didn't want to cause upset by ignoring his kindness. "Hey, Thurandír," she said, forcing the words to sound as genuine as his.

"I'm glad to see you out of those binds."

He stood at a cushioned chair. Thallon was behind him, unpacking the contents of his sack into a pile on the table. Potions, herbs, dried food, flint, a whetstone, and other various necessities were laid together.

"I'm sorry about that," Thurandír continued, dragging Neer's attention from Thallon back to the archer. His eyes seeped with remorse. "Aen'mysvaral can be..."

He struggled to find the right word and was befuddled by Thallon's explanation when the scholar said, "An idiot?"

Thurandír turned to him, eyes wide. "You can't speak about him like that!"

"Can't I?" He cut a sharp glare that dwarfed Thurandír's anger. "He's my brother. I have the right."

Thallon shoved several smaller items into his leather pack. "If we want to reach the ilitran in time, we should get moving."

The home was quiet as they packed their things and snuffed out the glowing embers in the hearth. Neer stepped to the back of the home, finding a short sword lying on the bed with other belongings Thallon had bought her. She slipped into the clothing and armor, pleased to find they fit nearly perfectly. The soft, evenly stitched clothing was more elegant and comfortable than any she had ever worn. She slid her fingers across her sleeve, admiring its softness.

"You ready?" Thallon asked, approaching the back of the home where she stood.

She nodded, and he stepped away.

"Thallon...," she started, unsure of what to say. "I'm sorry. Truly...for what happened last night. I don't..." She sighed, struggling to contain the emotions swelling in her chest. "We're friends. I don't want that to change."

With a subtle nod, he said, "We're good, Neer. Just work on it, all right? Use what Aélla taught you."

With a nod, she turned away. They moved across the home, gathered their belongings, and stepped outside, heading north, in the direction of the ilitran.

Neer trailed behind Thallon and Thurandír as they traveled until dusk, stopping occasionally to rest and eat. She winced at the burning in her thighs and aching in her feet. Her eyes scanned the forest, taking in its serenity and calmness.

Closing her eyes, she breathed in the woodsy aroma of fresh air and tree bark. The light sting of magic clung to the air, prickling her skin and filling her with energy. She had felt it since she arrived—the light surge of power. It was a constant feeling of strength and warmth connecting her with the forest and trees.

"We should camp here," Thallon stated, approaching a cluster of broken columns and crumbled stone walls.

Neer followed, and she winced as strong energy stung her skin, causing her hair to stand on end. Thallon dropped his pack and stretched with a groan.

"This should be safe enough from the kanavin," he said.

"What is this place?" she asked, crossing her arms and observing her surroundings. The painful sting of magic lessened into slight discomfort the longer she stood in its presence. "Why is there so much magic here?"

"Hmm?" Thallon turned to her with a quizzical look and then eyed the forest. "You can feel the energy?"

"You can't?"

"I guess I'm used to it. Nyn'Dira holds some of the strongest magic in the world. The entire continent used to be like this. Full of magical energy that connected all living things to one another."

He sat on a crumbled half-wall and dug through his belongings. Thurandír rested across from him, leaning against a crumbled ruin.

"The glowing Ko'ehlaeu'at trees are believed to be the source of all magical energy," Thallon continued. "No one knows exactly how they formed or *why* they hold magic, but the First Blood revered them as celestial. They worshipped them, made sacrifices and rituals in their honor."

He motioned to the ruins.

"This was one of their altars," he said. "It's protected by ancient magic. Creatures born of darkness, like the kanavin, cannot enter here."

Neer glanced around, examining every glowing plant and rustling branch. The forest had grown darker as the sun faded, leaving them at the mercy of the shadows and night.

Thurandír unwrapped his bread and dried meat, while Thallon retrieved a notebook and quill from his bag. He flipped through the pages.

"The Ko'ehlaeu'at are very sacred to our people. The Klaet'il still follow in the beliefs and rituals of our ancestors, but the other clans have moved beyond such credence."

Neer stepped to a nearby tree and touched its bark. She inhaled a slight gasp when a swirl of energy moved through her, ebbing and flowing like waves upon the sand. Neer felt the life of the world crashing through her, connecting her to every root and stem. The branches rustled, creating a gentle disruption that shifted through her core, like a ripple on water, falling weaker until it vanished. Animals wandered through the shadows, their soft footsteps pressing against her with warmth.

She retracted her hand and stared into the forest, perplexed at its emptiness and peace. There were no signs of any animals or disturbances, yet she felt them, however far away, through the energy binding them together.

Thallon wrote hastily in his notebook, his quill scribbling against parchment. Neer sat on the grass and leaned against a crooked pillar.

"What are you writing?" she asked.

"I've been taking notes on the longevity of the days. The sun set much sooner today than it did this time last Fisonaar.*"

"What does that mean?"

His eyes remained on the page, and he continued writing without a response. Neer and Thurandír shared a quiet glance before turning away. She wondered if Thallon had purposefully chosen to ignore her or if he was so wrapped in his writing that he hadn't heard. She had learned through her many years with Loryk that once a minstrel—or in this case, a scholar—set their mind to the pages, there was little to stop or distract them.

Thurandír glanced between them and timidly explained, "It means the darkness is growing."

"The darkness?"

He nodded. "Stuff like the kanavin and shorter days have all been prophesied since before the First Blood."

"Kanavin? Those are Creatures of Darkness, right?"

"Yeah. They're monsters twisted up by the imbalance of energy."

"Imbalance? What are you talking about?"

His eyes settled on the ground, grim with darkness. "Naik'avel."

Neer gulped through a dry throat. "Naik'avel is causing kanavin to rise from the energy of the dead?"

---

* Evaesh term for the autumn season.
While humans track time by days, months, and years, the evae track by day and season.
Their seasons are as follows:
Spring: Aeroniat, or First Light
Summer: I'Sylyasar, or Sun's Flame
Autumn: Fisonaar, or First Leaf
Winter: Malvainha, or Frost Fall

He nodded, still displaying a dark look that sent chills down her spine. Her eyes fell away, thinking of all the creatures she had faced. Spindra, wispers, khiut...None existed just years ago, yet now they were emerging, growing stronger and stalking the night. Creatures that once lived in storybooks and legends had come to life, filling the world with darkness and dread.

Their conversation came to a bitter end, filling the night with an inescapable chill. While Thurandír started a fire and Thallon scribbled in his notebook, Neer chose this time to meditate.

Resting on her knees, she pressed her fists together and closed her eyes. Energy moved through her like a shift in the wind, unbroken in its grace and tranquility. With her eyes closed, she didn't notice the subtle glow that had formed around her. Thallon and Thurandír lifted their eyes, amazed at the luminance. A small radius of plants brightened and dimmed with her every breath.

For a moment, she was free, the force of her magic melding with the energy of the forest. Her tattered and broken soul felt healed, and she could breathe.

She meditated for nearly an hour, before slowly opening her eyes and relaxing her shoulders. The weight of the world fell heavily against her, and she was reminded of the burden she was forced to carry. Of the misery and torment shackling her to the darkness brewing in her soul.

Her eyes flashed to Thallon, who was staring at her with his notebook in hand. Thurandír was beside him, gaping in wonderment.

"You...," the archer said, breathless. "It's true...You're...Drimil'Nizotl..."

Neer turned away with shame, hating to be labeled in such a way, especially by someone she viewed as an ally. A scuffle shifted the silence, and Neer lifted her eyes, finding Thurandír scrambling to find his bow.

At the sight of his sudden panic, she inhaled a sharp breath and lifted her arms, prepared to defend herself.

Before she could utter a sound, hot breath brushed against her neck from behind, and the sound of a deep, vibrating growl shook in her ear. Coarse fur brushed against her skin as a beast stood behind her.

She could see its large snout from the corner of her eye.

Her heartbeat throbbed in her veins. The sounds of the world were muted as she sat, immobilized by terror. The animal sniffed, and Neer held her breath.

It circled around. Thick paws patted against the soil, and her throat tightened when she met its gaze. A direwolf, thrice the size of any canine she'd ever seen, stood before her. Black fur cloaked its body, leaving it nearly invisible in the shadows. Grey-tipped ears and feet were the only other coloring it displayed, along with its vibrant sapphire eyes.

Neer stilled, watching the direwolf she had seen at the river glide to her front, never breaking her from stare. It stood before her, peering into her soul as if it could read her every thought. She felt something odd lingering between them. Something warm and easy. A gentle tug bonded them, and for a moment, she wasn't afraid.

Thallon and Thurandír were left speechless when Neer slipped her hand past its snout toward its ear. Fur brushed against her palm, and she inhaled a quiet gasp. The warmth of its skin eased her discomfort, and she smiled while patting its head.

For a moment, she wondered if it was truly an animal of the forest or if a creature of darkness had manifested into the shape of a wolf. The thought caused her to withdraw her hand, but as she did, something caught in her fingers.

Neer paused, examining the wolf's demeanor, and felt the string tied around its neck.

The wolf was still as she slid the string over its head. Her eyes fell to the woven trinket hanging from the necklace, and Neer was at a loss for words. The world stopped spinning. Nothing existed but the old tiaavan in her hand. *Her* tiaavan.

She dug through her pocket and retrieved Avelloch's matching trinket.

He was here. He had sent this direwolf to find her.

She met the animal's gaze. "Is he alive?"

The wolf snorted and gave a firm nod. Neer exhaled a relieved breath. She held the tiaavan close, not daring to let them go.

"Can you take me to him?"

Another snort.

She nodded. "Then let's go."

Chapter Fourteen

The Ilitran
Avelloch

"You are strong, my son. So strong and brave. Do not be poisoned by the misguidance of others. Walk tall and remain strong."

— Merethyl Líadrinel to her son, Avelloch

Avelloch trailed behind Altvára. His footsteps were silent as he moved quickly through the shadows, never losing sight of the raven. Two days had passed since he was approached by the dren'seol, who carried a letter from Klaud that told of Neer and Aélla's return to the forest.

Avelloch had known they were there and spent many nights searching for them. But now he was on the right path. A path that would bring them together once more. A path that would see him to her.

Altvára cawed from above, breaking Avelloch's thoughts. He peered upward and followed the raven, who veered left into a thicket of overgrown trees and shrubs. Purple light illuminated his sword when he fought through the vegetation, slashing branches and vines that obscured his path.

"Avelloch…"

His heart stopped when a voice whispered through the air. He became still. Listening, waiting. Riddled with fear, he breathed heavily, scanning his surroundings as he stepped forward. Twigs snapped underfoot, resounding through the silence like a crashing wave.

"Help me!"

The voice was directly behind, screaming. *Shrieking.* He turned and slashed his blade against flesh. A choked breath filled the silence, and Avelloch froze. His skin was ghostly white as he stared at his intruder. Her voice still rang in his ears, and her teal eyes begged for help.

But it wasn't her. It couldn't be. The forest was dense with kanavin. He knew it was a trick. Yet staring at her face, he was unsure. Confliction and terror rose to his throat.

Neer clutched her neck. Blood coated her fingers, and Avelloch caught her when she collapsed forward. She was cold as death itself, her weight light as a feather. He stared at her with wide eyes, and his body trembled with confusion and regret.

When he started to speak, Altvára dove from above, releasing an alarmed shriek. Heeding his warning, Avelloch released Neer and scurried back.

The shadow before him fell to the ground, twitching and groaning. Large boils formed across its skin, bubbling like water in a hot cauldron. Black mist rose from its contorted body, and it transformed into a sickly, grotesque creature. Oozing lesions covered its lumpy flesh, and its cracked lips curled inward to reveal slimy, yellow teeth.

"Don't die in there…"

Neer's voice vibrated from the creature's throat. They were the words she had spoken to Avelloch before they entered the Trials of Blood. He breathed heavily, gazing at the creature as it growled and twitched. Bubbles roiled across its skin, and it transformed into a woman. Her hair was solid white, and her smile was warm.

Her face, timeless and beautiful, was slashed and bruised. Blood poured from the lacerations marking her arms and chest. Her lavender nightgown held dark stains and uneven tears that revealed the broken, bloody skin beneath.

"Don't take him!" she wailed, her smile never fading. Her lips never moving as her bright eyes bore into his.

Avelloch was unable to move, listening to a voice that had haunted him since the day it was silenced forever.

"He has no magic!" she said. "I'll be of more value than this child!"

"Stop!" Avelloch growled, consumed with memories.

Her pained shriek vibrated through the air. Avelloch lunged forward and struck his sword through her chest. The creature squealed before stumbling back. Its twisted body was revealed before slowly fading to ash.

Avelloch sat on his knees, watching cinders drift through the air. His jaw was clenched tight, and his eyes burned with repressed tears. Never had he encountered a kanavin such as that. One that could manifest into his darkest memories. The image of his mother, blood-soaked and beaten, was burned into his mind. He had never seen her so broken and defeated.

It had been many seasons since she was taken. Since she sacrificed herself to keep him alive. He had pushed the thoughts away long ago, not daring to be consumed by the dread they left behind. But faced with her ghost—with the echo of what she would've been… it was too much to take.

"Fuck…," he growled. Wiping his eyes, he leaned forward with his hands on his knees. He closed his eyes and fought to regain his strength. The deep pit forming in his chest was heavy and swollen. But he wouldn't let it consume him. He had to push it away. There was no place left for emotion or anguish.

There was no time for regret.

With a deep sniff, he rose to his feet. Clouds blanketed the sky, shrouding the moons and stars. He examined the forest to be sure he was alone and then continued onward toward his destination.

Altvára was just ahead, leading the way.

The sun rose for the fourth time since Avelloch's journey began. He knelt by a creek, splashing his face, when a light breeze danced through the air. The trees sang a calm, peaceful melody, and sunlight beamed through the branches, signaling the start of midday. He glanced around, spying his surroundings. Wildflowers brightened the forest floor with pastel colors. Small animals rustled through the grasses, gathering food in preparation for the coming winter. Auburn leaves broke away from high branches, soaring gracefully through the air as they were carried westward.

Avelloch gathered his things and followed the call of the wind. Magic stung his skin as he headed further south. He broke through a dense wall of underbrush and came to a large meadow. In its center was the ilitran. The enormous stone pillar hovered above the ground, its jagged base glowing with red light.

As he moved past the tree line and into the large meadow, the harsh sting of magic enveloped him with pain. He stumbled forward with a grunt, stricken by its heat.

Unable to move, he was trapped in his agony. Deep grunts sawed from his throat, and he willed his body to move, forcing himself back into the forest. But his movements were slow, as if wading through molasses.

Suddenly, he was gripped from behind and pulled back into the tree line. He exhaled a deep breath and leaned forward, relieved of the pressure and sting of magic. The air was colder, and sweat dampened his skin.

A shadow lingered nearby, and he turned to find Klaud standing beside him. His eyes were distant and expressionless, his robes dirty and stained. Hair had grown across his face, making him appear filthier and unkempt.

"Klaud?" Avelloch asked, unsure if the man before him was truly his friend. He had seen too much of the kanavin to trust his eyes.

"It's me," he said in a voice coated with grief.

Avelloch stood straighter, his eyes still scanning Klaud's filthy appearance and expressionless eyes. "Are you all right?"

Klaud nodded wordlessly, his eyes veering to the ilitran.

Avelloch examined the floating monolith. "Is Neer with you?"

Klaud shook his head. "She's in Navarre."

"What?" he snapped, pulling Klaud's shoulder to meet his gaze. "Why didn't you tell me? They're going to kill her!"

"She's safe. They granted her passage to the ilitran. She's to rejoin with Aélla." Klaud's jaw tightened. "I told them she can be trusted."

He breathed heavily, drowning in remorse and sorrow. When he pulled back his sleeve, Avelloch glanced down at the gauze wrapping his hand. He studied the bandages for a moment, quickly realizing they were covering his right hand.

The hand they'd use to mark him as a traitor.

A *nesiat*.

His heart sank. Slowly, he lifted his eyes, and Klaud's anguish melted the anger that had consumed him. "Klaud...," he started, unsure of what to say, understanding his emptiness and solitude.

"I said that we don't know each other...but she called me a liar and told them everything." He paused, sliding his left hand over his right. "There was nothing I could do."

Avelloch turned away, his brows pulled together in sorrow. "Did she say anything...when you were branded?"

Klaud shook his head. Avelloch clenched his jaw.

"You didn't deserve this."

"I did."

Avelloch turned to Klaud, but he was staring at the ilitran, as if he could see through its outer walls to the prison inside.

Klaud sighed. "This is my punishment for betraying those who trusted me. For turning my back on the one who saved my life..."

He lightly gripped his bandaged hand, his eyes never veering from the ilitran.

"If I have to lose my morality to keep us all alive, then it's what I'll do...but I won't pretend my actions were noble. I won't act like the hero when innocent blood stains my hands."

Avelloch gripped Klaud's shoulder. Klaud never met his harrowing gaze, but Avelloch gave it all the same. "You are *not* the enemy here," Avelloch said. "What you did...not many could do. But I know why you did it."

Klaud closed his eyes, slumping forward in sorrow.

SHADOWS OF NYN'DIRA

Avelloch continued, "And someday, when this is over, your name will be remembered. Not for the people you hurt or the terrible choices you've had to make...They will remember you because you are the reason they are still alive."

Klaud didn't speak, and Avelloch didn't expect him to. He'd never seen him so lost. So broken. Avelloch understood this pain and never wished it on anyone, especially those he cared for. But there was nothing he could say that would erase the misery tainting Klaud's soul. He would have to see this through on his own. There weren't many throughout history who had received the fil'veraal[*], a punishment considered worse than death itself, and of those who had, Avelloch was the only known survivor of its shame and isolation. Hunger, the noose, or irreparable sorrow saw the others to their untimely graves.

Avelloch wouldn't allow Klaud to be among those who slipped away, just as Klaud hadn't allowed him to be when he received his own mark long ago.

Avelloch opened his lips to speak, but a shuffle came from behind, silencing his voice. Altvára soared through the limbs, landing softly on Klaud's shoulder. Behind him, trudging closer with thundering footsteps, was an enormous red beast. He was nearly two heads taller than Avelloch, with muscles to match.

"A vaxros," Klaud said, awestruck.

Avelloch was silent, staring at him with the same admiration and shock. He had only heard tale of their ferocity and large stature. But the stories paled in comparison to the man before him, who stood with a small, fiery creature on his shoulder.

Klaud asked, "Did you travel with Aélla?"

The vaxros nodded with a deep grumble. "Klod?" he asked in broken evaesh.

---

[*] The branded mark that labeled one as a nociat. While the scar itself was a telling sign of their banishment, it was also laced with magic that prevented its bearer from entering certain areas of the forest, forcing their life of seclusion.

Klaud and Avelloch shared a wide-eyed glance, astonished he could understand and speak their language. Klaud nodded, and the vaxros turned to Avelloch.

"Av-flick?"

"Avelloch," he corrected, still amazed.

"Av…lock." The vaxros placed his hand to his own chest. "I am Y'ven. This is Dru. We protect Master Drimil."

Klaud turned to Avelloch. "Aélla must've told him we would be here."

Before Avelloch could question him further, a pulse was emitted from the ilitran, sending a gust of hot air rolling through the trees. They stumbled back, hearts racing as they stared upon the floating monolith. The red luminance it once held slowly faded, and it receded back to the ground.

"She's ready," Klaud stated.

Avelloch inhaled a deep breath and then stepped closer, leaving Klaud and the others behind. Its magic was intense, though not nearly as harsh as before. He was able to withstand its heat as he walked across the meadow and approached the enormous stone pillar.

Standing at its base, Avelloch collected his dagger and drew a thin line across the scar on his palm. He stared at the blood, realizing how often he'd used it to unlock various tombs, doors, or magic.

Ignoring the pain, he slid his palm across the stone, and the ground quaked beneath him. The magic stinging the air subsided, and Klaud appeared at his side. Y'ven soon followed. The ilitran blazed once again with red light, sending waves of heat through the air. They lifted their arms to shield their faces.

A flash of light expanded from a narrow opening, and Aélla's shadow appeared amidst the haze. She stepped forward, and the light encasing them vanished as the door slid itself shut.

Avelloch closed his eyes, reeling from the wave of magic burning his skin. As his eyes readjusted, he glanced at his sister. She knelt in the dirt on her hands and knees. Sweat dripped down her face. Her back and shoulders widened with every deep breath.

"Azae'l," Klaud said, his sullen voice now thick with concern. He moved to her side and gently touched her face. "Are you hurt?"

She shook her head. "I'm all right."

He unlatched his waterskin and quickly passed it to her. She sat straighter, and Avelloch took note of her sweat-stained hair and clothes. Their eyes met as she sipped the water. She wiped her lips with a hidden smile.

"Brother," she said.

Avelloch knelt at her side. "You made it. You look good."

She softly smiled and then turned to Klaud, answering his questions before he had time to ask them. "We were attacked by the Nasir. I escaped with Thallon, and we received aid in a village nearby."

"But Thallon's with Neer," Avelloch said.

She turned to him with wide eyes. Her lips parted in sudden shock. "She's alive?"

"Yes," Klaud explained. "She's on her way here."

Aélla's expression was washed in relief. She sank forward, exhaling a deep, long breath.

"Aélla," Klaud started. "What happened in the desert? Why aren't you all together?"

Tears filled her eyes, and she fell into a state of despair. "I gained the powers of tre'lan Aenwyn, but I didn't have the strength to stop him." Her hands balled into fists, and she fought to contain her emotions. "Naik'avel is coming...We were too late."

She took Avelloch and Klaud's hands, not daring to look into their eyes as she said, "I failed."

Chapter Fifteen

Wayfarers and Wolves
Nerana

"A shadow in the night stalks its prey. The lone wolf travels; glowing swords guide the way. Ruthless and depraved, this monster does not speak. Alone in the wilds, restless, it sneaks."

— tales of the Zaeril

MOONLIGHT BRIGHTENED THE WORLD AS another day came to pass. Neer and Thallon had hardly spoken since she insisted on following the direwolf. She understood his anger. He had been made personally responsible for seeing her to the ilitran with no delays.

But she couldn't ignore the path set before her. One that would lead her to Avelloch and finally see them reunited. Though she was reluctant to believe in fate, all signs pointed to its divinity. She could find no other reason for his direwolf to have approached her. Neer had to follow it. She had to find him.

The thoughts escaped her when Thallon returned from the forest with two rabbits in hand. Blood stained their fur where he had cut their necks. The direwolf curled close to Neer, its coarse fur tickling her arm with every shift in the wind. Thallon glanced at the animal before taking his seat across the fire. Thurandír was beside Neer, eyeing the wolf with caution.

Thallon swiftly dressed the animals and shoved them onto the spit. The flames brightened, sending waves of heat and light through the forest. Neer turned to the wolf as it raised its head, its nose twitching at the scent of the roasting meat.

Neer curled into a cloak when a cold breeze carried through the air, and the wolf nudged itself closer, shielding her from the wind. "Does everyone have an animal companion?" she asked. "Aélla had a raven that guided us through the desert."

Her eyes flashed to Thallon as he scribbled in his notebook, purposely ignoring her.

"Not everyone," Thurandír said, realizing Thallon was refusing to speak. "Dren'seol are rare. Some say that only the purest of heart are able to feel the connection that binds you so intimately to nature."

Thallon scoffed in disgust. Neer turned to him, a sour look on her face.

"Are you going to keep moping, or can we have a conversation?" she said.

His quill stopped, though he continued staring at the page. When their eyes met, she lifted her brows, pressing him to speak. He slapped his notebook shut.

"You're risking my life by following that dog around."

"We'll make it to Aélla, Thallon."

"If we don't, I'll be branded a traitor! I'll lose everything!" His jaw clenched. "I risked my life for you in that council chamber, and this is how you repay me?"

"We're *going* to make it." She spoke through clenched teeth. "I can't ignore this. If he's out there—"

"Who?" He remarked. "*Avelloch*? You truly wish to throw my life away for that *meena'fromien*!"

Neer flinched when the direwolf released a deep, sawing growl. Its hair stood on end, and it stared at Thallon, sharp fangs exposed in a deadly warning. Neer recoiled, putting a slight distance between her and the furious beast.

"Thallon..." Neer started, her voice wavering as she eyed the direwolf.

He scoffed and shook his head. "If you knew *anything* about him, you'd stay far away."

The wolf rested its head on the ground. Neer clenched her jaw.

"I know you're upset that I'm trying to find him. You're afraid that—"

"I'm not afraid!" he snapped.

There was silence as she waited for him to continue. But he refused to speak further, keeping his furious eyes on the fire. Neer started to speak, producing a single syllable before Thallon's voice silenced hers with his rage.

"He's a traitor, Neer! Cast aside when he—"

"Enough!"

The flames burned hotter, splaying against the charring meat. She turned away, stricken by her anger. Crossing her arms over her chest, she fought against the pressure threatening to explode. There was a long silence between them.

"I don't want this tension, Thallon. You're my friend. We've been through a lot together. I swear...I won't let them banish you." She caught his glare as she continued. "We'll make it to her, I swear it."

"We've already gone off course. If the Eirean believe we've betrayed them, they'll—"

"Thallon," she said, her voice strong with promise. "I *won't* get you banished."

He turned away, focusing his attention on the cooking meat. Neer pulled up her knees and wrapped around them. Footsteps and fiendish growls echoed in the darkness. Chills crawled across her skin, and she examined her surroundings, fearful of the creatures lurking through the night.

Thurandír kept his fingers on his sheathed dagger. His eyes were glued to the direwolf. "I know that wolf," he said. "It belongs to the Zaeril."

"The what?" Neer asked.

"Zaeril. It's a *sitria*—a nickname."

"Like the one Aen'mysvaral has?"

"Kind of. Except, no one knows who the Zaeril is. Some people think he's just a myth. All we know is that he clings to the shadows and travels with a direwolf...just like that one."

Neer eyed the beast. Knowing it was connected so closely to Avelloch made her feel safe. Whole. She knew it

would lead her to him. Even if she wasn't entirely sure she was ready to reunite and face the man who left her behind.
Thallon added, "The Zaeril is nothing but a man, same as you and me." He removed the spit from the fire, tending to the meat, and muttered, "Though, the rumors of his soul being shredded by darkness are accurate."
Neer ignored him and returned her focus to Thurandír.
"What else do they say about him?" she asked.
"Nothing really. He's a shadow, a ghost. Prowling the night, slaughtering the lanathess or Klaet'il that invade our territory."
"He just slaughters them?"
"Yeah, but a lot of us think he's a hero. He does the dirty work the Eirean won't allow the avel to do." He accepted a helping of meat Thallon passed him. "If anyone knew he was *nesiat*"—he shook his head—"I don't know what they'd think."
Neer eyed the wolf, wondering what it and Avelloch had been through. Wondering how many people they'd killed—no, *slaughtered*—in the name of justice. When she first met Avelloch, he had been torturing people for information about the Nasir. People who had ruthlessly killed two young boys and shoved their bodies away like buckets of waste.
At the time, she thought it unforgiveable that he could inflict such torment and pain on someone else, but now, after seeing the massacres the Nasir and his followers inflicted on the innocent...remembering the look in the father's eyes as his own son's corpse charged at him...
She blinked her eyes, casting the thoughts away.
"You two must be close," Thurandír started. "You and Avelloch, I mean. A dren'seol is only loyal to their companion and the people they're closest to. My dren'seol is a fox named Isk. He's back home, though, with Aeraviin. She likes the company while I'm away."
"Is Aeraviin the girl from Navarre?"
A faint smile pulled his lip. "Yeah. She's my *see'nah*."
Thallon leaned back on his right arm, his scowl no longer present as he ate his meal. "Come on, kid," he said

with a mouthful of food. "You don't believe in that, do you?"

"You've heard of a see'nah?"

Thallon motioned to himself. "*Drek'vaggeá ahn'clave.*°"

"Oh yeah. That's right!" He took another bite. "What's a scholar of the First Blood doing with a lanathess, anyway? How do you two even know each other?"

"Saved her ass a couple of times out in the desert." The hint of a smile stretched his lips, and he took another bite, eyeing Neer. "Looks like I've saved your ass in the forest too."

"You can keep telling yourself that," she remarked, happy to find the tension between them fading.

Thurandír smiled, and they spent the rest of the night in quiet conversations.

The next morning, after a night of restless sleep, Neer awoke to find the wolf next to her. Its breath warmed her face, keeping the chilly air from stinging her skin.

She stirred before slowly rising. The wolf lazily followed, staring at her, then glancing through the forest. Neer rubbed its head, thankful for its protection and warmth.

Dying embers created the aroma of charred wood, and the smoldering heat lost its glow. Thurandír leaned against a tree, lightly snoring, while Thallon lay by the blackened logs. His mouth was wide open and seeping with drool. Neer and the wolf shared a glance, and she smiled at its humanlike behavior.

"You aren't as bad as you look, are you?" she said, rubbing its head.

The wolf closed its eyes, enjoying her loving strokes. She scratched behind its ears and under its chin before pulling her hands away. The wolf released a disappointed huff and then rested its head on the ground.

Neer lifted her eyes, basking in the warmth of the rising sun. She inhaled a deep breath, taking in the smell of natural wood and grass. The world was peaceful and quiet.

° In the language of the evae, Drek'vaggeá ahn'clave translates directly to *Scholar of the First Blood*

Birds whistled in the trees above, bringing life to a once quiet and slumbering land.

As she peered through the limbs, her attention fixed on a white raven perched nearby. Its light blue eyes were set on hers. Neer stared curiously at the creature, whose stare never faltered from her own. She wondered, for a moment, if it was a dreled, as its uniquely colored eyes weren't typical for an animal. But when the wolf rose with a vicious growl, Neer realized it was something more.

The bird quickly took flight, diving through the trees in its escape.

Neer turned when Thallon woke, rubbing his eyes with a yawn. "What's going on?" he asked.

"I don't know," Neer said. "I think someone's following us."

"What do you mean?"

Her eyes moved back to the limbs. "There was a raven. It was white with blue eyes."

Thallon leaned forward with a sigh. "It's probably the Eirean. They've got spies all over the forest and said they'd be watching us."

"They use dreleds?"

"No." He sleepily rubbed his face. "They're *stia'dyr*.° People who can see through the eyes of animals."

Neer sat for a moment longer, allowing Thurandír and Thallon to fully wake. After a short breakfast, they gathered their things and stomped out the embers. Clearing their campsite and searching the trees for any followers, they trailed after the direwolf, each step bringing them closer to Avelloch.

Morning faded into afternoon, and the warm day became dreary beneath a blanket of thick clouds. The scent of rain grew stronger with every gust of wind. Neer wrapped tighter into the white cloak, now stained with dirt

---

° Pronunciation: Stee-ah-deer

A title for those born with the rare ability to see through the eyes of an animal. While under their hosts control, the animal becomes white and obtains the eye color of the one controlling its will.

and grass. The thick material waved harshly in the gale, nearly ripping from her shoulders.

"We should find shelter," Thurandír said.

Neer clenched her teeth, not wanting another detour or rest. Her eyes shifted to the trees, and she watched the branches rustle and sway. "What shelter is around here?"

They followed Thallon behind a tree, shielding themselves from the wind as he collected a map from his pack. Neer and Thurandír leaned over his shoulders to get a closer look.

Thurandír pressed a finger to the parchment. "I think there's a hunter's cabin around here."

As they spoke, Neer leaned closer to study the map.

When voices rose through the ripping winds, she turned around, eyeing the forest. Her heart leapt in her chest, anticipating Avelloch's arrival. While Thurandír and Thallon spoke of their next move, Neer stepped away. The wolf followed.

"Neer?" Thallon asked.

"I hear someone," she said, still searching their surroundings.

He shoved the map into his pack. "What? Where?"

The wolf's ears perked, and it turned to the east.

"Do you hear them?" she asked.

With a low growl, the wolf lowered itself to the ground.

Fear rose in Neer's chest when she realized it wasn't Avelloch she had heard. The sound of gruff laughter erupted through the air, and Neer ripped her sword from its sheath.

Thurandír stood beside her with his bow in hand. Their eyes were focused ahead, waiting. More laughter mixed with the sound of pelting rain, and a chill ran down Neer's spine when the deeply accented voices of human men rang in her ears.

Neer raced forward, following their sounds. The direwolf was at her side, keeping in perfect stride. They rushed ahead, and the winds increased. As she moved closer to the sounds, she noticed white parchment was tacked to nearly every tree.

Slowing to a stop, Neer examined the nearest note, which displayed a large portrait of her face. Evaesh symbols were written across the top and bottom, stating:

Beware the humans!

This woman is not who they claim her to be. She is the key to our salvation. Do not return her to the lanathess. Do not regard her as your enemy.

The Broken Order Brotherhood seeks her return in good faith.

And we will find her.

Neer ripped the paper from the tree, rereading the words a dozen times. The Brotherhood was there, in the forest, searching for her. But she knew the voices she followed didn't belong to them. They were gruff and accented—the undeniable voices of deeply devout Ravinshire men.

The parchment crinkled in her fist. She shook her head, thinking of how Reiman had outwitted the humans. He had truly thought of everything, going so far as to inject spies into the Order to create these notes. Before he had stepped foot in the desert, her father was already several steps ahead, planning for this moment when the invasion would occur.

These humans, who had butchered and slain so many innocent lives in her pursuit, were unknowingly posting a plea for her salvation. The Order must've believed these notes to be a direct translation of their own perfectly crafted wanted poster. Neer was lucky the pious rulers had more power than they did wit.

Laughter broke through her thoughts, and she was quickly reminded of her path. Leaving the notes behind, she pushed through branches and leaves before coming to a halt at the edge of their camp. Four leather tents with open fronts were huddled together within the trees.

Several men were congregated around a campfire beneath the largest tent. Their long shadows lurked like wraiths in the night, flickering with every hiss and pop of the spewing flames. Gruff laughter echoed from their camp, igniting the flames of hatred in Neer's soul.

The men stirred stew in a cauldron and drank from wooden tankards. Their weapons were tossed aside, and no guards stood watch. Neer's eyes narrowed as they spoke, telling stories of their time in the forest. Among the larger, red-haired men were smaller, leaner fighters. They wore black leather armor, a stark contrast to the Ravinshire's filthy trousers and tunics.

"What 'appened to the others?" a man asked. "Them human camps were left empty. Dozens of 'em."

Another man spat into the fire. "Fuckin' pale-faces. Who else would it be?"

"Maybe it was the Child. She's a witch, after all."

"A blood demon," another man chimed in. "Probably stole 'em from their tents in the night or 'ad 'em all follow 'er into the woods with 'er magic."

Rain pattered loudly against the leather tents when the men fell silent. More drinks were passed around, and the conversation shifted as a drunken man stated, "Praise be, least she's leavin' the pale-faced bastards for us. I always 'eard these forest 'eathens were good." He laughed. "If only they didn't kick so damned hard!"

"Maybe if your prick weren't so small," another man jeered, lifting his pinky into the air, "you wouldn't 'ave to put up such a fight!"

The others cheered and laughed. A sour look stained the scarred man's face. He spat into the fire, guzzled the remainder of his drink, and then wiped his mouth with his sleeve. "Fuck off, Sal."

The others continued laughing, and the scarred man stood.

"Where're you goin'?" the others jeered.

"Takin' a piss. Lest' you want ter come and hold this prick you're gushin' about."

"Would"—Sal laughed—"if I could find it!"

Another roar of laughter erupted from the tent. The scarred man marched away with a huff. He stomped into the forest and stood alone in the trees.

SHADOWS OF NYN'DIRA

"Neer!" Thallon hissed, but she stalked forward, tucking herself deep in the shadows.

The wolf was a step behind, following her every move, working in tandem as she stepped closer to the scarred human. His grumbled voice became clearer, and she ducked behind a tree nearby.

"Fuckin' prudes," he muttered. "I'll find the Child myself and fuck 'er bloody. That'll show 'em."

His words sent waves of fury through Neer's veins. Magic sizzled in the air, stinging her skin, and winds raged as her anger strengthened.

The storm grew stronger.

With a deep inhale, Neer glared at the man before her, and then she sprung from the shadows.

Chapter Sixteen

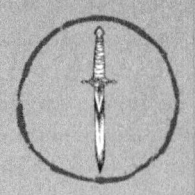

Blood of the Lanathess
Nerana

A twig snapped underfoot, and the man lifted his eyes. Their gazes met.

Neer plunged her sword through his chest and glared at him, wanting to inflict the pain he had caused so many others. The pain he wished to inflict on her.

He inhaled a wheezed gasp when Neer yanked her weapon from his flesh. Blood drained from his body. She stepped back when he collapsed to his knees.

"Gregor?" a man called from within the tent.

The others quieted and then stood at the edge of the canopy, scanning the woods.

With her hands at her side, Neer twirled her fingers, feeling the fizzle of heat erupt through her veins. Sweat beaded across her forehead as she coalesced her magic with the heat of the flames popping within the tent. The searing energy flushing her skin was numb to the rage sweltering inside, fueling her magic.

A rush of heat came from behind the men, and they turned around, watching the flames rise like an angry serpent. Two men fell back, while the others stared in terror.

Neer stood above Gregor's body, his blood staining her leather soles. She reached out toward the growing flames. Sweat trickled down her face as magic roiled deep inside. Neer pulled her arm back and clenched her fist. The flames followed, striking forward at the nearest man.

Screams echoed through the night when his body was engulfed with heat. Scurried footsteps splashed against muddy soil as his companions fought to extinguish the flames.

Weapons clamored, and the men trudged out of the tent, searching for their intruder.

"Come out, you 'eathen!"

Exhausted, Neer released the flames and exhaled a deep breath. She shared a glance with the direwolf and then turned to the humans. The wolf raced forward, silent as a shadow. It sprang from the darkness, tackling a man to the ground. Vicious growls erupted from its throat as it tore into the man's neck. The human's screams became gargled, and blood sprayed through the air.

Another man raised his axe, plunging it toward the wolf, but an arrow struck his head. He collapsed to the ground, twitching. Neer turned, watching Thurandīr flip across the ground and then release another arrow. A human shouting at Neer was thrown back with an arrow lodged in his eye.

His comrades turned to Neer, and she fell into a defensive posture. The first man approached, and Neer lunged forward, slashing her sword. He spun aside, evading her attack. She turned to him, her chest heaving as he growled.

"You fucking bitch!" he shouted.

Neer sliced her sword. It swung through empty air when the man leapt aside. He jabbed his rusted sword. She disappeared before the blade reached her skin, and the man swung his weapon around. Neer lifted her sword to block his hit, iron striking steel. The winds pushed the rain aside, whipping limbs and leaves through the air.

This was no ordinary man from Ravinshire. He was leaner, with steady eyes and well-equipped hands. Hanging from his neck, glistening with raindrops, was the crossed sword sigil of the Shadow Blades.

"We've got you now, *Child*," he growled.

Neer struggled against his strength. His blade slid against hers, moving closer to her throat. Her face turned red, and her teeth clenched. Trembling arms forced his weapon back, but her strength was waning. With a grunt, he shoved harder, sliding closer to her skin.

Neer pushed against his weapon. She prepared to teleport, when suddenly, her attacker was thrust to the ground. Neer staggered back, watching the wolf rip a hole in his throat. Its sapphire eyes met with hers. Blood dripped from its snout.

Two Ravinshire men charged, mud slinging from their boots. A vicious growl sawed through the air as the wolf lunged at them. The men yelped and quickly turned to run. The wolf chased them deep into the forest. Neer eyed the battlefield. To her left, Thurandír slid through the woods, ducking behind a wide trunk. He peered around, nocked an arrow, and then released it into the back of a man charging at Thallon.

Two humans swung their axes at the scholar, and he flipped aside. Thallon lifted his shield, taking the impact of their hit. With a pained grunt, he struck his dagger into the throat of the nearest man.

Neer averted her gaze to a mercenary charging at her. She lifted her sword and blocked a hit aimed at her chest, then flipped back. But the man lunged forward and jabbed at her stomach.

She lifted her arms, creating an invisible barrier shielding her from his attack. White lines crazed the air when his blade struck against her magic. A shockwave sizzled through her veins. Her fingers curled inward, and she groaned.

He spoke angrily while striking against her weakening shield. Neer fell to her knees, overcome with agony. The cold touch of his steel sent fire coursing through her, and the barrier dissipated.

A strong hand grabbed her throat, thrusting her against the tree. His lips pursed together as he glared. Neer's muscles ached, and her chest was heavy. Tired eyes displayed her anger, never faltering in her fury or hatred.

She glanced downward when he gathered a syringe from his pocket, and her eyes widened with terror. Weak hands clawed against his arm, fighting to be released, but her muscles could hardly push against his iron grip. Her lungs convulsed, begging for breath.

The needle moved closer to her skin, prepared to inject her with the magic-blocking serum, when a shadow appeared behind her captor. He turned to face his attacker, and a sword was pressed against his throat. His harsh words faded into gargled breaths when the blade slid across his neck, slicing deep enough to expose bone. The mercenary fell to the ground, choking on his blood.

Neer stared up at her savior. He was dressed in black, with a hooded cloak shrouding his face and hair. A tight mask covered his lower face, leaving only his eyes displayed through a veil of shadows.

The stranger pulled himself away when the direwolf growled from behind, still in a fight of its own. He raced to the wolf's side and jabbed his sword deep into a human's gut. Neer watched him slice through the remaining humans. His movements were nearly too quick for her to see, weaving from one man to the next.

Thunder rumbled across the sky. Lightning brightened the night. Neer watched through the heavy rain, her heart thumping in her chest. From the corner of her eye, she noticed Thurandír drawing back an arrow, aiming at the man in black.

"Don't!" she shouted.

His eyes cut to her, and he disarmed his bow, staring back at the man. Neer was silent, watching the stranger study the humans lying in the mud. Their deep wounds filled the grass with streams of red.

Neer drew his attention when she stepped closer. Rain dripped over her eyes and down her face. She breathed heavily, not daring to show her fear. Her grip tightened on her sword when she approached him.

He straightened, never drawing his weapon or preparing to defend himself as the tip of her blade pressed against his chest.

"Who are you?" she demanded.

He was silent and still as a shadow. Rain pattered against his cloak, washing it of the blood and filth. Neer pressed her blade firmer when he lifted his arm to his shoulder. Slowly, he sheathed his blood-coated sword into the scabbard on his back. Her heart throbbed as she waited, watching his fingers curl around the edge of his hood. For a moment, he hesitated, his shoulders rising and falling with every hard breath.

When he pulled it away from his face, Neer took half a step back. Her arms fell to her sides. The sword dropped from her fingers and splashed in the mud at her feet. Platinum hair, wet with rain, was half-pulled back and tied at the crown of his head. Dark blue eyes peered into hers. He didn't need to remove his face mask. She knew who was standing before her. The weight of confusion and anger lifted as she held his stare. And the world, for a moment, was still. Silent. Empty as her heart.

She stepped closer, their gazes never breaking. Her lungs never exhaling the breath caught in her throat. Her fingers gently curled around the edge of his mask, and slowly—painfully—she unveiled his face.

A wave of uncertainty surged through her. She didn't know how to feel. What to think. His dark eyes were unrecognizable in their sorrow and guilt. It had been so long since they had seen each other. Since he had abandoned her in Nhamashel.

But he was there now, standing before her, with the blood of her enemies soaked into his skin. His jaw tightened. Before she could speak—before she had the time to breathe, he said, "*Thir'gildrak me'nyen.*" His voice was gruff with pain. "Forgive me."

Her lip quivered, and tears burned her eyes. She inhaled a deep sniff, unable to face him. Unable to unleash the confusion and anger and sorrow she felt at his betrayal.

Avelloch was silent, watching her with bloodshot eyes, awaiting her judgement. But she didn't want to forgive or hate or understand.

"I don't...," she started, but the words were lost in her mind. For so long she had imagined their reunion, and now that he was there, she didn't know how to feel. "Why did you leave me?"

His posture slackened, and his eyes fell away. Lightning flashed, and thunder rumbled across the skies. The winds blew stronger, carrying the weight of dread and sorrow.

Neer turned aside and wiped her nose when Thallon approached. He touched her shoulder and glared at Avelloch.

"We need to move," he said. "Where are you staying?"

Avelloch exhaled a deep breath. Another clash of thunder shook the air. Neer closed her eyes. She wished Thallon would have kept his distance. She wished he wasn't there at all. At least, not while Avelloch stood before her, begging for forgiveness.

But she couldn't face him, not until she knew what she wanted. Avelloch opened his mouth to speak, but another voice echoed through the woods. And Neer's blood ran cold.

She glanced ahead, watching as Klaud came into view. Her eyes simmered with hatred. Only days before she had seen him, standing next to her, pleading for her freedom. As if he hadn't been the cause of her devastation. As if he hadn't *killed* the only person who truly mattered to her.

Her body trembled, and the world was red.

"Avelloch!" Klaud called. "Are you—"

Avelloch leapt forward, stumbling through empty air when Neer vanished. "Klaud!" he shouted.

Klaud disappeared just as Neer teleported behind him, jabbing her sword through the air where his chest would've been. He appeared to her left, looking around in a daze. Neer lifted her arm and expelled a powerful blast of energy. Klaud rolled across the grass. He vanished, reappearing several paces to the left. Neer released another wave of energy.

As he smashed into the dirt, Neer lifted her hands, preparing for another assault. But Avelloch grappled her from behind, pinning her arms to her sides. She screamed and fought against him. Using her magic, she broke free from his grasp. He fell back and gripped his arm with a groan.

Neer watched Klaud crawl to his knees.

"You bastard!" she exclaimed, her voice raw with fury and pain. The winds increased as her rage strengthened. Water whipped through the air in a vortex, slicing their skin. "You killed him!"

Her arms were raised toward Klaud, and he gripped his head in agony. She could feel the solidity of his skull as her magic pressed against it, squeezing.

He cried out, clutching his head.

"Neer!" Thallon screamed, racing to Klaud's side. "Stop this! You're killing him!"

She stepped closer, not hearing his words. Not feeling the sharp sting of water carving into her skin. Her eyes faded to black. Soulless and empty. Rage and fire filled her with power.

Avelloch blocked her path. "Neer!" he called, but she didn't react. Black veins formed around her eyes, crawling away like bolts of lightning. Her skin was pale, and her lips were held in a tight line. "Nerana!"

"Klaud?"

Avelloch froze when Aélla's voice came from behind. She dropped to Klaud's side and pulled him into her arms.

"What's happening!" she exclaimed.

"It's Neer!" Thallon remarked. "Do something!"

She gasped and turned to Neer. "Stop this!" she exclaimed. "Please!"

The winds increased, drowning out her panicked voice. Aélla's face twisted with pain. She lifted her arm and expelled a shockwave toward Avelloch and Neer. They were pummeled to the ground, rolling across the grass and mud. While Avelloch came to a stop, Neer vanished.

She reappeared above Klaud, striking her sword at his back. Aélla lifted her arms, and white cracks formed around the tip of Neer's sword where it met with Aélla's shield. From the ground, Aélla stared up at her, terrified and confused. Neer glared back, her black eyes fuming.

"Neer," Thallon started. "Please, you can't—"

Neer's eye twitched, and his words were silenced. She hadn't lifted a finger. Hadn't shifted her focus from Aélla's. Yet still, his voice was restrained.

Neer placed her hands upon Aélla's shield and sent waves of heat through her palms. Her palms glowed bright red, like a hot iron set in flames. The white cracks glowed orange as the heat of her magic intensified.

Aélla whimpered and groaned. She shook her head, tears streaming down her face. "Please…," she begged.

But Neer didn't stop. She didn't blink or flinch as her energy increased.

Aélla closed her eyes and clenched her teeth.

"I'm sorry…," she said, her voice strained. She released the barrier and clutched Neer's wrist.

The fires once raging through Neer turned to ice. Her blood froze as Aélla's energy melded with her own, swirling through her veins and into her chest, where it culminated into intense, ripping agony.

Neer shrieked and crashed to the ground, convulsing. Aélla collapsed, lying immobile, the rage of Neer's magic sizzling through her. The winds receded and the storm calmed when the darkness of Neer's eyes faded, and she fell silent and still.

Chapter Seventeen

Forgiveness
Avelloch

"*Trust no one.*"

— Eive to Avelloch

Rain fell from the sky, landing against Avelloch's bruised and bloody skin. He sat on his knees, staring at the others, wondering how this had happened. How easily Neer could have killed them all. Her black eyes, so full of hatred and rage, were vivid in his mind.

Aélla groaned, and Avelloch was pulled from his thoughts. His eyes shifted to his sister, who whimpered, still unable to move. Klaud was next to her, leaning over with his head in his hands. His arms trembled in his agony.

Thallon knelt over Neer, checking her pulse, while Thurandír carefully approached with his bow in hand. His cautious, terrified eyes were on Neer. Y'ven stepped forward, his wide eyes on the carnage of Neer's fury.

"Master Drimil," he said, marching forward. He knelt beside Aélla, unable to help.

Avelloch climbed to his feet and trailed toward the others. He sat next to Aélla, wishing to erase her pain. Her eyes were closed, and tears streamed down her face as she choked on her breath. Avelloch's jaw clenched, and he turned to Klaud, watching him writhe in his own torture.

"Klaud," he said, touching his shoulder. "Are you all right?"

Klaud groaned. "Aélla…"

Avelloch glanced at his sister. "I don't know...We need to do something."

"Do what?" Thallon asked. "There is nothing for this!"

Avelloch scanned the forest, searching for intruders. The direwolf slowly approached his side, staring curiously at Neer. "We need to find shelter," Avelloch stated. "If others come, we won't have the strength to fight them off."

Thurandír's wary eyes were fixed on Neer. "There is a hunter's cabin just north of here," he explained.

"Are you f'yet?" Thallon remarked. "We need to get Neer away from Klaud, and they all need a nes'seil! Her powers are too great for us to handle."

"Maybe we can help her," Thurandír stated. "If Drimil'Rothar can—"

"She's unstable, Thurandír! If Aélla didn't come, Klaud would be dead! She probably would have killed us too! Did you see her eyes? Her rage?"

"Stop it!" Avelloch hissed.

Thallon gawked at him. "What she just did was out of line, Avelloch," he argued. "Trying to kill him like that? Without even speaking to him?"

Thallon's gaze shifted to Neer, and confliction rose in his eyes. "She's too dangerous," he said. "Someone needs to contain her energy. They need to—"

"She stays with us," Avelloch said, his voice strong and demanding.

Thallon scoffed with a laugh. He shook his head and licked his lips. Simmering eyes examined Avelloch from head to toe. It had been ages since they had seen each other, and the absence seemed to have brewed an unbreakable hatred within Thallon. Avelloch could see it in his eyes—the resentment and fury. It had been this way since he was cast aside. The scholar didn't want to believe it at first, but eventually, he turned his back on Avelloch like everyone else.

"Come on, Thallon," Thurandír said, urging him to calm.

"She has to be contained," he said. "Otherwise, everything Aélla's working toward will be for nothing!"

Thunder rumbled across the sky, breaking their intense glare. Avelloch stood, weighing his decisions. He knew Thallon was right. Neer was dangerous. Her anger and power were stronger than he had ever seen. But he wouldn't allow her to be taken.

"We'll rest at the cabin," Avelloch said, his eyes fixed on Neer. "I'll stay in the woods nearby with—"

"If you think we're leaving her out here with you, then you're out of your mind!"

"Thallon...," Klaud begged, pain seeping through his voice.

"I don't trust him." His angry eyes cut to Avelloch. "If she's staying with us, then we aren't leaving her alone with him. And we aren't spending another second in this forest. Not until we can afford to fight."

Tired of the fighting and tension, Avelloch agreed. "Let's go."

He stepped to Klaud's side and extended his hand. Klaud grasped his wrist and was pulled to his feet. Mud and grass covered his cloak in filth. Avelloch tapped his shoulder and looked into his eyes.

"Are you okay?"

Klaud nodded with a groan and stumbled forward. Avelloch caught him, quickly wrapping Klaud's arm around his shoulders. A deep, sawing groan came from Y'ven, who lifted Aélla from the ground. Thallon attempted to carry Neer, but as he pulled her close, he inhaled a sharp wince and clutched his chest. Thurandír came to his side, pulled Neer into his arms, and then led them toward the cabin.

The forest fell cold, and the storm dwindled into a light drizzle. Avelloch walked the familiar path to the cabin, a place where many evae would go to find shelter during their hunts. There were several hundred of the small, one-room buildings scattered all throughout Rhyl territory. Avelloch had come to know many of them during his life, as he was forbidden to build a home of his own on Rhyl grounds.

When the silhouette of the small cabin came into view, Thurandír called, "Here it is!"

A small clearing housed the hunter's shack. Wooden barrels, an archery target, and a grindstone were spread out in front of the home. Two chairs and a table rested by the door beneath the porch gable.

Thallon stepped ahead of the group and knocked on the door. When there was no response, he stepped inside. The room was dark and quiet. A soft glow brightened the room when he ignited the oil lantern hanging from the ceiling. He then gathered firewood from a pile by the hearth and placed them into the fireplace.

Y'ven entered and set Aélla on the cot. The leather creaked beneath her weight, and she settled into place, whimpering. Avelloch was behind, navigating Klaud toward the table. He helped him sit and then stretched the ache from his back. He turned and watched as Thurandír placed Neer on the floor by the bed.

Light sparked from a flint as Thallon set the tinder ablaze. A gentle glow illuminated the room, lifting the darkness. Everyone turned to Aélla whimpering in her sleep, twitching with affliction. Klaud passed a potion to Avelloch.

"This will help," he said, "with her pain."

"What about you?" Avelloch asked.

Klaud leaned forward with his head in his hands. "There is only enough for one."

Avelloch clutched the potion in his hand, conflicted. But he knew Klaud would never take it, not while Aélla was in such torment. With heavy feet, he stepped across the room and gently poured the potion through Aélla's parted lips. Slowly, her body relaxed, and the light whimpers faded as she drifted to sleep.

He returned to the table, sitting across from Thallon. The scholar exhaled a deep breath and leaned back in his chair.

"So," Thallon started, his voice thick with resentment. "It's been a long time, Avelloch...I heard you were in lana'thoviin.° It's how you met Neer."

Avelloch remained silent, glaring.

Thallon licked his teeth. "We could be banished for just talking to you."

"Then stop talking."

Their eyes met, and Thallon chuckled darkly. "Clever. Tell me, are you—"

"Stop," Klaud said, his voice weak from pain. "There is enough distrust and anger between us...Fighting will solve nothing."

"You're too passive, Klaud," Thallon sneered. "He's a sick bastard for what he did. They should have hanged him like all the others."

Avelloch shook his head and turned away. He had heard it all before—the hatred and threats. The words had grown meaningless overtime. Coming from Thallon, they were expected.

Thurandír stepped across the room. In his hand was a glowing crystal; its blue light shone against his eyes. As he stepped closer to Neer and Aélla, its glow brightened. He stared curiously at it, watching it dim the further he moved from them.

"What is that?" Thallon asked, his voice still steeped in anger.

"I don't know," Thurandír said. "It was at the lanathess camp. They had dozens of them."

"Let me see it."

Thurandír passed the stone to Thallon, and he examined it. His brows pulled together, twisting it in his hand. "These are *lyansthaa*. They can only be mined in Anaemiril. How did the humans—"

His voice was silenced when a deep thud shook the cabin door. Everyone jumped when the wooden entry rattled. Avelloch held his swords in hand, waiting. His heart

---

° Pronunciation: Lah-na tow-veen

In the language of the evae, Lana'thoviin translates roughly to mean *human territory*

pounded harder than the raging storm as he anticipated another attack. Narrowed eyes veered to Aélla and Neer when Y'ven stood before them, a strong and immovable guard.

Thurandír crept by the hearth and nocked an arrow as winds battered against the walls, and thunder shook the air. Low sniffing sounded through the pouring rain when a creature stalked their shelter. A slow, clicking growl moved east as their intruder searched for its prey.

Its threatening sounds disappeared, and everyone released a sigh of relief. Thallon closed his eyes.

"The balance is shifting," Thallon said, staring once again at the softly glowing stone. "If we don't take this seriously, then everything will fall."

Avelloch exhaled a deep breath. His eyes fixed on Neer, Thallon's words replaying in his mind. Turning away, he sat in silence, becoming lost in his thoughts as he stared into the flames, waiting for the others to wake.

Chapter Eighteen

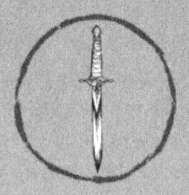

Lost
Nerana

"Do not allow corruption to pull you asunder. Find truth in the Light and never be led astray."

— Rotharion, *The Book of Light*

Dawn broke through the clouds, and sunlight peeked through the windows of the small cabin. A bright stream of warmth crawled across the floor, traveling closer to Neer before gently caressing her face. She stirred, then slowly woke and rubbed her tired eyes.

Neer looked around and then sat up with a quiet gasp, staring at the unfamiliar surroundings. Her quick pulse reduced when she spotted Thurandír nearby. Embers burned in the hearth, where he lay asleep next to Y'ven. Her jaw dropped at the sight of the vaxros, and her mind swirled with confusion. Across the room, Thallon leaned forward with his arms folded atop a table. His mouth was open, and he lightly snored.

And leaned against the door, his feet nearly touching her, was Avelloch. His head had fallen aside as he lay asleep. Neer gripped her forehead, struggling to remember how she came to this place. All she could recall was Avelloch approaching her in the forest, and then there was nothing. Not a whisper of what happened next.

But something was different. Inside her chest, where her magic festered and grew, was cold and bleak. She was heavy with emptiness, as if all the air had been pulled from her lungs. She sat up, brushing against Avelloch's outstretched legs and causing him to stir.

He lazily opened his eyes with a sigh. The sleep that weighed his expression lifted when he noticed Neer staring at him. He drew his legs inward and sat up, staring at her with cautious eyes.

"Hey...," Neer said, her voice was quiet.

Avelloch's jaw clenched. "Hey."

She ran her fingers through her hair and scanned the room. "What are we doing here? What is this place?"

They turned when Thallon repositioned in his sleep. Neer stiffened, hoping he wouldn't wake. Hoping she could have this time to speak to Avelloch without interruption. As he started snoring, she released her breath.

Her eyes shifted to Avelloch when he asked, "Would you care to walk with me?"

The floor creaked when they stepped out of the home. Neer closed her eyes, allowing the sun to melt away the chill in her bones.

They stepped away from the cabin, wandering through the quiet, peaceful wood. She walked with her arms crossed and glanced at his face. It felt like a lifetime since they had last seen each other, and the time had made her question everything.

"Avelloch," she started. "I don't...I'm not sure what to say. After Nhamashel, I thought that..." She crossed her arms and turned away, confused and overwhelmed.

Avelloch was silent for a moment, his eyes never meeting with hers. His posture rigid and jaw tense.

"I just woke up alone," she continued, "with Loryk. And you were gone. You took the arun and —"

"It wasn't my choice." She was silenced by his voice. "I had no idea he would take the arun from you. I tried to stop him. I tried to stop *you*, but I—"

"Stop *me*?" she asked, conflicted.

Her throat tightened. Sorrow weighed her feet, and she came to a stop, unable to find the strength to move forward. Avelloch stood beside her, watching as she struggled to find the words. "I lost control...didn't I?"

H.C. NEWELL

He pulled off the glove covering his right hand. Neer was motionless, and her heart sank when his flesh was revealed. Thick black veins painted his limb with darkness. They swirled upward from his hand like a web of shadows, reaching his elbow where it faded into healthy, unblemished skin.

He stared at his injured arm. "I tried to stop you," he said. "But you were lost. When he died you just...You were lost, Neer."

She touched his arm, haunted by what she was seeing. "Did I do this?" her voice was hardly a whisper.

"You were lost."

Her lip quivered. She thought of her night in Nhamashel, when she awoke to find the cave had crumbled around her. Trees were stripped bare, their bark cracked and lifeless. Grass had turned to ash beneath her knees where she sat, crippled by her grief and confusion. She never understood what happened that night, but always knew that, somehow, it had been done by her. Whatever rage and pain she felt was unleashed in that cave.

The thought clung to her chest like a heavy weight, pulling her lungs and stealing her breath. She didn't remember much from her time in Nhamashel—many of the events from the Trials were a blur of visions, blood, darkness, and pain...so much pain.

"You should stay away from me. Everyone should—" She sniffed and turned away. "I don't know what's happening to me." Tear-filled eyes met with his, and he was shattered by her anguish. "I don't know why this is happening."

Avelloch took a cautious step closer. Neer stared into his eyes, wanting him to believe her. Wanting *someone* to trust. But her memory of that night had failed her, and she was left to rely on faith alone. And in her years, she had learned that faith was a lie. Its comfort no longer soothed the unrest simmering deep in her soul.

Her eyes fell away when he reached back and unsheathed his sword. Dark fingers swept across its smooth edge, his eyes gazing at the purple light. With a glance at Neer, he offered it to her. "This is yours," he said.

SHADOWS OF NYN'DIRA

She accepted the weapon she had thought was lost. The one that had protected her in the desert and gave her comfort in his absence. Behind his shoulder was its twin, resting in the sheath across his back.

"Why weren't you there? In Aragoth."

"I couldn't be. Not with who I am."

She shook her head and shoved the weapon back into his hands. "I don't want this. I don't need your pity."

Avelloch tenderly placed the sword into her hand and wrapped her fingers around its hilt. "It isn't pity. There are many things that I regret...but none compare to the pain I've caused you."

Purple light emitted from the sword, shimmering against her watery eyes. "I want to believe you...but I can't even trust myself anymore."

"Neer, I—"

His words were interrupted when she shook her head. The excuses and promises and guilt made her sick. She crossed her arms and turned away, happy he didn't press her further.

The forest was quiet, peaceful. And for a moment, she felt calm. But peace was fleeting, and when voices rang in her ears, the solitude had passed. She turned away, searching for their intruders.

Avelloch was by her side with his hand on the hilt of his weapon. She watched him from the corner of her eye, comforted by his presence. Eased to know someone was truly, *genuinely* on her side.

The voices grew louder, followed soon by gentle footsteps. When Aélla's soft soprano touched her ears, Neer closed her eyes, thankful that a friend was nearby. Thankful that another fight wasn't waiting around the corner.

"They were with you?" Neer asked Avelloch. "Aélla and Y'ven?"

He nodded.

"What happened last night?" she asked. "Why don't I remember anything?"

The muscles of his jaw rippled, and he struggled to find the words.

"Avelloch," she pressed. "What happened?"

"You attacked Klaud."

A deep pit formed in her stomach. She closed her eyes, preparing for the worst. All the nights she had spent wishing for his death, for him to feel a shred of the pain he inflicted upon her…it might have come true. And the thought was more devastating than she imagined it would be.

"Is he…," she forced the words out, though they were like acid on her tongue. "Did I…"

"No," he said, and she released a deep breath. "Aélla stopped you."

She shook her head, feeling the weight of her energy and rage. "I didn't mean to. I…"

Avelloch reached out to touch her and then retracted his arm. "We'll figure this out," he said. "You aren't alone."

She turned to him with tear-filled eyes. "Thank you."

They stood together for several minutes, accepting the warmth of each other's company. She didn't know how she felt, not entirely, but she knew she needed him there. Whether as a friend or fighter or something more, she felt safe in his presence. Whole. The weight of the world was lifted when he was near, and she could breathe.

The voices humming through the empty wood became louder, and Neer smiled at the sound of Y'ven's gruff voice. She peered through the trees, eager to see her friends and have everyone together again. When his large stature came into view, Neer took half a step closer.

Limping next to him, clutching her ribs, was Aélla. Her long hair hung loosely across her shoulders and back. She appeared tired, with dreary eyes focusing more on her feet than the world ahead.

Dru's aura brightened when she spotted Neer. Her tiny fists wriggled in front of her face before she vanished into a stream of orange light. A trail of small embers wisped through the air before her small body smacked against Neer's cheek.

Neer laughed while gently stroking her back. "Hey, Dru," she said.

"Ürok!" Y'ven called.

His wide grin caused a fresh scar on his face to wrinkle. Neer stepped forward, and Y'ven reached out to take her forearm. She studied his left hand before flashing her eyes to his right. Her heart jolted when she noticed the bloody, misshapen bandages. He followed her gaze and then lifted his injured arm.

"Shadosalaan[*]," he explained. "Poisoned."

"The wisper...," Neer said, remembering the night he was attacked by the ghoulish creature of darkness. It had cried out in the night like a child, luring them closer before attacking. "You haven't healed?"

He shook his head but then lifted his left hand into a tight fist. "I am strong. Warrior."

Neer smiled, happy to see his strength and resilience hadn't faded.

Aélla stepped forward, and Neer hugged her tight. They stood together in a strong embrace.

"It is good to see you again," Aélla said, backing away. Her smile faltered, and she lifted her hand to Neer's face, touching the deep mark across her cheek.

"What's a warrior without a few scars?" Neer remarked, then glanced at Y'ven's arm. "Or broken pieces?"

He shook with rumbling laughter. Neer backed away when Dru darted toward her, hovering inches away and spewing with anger. She pointed a tiny finger at Neer, her aura and flames brightening with her every foreign word. Y'ven calmly pulled the faeth away, her squeaking voice never fading as she scolded Neer for making light of Y'ven's injury.

Aélla wrapped her arm around Neer's, and they walked toward the cabin. "I see you've reconnected with Avelloch."

Neer shared a glance with him. "He's your brother?"

She nodded. "I'm sorry I didn't tell you. I wasn't sure how you felt about him, and I didn't want that to affect our friendship."

Neer pulled away. Staring at her feet, she asked, "And Klaud?"

---

[*] Pronunciation: Shad-oh-sah-lahn

In the language of the humans, Shadosalaan are referred to as creatures of darkness.

Aélla was silent. Her hands twisted nervously at her waist. "He and I…are very close." She closed her eyes. "You do not understand the pain he carries."

Neer clenched her jaw and turned away. She hadn't the energy for an argument, but the mere mention of Klaud's name caused her blood to boil.

"We are worried about you," Aélla said, her voice strong and confident. "What happened last night…it cannot happen again. Do you understand?"

"Aélla, he—"

"I know." Their eyes met. "I know everything. But our feelings and resentment don't matter. We have to let it go. And if you can't do that, then you can't be with us."

Neer closed her eyes. Her chest swelled with anger.

Aélla continued, "There is a lot of hostility and distrust between us, but if we're going to survive, then we need to come together."

Neer stepped away, shaking her head. "How do I know that the knife he uses to defend me won't someday stab me in the back?"

Aélla bowed her head in shame. "We need each other, Nerana. But above all else, we need peace. Forgiveness is stronger than vengeance. If you don't control your emotions…they will control *you*."

Neer inhaled a deep breath. She didn't want to admit what Aélla said was truth, but they had all seen it firsthand—the toll her rage could take. She had to let this go. Her anger wouldn't bring him back. It wouldn't absolve Klaud of his betrayal, but it could free her from the darkness tainting her soul.

Through forced resolve, Neer said, "I don't know how."

Aélla smiled and touched her shoulder. "I can help you."

Calmness and the slight tingle of magic settled into her bones, and she peered into Aélla's soft eyes. It was a peace she hadn't felt for many, many years. With a light nod, she agreed, though she knew the path to mercy would be difficult. The hatred she felt for Klaud ran deep, but if she could overcome it, maybe the pain shredding her soul would mend.

SHADOWS OF NYN'DIRA

They walked in silence to the cabin, and Neer's stomach twisted when it came into view. Low voices echoed from inside the home, and she came to a stop.

"Come on." Aélla took her hand, and the turmoil festering inside calmed.

Neer glanced at their hands, wondering if Aélla's magic had altered her mood. When Klaud's voice whispered through the air, her thoughts were fractured, and she refocused her attention on the cabin.

At the door, she could hear him speaking to Thallon. Their voices were light and friendly. Aélla turned to her with a reassuring nod and then calmly stepped inside.

Thurandír sat on the edge of the cot with his hands together. His eyes flashed to Neer, and he straightened, becoming instantly alert. She was saddened by the fear in his dark blue eyes. Thallon stood by the door with his arms crossed while Klaud sat at the table, grinning softly as they spoke of their childhood.

Neer stared at him, surprised by his disheveled appearance. Black hair covered his lower jaw, and his eyes were dull with pain. His hair fell messily across his shoulders, and he leaned forward, sitting with his head propped against his hand, as if cradling it in pain.

Klaud met her gaze, and she was glad for Aélla's presence, which kept her anger at bay. Though, it festered and boiled deep inside, fighting to be released.

The cabin was silent. No one moved. They didn't breathe as Neer and Klaud stared at one another.

"Nerana, I—"

She stiffened, and a tremor of magic rumbled through the air. Her jaw clenched and chest ached as energy churned and simmered deep inside. She swallowed the lump in her throat, forcing her anger aside.

Klaud closed his eyes and exhaled a deep breath. Slowly, he stood, and Neer watched him with guarded eyes. Her heart raced and rage simmered when he stepped closer, and she took half a step back when he knelt before her with his head bowed.

The world was still when she looked down at him, speechless.

Everyone held their breath as he put his fate in her hands. The silent gesture of trust sent waves of tension through the air. Neer fought against the instincts demanding her to end his life. Loryk's cold, bloated body flashed through her mind. Her heart sank with emptiness and grief. Klaud had caused this. He chose to betray them.

He chose to murder an innocent man.

Avelloch and Thallon watched with worried eyes. No matter their fear, they knew not to intervene. This was Klaud's decision—he had put his life in Neer's hands, accepting whatever fate she would choose to give.

But this was no honorable sacrifice. She didn't care about his guilt or regrets. Loryk was gone. He'd never laugh or sing or dance again. The thought of Klaud's death—his body lying lifeless on the cabin floor—sent waves of relief through her. And that wave of peace, however brief, melted the anger scorching her dying heart.

Slowly, she reached out to him, feeling the warmth of his scalp as her fingers hovered inches above his ebony locks. She grasped onto the sliver of tranquility washing through her, knowing his death would calm the storm that raged within. He couldn't get away with this. He wouldn't. Not while she was still breathing. Loryk would be avenged. Everyone she lost would find peace. She would make sure of it—one blood-soaked dagger at a time.

Her hand trembled over his head, and she fought to do what was right. To push away the anger and forgive. Everyone watched, waiting for her to make her judgement. A judgement they all knew would be met with vengeance and pain. But this wasn't the path she wanted to take. The pain of loss was too great to inflict upon the others. Yet still, the desire to end his life was too overwhelming. Like an itch that couldn't be scratched, she *had* to kill him. Her soul yearned for his death.

Icy magic festered and burned deep inside her chest. She fought against it, grunting as it tore at her soul, begging to be unleashed. Aélla whimpered, holding tightly to Neer's wrist, unable to withstand the pain of Neer's twisted energy.

SHADOWS OF NYN'DIRA

But Neer had grown used to the agony and torment. It never faded, each day bringing a new wave of sorrow and resentment.

"Forgive," Aélla whispered through a strained voice. "You write your own destiny."

Neer closed her eyes, and a tear slid down her cheek. She wouldn't allow herself to be consumed by her rage. Her vengeance was meant for more than Klaud. She'd save it and allow that anger to fester, using it on the Order and High Priest.

With a deep exhale, she opened her fist and hesitantly placed her hand upon Klaud's head. The silent act of forgiveness sent waves of relief throughout the room. Aélla carefully released her grip on Neer's arm and took a step back.

Klaud stood and looked into Neer's eyes. He bowed his head in a sign of respect and returned to the table, putting much needed space between them.

"There is a lot of hostility between us," Aélla stated. "But our paths are far greater than the resentments we hold."

She glanced around the room. Her eyes settled on Neer, who stared at the ground, unblinking.

Aélla continued, "We *have* to trust each other if we're going to survive. There is enough unrest in this world. I won't have it strengthen through us."

Thallon stepped forward and placed his right fist over his heart. "I'm with you, Drimil."

Y'ven straightened, following Thallon's gesture with his left hand. "Drimil."

Dru stood on his shoulder with her right fist on her chest. Avelloch and Klaud shared a glance and slowly lifted their arms, showing their respect to Drimil'Rothai. Thurandír glanced at each of them, seemingly unsure, before taking the vow.

Aélla's lips curled into a sad smile, and tears glistened in her eyes. She glanced at each of them, before turning to Neer. Their eyes met, and Neer was taken aback when the evae placed her fist on her own chest and smiled. "We are with *you* too…Master Drimil."

Neer's eyes widened. She glanced at everyone, contemplating her fate. After the turmoil and strife and anger, they still vowed to protect her. Vowed to stand by her side, no matter the cost.

Thallon smiled with a nod, reassuring Neer of Aélla's words. They were with her…until the end.

Neer curled her fingers into a tight fist and placed her hand over her heart.

Chapter Nineteen

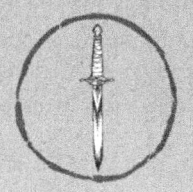

The Path of Salvation
Nerana

> *"It is with Galdir's unrivaled power and purity that our world has not yet fallen. But make no mistake, this world is not indomitable, and should the hammer strike with enough force, we, too, shall fall."*
>
> – Prophecy of Naik'avel; An'feindro'l,
> First Blood scholar of energy and time.

NEER SAT ON THE FLOOR of the cabin, leaning against the wall. Firelight flickered within the hearth, sending waves of orange light dancing through the small room. Through much argument with Aélla, Klaud had departed long ago to hunt, claiming the fresh air would do him good. Aélla lay on the cot, reading one of the many books left for travelers. She pressed a hand against her aching ribs and released a quiet groan every so often. Avelloch sat at the table, stitching a hole in his leather gauntlet.

With a sigh, Neer moved to the table and sat in a chair across from him. "So, what's our next step? We can't allow the humans to keep pushing forward."

Aélla closed her book and sat on the edge of the cot. "The avel can handle the lanathess," she stated. "We need to focus on our journey."

"What?" Neer retorted. "You and I are two of the most powerful people in the world. How can we sit by while everyone else fights?"

"We have to focus," Aélla said. "Keeping our energy under control is far more important than fighting."

"I can't just sit around while others die for me!"

Aélla closed her eyes and placed her hands on her thighs.

Avelloch glanced at her, and said, "The invasion is still manageable. They're sending children and ill-equipped men."

Aélla added, "Galdir° also protects us. Its magic fortifies Nyn'Dira."

Neer bit her tongue, knowing that arguing was futile. "Okay," she pushed the words from her throat. "So, what do you suggest we do?"

Aélla hesitated. She was quiet for a moment before approaching the table and sitting in a vacant chair. Her eyes were distant as she explained, "The magic here is dying...If we can't find a way to protect it...then the lanathess will be able to invade at full strength."

"How can we do that?"

More silence. Aélla's face paled and eyes were unblinking. "We need to stop the Nasir. His power is growing, and with the ring, he's close to unstoppable. The more he uses it...the more imbalanced the world will become."

Neer gulped down her fear. Her eyes shifted to Avelloch, who became stiff with deep, unrivaled fury. Her brows pulled together at his sudden anger. Before she could ask, Aélla continued.

"But first, we have to strengthen the magic of the Ko'ehlaeu'at trees. They cleanse our energy, keeping it in balance." She paused with sorrow. "We need to get to ydris territory and approach Galdir. I can use my energy to strengthen its magic. It may give us time until I can make it to tre'lan Rothar."

Neer leaned forward with her head in her hands. Her mind reeled. "Is there no option? We can't just track down the Nasir and take the ring back?"

"No. Our priority has to be the trees. If Galdir dies...this is over."

° Galdir is the mother of all the magical Ko'ehlaeu'at trees.

Avelloch repositioned and crossed his arms. "Ydris territory is heavily guarded, but we can go southeast to Galiendör. If you teleport, you can—"

"No!" Aélla retorted. "Teleportation is too unstable. It takes too much energy. And I'm not separating from everyone again. If something happens to one of you while I'm away..." She shook her head, determined. "We're staying together."

Avelloch reached over and clutched her arm. Aélla closed her eyes, calmed by his protectiveness and strength.

Neer glanced between them, considering their journey and what lay ahead. "Aélla," she started, "I know that we're here for you, but I've my own mission to fulfill. I have to get to the realms and strengthen my magic."

Aélla nodded and gulped down her words. "I understand. Once I've added my energy to the strength of Galdir, we can continue on our path."

"Are there any realms in the forest? Where are they located? Show me a map."

Aélla and Avelloch shared a wary glance. He collected a linen map from his pack and straightened it over the table. Neer stood, leaning over it with her hands splayed against the wooden surface. She studied the evaesh map, which was different from any she had ever seen before. Evaesh symbols littered the page, with Nyn'Dira being full of territorial lines, rivers, villages, and ruins. Laeroth, however, was empty. There were no titles labeling each region, no marks to signify the temples or other landmarks. It appeared as barren as Nyn'Dira on human maps.

There were only two areas within her home country that were present: the colleges of Styyr and the Temple of Rothar.

Her eyes narrowed as she studied further, noticing five more landmarks were located in a wide circle around the continent.

"Are these the realms?" she asked, turning the map to view it easier. Her jaw dropped when she recognized the names tied to each realm. Pointing to the colleges of Styyr, which were now destroyed, she read, "Tre'lan Rothar...Is that the Realm of Light?"

Aélla nodded wordlessly.

Neer's brows pulled together. She dragged her finger to the next pillar, located deep within Skye, where the Temple of Rothar was located. "Tre'lan Nizotl..." Her words were hardly a whisper as confusion whirled through her.

Nizotl. The Divine of trickery and deceit, known for meddling in human affairs and casting magic upon the world. The Shadow Blades and Mystic Nine[°] revered him as a savior, finding refuge in his Temple and praying at his statues.

But to the others, the Order and those who followed in the New Ways, Nizotl was considered the Divine of darkness. A ruthless, cunning, vicious being who preyed upon humanity. He sought nothing more than power and vengeance.

Neer gazed at the map, perplexed. The seat of power — humanity's most sacred temple — had been built around the realm of dark energy. Her touch lingered on the Temple of Rothar, where the realm was located. Rothar was the overseer of the immortal planes. A god of gods.

The Divine of grace and *light.*

Neer blinked when the door burst open, and her confusion melted into discomfort.

From behind, Thallon stepped inside with Thurandír. Their voices were cheerful and loud as they spoke of different things. Thurandír sat on the cot, and Thallon approached the table. He bit into an apple and wiped the juice from his chin.

"What's this?" he asked, pulling the edge of the map toward him. "Oh, a map! Are we finally coming up with a plan?"

"Yes," Aélla explained. "Tomorrow, we will leave for Galiendör."

[°] The Mythic Nine are a shadowy cult known for performing dark spells and incantations, including necromancy, poison, energy draining enchantments, and energy blocking potions.

While many believe the Mythic Nine work against the Order of Saro, the Priests and shamans have been known to use their potions and magic.

SHADOWS OF NYN'DIRA

Thurandír said, "My hometown is on the way. Could be nice to stop by. See how my parents are faring in the invasion."

Aélla smiled. "That would be nice."

Thurandír grinned and then shifted his eyes to Avelloch and Neer. "The e'liaa are welcoming of everyone. You should have no trouble finding a hot meal and warm bed."

Thallon sat on the floor, finishing his fruit. "Beats the hell out of bed rolls and burnt rabbit."

A hidden smile pulled Neer's lip as he teased her for carelessly burning one of their meals days prior.

With a laugh, Thallon called, "Finally! A damned smile."

"Come on," Thurandír stated while walking to the door. "I told the vaxros I'd train with him. He needs to strengthen that arm if he wants to fight."

Thallon plopped onto the cot, ignoring the light rip of the old leather beneath his weight. "I've had enough fights. A and I can discuss what's to come. My notebook is full of theories."

Aélla nodded in agreement. "Yes," she said. "There is a lot we should talk about."

"Neer?" Thurandír pressed. "Avelloch?"

He cheered as they stepped across the room and grabbed their boots. With a beaming smile, Thurandír excitedly led them outside to a nearby clearing, where Y'ven stood alone. He grunted while swinging a sparring sword through the air. His right arm was secured to his chest in tight bandages, and he leaned forward with a slight limp.

While Thurandír collected a sparring weapon from the wooden crate, Avelloch asked, "You want to fight against a vaxros?"

The archer gave a wry smile, and with a shrug, he quipped, "Why not?"

Thurandír trotted away, taking his place before the warrior thrice his size. Neer and Avelloch shared a glance.

"He *is* a warrior with your people," she explained. "Stationed under Thallon's brother."

Avelloch's brows pulled together, and he watched as Thurandír fought against Y'ven. "He's a kid."

"I was fighting with the best at his age."

His eyes cut back to her. A half-smile brightened his eyes, and Neer fought to contain her own, though it still showed in her scrunched lips.

They lifted their eyes to Y'ven when he released a rumbled growl and struck at Thurandír's side. The evae ducked, flowing smooth as a clean river beneath the vaxros's heavy swing. He then smacked Y'ven's shin with his weapon and turned on his knee, jabbing the edge of the weapon against Y'ven's lower spine. The thick yellow scars across Y'ven's back gleamed in the sunlight.

Neer watched with sullen eyes, noticing Y'ven's slowed movements and yellowed skin. She glanced at the bandage on his arm, noticing the dark red and yellow stains seeping through the linen. Thurandír was an avel fighter, but he was young and should have been no match against an al'yavan warrior.

But Y'ven was losing. Badly. Missing nearly every swing as Thurandír rolled and dodged around his painfully slow movements. Y'ven breathed heavily, riddled with exhaustion.

"Maybe we should stop," Neer called.

"No way!" Thurandír retorted, swinging his sword.

They continued, with Thurandír easily predicting and evading Y'ven's sloppy movements. He had lost his confidence, and with every missed swing, rage grew in his eyes. With a vicious shout, Y'ven slashed his sword downward and cut to the right, attempting to take Thurandír by surprise.

The quick fighter danced around his movements, smacking his wooden sword hard against Y'ven's wrist. They came to a stop, chests heaving, sweat dripping down Thurandír's face. He stepped back when Y'ven furiously tossed his sword aside and released a deadly roar.

"I cannot fight!" he said in his native language. "I am *weak!*"

Thurandír's terrified eyes were glued to the raging man before him. Noticing his fear, Y'ven's lip twitched, and he marched into the forest with Dru.

Neer chased after them, calling out his name. Y'ven ignored her pleas, trudging angrily through the dense underbrush.

"I thought the al'yavan didn't cower in defeat!" she exclaimed, and he came to an abrupt stop. Fear trickled through her, muddying the confidence she desperately clung to. But she wouldn't allow his rage to frighten her, not now, when he needed someone on his side. "Have you come this far to give up now?"

A low, rumbling growl seeped through his clenched teeth.

"You are a warrior, Y'ven! You lost everything to be with your bond mate, and you survived. You fought to restore your honor, and you survived. You were bitten by a creature of darkness, and you will *survive*."

Her lips pursed together, and she gazed at him, waiting for their eyes to meet. Once they had, she clutched his arm and said, "Don't let this be your downfall. You're greater than this. Stronger than it. A true warrior wouldn't let this best them."

His jaw clenched, and rage spewed from his fiery eyes. "Dishonored, Ürok. A warrior who can wield no blade is no true warrior at all."

Neer yanked the heavy battleaxe from his belt loop and forced it into his thick hand. She curled his fingers around the steel handle and stared into his eyes. His anger faded as he glanced between her eyes and the blade in his hand.

"Do *not* let this defeat you," she said. "You are more than this, Y'ven."

He stared at the battleaxe, and his fingers tightened around its handle. Dru was on his shoulder, glancing warily at his face, reading his expression. He turned to her, and she gave him a stiff, reassuring nod. With a grunt, he returned the gesture and stood taller with pride.

Neer clutched his shoulder with a tight smile and then returned to the cabin, allowing them a moment alone.

As she stepped through the foliage, her eyes fell to the two figures standing in the clearing by the hut. Sunlight brightened Avelloch's hair as he stood with Thurandír, teaching him different sword techniques.

After several jabs and slashes, Avelloch nodded with approval. Thurandír chuckled with pride, his beaming smile brighter than the sun. He scanned the clearing before spotting Neer.

"Come on, *lanathess*," he said before tossing a wooden sword her way.

She caught it by the blade and then flipped it into her palm, clutching her fingers around the hilt.

With a smile, Thurandír said, "Want to try your luck against an avel warrior? I'll bet a drimil'lana° can hold her own against an evae."

She smirked. "I can hold my own against *you*."

"Oh-ho-ho!" he laughed. "You're on!"

Neer smiled and got into position, her fingers wriggling against the wooden shaft. Thurandír withheld a grin and then lunged forward. Neer smacked his weapon and jabbed at his chest.

He spun aside before swiping at her neck. She leaned back and he cut upward, smacking her face. Neer stumbled forward when pain stung her lip. The taste of blood filled her mouth. She wiped it away with her sleeve, dragging crimson across the fabric.

Thurandír smirked and then twisted the weapon, falling into a defensive stance. They continued fighting, striking against each other's legs, chests, and faces. Beads of sweat dripped down Neer's face, and she danced around the quick-moving evae, matching his footfalls and anticipating his strikes. As he lunged left, she jabbed right, and they ended their fight in a stalemate, holding their weapons to the other's chest.

Thurandír breathed heavily, a wide smile brightening his youthful face. He reached for Neer's arm, and they shared a firm shake. "You're good," he said, tossing the weapon into its box. "Guess that magic really comes in handy."

She gave him a daring look. "Who said I was using my magic?"

° In the language of the humans, drimil'lana translates to mean *human magic user*

His expression fell and eyes widened. Before he could speak, the direwolf approached. Thurandír shuddered and took half a step back, while Neer remained calm. She turned to Avelloch, who stood with his arms crossed.

"You've improved," he said.

Neer shrugged. "I suppose being chased and captured and fighting through magical realms has been paying off."

She tossed her weapon into the box and drank from her canteen. Avelloch was quiet, keeping his eyes focused on Neer. Seldom their gazes would meet, the vulnerability bleeding through like a cold draft in the winter. He clutched his gloved, blackened wrist, rubbing it slightly as if to ward off an onset of pain.

Guilt washed through Neer, dragging her heart to her toes. "Can you still fight with it?" she asked, studying his arm.

"Hardly," he said.

"Maybe we can train and get you better."

She gently clasped his forearm, which felt much stronger than it looked. Closing her eyes, she focused on her energy. The warmth swirling inside turned to ice, and they both pulled away with a pained gasp. Their eyes met, and she quickly turned away, realizing she couldn't heal him. The damage was irreversible.

His eyes fixed on her, and he rubbed his wrist. "If we do any training, it'll be to get *you* better."

She turned to him with a furrowed brow.

"I defeated you with one arm before," he said. "I can do it again."

She thought back to their sparring session in Laeroth, when he didn't try and still easily defeated her. A bashful smile pulled her lips. "You can't even handle a bit of healing magic, *Zaeril*."

He chuckled. She watched the smile dance across his face, happy to have him nearby. Happy to know things between them were mending.

"It means wolf, right?" she asked, not wanting their conversations to die. "Because of your drink...sole?"

His smile widened. "Dren'seol," he corrected. "His name is Blaid."

"Blaid. Why am I not surprised?"

He wiped his smile away and said, "We met when I was a child. I was…injured. He brought me a dagger to hunt and protect myself with. The name just fell into place."

"Why not Dagger? Or Killer?" Their eyes met. "Shadow?"

He parted his lips to speak, but Klaud's voice echoed nearby. They turned aside when he appeared through the thicket of trees, speaking to Aélla, who stood at the cabin, scolding him. She had told him not to hunt until his headaches subsided, but he insisted, wanting to feel useful.

Neer and Avelloch stood in a comfortable silence. He hesitated before stepping toward the cabin. Neer took his arm, and they stood close. Her heart raced. She didn't want their time to end. Didn't want things to fall back to the way they were.

She clutched the tiaavan around her neck and slipped it over her head. Avelloch gently clasped his fingers around its edges as she passed it to him. His eyes set on the red rocks and misshapen design.

"It's a good thing you're a thief," Neer remarked. "Or we may have never found each other again."

His thumb traced along its edges. "Something just told me to hold on to it…that maybe it could bring you peace someday."

She smiled. "That's pretty noble thinking…for a thief."

Chapter Twenty

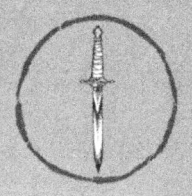

Reflections of Pain
Nerana

"The reflection of time is carved in stone, unable to be obscured."

— Vethad, *The Book of Time*

THE WORLD WAS QUIET with moonlight and shadow as Neer lay asleep with her head on Avelloch's shoulder. Chaos and pain filled her mind as shadows embraced her with ice.

She sat up with a gasp and scanned the hut. Everyone slept soundly, purple moonlight filtering in through small cracks in the ceiling. Neer rubbed her face and quietly stood. Her eyes moved to Avelloch, who lay peacefully in his sleep. She took one last glance at the others and then slipped outside to get some air.

Heading for the trees, she noticed a figure lingering nearby, like a cloud of impenetrable darkness against the grey shadow of night. Her heart skipped, and she came to a stop. Slowly, she forced herself to look in its direction but found nothing in its place. A deep breath escaped her lungs, releasing her fear and slumping her shoulders.

Neer took another step toward the thicket of trees and halted when a voice cut through the silence. It was gruff and angry. She followed the noise, tucking herself into the shadows to stay hidden.

"Stop!" an adolescent boy called. "Please!"

"You're weak!" a man growled. The deep thud of a boot sinking into flesh was followed by a pained grunt. "Pathetic! It should have been you who was taken!"

Neer grabbed her dagger and moved quicker, determined to find them. Her footfalls halted at the sight of a man and young boy, no older than fourteen, in the woods ahead. The boy was curled on the ground with his arms covering his face. He trembled, begging the man to stop.

The figure standing over him was stiff with fury, tall and built like a warrior. His thick fists were held at his sides, and his jaw was clenched so tight, the muscles were exposed through his skin. Dark hair hung across his shoulders, shielding his face from view.

"Get up," he growled, and the boy whimpered, pleading. "Get up, you *kila grot fiin*!"

"Hey!" Neer called, charging from the shadows.

But the man didn't respond to her presence. Instead, he grabbed the boy by his collar and lifted him from the ground. Neer stared at him, recognizing his white hair and blue eyes. He was small from starvation. Dark circles rested beneath his young, tired eyes.

"Fight me," the man said. "Go on!"

The boy stumbled when he was shoved back. He stared at the ground, sobbing. "Please…I didn't mean to do it!"

"You want to be a man, Avelloch? You want to prove yourself a warrior?"

The man struck Avelloch in the face with his fist, and Neer lunged forward, shoving his arm, but his flesh was an icy wind as she slipped through him. Stumbling forward, she caught herself and turned back, watching him stalk closer to the quivering boy.

Avelloch crawled back, terrified. He choked on his breath, tears gliding down his cheeks. Neer was frozen. She had to help him. Had to figure out a way to stop this from happening.

But it was a dream. A fictitious illusion conjured by her imagination. This wasn't real. It couldn't be real.

SHADOWS OF NYN'DIRA

Moonlight glistened against a dagger that was yanked from the man's sheath. He moved closer to Avelloch, who lay defenseless on the ground, pleading.

"Get up," the man growled.

"This isn't real...," Neer whispered, her heart throbbing. "It isn't real..."

Avelloch cried out when the man yanked his hair and forced their eyes to meet.

"Father, please...," he begged.

The man hissed. "You are no son of mine."

Neer leapt forward, reacting on instinct, as the dagger sank into Avelloch's chest, piercing his heart. Magic erupted through her, shaking the trees as it pulsed from her palms, crashing into the man. He was thrust aside, flipping atop the grass before smacking his head against a rock.

Avelloch lay in the dirt, blood bubbling from his lips, his life draining. Neer fell to his side and dipped her hands within the cold, empty air of his chest. She had to save him. He wouldn't die. Not like this.

Magic raged inside her, swirling with blistering heat, and she pushed her health into his body, a body she couldn't feel. But his energy was alive, twisting and converging with her own. Her magic moved through the illusions and dreams—it was saving him.

As the wound slowly healed, she apported the dagger from his chest and tossed it aside. Sweat dripped from her face as she expelled her energy. Her body weakened and muscles shrank. Once the wound in his heart was fused, she collapsed to the ground, weak.

Black fog crept over the land like a slow-moving wave as Neer lay on her side, watching Avelloch take slow, steady breaths. His eyes were closed, and blood seeped from his parted lips.

Neer opened her mouth to speak, but a deep pressure weighed against her, stealing the breath from her lungs. She fought against it, unable to move beneath the tonnage pinning her to the grass. The shadows began to quiver, sending small vibrations through the air, standing her hair on end.

And then a voice, deep and rumbling, split her mind, rattling her thoughts as it spoke from within.

Summoned and chained, a path must you walk
Tired…broken…alone in the dark.

Tendrils of fog crawled across the ground, slithering closer. She breathed quickly, watching them encroach upon her, weaving slowly through the darkness. Before their icy sting touched her skin, Neer broke free from the crushing pressure and leapt to her feet. The shadows quaked as she ran, going as far as her weak legs would take her. But her body was frail from expelling her energy, and she knew she wouldn't make it far. Her lungs burned as she pushed herself beyond exertion, determined to survive.

In the distance, a bright glow caught her eye, and she moved quicker, never looking back at the serpentine shadows chasing behind. She held her breath when a glowing wisteria came into view. Neer broke through its limbs and fell to her knees when her legs collapsed. She caught her breath, hoping beyond hope that the light would keep the darkness at bay.

After taking several heaved breaths, Neer lifted her eyes to view her surroundings. She spotted four shadows lying nearby, and she lurched back, finding herself in the midst of a small group. Two men, both humans, and a woman with red hair lay against the tree trunk, asleep. She stared further, and her jaw fell open. These weren't just any humans; they were faces she knew: Wallace, a brawny warrior with the brotherhood, and Coryn, her childhood friend.

Confused, thinking herself mad, Neer turned to the final shadow, and her breath caught in her throat. Ten feet away, unaware of her presence…was Gil. He sat alone, staring at her wanted poster.

Neer reached forward, tears stinging her eyes. "Gil…" Her voice was silenced as soon as it left her tongue, sucked into the void of her visions. Her fingers dipped through his shoulder when she attempted to touch him, and she pulled her hand away.

His fingers grazed over the drawing of her face, and he released a defeated sigh. "Where are you, child?"

SHADOWS OF NYN'DIRA

A light rustling came from beyond the limbs, and Neer inhaled a sharp breath. She turned with her weapon out, her body trembling as tendrils of darkness edged along the tree, never breaking through its barrier.

The thunderous voice returned, and Neer collapsed to her knees, clutching her ears as it spoke from deep within her mind.

In the darkness we lie in wait...
Shadows unbroken, untethered, untamed...
Seek to find the power's alight...
A soul is torn and welcomes the night.

Neer closed her eyes, and the weight of the world crashed over her. With a grunt, she sank further to the ground, unable to withstand the force of life as the visions faded. Lights shimmered from the wisteria, and she sat alone, no longer in the presence of her old friends. No longer comforted by the warmth of a familiar face.

Her body trembled with intense fear as the threads of her sanity were slowly unraveling. She gripped her head and closed her eyes. Her palm smacked against her scalp as she beat against her skull, attempting to force the illusions from her mind. Neer couldn't understand what was happening and found the lines between reality and illusion starting to blur.

With a huff, she dropped her arms to her sides, and her shoulders slumped forward with exhaustion. Eying her surroundings, she knew she had to find her way back to the others before they realized she was missing. Whatever was happening to her, they couldn't know. Not until she understood it herself. For now, she needed to keep this inside; otherwise, the fear and doubt they held would deepen into distrust or contempt.

They would see her as a demon, just like all the others.

She lifted a shaking hand to the curtain of glowing limbs. A hard knot formed in her throat, and with a deep breath, she parted the branches and peeked into the forest. The world was dark, and not a sound crept through the sleeping woods. She sat for a span, waiting for the mind-crushing voice to return and whisk her into another realm of haunting illusions.

Insects chirped, and glowing plants rustled in a soft breeze. Warm energy swirled through the air, drenching her with a sense of peace. Neer inhaled a deep breath, trusting the wind, and convinced herself that the monster from her visions had truly been nothing more than a shadow from her mind. Feeling a bit lighter without the weight of fear and uncertainty clinging to her shoulders, she broke through the limbs and stood in the forest. With one last glance at the glowing wisteria, where Gil and the others once sat, Neer set off in search of the cabin.

The night grew colder as she wandered through the empty woods, and a heavy silence fell over the sleeping lands, deepening her solitude. Her only company was the sound of her footsteps trudging against the soil. Neer had no idea where the vision had taken her, and without a map, she was entirely lost, left at the mercy of the forest. There was no wind or magic to guide her back to the others, so she walked alone, depending on instincts and luck to see her reunited with the others.

A lot of luck.

Tired legs carried her further through the forest. She stepped over large, moss-covered boulders, the deafening silence lifted by the faint rumbling of a waterfall. Hoping to find her bearings and quench her growing thirst, Neer followed the sound. It grew louder, erasing the silence as she came to the edge of a pond. A light breeze rose from the water cascading down jagged rocks and crashing into the small lake below.

Neer stepped through the overgrown embankment and knelt atop slippery rocks. After taking several gulps of water, she leaned back and examined her surroundings. For a moment, she thought she recognized this place, though she knew she had never been there before.

Curiosity pulled her closer to the falls. Tall grass waved gently in the breeze sweeping from the waters. She followed the overgrown trail to the edge of the rocky hillside holding the falls. The familiarity was overwhelming. She knew she *had* been there. Glancing around, studying the rocks and breeze and smell, the realization struck her like a sharp knife.

The Trials had brought her there, with Loryk and Avelloch. It was the place Klaud had drank the poison that nearly killed him. This was where she saved his life.

Damp stone drained the warmth from her skin as she placed her palm upon its uneven surface, hoping to find answers. Praying the energy flowing through the world would guide her in the right direction. She felt a swell of magic ebbing and flowing, like slow, relaxed breaths. Every slight breeze or drop of water breaking the surface of the pond rippled through her.

And beneath the calming rhythm, a gentle patter, like the quick thrum of footsteps, pressed against her. It was soft, a whispering touch that grew stronger with every footfall. Her heart beat hard against her chest.

Someone was drawing closer.

Neer turned around and reached for a sword that wasn't there. Her heart skipped when a shadow stalked closer. Platinum hair glowed in the moonlight, and Neer exhaled a deep breath when Avelloch's figure came into view. A look of confusion pulled his face. Blaid, who had led him directly to Neer, slowly receded into the darkness of the forest.

"Neer?" Avelloch asked. "What are you doing out here?"

Thoughts raged through her mind. She clutched her chest, not ready to reveal what had truly dragged her so far into the forest. "I just needed a walk and got turned around."

His eyes narrowed with suspicion, and she held her breath, hoping he wouldn't press her further. A look of disappointment flashed through his eyes before he turned away. He fixed his attention on the falls. "Did the forest lead you here?" he asked.

"No."

Avelloch slowly nodded, and his eyes became distant, as if in deep thought. Neer studied him for a moment. She followed his gaze, which landed on the waterfall.

"Do the others know I'm gone?" she asked.

"No. I woke when you did. When you didn't come back, I knew something was wrong."

He was quiet for a moment. "We should get back. The others—"

"I'm not worried about the others."

He stole a glance at her, but she fixed her eyes on the shadows surrounding them. With another at Neer's side, the forest no longer held an air of contempt or endlessness. She was safe, and when they were ready, they'd find their way back to camp. For now, she wanted to enjoy the solitude: the glowing flora and streams of light dancing through the crashing waters, bright moonlight that filtered through the trees, gifting the world with a beautiful purple hue. The ground beneath her feet that illuminated with every step.

"Nyn'Dira really is something else," Neer said.

She caught Avelloch staring at her and turned to meet his eyes. There was comfort in his presence. Warmth and security. She couldn't ignore it. Didn't want to. The nights she had spent wondering if he had betrayed her seemed so long ago, now that he was there, at her side. Ready to protect her from the world and its nightmares.

"Thank you for finding me." She paused and then rolled her eyes. "Again."

"You leave an easy trail to follow."

She smiled. "Easy when you have someone else sniffing it out for you."

He chuckled and slid his hands into his pockets. Neer admired him for a moment, noticing his disheveled top and messy hair. He was undeniably handsome, as was true of most evae. But there was something more to Avelloch that drew Neer close. He wasn't like the others. He was alone and different, just like her. He understood her pain, and despite all she had done, he cared. Truly, deeply cared. She felt it through her body and soul. No matter the cost, he'd fight for her, just as he had done in Laeroth and the Trials.

Just as he was doing now.

With a relaxed smile, Neer bridged the gap between them. She wrapped her arm around his and leaned her head against his shoulder. They were silent for a while, watching the moonlight reflect against the pond and dance across the trees.

"Where are we?" Neer asked, breaking the long, comfortable silence.

"This is Aesgrot," he explained. "I used to come here as child."

Neer turned to him. "With Klaud?"

"And Thallon."

Neer snorted, though she hadn't meant to.

He responded with a knowing look, one that silently agreed with her shock and laughter. "The three of us were inseparable," he admitted.

"That's...surprising."

He nodded. "This was once our favorite place in the world."

Neer smiled. "Why here? It's just a pond."

A crooked smile pulled his lip, and he glanced at her with a flare of excitement. "That's on a strict need-to-know basis."

"Oh yeah?" she mused. "Can't go spilling your secrets or they'll kick you out of the club?"

"Something like that."

Her face flushed and eyes beamed. She lifted her finger. "What if I *pinky promise* not to tell anyone?"

Avelloch glanced at her outstretched pinky with a look of curiosity. Riddled with confusion, he gently touched the end of her finger with his own, and her laughter mixed with the sounds of the crashing water. She hooked their fingers together and peered into his eyes.

Her smile widened when he laughed and said, "You can't break the pact, *meena'keen*. Once a brother, always a brother."

"I don't have to make a blood sacrifice, do I?"

He chuckled. "Not after Thallon nearly cut off his finger."

"You're joking."

With a wry smile, he took her hand and led her along the rocky embankment. Their feet slipped over algae-coated rocks as they approached the roaring waterfall. Avelloch carefully stepped onto a narrow ledge leading behind the falls. Neer clutched his hand tighter and followed, her eyes wide with wonderment as they shimmied along the base of the rocky hillside. Mist from the falls shielded them from the world, coating her skin and dampening her clothes. The sounds of falling water resounded against the wall, drowning any whisper of outside noise.

Avelloch stepped onto a narrow alcove in the wall and guided Neer to his side. They stood together on the uneven platform, and Neer looked around, studying the empty space. A cold chill crept across her skin, and the coolness of night embraced her with a gentle caress. She crossed her arms, fighting for warmth.

"This is…cozy," she said, hoping her attempt at a compliment was convincing.

Avelloch raised a brow, and she knew it wasn't. She stifled a smile. He stepped to a large piece of tree bark leaning against the rocky wall. It was just over half his size and covered in mold. The wood creaked when he moved it aside, revealing a hidden entrance in the wall.

Darkness swallowed him when he stepped inside, and Neer stood alone, staring at the cave. Her quick heartbeat throbbed through her veins. She inched closer but couldn't bring herself to enter. Her eyes veered to the waterfall behind. It was far enough away that she was no longer swept by its mist, yet close enough to feel the coolness of its presence.

Her heart leapt when a spark ignited within the cave, brightening the entrance. Twice more the flame flickered before warm amber light filled the void. Avelloch returned to the entry and reached for Neer's hand. She wiped her clammy palms against her trousers, too nervous to accept his touch. Her eyes fixed once again on the waterfall and then to the ledge that would lead her back to the forest.

"It's safe," he said, noticing her panic. "Trust me."

Neer hesitantly placed her hand in his. As he took it, she pulled away. Their eyes met, and she asked, "Is this…Is it part of Anaemiril?"

His confusion softened into pity. "No," he said.

Through a deep breath, Neer took his hand and entered the hidden cavern. Fire roared from a torch on the wall, allowing her to see each of the surrounding walls. The hollow was small, with enough room for two or three adults to fit comfortably. To the left was a small cot and two bedrolls. A bookshelf and chest full of toys and books were to the right. In the center of the room, littered with scribbled parchment, was a square table and three chairs.

She exhaled a sigh of relief, thankful they were in the confines of a non-magical cave.

"What is this place?" she asked through trembling, purple lips.

Avelloch stepped across the room to the bookshelf and collected an old fur blanket from its wide drawer. He returned to her side, and Neer removed her top, hanging it on the wall beside the torch, hoping it would dry.

"You aren't freezing?" she asked, bundling into the warm furs.

"I'm fine." Avelloch crossed his arms. "This is just a cave," he explained, answering her question. "We found it as kids."

A smile replaced the fear staining Neer's face. She stepped to the wall, admiring the childish drawings tacked to the stone, creating a mural of the past. They ranged in skill from stick figures to fully drawn heroes with bows and swords.

She pointed at the worst one and guessed, "This is Klaud's."

With a laugh, Avelloch moved to her side. "How'd you guess?"

Neer shrugged. "He doesn't seem like the artistic type." She studied the next, which was eccentric and abstract. "Thallon."

Moving down the wall, she found a colored drawing of a wolf. It was impressive, with beautiful detailing surpassing most children's art. The animal was standing in the forest. Its head was high and snarl was vicious.

The parchment crinkled when Neer gently tore it from the wall. She studied the picture. "Is this Blaid?"

She handed the page to Avelloch, and he inspected the drawing. While staring at the parchment, he walked across the room. His shadow cast against the wall as he sat on the

179

old leather cot. "I drew this before I met him," he said, riddled with memories. "Feels like a lifetime ago."

"Growing older sure is fun, huh?" Neer stepped through the room, examining the toys and old sparring swords. "Soon, you and I being here will feel like a lifetime ago."

She collected a sword and flipped the weapon into the air before catching it again. The old wood was thin and light, perfect for a child. With a quick swipe, she imagined herself being part of their secret hideaway.

"I never had a place like this," she said, hoping to lighten the somber mood.

Avelloch placed the drawing aside and leaned forward with his forearms against his thighs. His hands were clasped together, and he watched her stalk the room, oddly comforted by the ghosts of his past.

"I don't remember much before the Brotherhood," Neer continued. "Loryk and I were inseparable, as you could imagine. But he was too spooked by the woods to go adventuring for fun."

With a look at one last drawing, Neer turned away. She placed the sword onto the table before moving to Avelloch's side.

"So," she said, taking a seat next to him. "How many girls have you had in this coveted hideaway?"

He snorted. "Wouldn't you like to know?"

"I imagine you convinced them here to ogle at your wooden swords and whatever the Hells Klaud drew on the walls."

Their eyes met, and he quipped, "It worked on you."

"Don't flatter yourself, *Zaeril*. I got you into the Trials. This is just a courtesy visit."

He turned away with a growing smile. Neer's face burned, and her grin was impossible to hide.

She bundled tighter into the cloak when a draft moved through the cave. Her body trembled and breathing was uneven. "Tell me again why you three decided to make a secret hideout in the frozen depths of Hell?"

Avelloch walked across the room and retrieved the torch. Its warmth soothed the chill in her bones, and she exhaled a sigh of relief.

"You should really take this off," she said of his wet tunic. "It's too cold to—"

A hollow pit formed in Neer's gut when she noticed a scar peeking through the untied opening of his black tunic. She studied the faint blemish in the center of his chest.

Directly over his heart.

Chills crawled across Avelloch's skin when Neer pulled back the loose collar of his tunic and touched the faded mark. Her wide eyes were fixed on the scar.

"It was real...," she said in the human tongue.

Her voice was a whisper on the wind. Avelloch gently clutched her wrist, and she was jolted from her thoughts. Realizing how intrusive she had been, she attempted to back away, but his tender grasp kept her in place.

She met his gaze, fearful, but all she found was confusion and pain. Tears welled in her eyes as she recalled her vision. A vision she had believed was nothing more than a figment of magic meant to lead her far from the others. But it was more, and she was stricken by the realization that whatever was haunting her had somehow dragged her through time.

It led her to Avelloch that night...and she had saved his life.

"Neer?"

His voice fell on deaf ears. Her wide eyes, full of welling tears, stared through him. Fear had encased her, made her immobile and absent.

"Neer," Avelloch said. He gripped her shoulder with a firm shake.

She flinched with a gasp. His guarded eyes bore into her, waiting for an answer she wasn't ready to give. Grasping at whatever thought would cling to her tongue, Neer asked, "How did you survive this?"

Avelloch slowly released his grasp, but Neer kept her hands close to his chest—too afraid to put space between them for fear of her visions coming back to life and pulling her far away. His shoulders relaxed and head dropped slightly.

A strained voice chiseled through the air when he said, "I don't know."

Neer's throat tightened. More tears. More madness roaring just beneath the surface. "Maybe the forest—"

"The forest can't heal you on its own. It can't bring you back from death." His voice was forced and direct. "I don't know who or what saved me that night. But whatever it was…I wish that it hadn't."

Neer's jaw dropped. Tears flooded her eyes as she looked at him, watching the firelight reflect in his cold, dark eyes. The regret she felt was outweighed by sorrow. Neer sniffed and wiped her face.

"Well, I'm glad it did," she said. "The world would be far lesser without you here."

Avelloch was silent for a moment. His eyes were distant and unblinking as he became lost in thought. Eventually, he blinked them away and then carefully placed the torch onto the ground. The cot creaked when he turned to Neer, and a warm touch caressed her cheek as he gently wiped her tears. He softly kissed her forehead and pulled her into his arms.

Chapter Twenty-One

Ik'Erithaan
Nerana

> "Take heed! The true identities of our beloved overseers have been made known. Leirin, the Goddess of Purity and Health, and Aenwyn, the Goddess of Nature, shall henceforth be known as Kirena and Numera, respectively. Give grace to the Circle and have faith in the Light."
>
> – Proclamation of the New Ways, the Order of Saro

Days passed as the group headed east, toward their destination. The sun rose in the sky, gifting the world with a warm embrace, and they paused to make camp at midday. Neer stood alone, staring up at the cloudless blue. Branches swayed in a soft breeze, creating a beautiful melody that filled her with calmness and peace.

But she couldn't push away the dread plaguing her every thought, consuming her with doubt. The haunting visions and voice that shook her mind sent waves of uncertainty and pain through her soul.

Grass rustled from behind, and Neer turned as Blaid came to her side. Sapphire eyes met with hers, and she exhaled a calm breath. The beast, which stood half her height, nuzzled his head into her hip. She scratched between his ears.

"You coming to check on me?" she asked. "Seems to be what everyone's doing these days…keeping their eyes on me. Waiting for me to do something horrific."

Her fingers stopped as her mind wandered.

"Maybe they're right. Maybe I *am* a monster."

"You aren't a monster."

Neer and Blaid turned when Aélla stepped closer. She tossed an apple to Neer with a half-hearted smile. Juice spilled into Neer's mouth when she took a bite of her meal. Aélla kept a measured distance, glancing at Blaid, who remained at Neer's side, protective and strong.

"He seems to like you," Aélla said. "Avelloch is the only person he's ever shown kindness for."

Neer glanced at the wolf, wondering why he held such a deep, unspeakable bond with her. He was ferocious and quick to anger, yet she felt comforted and safe in his presence. There was a silent trust between them, one she had never felt with an animal before.

"How are you feeling?" Aélla asked.

"Alone…confused…like my body and soul are fighting against each other."

"That happens. As drimil, we are gifted and cursed with the burden of magic."

"Do you feel it too? The constant battle within yourself."

Aélla nodded softly. "Everyday."

Neer turned away, relishing in her words. It was a comfort to know she wasn't alone, even if it meant another had to endure this torment.

Neer closed her eyes. "I've been thinking…about fate and my path. What I should do."

Aélla was silent, waiting with patience as Neer struggled to speak. With a deep inhalation, she turned to Aélla, eyes heavy with sorrow.

"Maybe it's time for me to be on my own. What I did to Thallon and Klaud…the things that are happening to me…the people that want me dead…I'm too dangerous to be around." She paused. "If one of you lost your lives because of me, I'd never forgive myself."

Aélla stepped closer. "We're a family, Nerana. All of us. Me, Klaud, Avelloch, Y'ven—we are *all* dangerous to be around. Every one of us has a target on our backs. Whatever is happening to you—we will figure it out together." Another step. "You are not alone."

Neer stared at the apple in her hand, hollow and broken. "Then why do I feel so alone?"

Blaid stepped aside as Aélla placed her hand on Neer's shoulder. Warm energy washed through her, soothing the ache in her soul. The turmoil and confusion faded into peace, and she exhaled a calm breath.

"We may not understand," Aélla said, "but we are here."

Neer turned to Aélla and clutched her hand. "Thank you."

Aélla nodded. "Now, let's practice your meditations."

Day faded to night as Neer struggled against her tormenting thoughts and visions. When the moons rose higher, giving life to the glowing plants and darkness, Neer returned to the group with Aélla. Thurandír offered Neer a handful of berries when she sat next to him. She nodded in thanks before feasting on her snack.

"I still can't believe it." Thallon chuckled.

"Believe what?" Aélla asked with a smile of her own.

Y'ven added, "Stories. Childhood games."

Aélla turned to Klaud with quizzical eyes, and he explained, "We were talking about Aesgrot, when the three of us had a hideout there."

Neer and Avelloch shared a glance, choosing to keep their night hidden from the others.

"The Flying Bandits." Thallon laughed. "Whose idea was it to call ourselves that anyway?"

"Yours," Avelloch stated, though there was a hint of ease to his otherwise emotionless tone.

Thallon burst with laughter, followed soon by light chuckling from Avelloch and Klaud.

Neer smiled, thinking of her own childhood. "You three were friends?" she asked.

"Brothers," Thallon explained. "We did *everything* together. Fighting over girls, fighting over who was the strongest, fighting over who would take charge in our make-believe games."

Aélla giggled. "There really was a lot of fighting back then."

Klaud smiled. "There was."

"Yeah," Thallon said to him, "and you always came out on top with that damned magic!"

"And you were always jealous."

Everyone laughed. Thurandír added, "It must be nice to be together again. I've heard only true friendships can survive so much time."

Their smiles slowly faded, and tension infiltrated the easement of their conversations. Thallon cleared his throat before taking a drink from his canteen. He wiped his lips with his sleeve and turned away. "You'd think," he said. "But after Avelloch was banished, Klaud took his side, and we just fell apart."

There was a deep silence, only lifted by Thurandír when he asked, "You didn't?"

"Didn't what?"

"Take his side."

Thallon lifted his dark, glaring eyes to Avelloch. "I don't side with murderers."

A cold breeze shifted the wind, bringing the chill of sorrow and contempt. Neer stared up at the limbs, curious of the emotions sweeping through her. She inhaled a deep breath and then released it quickly after.

"My friends and I had a secret hideout too," she said. "Well, more of a meeting place, I suppose. Jenna, Sadie, and I would always go to the Hog's Den after dark."

"Hog's Den?" Thurandír asked with a chuckle. He took a sip from his canteen, and the others listened with quiet smiles.

Neer grinned, happy to relive one of the few good memories she still had. Though she hadn't thought of it in many years, it was still present in her mind, as if the laughter and peace had never faded…as if the friends she once thought so fondly of were still alive and well.

Shaking her head, she focused once again on her story, and said, "It was old man Dej's pen. Rotten thing was old and smelled of piss." She laughed, being swept away by her memories. "The hogs were *massive*"—she stretched out her arms to showcase their width—"and I was convinced by a boy in town that if you saddled one, you could surely ride it."

"No!" Aélla giggled.

Neer's cheeks were flush with laughter. "Truly! We wrestled those things all the time, coming home covered in shit and mud. It wasn't until Sadie fell off and cracked a rib on the trough that we had to come clean."

Thallon said, "You're lucky to be alive. Those things could've killed you!"

"You sound like my mother."

They shared a playful glance before she turned away.

She caught sight of Avelloch's smile, and her grin widened. "I bet you could've saddled one," she teased.

He laughed with a full, happy grin. "I would've tried."

"Oh," she teased. "Mr. stone-faced assassin has a wild side, does he?"

"Avelloch was fairly wild back then," Klaud added. "If we were in trouble, it was usually because of him."

Neer felt a tinge of anger slide down her gut. She kept it inside, forcing herself to accept his company.

The internal struggle was lifted when Thurandír's much happier tenor rang through the air. "Really? The *Zaeril* was once a *lyena faa**?"

Avelloch hid his smile beneath the spout of his canteen, coolly taking a sip while staring into the forest. Neer studied him for a moment longer, thinking back to the child she had witnessed in her dreams. His white hair blazing in the darkness as he lead his friends deep into the forest, speaking with rambunctious authority as Thallon fell behind. The joy once filling his eyes was now hollow and broken. Even beneath the light of his current smile, there was shadow and pain.

His eyes slowly drifted to hers, and she was suddenly aware of how long she'd been staring. But she didn't turn away. Instead, she held his gaze, knowing the truth of his anguish. His eyes were open, allowing her to see the deepest parts of his soul, but still, the answers were unclear. Neer didn't understand why he was banished. She couldn't make sense of why his father would attempt to kill him.

---

* Loosely translated, this term is meant to describe an unruly or "wild" child

Emotions swelled within her, culminating in her throat, begging to be set free in an influx of questions that didn't seem to have answers.

His lips parted, and just as he spoke, Y'ven's gruff voice broke the silence. "What is *hog*?"

The tension building between Neer and Avelloch melted like ice beneath the sun. Everyone turned to the vaxros with vibrant smiles, and after a too-long discussion explaining the meaning of a hog, they spent the rest of the night lost in old memories.

Tired feet marched across sodden soil, and rain dripped from the sky. Two days had passed since their journey began, and Neer was desperate for a rest.

"How much farther until we get to your village, Thurandír?" she asked, wrapping tighter into her wet cloak.

"Close," he said, walking alongside her. "We should be there soon."

Y'ven trudged behind, his feet sliding against the dirt and eyes struggling to stay open. Dru was perched on his nape, hiding within his thick hair. Only her soft glow could be seen through his dark locks. Next to him, keeping with his slow stride, was Aélla. She pressed her hand to his chest every few yards, healing him with magical flames. But the sun was tucked behind a blanket of grey clouds, leaving the vaxros weak and dreary.

Neer averted her eyes ahead, noticing Thallon and Klaud. Avelloch was a step behind them, listening to Thallon's constant gripes about the long journey and weather.

"I'm ready for a nice warm bed," he said, shivering. "Hey Aélla! Neer!" He turned back to view them. "Why don't you two do some magic and get us there faster?"

Neer's glare caused him to laugh.

They continued on, trailing up stone steps that wound through the hillsides. Amber and gold leaves were vibrant with moisture. Thorned vines lay atop the grass, growing toward a large statue of a woman. She sat alone with her hands cupped together, catching the rain. The evergreen vines coiled across her lap and chest. She had short hair and wore a crown of roses. Her head was tilted downward, and her eyes were closed. Deep cracks had settled into the stone. Surrounding the statue was an ocean of swords staked into the soil. Many appeared ancient, with eroded pommels, rusted steel, and deep cracks down the blades, while others were newer, holding little to no imperfections.

Thurandír noticed Neer was staring, and said, "That's Kirena. She was the most famous Drimil'Leirin."

Neer glanced at him with her brows furrowed. "Drimil'Leirin?"

"The drimil of vitality and healing. People come from all over for *Arnikvia*. It's a ceremony that happens every First Leaf." He paused. "Some believe just being in the presence of her statue can cure them of their ailments and pain."

Neer pondered for a moment, considering his words, and then asked, "Does it?"

He smiled. "I guess that's for you to decide."

"What about the swords?"

"Oh...those are for the fallen. After someone dies, their sword is left to mark their life and passing."

Her eyes remained fixed on the statue and swords as she climbed the steps, returning to the thicket of trees. Cabins were spread throughout the woods, with fences bordering dirt-laden training fields and archery targets.

"It's just ahead!" Thurandír exclaimed, boasting with excitement. "I bet my father will be happy to see me traveling with Drimil'Rothar! And my mother will want to meet you, Neer. She's a human too."

"Really?" Neer asked, elated to know one of her own was nearby.

"Yeah! The c'liaa are half-human, after all. We've got a village full of them."

Neer chuckled as he continued chattering, pointing at everything and reliving old memories. "I have a little sister," he said. "I think she'll like the little one with the vaxros."

"Her name is Dru," Neer said with a chuckle. She glanced at Y'ven when Dru's glowing light burned bright in deep offense.

Thurandír continued, "My brother will have a new baby soon. If it's a boy, they'll name him Thurnin! That's after me!"

The others listened quietly as he bounced with excitement.

Up ahead, Avelloch peered at the village with narrowed eyes. He looked around, examining every quiet home and empty field.

"Avelloch?" Klaud asked, his voice nearly undetectable beneath the pattering rain and Thurandír's never-ending voice.

They shared a glance, and Avelloch said, "Why is no one here?"

Klaud's face twisted with confusion. He looked around, realizing how empty and silent the homes were. Vegetables had begun to wilt in their gardens. Doors were left open, and the quiet of solitude crept in as everyone stalked forward. Nothing but the thud of their boots was heard against the rustling leaves above.

Thurandír's voice became hushed. The light in his eyes slowly dwindled. "Where is everyone?" he asked.

"Maybe they evacuated to Navarre," Aélla suggested, hopeful.

Thallon added, "It's possible. Plenty of people are fleeing from the invasion."

They came to a large stone bridge. Far below was a wide river. Waterfalls crashed to the east, cascading down the sloped hills. On the far side of the bridge was a sprawling village. Roads of cobblestone led to houses and shops of wood and stone. Flower beds gave color to the desolate town.

Y'ven stumbled aside and quickly caught himself against the side of the bridge. His skin had turned yellow, and his eyes were dim. Aélla rushed to his side, keeping him steady.

"We need to get him to a fire," she warned.

While the group found an empty tavern nearby, Thurandír stepped into the streets. He examined the quiet village.

"Hello?"

His strong voice echoed through the empty streets. Breathing heavily, he ran ahead, weaving down one path to the next. Thallon and Klaud chased after him, while the others stayed behind, guiding Y'ven through the narrow doorway.

"Thurandír!" Aélla called.

Thallon and Neer chased after him, running through empty streets and down lonesome alleyways. Across the village, Thurandír stood alone, gazing up at an empty home. The door was ajar. Not a sound came from inside.

"Where are they?" Thurandír said. "How could—"

"Help..."

They turned when the faint voice called out from behind.

Thurandír ran down the street, chasing after it. Around the corner, he knelt on the ground, cradling a wounded man in his arms. Blood stained his filthy face and chest. Dark red poured from the deep wound in his side. He was a human, with tan skin and light hair covering his face.

"What happened?" Thurandír said, holding back tears. "Come on...You can tell me..."

The human wheezed and choked on his blood. Thurandír held him close. He gently wiped the matted hair from the man's forehead as tears streamed down his face.

"Ricard!" he cried as the man struggled to breathe. Thurandír turned back to the others, and shouted, "Get Aélla! Go!"

"I can help him!" Neer stated.

As she stepped closer, Thurandír threw up his arm. "No!" he shouted. "Stay away from him!"

Thallon argued, "She can help!"

"I've seen what she can do!" His voice was raw with pain. "I don't want her touching him!"

Neer watched him for a moment longer, stricken with guilt. Without speaking, she stepped away, marching through the village in the direction of the tavern. The painful words he had spoken repeated in her mind, reminding her of how untrusted she truly was.

As she stalked through the lonesome streets, her thoughts were infiltrated by soft voices echoing from nearby. Neer looked around, searching for survivors, but the village was empty. Not a soul wandered the quiet alleys or desolate homes.

The voices remained, swirling through her mind, trapping her thoughts with their haunting words. Chills rose across Neer's arms and neck. She followed the voices, heading east as they grew stronger, leading her to the center of town, where a large building stood tall at a fork in the road.

Neer took in the sight before her, and dull pain pulled at her chest, tugging with a sense of agony and dread. Bound ankles held the weight of several bodies hanging upside down above the street. Dark red stained their chests where a single stab wound had punctured their hearts. Their faces and hands were bloated or burst open. Swollen eyes bulged from their sockets.

A quiet wind swept through the streets, and creaking ropes chimed with the haunting songs of death. Neer stared at a woman's marbled face. Her eyes followed a raindrop sliding down her cheek and dripping into a red puddle below. Rain mixed with the blood, creating streams of blood that flowed through the cobblestones.

Neer stood alone, staring at the faces of the villagers. Their weeping, terrified voices begged for mercy. Mothers cried for their children, while fathers were angered or riddled with guilt. She felt it all, every emotion that had been present in their deaths.

The voices penetrating her mind were shattered by the sound of a low, gargled grunt. Neer stiffened, too fearful to move. She had heard such a sound only once before—back in Galacia, when Avelloch had cut down two men after they had slain two innocent boys.

Neer clenched her teeth, hoping she had misheard. Her lungs burned and eyes filled with hot tears. The ropes creaked harder, and Neer lifted her eyes.

She reached for her sword when low growls slithered from the throats of the dead, and they slowly came back to life.

Chapter Twenty-Two

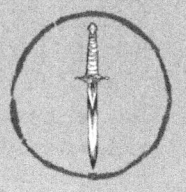

Free Us
Nerana

Rotten, swollen lips opened, and clouded eyes darted in every direction. Nearly half of the bodies started to reanimate. Ice burned Neer's chest, and she lurched forward, clutching her heart. She was cold and empty as death. Their voices reached out to her, slicing through her mind like shards of broken glass.

"*Fohl'nok melän…*"

The world began to shake, and she gripped her head. A flash of darkness overtook her vision. As soon as it came, it disappeared, and she sank to her knees, encumbered by the weight of hopelessness and dread.

She curled forward on her knees, digging her nails into her scalp, drawing blood. The pain inside was immeasurable. It sank deep into her bones and fizzled through her veins, like a roaring fire.

Another flash. More pain. The figure of a man appeared in her mind. He reached out a hand.

"*Fohl'nok melän…,*" he said.

Neer stared at him, fearful. The pain was unbearable. She needed this to end. The weight of ice and death and fear was too much for her to take. His palm hovered inches from her face. It was all she could see of his body, which was shrouded in a dark, hooded cloak.

A wave of agony crashed over her, and the bodies she couldn't see began to thrash. Neer winced and reached for his grasp. The coolness of his fingers stung her skin, but before she could take his hand, the darkness vanished.

Neer inhaled a sharp gasp, warmth and light overcoming the bitter void. She was weighted by reality and sank further to the ground, relieved of the misery that had consumed her.

"Neer?" Avelloch called.

He knelt before her, panicked. His touch was gentle against her shoulders, but his eyes were steeped with worry. Klaud was next to him, displaying the same concern and fear.

Neer pushed herself up. Tears wet her face. Her dark eyes had returned to their natural color. But the faint black veins remained. Avelloch carefully touched them with his thumb. Neer met his gaze before glancing behind him, where a wooden cart now hid the bodies from view. She leaned aside and witnessed the horror lying beyond their overturned shield.

The corpses that had begun to stir were no longer hanging with the others. Instead, they were spread across the streets, their flesh in thick lumps and limbs in pieces. Thick blood stained the cobbles and walls, and the sweet stench of rotten meat sank deep into Neer's gut, causing her to retch.

She leaned over, vomiting air, and then crumbled forward, clutching her stomach and wincing with pain.

"We can't tell him," she said. "Thurandír can't know about this."

Avelloch passed her a waterskin and pulled her hair away from her face. "We can't avoid this. He's going to find out."

Her eyes shifted to the streets, and she quickly turned away. "How did this happen?"

He stiffened. "The *haeth'r* do this after you kill them."

Neer clenched her jaw, thinking back to Galacia, when the boy had reanimated. Avelloch sliced through his neck and kicked his body into the water. He then pulled Neer behind cover, just as he did in this village, as its body exploded with acidic flesh.

"How did you know I was here?" she asked. "Where are the others?"

He and Klaud shared an equally confused glance, and Avelloch said, "We heard you screaming."

She turned to him, matching his look of confusion. More tears burned her eyes, but she quickly wiped them away. "Come on," she said. "We should get back to the others."

"Neer."

He stood and caught her arm as she stepped away. She inhaled a deep breath and became rigid, not wanting to speak of what happened.

"You don't have to run from this. We can't help you if you won't tell us what's happening."

Her lip quivered and eyes burned with tears. She turned to him, wishing he could understand. Her chest convulsed, and deep, heavy sobs threatened to escape. But she choked them back, determined to remain strong. Unwilling to reveal the truth—to have him or the others view her as a dangerous monster. "I'm scared, Avelloch."

She fought against the tears, but the weight of terror and grief became too much to bear. Sputtering and sobbing, she leaned forward, falling into his arms.

"I'm so scared…"

Klaud quietly stepped away as Avelloch held Neer close, rubbing her hair as she cried. His expression was taut, and his hard eyes slowly scanned the village, taking in the devastation surrounding them. He turned to Neer, burying his face in her hair and pulling her close.

"*Malidrei alessiri*," he whispered. "You aren't alone."

His arms tightened around her, and she felt the weight of his embrace and thrum of his heart as their bodies pressed together.

"You're not alone."

Late into the evening, everyone sat in the long hall of the Cobbles and Kay Inn. A bar stained with ale rings stretched across the backwall. Bottles and jugs of spirits were displayed on open shelves. Empty tables and chairs were reminiscent of the life that once filled the room with laughter and songs.

 A large fireplace rested along the right-side wall, where fires rose atop a stack of wood. Dru hovered within the flames, her aura brighter as the heat rejuvenated her strength. Y'ven sat on his knees in front of the hearth, creating a deep shadow that swallowed many of the tables behind. In his hand was a ball of flames. He sat in undisturbed meditations, the flames pulsing with his every deep breath.

 At a table nearby, bathing in a sliver of flickering light, Neer sat with the others. Thurandír was across from her, peering downward with distant eyes. Stray tears slid down his face as he was entranced by pain. Thallon leaned forward with his head in his hands, while Klaud drank heavily from a bottle of wine.

 "This is such shit," Thallon exclaimed. "It's fucking—!" With a growl, he smacked the table, and everyone flinched.

 Aélla touched his arm in a comforting gesture, and he pulled away with a huff.

 "Who would do this?" she asked. "Was it—"

 "The Klaet'il," Thurandír stated. His voice was hollow and bleak. Another tear fell from his vacant eyes. "Ricard said it was the Klaet'il."

 Klaud took another gulp of wine, while Neer and Avelloch shared a glance. The room was silent, lingering with dread. The Nasir had the ring, a dangerous and powerful weapon, yet he hadn't used it. Not here, at least. The bodies were too intact for any creature of darkness to have slain. Their wounds were made by swords, not claws or fangs.

 And Ricard, the man from the alley, would have mentioned the creatures had they attacked the city. But the most damning of all wasn't the bodies hanging in the streets—it was the ones who were missing. They were gone without a trace. Cups half-full of ale sat on the tables of the tavern, and a dirty washcloth was atop the counter, as if everyone had left in a hurry.

 Throughout the day, while Thallon tended to Thurandír, the others scoured the homes, searching for survivors. Instead, they were greeted by empty homes and silence. Bone-shattering silence that reminded them all of the cruel fate the others might have endured.

"I'm going after them," Thurandír said, breaking the long, insufferable quiet.

"Thurandír," Aélla started, "we can't go rushing off after the Nasir. We need to figure out what he's after and why he came here. If we—"

"My people are *gone*!" His loud, raw voice shook the air.

Y'ven fell from his meditations at the sound of Thurandír's strained voice. He turned back, watching the others as they sat quietly, too grief-stricken to speak. Thurandír trembled. He breathed heavily and wiped his eyes, which produced a constant stream of glistening tears.

"You can sit here and pretend to care, or you can do something!"

No one spoke, and his face twisted with disgust. Thallon reached out as Thurandír left the table. The archer smacked him away and then marched through the room before disappearing behind a doorway.

Everyone gazed at the door. Their eyes were heavy with sorrow and pity.

They refocused their attention on the table, and Aélla said, "Why would the Klaet'il do this?"

Klaud leaned forward with a heavy sigh. "It's possible they're targeting the lanathess," he said. "There were nearly two dozen hanging in the village center."

"What?" Aélla and Thallon said with a gasp.

Neer nodded silently when they glanced at her, searching for the truth.

Avelloch added, "They weren't only human, though. There were evae too."

Klaud said, "I don't suspect the Klaet'il would attack evaesh villages without cause. The e'liaa aren't under the protection of the Eirean." He paused, his eyes becoming sullen. "Not in the way they should be."

"It's no secret the Klaet'il have always resented the e'liaa," Thallon said. "They could be taking out their anger of the invasion on them."

Avelloch leaned forward and shook his head. "When we searched the village for survivors, no one found a trace. No blood, no missing items, no messes left behind." He paused. "It's as if they just disappeared. Cupboards were stocked and dressers were full."

"What does that mean?" Aélla asked.

"I don't know. If the e'liaa evacuated, they would have taken provisions."

Neer stated, "Maybe they fled. Saw what was happening in the village and—"

"No," Klaud interjected. "The Klaet'il had time to tie up their victims with no other evidence of a fight. Whatever happened to the villagers...it had already been done before the others were left to hang."

More silence. Their words rang loudly in the heavy air. Had the village been evacuated, the residents would have carried food and provisions. They'd have left their homes in a hurry, creating a mess in their haste. But they hadn't evacuated, and they weren't murdered.

They were taken.

No one said the words aloud, but they knew. Deep in their souls, they understood the harrowing truth. Whatever the Nasir had planned, it involved living captives. They had taken everyone and left behind those who resisted.

Neer raked her fingers through her hair. "We can't let them get away with this," she said. "They can't just attack entire villages!"

Klaud said, "I've sent Altvára to the Eirean with a note. Hopefully, they'll trust my words and send aid."

Thallon scoffed. "Good luck with that. Aélla should just teleport there and speak to them directly."

"No," she responded. "I don't want us to separate. Things are too unstable. If you had to flee while I was gone, we may never find one another again. I have to focus on getting to Galdir."

Neer shook her head in disbelief. "These people were taken captive!" Her eyes simmered with resentment and anger. "The longer you choose to ignore it, the longer they'll be victims of the Klaet'il."

"Nerana, we can't—"

"Fuck doing what's 'right'! We need to find them before it's too late."

No one argued. No one agreed. They simply remained silent. With a scoff, she stood, condemning them all with her hateful eyes.

"Some saviors you are. The world is in great hands if *this* is how you choose to keep the peace."

"Neer—" Thallon started, but she quickly interrupted.

"No! I don't want to hear about how unstable or dangerous or impulsive I am. I'll watch this world burn before I allow innocent people to be tortured or imprisoned. You can all sit here and feel justified because you're following *Drimil'Rothar*, but if she's unwilling to compromise in her beliefs, then she's no different than the others!"

Before they could utter a response, she left the room.

The next morning, before light touched the world, Neer sat alone by the hearth where embering logs billowed with smoke. She leaned forward with her pack and weapons resting at her side. Her mind was focused on the villagers and where they could be.

When footsteps pattered across the wooden floor behind, Neer was jolted from her thoughts. She turned around and was swept with confusion. Walking through the Inn, carrying his pack and weapons, was Avelloch. His eyes scanned the room before falling to Neer's, and he slowly approached her side.

She watched as he sat beside her, leaning forward with his arms bracing his knees. Firelight reflected against his clean hair and skin.

Neer studied him for a moment and asked, "What are you doing?"

"Coming with you."

Her heart sank. "You don't have to do that. Your loyalty should be with Aélla, not—"

"My loyalty is mine to choose." Their eyes connected, and the weight of confusion lifted from her shoulders. "I won't allow innocent people to suffer."

Neer nodded with approval. She leaned back against the cushioned bench and stared into the flames. "Do you think the others will come?"

"No."

A sigh escaped her throat, and she leaned her head back to stare up at the ceiling. "They'll be angry if you leave, you know?"

The cushions shifted when he sat back and crossed his arms. Neer glanced at him through the corner of her eye, and he responded with a wordless shrug.

Dancing firelight gave life to the room as their conversation came to an end. The logs collapsed when heat turned them to ash. Too many thoughts raced through Neer's mind as she worried over the civilians and their fate. But the most pressing concern was for Thurandír. She understood the weight of losing everything—of finding her home in ruins and her people gone.

Before she could fall too deep into her sorrow, the sound of heavy boots clunked against the floor behind. Neer and Avelloch turned at the sudden noise, which was loud against the quiet that had overtaken the large room.

Thurandír stalked across the hall, focused. He carried his weapons and pack, marching to the door. The happiness once brightening his face had faded to dread.

"Hey," Neer said as she stood.

Thurandír halted, the sullen look still present on his face. He didn't speak when their eyes connected. Didn't show a sense of shock or confusion at her and Avelloch's presence. The others had fallen asleep hours ago, tucking into their rooms for the night.

Realizing he had nothing to say, Neer continued, "We're going with you."

"I don't need your help."

"Thurandír."

He released an angry huff when Neer stepped to his side.

"Don't do this on your own," she begged. "You need help."

His eyes fell away and lips pursed. "Fine. Let's go."

SHADOWS OF NYN'DIRA

Neer and Avelloch followed him outside. They walked silently through the village, haunted by its silence. Thurandír kept his eyes forward. His jaw was clenched, and Neer wished more than anything to relieve him of his pain.

Outside of the village, they entered the forest. A slight shift in the wind beckoned them east, and they followed. The world was drenched in purple moonlight, helping them to see through the thick underbrush. Limbs swayed above, causing the shadows to dance and leaves to chime with soft, calming melodies.

Energy swirled through the air with every light gust of wind, and Neer breathed in its warmth. For a moment, she felt calm and at peace. The weight of the world and all of its terrors didn't seem to matter with the forest embracing them in its protection. Another breeze whisked simmering energy through the air, and the slight sting of magic caused chills to form along Neer's arms and back. She glanced around, watching the trees. Her lips drew into a smile when she realized the forest was doing more than providing warmth and melodic tunes. It was gifting them with peace. The magic that clung to their skin was inhaled in their lungs, easing the sorrow that carried them forward.

It felt their pain and attempted to erase it.

Neer scanned the forest, entranced by its beauty and the deep connection it held to its inhabitants. Her eyes scanned the horizon, admiring the glowing plants and buzzing fireflies, when she noticed a shadowy figure lurking nearby.

A light gasp filled her lungs, and the others came to a sudden halt. They looked west, toward the approaching shadow. Weapons clattered when Thurandír drew an arrow, prepared to fight. The glow of Avelloch's sword brightened his face as he unsheathed his weapon.

Neer held her breath, watching the creature stalk forward. When moonlight cast against the silhouette of a direwolf, she slumped forward with relief.

Avelloch slid his sword back into its scabbard on his back. "Blaid," he said.

The wolf held Avelloch's gaze as the gap between them dwindled. He then turned to Neer. She looked into Blaid's sapphire eyes, comforted by his presence.

"Come on," Thurandír pressed. "We need to keep going."

Neer tilted her head aside, urging Blaid to follow as she and Avelloch trailed behind their leader.

The silence of dawn faded into a bright and sunny evening as they trekked further west, stopping for a rest by a creek. Neer and Avelloch refilled their canteens, while Blaid lapped the water. Thurandír was nearby, sharpening an arrow. He slid a whetstone against the steel, growing angrier with every stride.

"Thurandír," Neer started. He glanced at her, and she asked, "You okay?"

"My entire village is gone…I grew up with Ricard." He shook his head, refocusing on his arrowhead. "I can't let the Klaet'il take them! What kind of warrior would I be if I gave up on my own people?"

Neer started to speak, but in his misery, he spoke over her, shouting as tears formed in his eyes.

"I left my brothers to walk with Drimil'Rothar, and she turned her back on me! They all did…" His lip quivered, and more tears spilled down his face. "I should've let you help him…He could've survived…I killed him…"

He dropped the arrow to the ground and hugged his knees. Sputtered sobs choked from his throat, his agony unleashed. Neer crawled to his side and wrapped her arm around his back.

"I'm never going to find them…," he cried. "My whole family's gone."

Neer rested her head on his shoulder as he bawled. His shoulders shook and breaths were choked as his grief unleashed in waves of agonized weeps. Neer remained at his side, gifting him with words of hope and encouragement. She knew the chances of finding his people were slim, and should they never find his family, she would be there, able to comfort him in ways most others couldn't. She had lived through this agony. Was strengthened by its pain. But

Thurandír was good. He was innocent and kind, and she feared he might not recover from such anguish.

"Come on," she said, rubbing his back. "We've got to keep moving."

After several minutes, Thurandír straightened and wiped his eyes. With a low sniff, he collected his belongings, and they continued onward. Neer kept in stride with Thurandír, watching him from the corner of her eye. Avelloch and Blaid were a step behind, silent as a shadow.

"Where are we headed?" Neer asked, breaking the long and dreary silence.

"Ik'Navhaa,*" Thurandír explained, his voice thick with grief. "It's another e'liaa village. My people may have fled there, or the others might know what's going on."

The conversation came to a bitter end as Neer was lost for words, knowing nothing could ease his suffering. Thurandír focused on the forest, and they were silent for a while, drenched in sorrow.

Soon, he said, "I'm sorry about what I said to you back in the village. I know you're a good person. I was just—"

"It's okay. You were hurting. Can't say I haven't done worse."

He exhaled through his nose. "I guess not."

Scattered homes were present throughout the forest as they neared the village of Ik'Navhaa. They wandered by cottages tucked deep into the woods, and Neer's heart sank. The homes were silent and empty. Wooden swings hung from tall trees, a desolate shrine to those who once lived in its comfort.

Thurandír felt it too—the emptiness and sorrow. But neither would speak of it aloud. The harrowing thoughts were too great to bear. Their only hope lay in the survival

---

* *Ik* is a term roughly translated to mean disgraced one.

It isn't the name the e'liaa gave themselves but is used to reference their villages. Over time, the e'liaa adopted the prefix, finding it easier to coexist with conformation than opposition.

Because of the evae's prejudiced views, Thurandír is the first e'liaa to be accepted as an avel warrior. His commander, Aen'mysvaral, lost a lot of respect from his people when he chose the half-blood to join his ranks, forcing Thurandír to work harder than most to prove his worth.

of these villagers—that maybe his loved ones were taking refuge nearby or preparing to fight back against their attackers.

Mist sprayed through the air when they walked alongside a river, following it closer toward the village. Neer turned away, holding in a silent retch when the faint odor of rotten flesh stung her nose. She held her breath and clenched her teeth, praying to the gods that the smell didn't come from more villagers.

Her eyes flashed to Avelloch, who walked several paces behind. A deadly glare was seared across his face as he scanned the forest, searching for the source of the acrid smell. The hair on Blaid's back stood tall.

Neer breathed heavily, fearing the worst. The intense aroma grew stronger, burning her eyes as they stalked closer to a logging mill. Thurandír was silent. He walked with forced steps, dragging himself closer, tears burning his eyes.

"We can go alone," Neer suggested. "So, you don't—"

"I need to see it."

With a silent nod, she continued on, following in his lead. Blaid was at her side, keeping an eye on the forest. Neer covered her mouth and nose as they approached the mill. With every step, the gentle chime of leaves was replaced by the loud buzzing of flies. Stains of dark red spattered the grass and wooden posts of the mill. Small chunks of lumpy, red flesh were strewn across the dirt, as if more bodies had exploded.

They moved closer to the open mill, and the sight of several bodies, thrown into piles, came into view. Thurandír came to a stop, unable to breathe as the smell of decay and view of the slain villagers overwhelmed him. He leaned forward against his knees and expelled what little contents he had eaten that day. More sobs escaped his tightened throat, and he covered his face, consumed with grief.

Neer gripped his shoulders in an attempt to comfort him. She shared a glance with Avelloch, silently begging for help. For a way to ease Thurandír's pain. But there was nothing they could do.

Avelloch peered at the mill and then slowly approached. Blaid was at his side, scanning the carnage of the vicious attack. He covered his nose with his arm and stepped onto the wooden platform. Brain matter and bits of flesh squished beneath his boots as he stepped through pools of thick, sticky blood.

Two piles of bodies rested on either side of the mill. Upon further inspection, Avelloch closed his eyes. He appeared to nearly faint, standing for a moment and swaying with sickness. Forcing his eyes open, he gazed at the partial remains of the villagers, all of whom had been sawed in half by the mill. Left legs and arms were tangled together in the mess of bodies lying before him. Resting on the opposite side of the mill, coated in larvae and flies, were the victims' other halves.

Organs were split and leaking from the serrated bodies. Fragmented bones spread across the mill with the crimson spattering the floor and wooden beams. Avelloch was frozen. His eyes were dark and body was stiff.

Seconds passed before he turned away and approached the others.

"What is it?" Neer asked, noticing his paled face and horror-stricken eyes.

He softly shook his head, unable to speak. Thurandír's face twisted, and he clenched his teeth, fighting back more tears. Neer rubbed his back and led him forward, passing the mill to head closer to the village.

Thurandír kept his eyes forward, not daring to look at the massacre. His eyes were wide, and he breathed slowly, struggling to stay calm. Every step was like walking through thick mud. Their feet were heavy as they forced themselves forward.

Neer glanced aside, noticing the mangled bodies and burst entrails. She pursed her lips and kept her eyes ahead. The forest was silent and heavy with the weight of death. Moonlight overtook the sun, and dusk crept over the land. Neer crossed her arms, knowing they had more to worry about than the Klaet'il now that night was upon them.

At the settlement, where several dozen homes were spread throughout the forest, they found six bodies hanging upside down. A deep stab wound opened each of their chests, staining their bloated faces with dried blood. Neer fought through the voices and pain. But they crept in, gripping her soul and splitting her mind with their desperate cries.

She grunted and wheezed. Her eyes squinted, and sweat formed across her temples. Thurandír looked at her, his brows furrowed.

"What's wrong?" His voice was as bleak as his grief-stricken eyes.

"I…" she started with a grunt. "I can…hear their voices."

His jaw dropped. He turned to the bodies with worried eyes. "What are they saying?"

She shook her head. "Nothing. Let's keep going."

He stood before her, blocking the path. "Tell me. Please."

With another wince, she said, "They're just…afraid. Some are angry. I can't really—" She gasped and stumbled forward.

Blaid leapt forward to catch her fall. Thurandír was at her side, touching her shoulder. Their eyes met, and they shared a silent nod.

Returning their attention to the city, Thurandír continued on, no longer needing the words of the fallen to ease his pain. Avelloch came to Neer's side, and they walked together through the blood-spattered village. Sigils of the Order were painted across several homes. Innards were dragged across the ground, torn apart. Faces were mauled and chests were clawed open.

"The kanavin have been here," Avelloch said quietly.

Before Neer could speak, the sound of tearing flesh echoed from nearby. He grabbed her arm to keep her still. Thurandír halted, and everyone held their breath. Avelloch's wide eyes were focused in the direction of the noise, where the sound of hungry grunts and crunching bones rose from the alley.

Blaid lowered to the ground with a deep growl, and Neer and Avelloch collected their twin swords. As they stalked ahead, searching for the source of the noise, she lifted her hand to Thurandír, commanding him to stay behind. But he ignored her, choosing to follow as they slowly rounded the corner.

The sounds of ripping flesh were followed by thick, slopped chewing as a body was torn apart. When the creature came into view, Neer was washed of all feeling or strength. Her body numbed, and she stared through the alley, where just ahead, ripping into the flesh of a deceased woman, was the gaelthral, Thorne's mutated body. Organs burst as it chewed on the woman's remains. The gaelthral lifted its head, pulling a muscle with its teeth until it snapped.

Neer inhaled a shallow breath, and the gaelthral came to a sudden halt. A deep growl vibrated from its throat, and it turned, setting its solid black eyes on her.

Chapter Twenty-Three

Tek'Brenavath
Nerana

The ground quaked as the gaelthral charged. Sharp claws carved into the soil as it moved closer, smashing into walls in its fury. Neer shoved Thurandír aside and then disappeared. Wood splintered when the gaelthral smashed into the cabin where the archer once stood. Its head shook, and it backed away, rumbling with furious growls.

Neer reappeared in the air above the gaelthral. She fell onto its back and thrust her sword deep into its spine. The gaelthral thrashed and roared, attempting to buck her off. Neer held tightly to the sword still lodged in its body as she was whipped back and forth.

Her body ached, swinging from left to right. She closed her eyes, trying to teleport, but the images were muddled beneath her pain. Clenching her teeth, she forced herself to focus. When the images of the village were clear enough in her mind, she inhaled a deep breath and vanished.

Her body dropped to the grass nearby, and she released a groan. Pain rose from her abdomen where the jump had torn a shallow incision across her flesh. Blood soaked into her armor, warming her skin. Every movement brought another wave of burning agony. She crawled to her knees, pushing away the pain that rippled through her.

The gaelthral stood at the opposite end of the alley, releasing a screeching roar that chiseled through the air. Neer covered her ears and leaned forward. Homes shattered when it pummeled the walls, struggling to remove her sword from its back.

Dust thickened the air as the homes were crumbled and smashed. Neer's glowing sword remained deep in the gaelthral's flesh, protected by the fragmented spines and antlers protruding from its back.

A dull pressure touched Neer's nape, and she was pulled back. Her mouth was covered, and she was dragged through a doorway. Thurandír swiftly closed the threshold, and the room was masked in dark shadows. Only the lone window, staring out into the village center, allowed a stream of purple light to enter the small home.

Avelloch released his grip on Neer's shoulders and mouth, and she stepped aside, gripping her abdomen. Blaid stood guard beside her, snarling when the gaelthral's shadow raced by the window. Its pounding steps receded across the village before another home was destroyed.

"What is that thing?" Thurandír whispered. "How can we take it out?"

Neer withheld a groan. "We can't. Not alone."

"We have to do something before it—"

"Be quiet!" she hissed.

Thurandír fell silent. His fearful, pleading eyes were fixed on Neer. Outside, the gaelthral roared. Its powerful voice caused objects within the home to rattle. Avelloch peered through the window, watching the gaelthral slam into another house. His eyes widened, and he raised his swords.

"Someone's here!" he exclaimed.

"What?" Neer asked.

Thurandír was instantly at his side. He opened the window and drew an arrow. Neer hobbled to their sides, feeling the warmth of blood soaking the hem of her tunic beneath her armor. Gazing through the village of splintered wood and crumbled walls, she spotted the gaelthral. Its enormous body was a shadow in the darkness, only able to be seen by the moonlight glowing against its curved, spiny back. The creature was crouched on the ground, snarling at the seven figures surrounding it.

"Wait." Neer placed her hand on Thurandír's shoulder. She looked closer, noticing these figures appeared evaesh and wore dark leather armor. The Klaet'il often wore minimal clothing as a way to prove their fearlessness and to showcase the markings that covered their bodies from head to toe.

"Are they evae?" Neer asked.

Avelloch and Thurandír shared a confused glance, but Neer didn't notice as she leaned forward, bringing herself halfway out of the window. Her squinted eyes fixed on an enormous warrior with large muscles and a thick greatsword. He was nearly a head taller than the other men. She studied him for a moment, feeling as though she recognized his figure and brawn.

Before she could clearly make him out, a light rumble shook the ground. Neer glanced from left to right and then inched back into the cabin. Avelloch stepped forward with his swords held before them, anticipating another attack.

Tremors shook the walls, becoming louder with every footfall that caused them. The evae calmly parted when the enormous shadow of a mammoth trampled forward. Neer watched with a racing heart, unable to believe what she was seeing. The mammoth raised onto his hind legs and then slammed into the gaelthral.

Thurandír drew back his arrow.

"Don't!" Neer exclaimed with a gasp.

He lurched forward, stopping himself. "What?"

Her mouth was dry and throat was tight. She watched the warriors fighting against the gaelthral, slashing and jabbing into its sides, while the mammoth continued its assault. A single woman was among the hoard of men. She was smaller than the rest, flipping toward the gaelthral while it fought against the others, moving almost too quickly to see. Moonlight glinted against her sword as she slashed deep into the gaelthral's ankles. Smoke bled from its nearly severed foot.

The creature unleashed a hellish shriek and then collapsed. Neer stumbled when the ground quaked. The fighters shouted with strong war cries and raced forward. The much larger man, who was wearing a steel breastplate, charged at the gaelthral, shouting with a deep, sawing voice as he raised his enormous sword. The creature whipped its head in his direction and snapped its jaws. Sharp fangs tore through the air, scraping against the man's chest plate with a reverberating screech.

The man spun aside and swiftly jabbed at the gaelthral's eye. As the blade drew nearer, the beast whipped its head aside, and the longsword plunged deep into its shoulder. A thunderous roar erupted through the air. Dirt and grass were ripped from the soil as the gaelthral thrashed, attempting to stand and fight.

The mammoth trumpeted, and the fighters scattered. Quick steps pounded against the soil as the beast approached the gaelthral. It lifted its front legs and slammed against the creature from above, pinning it to the ground. The gaelthral's injured paws clawed against the dirt, unable to gain leverage with its sliced ankles. Smoke rose from the broken spines and antlers across its back, blocking the moonlight and drenching the village in a cloud of darkness.

The large fighter climbed up the gaelthral's leg and stood on its back. Moonlight glimmered against his sword lifted above his head. He sank his blade deep into the gaelthral's neck, severing its spine. A squealed shriek filled the air, before the world fell intensely silent. Its body slumped into the grass, and heavy smoke billowed from its enormous body.

"Wallace!" the woman shouted from below.

Neer's breath caught in her throat. She knew that name. She knew that fighter. Her gaze was fixed on the shadows surrounding the gaelthral. Her heart leapt in her throat, hoping it was true. These men weren't evaesh warriors or human invaders.

They were with the Brotherhood.

Wallace, still standing atop the gaelthral's back, glanced around as the creature faded to ash. Before he could move, the mammoth's trunk wrapped around his body and placed him on the ground. Everyone was silent. Soot drifted through the air, clinging to the destroyed homes and painting the world in deep shades of black.

Neer turned aside when a flash of light engulfed the mammoth. The village brightened, as if the sun had suddenly risen, only to set just as quickly. The world seemed darker now that the light had disappeared. And standing in the place of the mammoth, bare-skinned and proud as ever, was Gilbrich.

Avelloch and Thurandír turned quickly when Neer exhaled a choked breath. Emotions crashed over her, drawing tears to her eyes. She stepped forward, placing her hands against the windowsill while gazing at the family she never thought she'd see again. Her lip quivered, and she shook her head, thinking herself mad. This must be another trick—an illusion given by the magic of this forest. Something to pull her further into the chaos that swept her soul, filling her with agony.

But the vision never faded.

The warriors remained in the village, speaking quietly to one another and passing Gil his clothes. His voice sent shockwaves of relief and confusion through Neer's soul. The dreled slipped his clothes over his hairy body and then stood at the mound of ash with the others.

Avelloch and Thurandír reached out when Neer climbed through the window and ran into the streets. Dust billowed around her boots when she quickly approached the group, forgetting her injury and pain. Her body was numb, but she stepped closer, viewing all the familiar faces. When a man in white armor turned to her, their eyes connected, and she nearly dropped to her knees in relief.

"Neer?"

His confusion transformed into a genuine smile. Coryn, her childhood friend, pulled her into his arms. Neer winced, and he quickly backed away, gazing at her stomach, which was covered by a perfectly dry, intact chest piece. "Have you gone and hurt yourself again, woman?" he remarked.

Neer chuckled and wiped the tears from her eyes. "Old habits die hard."

With a laugh, he gently hugged her again, being careful not to disturb her injuries. "I'll have a look at it soon," he explained. "Can't leave old Gil waiting."

SHADOWS OF NYN'DIRA

Neer's smile was wide as the dreled stepped forward. She sank to her knees and pulled him into a long embrace. His large hands patted her back.

"'Tis good to see you, child."

Neer sniffed, unwilling to let him go. There were few comforts she had left in this world, and his presence was one she had difficulty parting with. Eventually, they backed away, but she kept her hands on his shoulders. Her eyes shifted to three scarred claw marks stretched across his left arm.

He said, "Seems we've both put up a good fight."

Neer glanced at him, confused, and he pointed at the deep scar across her cheek. She gently touched it, remembering how she had received it in Aragoth, when she fought against Thorne.

"What are you doing here?" she asked.

"What's it look like? Fightin' in this blasted war o' yours!"

The light faded from her eyes, and she turned away, feeling suddenly vulnerable. "You're fighting the humans?"

"Was. Now Reiman's got us trailin' these evae around. Bah!" He waved his arms dismissively. "'Tis a waste of time. We all know he's just searchin' for you, same as everyone else in these blasted woodlands."

Neer crossed her arms over her chest, her eyes on the ground. "You've come to find me...You want me to fight with you."

"Well, now, why wouldn't we?" He stepped closer. "Bein' with these tree-lovers hasn't made you soft, now, has it?"

A smile tugged the edge of her lip. "I've always been a little soft."

He rumbled with laughter. "That you have, child. Took many a years to turn that heart of gold into stone." He paused. "Never seemed to work, though. You've always had a soft spot for the pure and innocent."

"It's a wonder I care so much for you, then."

Gil gave her a quick, light-hearted glare.

213

Footsteps approached from behind, and the humans quickly drew their weapons. Neer stood and turned, finding Avelloch, Thurandír, and Blaid stepping forward. An arrow was nocked in Thurandír's bow, though he held it at his waist, prepared for a fight should they see to attack him. Avelloch was guarded, clutching tightly to his swords. He cast a menacing glare that caused the others to take half-a-step back.

"They're with me," she explained of the humans, though it didn't settle the fury in Avelloch's deadly eyes.

Gil marched forward. He rubbed his bottom lip, eying the evae and wolf. "I know these two and that wolf of theirs."

Neer glanced between them, surprised. "You've met?" she asked.

"Aye," Gil said with a nod. "They burst into our camp, chompin' at the bits after some blasted creature of the night came lookin' for us."

"What?" she said with a gasp, glancing between them.

"Don't worry, lass," Gil said. "That'n there took care of 'im."

Her eyes shifted to Avelloch when Gil pointed in his direction. Her brows pulled together, but before she could ask, Gil continued.

"Where's the rest of your mighty crew, anyhow? Surely, you aren't traipsin' through the forest fighting elves, monsters, and milk-drinkin' pissers with just the four of ya."

"We left them." Gil turned to Neer, curiously, and she continued, "They're too focused on their mission. Thurandír's village was attacked, and they'd rather ignore it than help."

"Shame. 'Tis good we found you when we did. The Brotherhood needs you, child. We've got to get you away from this blasted forest and into the care of the scholars! Before that pious prick invades in full!"

Neer translated, and Thurandír asked, "He's truly sending an army?"

Gil nodded. "Got an armada of Knights waitin' at the border."

"Then why haven't they attacked?"

Neer said, "They can't. Not while there's magic protecting your lands."

Thurandír turned away. "The magic won't last for long if the Klaet'il are attacking our people and the lanathess are preparing a full-scale invasion."

"'Tis why we need to act quickly!" Gil exclaimed. "We've got word of an attack that's bein' planned by the evae. Reiman's workin' up a strategy now for it."

Neer's heart skipped. "Reiman's here?"

"Well, o'course, he is! Been fightin' alongside us ever since he saved your hide back in the desert." He turned to Thurandír. "You'd best follow us if you want to help findin' your people. We'll be makin' our way south soon enough. If there are captives, we'll be sure to find them."

Thurandír gave a stiff nod. The fire in his eyes burned hotter than the freshest flame. He was ready to find his people or avenge them.

Gil returned the gesture. His eyes shifted to Neer, and he said, "Come now, child. We'd best be gettin' to work. Don't want Reiman gettin' his knickers in a bunch, now, do we?"

When Gil stepped away, Wallace, the enormous warrior, took his place. Neer was silent as he held out her sword. She accepted it and gave him a thankful nod. He returned the gesture before following Gil and the others northward. Thurandír glanced at Neer, and she smiled.

"This is the Brotherhood," she said. "They're good people. You can trust them."

"If they lead me to my family, then I'll do whatever they want."

"Don't say that too loudly, or you might regret it." Neer playfully turned to Coryn as he approached.

He gave a halfhearted glare. "Can you make it to camp?" he asked.

"Depends on how far it is," she said, clutching her stomach.

"Just north. Not far."

She nodded. "I should be okay."

They walked the pathless woods, heading through thick underbrush and climbing large slopes filled with rocks. The darkness of the forest was overwhelming, and everyone was on alert. Their eyes scanned the shadows, searching for any creatures that could be lurking in the shade.

Neer kept close to Blaid, finding his presence more calming than the others. He remained at her side, gifting her with his heat as the night fell colder.

The heavy silence that gripped the land was broken by the calming chime of trickling water. Streams of glowing water reflected light through the trees, making the forest feel more alive. Everyone breathed a sigh of relief, as the world, for a moment, felt peaceful and safe. The light would keep any creatures of darkness at bay, and it allowed the others to better view their surroundings. Neer studied the forest, taking in its wonder and beauty. The towering trees were like sentries guarding the people from harm. Warm magic clung to the air, pulsing with the life of all living things beneath the expansive canopy. Moonlight trickled through the thick leaves, creating columns of soft light that obscured the darkness.

"It really is beautiful," she said, her voice a whisper.

Moving further north, they passed by ancient stone walls and tall, fragmented pillars resting throughout the woods. Small Trees dotted the landscape, filling the shadows with specks of glowing light. Glimmering petals danced through the crisp autumn air with every light breeze.

"This is *Lochlánaa*," Thurandír explained. "It was an alveryan library."

Neer gaped at an enormous half-buried wall, which was taller than any building she had ever seen. It was beautifully crafted, with chiseled embellishments outlining every window. Thick, leafy vines encased most of its surface, and roots from the surrounding Trees twisted through the stone walls.

Murmuring voices filled the silence, and Neer lifted her eyes, noticing a large encampment ahead. Human soldiers, wearing the pendant of the Broken Order on their breasts, wandered the peaceful woods. She watched them sharpening weapons or playing cards at tables and realized the camp didn't make up even half of the soldiers at Reiman's disposal. They must have been scattered through the forest or fighting back home.

The musky aroma of leather filled her nose as they approached dozens of tents spread throughout the wide area, the largest of which rested in the center. Its entry was rolled up and pinned at the top, allowing its interior to be seen.

Neer's eyes fell to the man inside. He leaned over a table with several others, staring at the contents below. His low voice carved through the air with unshakable authority, and Neer smiled. Reiman moved figures around a map while speaking to the others.

Gil entered the tent with Wallace, and Reiman's focus shifted to them.

"Got a bit of a surprise for you," the dreled stated.

He turned to look at Neer, and Reiman followed his gaze. When their eyes met, the tension fell from his shoulders. He quietly excused himself to approach Neer and wrapped her in his arms.

"My child," he whispered, squeezing her tight. His hands moved to her arms, and he looked her over. "I'm glad you're all right."

"You too," she said.

With a nod, he ushered her toward his tent. "I see you've lost favor with Drimil'Rothar," he said.

Neer clenched her teeth. "We just didn't see eye to eye. Once we find Thurandír's people, we'll make our way back to her and the others."

Reiman eyed Avelloch and then Thurandír, who walked alongside them. "Those were your people?"

Thurandír nodded.

Reiman inhaled a slow breath. His attention moved to the tent, where his men continued plotting their movements. "We've received word of another attack taking place two days from now. We don't know what the Nasir has planned, but we'll find out. Rest assured, if your people are alive, we'll find them."

Thurandír added, "I'd like to help. I grew up here, so I know these villages inside and out."

Reiman met Neer's eyes, silently questioning Thurandír's loyalty. She gave a confident nod.

"He wouldn't be here if I didn't trust him," she said.

With another look at Thurandír, Reiman gave an approving nod. "An ally of one is an ally of us all."

As they approached the tent, Neer stumbled with a wince. She leaned forward, clutching her stomach. Reiman halted. He turned to Neer and snapped his fingers. Two men quickly approached and stood at attention.

"Remove her chest piece," he commanded.

They did as they were told, carefully untying her armor before pulling it away from her body, revealing her blood-soaked tunic. Reiman kindly lifted her shirt to examine the wound.

"What's this?" Gil remarked, stepping closer to examine the deep flesh wound. "You've been wanderin' around all this time with no ointments or proper gut to seal that wound?"

"I'm fine, Gil."

"I've got a right mind to swat your rear red!" He pointed a stubby finger at her. "How many times do I got to tell ya, lass? Think before you act. Coryn should've patched you up good before walkin' all this way."

She groaned, portraying a sense of pain far more intense than was true. "He said it wouldn't be far."

Gil turned to Coryn, red-faced and angry. The healer took half a step back, suddenly terrified of the man half his size. While the dreled rebuked him for being so careless, Coryn glanced at Neer. His wide eyes fell into a glare as she withheld a smile, watching Gil berate him.

Neer turned her attention to Reiman when he stepped close. "It's a flesh wound. Coryn, take her to the springs. The water should heal her."

"Yes, sir, Master Reiman," he said, quickly stepping away from the harsh words of the still-angry dreled.

Reiman placed his hand on Neer's shoulder and gifted her with a hidden smile. "It's good to have you back."

She smiled. "Good to *be* back."

Emptiness filled the warmth inside when he stepped away, returning to his duties. Thurandír stood at the table within Reiman's tent, while Neer was led away. She shared a glance with Avelloch, who was reluctant to trust the others. Her head tilted toward Reiman's tent in a silent notion for him to enter and join the war party.

He gave her a slight nod, shot a glance at Coryn, and then entered the tent.

"Thanks for that one," Coryn griped. "I forgot how insufferable you can be."

Neer chuckled and then stumbled forward, clutching her side with a groan. Coryn leapt to her side, but his panic was washed with bitterness as she began to laugh.

"You make it too easy," she said.

"Come on," he said with a bit of spite to his voice. "You always know how to get yourself into some kind of trouble, don't you?"

"What's life without a few stories and scars?"

"A long one," he retorted.

A scrunched smile brightened her face as she sat by the water's edge. "A boring one," she added.

"I guess that's up to the one living it, yeah?" He sat on his haunches and stared at the glowing pool before them. "You need some help? Or you going to go crying to Gil if I don't stitch you up proper?"

"I didn't go crying when you patched me up in Valde."

"There's a first time for everything." He smiled. "I'm surprised you're still running around with the elves, though. You were always wild, but I didn't think you'd go off to the forest like this."

Neer swept her fingertips through the water, watching as tiny ripples danced away from her touch. "It's fitting, though, don't you think?" Her teal eyes flashed to his. "A demon among demons."

His brows lowered with disapproval. "You're getting grumpy in your old age."

Neer chuckled. She removed her hand from the water and wiped the wetness on her trousers. "Must be why I'm so dark and scary now."

"Don't kid yourself, *Child*. You've always been dark and scary."

Neer shook her head with a grin. It was a comfort being in the presence of an old friend, one who could share memories and speak of things the others could never relate to. During their childhood, she and Coryn would often sneak into the bakeries to steal pies or squash vegetables in Angie's garden. They'd get a good lashing for it, but once the wounds would heal, they'd be back at it again, dragging Loryk or others into their games.

"Well," Coryn said while standing, "I'll leave you to it. Don't want that scary-ass elf with the dark eyes coming after me."

Neer laughed. "You're sitting here with the child of Nizotl herself, but you're afraid of a little evae?"

His head cocked aside with a glowering, exasperated look, one that told her how incredulous he found her statement. "If he hasn't killed you yet, then he must have nerves of steel."

Neer laughed.

"That one's got death in his eyes. You can see it." He shivered dramatically.

Neer shook her head and tossed grass at him, forcing Coryn to retreat back to camp. She watched him step away with a gleaming smile.

Left alone, secluded behind a thicket of bushes and trees, Neer carefully removed her top. Blood coated her skin, staining her stomach and the band of her trousers in deep red. Her fingers ran along the shallow cut stretching across her right side to her navel.

She knelt by the water and cupped it into her hands. When she bent over, the pain was immeasurable. Her arms shook, causing her to spill water across the grass. With a huff, she leaned back, relieving the pressure in her side.

With a glance around to be sure she was alone, Neer removed her filthy clothes and tossed them into a pile. She then crawled into the glowing water, wincing as the surge of energy fizzled and popped against her shallow cuts and deeper wounds. Blood swirled through the water like mist, oozing from the cut on her stomach.

The pain subsided, and she slid a hand across her side, feeling the fresh scar where her flesh was once split. Exhaling a relieved breath, Neer sank further into the water. She stared up at the stars and listened to the sounds of familiar, happy voices echoing from all around.

Basking in the peace she knew might never come again, Neer closed her eyes and soaked in the solitude, allowing the warm sting of energy to ease her pain.

Chapter Twenty-Four

Trials of War
Nerana

"All living beings are born of equality."

– Tenet of the Broken Order Brotherhood

The next morning was spent with Reiman and the officers. Neer stood alongside Avelloch and Thurandír, who were invited to join in the planning of a pre-emptive assault at the village of Ik'Nharaii.

"How did you get this intel?" Avelloch asked, staring at the map.

Reiman said, "Our spymaster, Morganis."

He motioned to the side of the room, where a woman with short red hair sat on a table, picking her nails with a knife. Her left leg hung over the edge, swaying without a care. Her eyes lifted to the others as they turned to face her. A wry smile pulled her lips, and she sat straighter.

With her eyes fixed on Avelloch, she said, "So, we meet again, *Aegrandir*."

His jaw flexed and eyes were glazed with anger. Neer glanced between them, wondering how they knew each other. Her eyes flashed to Reiman, who matched her look of shock and confusion. He stared at Avelloch for a second longer, before clearing his throat and reclaiming his composure.

SHADOWS OF NYN'DIRA

"I've sent Morganis and Gilbrich to scout the area," Reiman added. "They've been tracking the Klaet'il's movements for several days."

Thurandír asked, "So, you saw the villagers being captured?"

Morganis turned to him with a bored expression. "Are we allowing children into our ranks now, Master Reiman?"

Thurandír's face twisted with sudden anger. Everyone flinched when he smacked his hands against the table, causing the figurines to tumble aside. "I'm an avel warrior! Better than any of these lanathess! And I'll find my people, with or without you."

With a sly smirk, she leaned back and began picking at her nails once again. "No," she said, never veering from her fingers. "We didn't see them."

The silence was deafening as they stood around the table, waiting. Neer placed her hand on Thurandír's shoulder, but he quickly shook it away. She exhaled a deep breath, searching for the right words to say. It was dangerous to have the humans and evae together like this, as neither had much trust for the other.

The figurines were set up in their respective places, and Avelloch said, "The Klaet'il don't fight like the rest of us. Their patterns are unpredictable. Even with a stia'dyr° or dreled, it would be hard to follow their path like this."

Avelloch lifted his eyes to Reiman, who hid his anger well. But it was there, brimming beneath the surface. Neer could see it in his eyes. It was the look he had always given her when she would question his motives or wit.

Retaining his composure, he said, "What would a fallen warrior understand about the trials of war?"

"You tell me," Avelloch responded, matching Reiman's dark stare, unwilling to back down beneath his power and authority. "What self-respecting evae would defect to lana'thoviin and create civil unrest with the humans?"

Everyone fell silent. Not a soul dared to speak beneath the pressure of their furious glares. Neer gulped down the lump in her throat and glanced between them. Avelloch

---

° Stia'dyr are evae who hold the incredibly rare ability to control and see through the eyes of an animals.

held Reiman's gaze, refusing to back down. It wasn't usual for someone to stand up to their leader, and Neer was surprised Avelloch had shown such resolve against him.

"I've invited you as welcomed guests into this sanctuary," Reiman said. "We've given you food and shelter and have risked our lives and men to protect your people from this invasion." His dark eyes burned into Avelloch. "Don't misunderstand my power. If I were truly your enemy, this forest would have already fallen."

Avelloch's eyes narrowed, and when Reiman stood taller, he followed. Wallace reached for his weapon, and Thurandír clutched his bow.

"All right, now," Gil called. "No need to go buckin' up to one another. You evae're worse than me wife when she's in need of a nice shite."

Neer gently touched Avelloch's arm. "Why don't we all just calm down?" she said. "There's no need for such hostility."

Reiman closed his eyes and leaned against the table, but Avelloch remained tense. His shoulders were squared and lips were pursed. Neer glanced between them, hoping this feud wouldn't last. She knew her father was a proud man. He'd never apologize to Avelloch in front of the others, and having a stranger undermine him was more than pressing. But Avelloch refused to give in to those he didn't trust.

Neer's voice cut through the silence as she said, "Reiman can be trusted, Avelloch. He's on our side."

His jaw clenched, and for a moment, she thought he was going to speak, but he remained silent, turning away with a nod.

Determined to end this feud, Neer returned her attention to the table, and asked, "What's the plan?"

The tension faded, and everyone refocused on the map. Avelloch stood beside Neer, their arms touching and faces close. She glanced at him, but he ignored her, choosing instead to focus on the conversation.

Reiman explained, "We'll have two groups enter from the east and western gates. Our forces will be divided, but it's the best approach. We can secure the borders and defend the village from the inside before the Klaet'il invade.

We can protect the village and be a step closer to finding Thurandír's people."

"Do the Klaet'il have a camp nearby?" Avelloch asked.

Morganis said, "No. As you said, they're unpredictable. We have no idea where they're hiding out."

Charlie, a human soldier, leaned forward, surveying the map. "We should wait," he suggested. "They'll have to move soon. Mor and Gil can watch and track their positions."

Reiman nodded with thought. "Yes, that's very good. I'll have six scouts in these areas. Morganis, you go south, see what you can find there."

Wallace asked—and Neer translated to evaesh, as she had done throughout the meeting—"The Klaet'il won't have spies surrounding the village?"

"Maybe," Avelloch said, staring at the map with a finger to his lip. "We need to be ready for anything."

"Such as?" Gil pressed.

"Hard to say." Avelloch crossed his arms. "They could use poison darts or potions to put everyone to sleep before moving in. Set the village on fire. Ambush from all sides and overwhelm us." He paused. "This could be a trap. The Klaet'il aren't fools. They could know we're coming."

Reiman nodded. "I'll take everything into consideration, and we'll reconvene tonight. You're all dismissed."

Neer followed when everyone stepped away.

Reiman called, "Nerana."

She gave Avelloch and Thurandír a reassuring nod, and they reluctantly left the tent. Neer watched Gil and Wallace exit behind them. Reiman leaned against the table with his eyes focused on the map. Callused fingers were splayed against the wooden surface.

They were quiet for some time, but she didn't mind. It had been far too long since the two of them had spent time alone. While she hoped he would invite her to sit for a quiet conversation and a glass of wine, her wit told her otherwise. Reiman wasn't an affectionate man. Even in her youth, he had been tough and firm. She didn't expect him to be anything less now that they stood on the edge of war.

"What do you think of these plans?" he asked.

She stood for a moment, stunned he would ask her advice. Her eyes shifted to the map, studying the figurines and their positions. War strategies and politics weren't her strong suit. Reiman knew that, so she answered the question he had truly meant to ask.

"Avelloch knows what he's talking about."

Reiman made a quiet *hmm* sound with his throat. "And you don't believe your judgement has been clouded by your affection?"

"Whether I trust in you or him, it's all the same. Avelloch's one of the best fighters I've ever seen. You should trust him."

He quietly stepped away from the table. At the back of the tent, Reiman poured himself a cup of water and sat in an oversized chair. He motioned to the chair next to him, and Neer took her place at his side. She was offered a cup of water and kindly accepted. Her fingers traced around the wooden rim as she waited for him to continue.

They were quiet for some time before he said, "I know you two were together last night."

Her jaw clenched, hating that he was reprimanding her, like a child sneaking out after curfew. Once the meetings were over and the camp was made to rest, she and Avelloch had walked away, spending their night alone, away from the humans and war.

An argument was on her tongue, but before she could speak, he stated, "I won't delude myself into believing that you haven't forsaken your duties to the Brotherhood for Drimil'Rothar and her companions." He paused with intent. "But you have made vows to us. Swore allegiance *to us*." His disappointed eyes bore into hers. "Have you lost your way?"

"I can fight alongside both of you," she argued. "I still seek to destroy the Order."

"Then tell me, what are you doing to strengthen yourself? How do you plan to defeat the High Priest if you're working toward Aélla's goals and not your own?"

Neer leaned forward with her elbows on her knees and closed her eyes. "I'm not—" She paused to gather her thoughts. "I'm not sure what to do, Reiman. I know that I need Aélla if I'm ever to control this madness growing inside me." She shook her head. "But I have no direction. I don't know where to go."

"That's because you aren't fighting for yourself."

She scoffed and rested her chin on her folded hands. Staring blankly ahead, she said, "It's what I've always done, isn't it? Fight someone else's war. When will my life be mine? When will I ever get a choice?"

Dark thoughts loomed in the back of her mind. Thoughts of vengeance and fire and war. They were once her truest desires, to destroy those who had caused her so much agony and strife. But she now understood there was a different path. One that saw forgiveness and light and peace.

She couldn't allow the Order to get away with all they had done, but each day, the darkness always brimming beneath the surface rose higher. Now, it was unleashing in waves of devastation that nearly cost her friends their lives. She had seen the effects of her rage—the scars and bruises it had left behind on those she cared for most.

Reiman's voice broke through her thoughts, and she turned away with a blink.

"You're strong, Nerana. One of the strongest women I've ever known." He leaned closer. "You don't need Drimil'Rothar or anyone else to help you find your way. Find strength within yourself, and then you'll be set free." Another pause. "The Brotherhood needs you. We can't win this without your help. But the choice is yours, and I trust that you'll be wise in making it."

She considered his offer, surprised to hear him speak so openly. His words sank deep into her soul, repeating in her mind along with everything else she had ever learned from her time with the Brotherhood. The High Priest couldn't be killed by conventional methods. He had to be stopped with magic. She had witnessed it firsthand in Llyne, after she stabbed through his heart and he stood, blood pouring from his chest as he watched her flee.

Reiman was her family. The Brotherhood was her home. She couldn't turn her back on them. With a sigh, she said, "I was told to enter four realms in order to defeat the

High Priest. Aélla had ventured to three before we met. The remaining four must be the ones we're meant to enter together." She paused with thought. "Once I've done that, I'll have the strength to fight against the High Priest. My magic will be unstoppable."

He nodded. "You've entered tre'lan Aenwyn in Aragoth, so I can assume you'll be heading toward tre'lan Zynther in the days to come."

"Tre'lan Zynther?" she asked. "But that's—"

She was interrupted when an officer stepped into the tent. "Master Reiman," he called, "the elves are here."

Reiman exhaled a deep sigh. With a gentle nod, he followed his soldier outside, and Neer was left alone. She stepped to the table to examine the map. To the east was a dark section of the forest, as if all the trees had been burned. The scorched trees nearly separated the Rhyl and Klaet'il territories from one another. The word *Ney'tarra* was written in beautiful evaesh calligraphy within the darkness.

"Nerana," Gil said, peeking his head into the tent. "Best hurry your hide out here!"

With a furrowed brow, Neer followed him outside, where a group of evaesh warriors stood with Reiman and several officers. Fury stained their long faces and dark blue eyes. Their angry words laced the air, slicing through the humans' brash voices.

Neer stepped to Reiman's side and asked through the chaos, "What's going on?"

Reiman ignored her. Speaking to the evae with a powerful voice that silenced the others, he demanded, "Why are you here?"

The evaesh leader, with dark, plaited hair, said, "We've been investigating the disappearing villagers." His lip snarled. "First, the lanathess camps were left bare, and now our own people are vanishing!"

Another evae pointed at Reiman and said, "Why have you led a fleet of lanathess into our lands?"

"Drimil'Nizotl!" a gruff voice tore through the crowd.

Wallace and several guards drew their weapons when an evaesh warrior broke through the crowd. His eyes were

SHADOWS OF NYN'DIRA

set on Neer, and she stiffened as a dagger was pressed to her throat. Dark blue eyes glared into hers.

"You are the one they seek," he hissed. "We can end this now. No more lanathess. No more bloodshed."

As Reiman spoke, the man's face twisted with hatred. The blade tugged against Neer's skin, and she vanished. The man glanced aside as she reappeared to his left, pressing the tip of her sword against his side. A shallow cut left a line of blood drizzling down her neck.

Reiman placed his hand on Neer's shoulder. His eyes darted from the angry warrior to the evaesh leader. "We are not your enemy," he stated. "Have the Eirean taken measures to prevent these invasions? Have they put their warriors on the front lines to guard the villages and stop the Klaet'il?"

He paused to examine the faces of everyone around him.

Standing taller, he said, "The Brotherhood is here to defend our lands against the madness that has plagued us all. We fight against the injustice set upon us. Humanity, evae, vaxros, dreled—we are all the same. We fight for one purpose: to protect our homes."

The man who attacked Neer said, "How can you preach of protection when you've brought war upon us?" He glared pointedly at her, his eyes seething with hatred. "Her very existence will be the death of us all!"

Neer took a step closer, overcome with fury. The clatter of metal filled the air when the evae readied their weapons, and the humans followed.

"I'm not the enemy here!" she sneered.

"Enough!" Reiman called. "We are here to find your missing people! The Klaet'il have begun their invasions, and we plan to know why. If you choose to fight against us, then there will be nothing but more bloodshed. Lay down your arms and allow us to work together in peace."

Neer breathed heavily, glaring at the man who had threatened her life. His anger was pure and unbroken. Slowly, the others lowered their weapons. He was the last, forcefully relaxing his arms under the order of his superior.

But his eyes never shifted from Neer's. Stuck in an endless battle, she held her ground, never showing a sign of weakness or fear.

The avel leader turned to his men. They spoke for several minutes, mentioning Drimil'Nizotl more than once. Tension born from lifetimes of distrust rose between the opposing groups.

After minutes of discussion, the evae turned to face Reiman.

The evaesh leader said, "How can we know you're to be trusted? You stand with Drimil'Nizotl and a band of lanathess at your back, yet you speak of fighting alongside our people."

Reiman straightened and placed his hands behind his back. "Nerana is a guardian of Drimil'Rothar, who I'm certain will be making her arrival to this camp shortly. She can attest to our alliances."

The leader's eyes shifted to Neer. "This lanathess is no guardian. She is the cause of this war. The catalyst for naik'avel!"

"I'm trying to help you!" Neer retorted.

Reiman lifted his hand to quiet her. "Nerana," he said, "you are no longer needed here. Excuse yourself."

"But—"

"Now."

She cast a hateful glare at the warriors and then marched away.

Chapter Twenty-Five

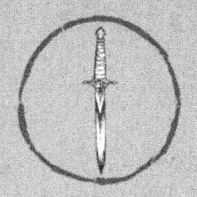

A Rightful Respite
Nerana

"What's the use in livin' if you don't got no songs to sing?"

– Ebbard of Rhys

FLAMES POPPED ABOVE A LARGE campfire, sending embers into the air. Neer sat by its heat at a long wooden table with Avelloch, Thurandír, Gil, and several others. Four dozen soldiers rested around two long tables, drinking and telling stories. Their boisterous voices filled the quiet forest with gruff laughter and snide remarks.

The evaesh warriors huddled around the glowing trees. Some were on their knees in deep meditations, while others spoke quietly to one another.

Cold air drifted across camp as the sun began to set, leaving the world dark. The Trees kept the air warm with magic, but it wasn't enough to offset the chill of late autumn. Soon, winter would be upon them, and Neer shuddered at the thought of the cold and snow.

"Pass me that satchel, would ya?" Gil asked.

A soldier passed him the jeweled garment, and Neer gazed at it for a moment.

"Is that Loryk's?" she asked.

"Aye," the dreled stated. "Blasted thief always knew how to find the best of things."

Neer reached for the satchel, and Gil handed it to her. She examined the beautiful material, remembering the day he had stolen it from the cave in Vleland.

"What's that?" Thurandír asked.

Neer explained, realizing he and Avelloch couldn't understand her conversation with the others. "My friend found this in Anaemiril."

His eyes widened with shock. "You went to Anaemiril?"

She nodded. "Twice, actually."

His jaw dropped.

"Don't look so surprised," she remarked with a grin. "It was Avelloch's idea. I had to go in and save him."

Thurandír glanced at Avelloch, searching for the truth. Avelloch gave Thurandír a playful shrug and then gulped from an alehorn. Neer stared at him for a moment, taking in the dark color staining his hair, hiding his platinum locks in an attempt to conceal his identity from the evaesh warriors. Had they known he was a disgraced and banished nesiat, they'd lose all faith in their fragile alliance with the Brotherhood.

Neer passed the satchel to Thurandír, who was eager to see a relic from the First Blood tombs.

As he examined its beautiful stitchwork, a familiar voice came from behind. Neer and Avelloch turned when Aélla walked through camp with the others, following behind Blaid. With suspicious eyes, the soldiers watched the group walk by. The evaesh leader trailed behind, eager to speak with her and learn the truth of her alliance with Reiman and the Brotherhood.

Aélla approached Reiman's tent, and the guards greeted her with their weapon's drawn. Y'ven stood, ready to defend, but Reiman quickly called them to disarm. He stepped out of the tent and bowed to Drimil'Rothar. They spoke for a moment, appeasing the avel leader's questions before he stepped away with a respectful bow.

Returning to his men, Reiman spoke briefly to Aélla. He then swung his arm in Neer's direction, and the others turned to view her sitting by the fire. Their guarded expressions became relaxed. He waved his arms openly toward the camp, undoubtedly inviting them to stay.

Many of the soldiers sneered and quickly left the table as the evae approached. Neer stood when they came closer.

"There you go again," Thallon stated with a shake of his head. "Are we going to have to tie you up next time, lanathess?"

The tension faded at his playful words, and Neer cast him a glare. "Aren't the evae supposed to be quicker than humans?"

He ruffled her hair as he stepped by and took his place next to Thurandír. Avelloch stood by Neer as Aélla and Klaud approached.

Aélla's hands twisted together at her waist. She stared at the ground with slumped shoulders. "I'm sorry," she said, her eyes darting between Neer and Thurandír. "You were right. I know that preventing naik'avel is our priority, but I can't lose sight of what's important."

Neer watched her for a moment, noticing the defeat and shame in her eyes. She understood this path wasn't easy, especially for Aélla, who sought to defeat a much greater threat than Neer would ever hope to fight. And she did so while retaining her dignity and holding close to her vows.

Aélla's eyes lifted when Neer extended her arm. She appeared stunned, unable to believe Neer had forgiven so quickly. When their eyes met, Neer smiled.

"We're in this together," she said. "*Senavae.**"

With a light grin, Aélla gripped her forearm. As they pulled away, Thurandír stood and extended his arm. Aélla looked into his eyes and then lowered into a deep bow. Thurandír watched her with confusion and awe. Their eyes connected when she rose, and she placed her hands on his shoulders.

"I'm with you," she vowed. "Just as you are with me."

His jaw clenched, and he gave her a stiff nod. "Thank you, Master Drimil," he said. "That means a lot, coming from you."

She smiled and then turned when Avelloch asked, "Did you hear from the Eirean?"

Aélla shook her head in despair. Avelloch scoffed and shook his head.

---

[*] Evaesh term meaning *sister*. Much like the term, *brenavae*, which means brother, it is commonly used amongst those who hold no blood relation but share a close bond.

"Fucking cowards. They're too afraid of Naisannis° and the Nasir to do anything."

Before she could respond, Klaud stepped closer, interrupting their conversation when he gripped a lock of Avelloch's dark hair. Their eyes met, and Klaud raised a brow. "You'll have to do better than this if you want to look like me, brenavae."

Avelloch laughed through his nose and shook Klaud's hand away. "It'll take a lot more trying to be as ugly as you."

Klaud shook with laughter. He gripped the back of Avelloch's head and pulled him close, resting their foreheads together. They stepped away with bright smiles, and everyone breathed a sigh of relief, happy to be in familiar company.

Klaud placed his hands on his hips and looked around, studying the strangers with a curious eye. "Why is a lanathess brigade here?" he asked. "What do they have to gain by fighting against the Klaet'il?"

Neer explained, "It's the Brotherhood. Our leader's evaesh."

"And they're working together with avel warriors?"

"For now. It won't last, though. Most of them want my head."

Aélla examined the three evaesh groups, which totaled no more than six warriors each. "We won't let that happen."

Flames spewed as a soldier removed roasted meat from a spit above the central firepit. He set them aside to cool.

"Smells good," Coryn stated while stepping by the cook.

He then casually made his way toward the group with a bright smile. Firelight glistened against his blond hair as he placed a jug of ale and an armful of wooden tankards atop the table.

° Naisannis Tormaris is the Eirean leader of the Klaet'il. While the Nasir is a notable figure, and many follow his every word, Naisannis holds all official authority and power over the clan.

"You're a fine-looking bunch," he teased. "Never thought I'd see a sack of people drearier than you, Neer."

She glared with a hidden smile. "It's a true mystery why I never kept you around, Coryn."

He chuckled and filled a tankard with ale. "I think Loryk was more than enough. That dog was always barking about something, yeah?"

Neer accepted his offering of ale and took a sip. She retched at its bitter taste.

"What'd you expect?" Coryn argued before passing a mug to Gil. "We aren't in Llyne anymore."

"Tastes like piss there too," Neer remarked.

Coryn shook with laughter. He reached across the table to offer the others a drink but came to a halt. His jaw dropped and eyes were wide. "God's body...is that a vaxros?"

Y'ven straightened, clearly recognizing the familiar word. Neer forced down another gulp of ale and wiped her lips.

"That's Y'ven."

Ale splashed against the table when Y'ven snatched a drink and chugged it without a wince. Thallon gave his drink a sniff and promptly handed it to Thurandír.

As the night grew longer, everyone was out of their wits and full of gleeful conversation. Gil had excused himself, leaving Neer alone with Coryn and her companions. Dru hovered in the fire, covering her ears at everyone's roaring voices. Several groups had begun singing giddy war songs, and soon, the forest was full of loud, boisterous voices.

Coryn and Neer shared a glance before joining in, performing the chant they'd known since childhood.

> "Broken, weary, suffering,
> We men are weak and wandering.
> Led by an elf, who would have known,
> This broken town would be our home!
>
> The Gods are good, or so they say

> We brothers here have 'lost our way.'
> No sounded sleep we'll have tonight
> For we fight 'til the morning light!
>
> So raise your sword and drink your ale
> Say goodbye to your Annabelle.
> For when we feast in hell at morn,
> Old Beinon's life will be no more!"

Neer and Coryn laughed and raised their mugs. Whistles and cheers resounded through the quiet woodlands. Aélla, Thurandír, and Thallon looked around with wide smiles.

"The lanathess sure know how to have a good time," Thallon remarked.

Klaud stated, "They're unusually rowdy, considering the battle we face."

Y'ven grumbled. "There are no fights. No bloodshed."

Neer playfully shook his shoulder and took another drink of ale, no longer able to taste its bitterness. "Many of us may die tomorrow," she said. "What better way to blow off steam than a night of good music and heavy drinking?"

"I'll drink to that!" Thurandír said, tapping her mug with his own.

A group gathered together near the center of camp. They beat on drums and played lively music on their lutes. Laughter filled the open space while soldiers began dancing and wrestling in the dirt. Coins clinked and knives tapped across the tables as people wagered on pinfingers and cribs.

Thallon and Thurandír boasted with stories, pulling the group into everlasting conversations and laughter. While they spoke, Neer watched the musicians play. Her heart thrummed with every pluck of the lute strings. For a moment, the grief she had so forcefully pushed away came to the surface. Being amongst her people, with so many she knew and loved, suddenly felt wrong.

Avelloch watched her sink further into the desolation of her mind. With a glance at the musicians, who were now surrounded by dancing men and women, he turned and reached out his hand to Neer.

She blinked her thoughts away and quickly wiped her eyes. With a quick glance at his hand, she became confused.

"Come on, *meena'keen*," he teased. "Let's dance."

A smile erased the despair clinging to her eyes. She took his hand and was led to the dance floor. The world spun as her senses were dulled. Music pulsed through the air, throbbing with the beat of her heart and rhythm of her feet against the grass. Laughter she hadn't felt in years echoed from her lips as she was spun and dipped.

Avelloch pulled her close, a drunken smile etched on his face. Her gaze was ripped away when they were pulled into the group dance, holding hands with everyone as they bounced and skipped together in a wide circle.

Thurandír excitedly squeezed into the formation, taking Neer's hand and dancing along without a skip in his stride. The others remained at the table, laughing and sharing drinks. Y'ven lay on the grass in a drunken slumber.

"The evae have no rhythm!" Thurandír said. He and Neer glanced at Avelloch, who was focused on his fumbling, uncoordinated feet. "Good thing the Zaeril doesn't have to dance his way through battle!"

Avelloch's unsteady glare caused them to erupt in a fit of laughter. They continued dancing with the others, giggling as Avelloch struggled to keep up with the quick-footed humans.

As the song came to an end, the group dispersed, and Thurandír pulled Neer away. She gave Avelloch a wry smile as she was twirled and led through the crowd.

Late morning came, along with the sound of retching, hungover men. Neer was alone, examining the map in Reiman's tent. She studied the formations and plans, hoping their casualties would be fewer than the Klaet'il. But she knew they would lose men. A lot of men. The Klaet'il were among the most vicious fighters in the world, and they didn't fight with honor, which made them unpredictable and dangerous.

Humans didn't stand a chance against the weakest of evae, yet they were there, fighting alongside their leader. A man who had given up his home for a chance at freeing the people he was once taught to hate. Neer knew evae and humanity would never see eye to eye, but she had hoped Reiman could carve a new path. One that saw coexistence and peace throughout the continent.

And that would start by ending the Order of Saro. But there would be no redemption if the forest burned at the hands of the Nasir. All life was equal. That was a tenet of the Brotherhood, one they vowed to protect. While the Order waited along the borders to invade, Reiman defended those the Eirean had turned a blind eye toward. He would bridge the gap between the races, and together, they'd fight against the Order, freeing their lands and uniting the peoples as one.

"Scout ahead," Reiman said, entering the tent with Gil and Morganis. "Be discreet. I'm under no belief the Klaet'il haven't sent spies to watch the village."

He glanced at Neer, who was still studying the map.

Gil added, "Should we collect more water for the men?"

"Get it done."

Gil and Morganis marched away, leaving Reiman alone with his daughter. He stepped to her side, watching her with a careful eye. "Finding flaws with the battleplans?" he asked.

Neer straightened and crossed her arms. "Just worried we'll lose a lot of people. The Klaet'il are much stronger than us."

"Don't underestimate our abilities. We've made it this far with minimal losses."

"They've been shitting themselves all morning."

He chuckled. "And you haven't?"

With a sideways glare, she refocused on the map. "I've seen too much battle to be bothered by its outcome."

"What may be, may be."

Their eyes met as he recited the same proverb he had repeated throughout her youth. Its message once rang loudly in her ears, helping her shove aside her worries and regrets. But time had forsaken its meaning, and she now realized that turning her grief into rage was far from the path she sought.

Refocusing on the map, she asked, "Where do you want me in this formation?"

He stood at her side. "Here," he said, pointing at the eastern gates. "Now that we have the elves, we can split into three groups. The Brotherhood will be here at the eastern gate, while the elves will enter from the west."

"Who is this?" she asked, pointing at a figurine in the northern section of the village.

Reiman picked up the figure and slowly spun it between his fingers. "I've spoken to Aélla. She and her brother will enter the village on their own, from the north."

Neer's blood ran cold. She glanced at Reiman, waiting for an explanation. He gently set the figure back in its place, and said, "They'll go directly to the earl's longhouse and protect the leadership. If the Klaet'il are going to invade, the earl and his family will be their target."

"Aélla's fighting?"

"I tried to keep her off the battlefield, but she's nearly as stubborn as you."

Her eyes fell to the map. "Where are the others positioned?"

"The elves will be together. You and Y'ven will be with the Brotherhood."

"The elves don't have enough men," she said. "Send some of ours their way to even out the formations. Doesn't matter if they don't like it—they've agreed to work together."

Reiman repositioned the figurines to Neer's approval.

She gazed at them. "I don't want Avelloch and Aélla going alone," she said. "They need more people."

"They need to be discreet. Aélla should be kept away from the battle, and she specifically chose her brother."

"I don't care." She spoke with an authority nearly identical to his own. "Give them more support. If they're ambushed, they won't stand a chance."

Reiman glared. He scratched his lip, contemplating his words.

Before he had the chance to speak, Neer said, "This isn't a debate."

Fury blazed in his eyes. His chest puffed and lips pursed. "Have you lost all wit?" he hissed. "Get out. Now."

Neer stood her ground, though she had never seen such anger in him. For a moment, she was afraid, looking into the eyes of someone much darker than she had ever known. Reiman had always been feared by the others for his authoritative presence, but he had never shown that side of himself to Neer. Even during her youth, when she was given severe punishments for showing the slightest signs of weakness, she was never afraid of him. His lessons were always given with purpose and followed with compassion.

She breathed heavily, feeling as though all the air had been sucked from the room. Crushed by the weight of his anger, Neer marched away.

Stepping outside, she walked past Morganis, who sat beneath a glowing Tree. Her legs were crossed and wide eyes were glowing white. Neer paused and eyed her curiously, never having seen anyone meditate in such a way.

"She's *stia'dyr*," Thallon said, approaching Neer from behind.

"What?"

Neer glanced at him and was taken aback by his appearance. He wore dark armor with a fur shawl. Green lines were drawn across his nose, cheeks, and forehead, giving him an intimidating look.

Thallon bit into a vegetable and said, "Stia'dyr. She's able to see through the eyes of an animal. It's pretty rare to be born with such a gift."

Neer thought for a moment and quickly remembered the white raven that had followed them through the forest when they first set off to find Aélla. "Do the Eirean have a stia'dyr?"

"All the men and women who were lined against the wall in their temple were stia'dyr."

Chills ran down her arms. "They just keep them there as servants?"

SHADOWS OF NYN'DIRA

"Some believe it's an honor to work so directly with the Eirean." His eyes veered to Morganis. "I guess she slipped through the cracks."

"Lucky her."

Thallon patted Neer's shoulder and then quietly walked away. Her eyes followed as he wandered through camp, and she noticed Y'ven sparring with Wallace. Dru hovered nearby, watching with fearful eyes as he struggled to stand upright. His eyes were dreary with sickness as the poison continued to spread through his veins.

Fear trickled through Neer's gut as she worried for his safety. She had hoped he would choose to stay behind, but Y'ven was a warrior. Death in battle was a vaxros's greatest honor, and he wouldn't allow his brothers to fight while he stayed behind.

Not wanting to disturb Y'ven, Neer scanned the camp, searching for the others. She spotted them kneeling by the spring together with the other evae. Men and women are all disrobed from the waist up, aside from Aélla, whose mamillare was wrapped securely around her chest.

Neer curiously approached them, watching as they washed their faces, arms, and chests. Large pitchers were filled with water and poured over the backs of their companions. Thurandír splashed his face and then blew his nose into the water one nostril at a time. Many others did the same. Those who had cleansed themselves pulled their hair into overlapping braids and painted their faces with black, red, or green designs, giving them fierce, intimidating appearances.

"What are you doing?" Neer asked.

Thurandír glanced up at her. "*Rad'fyir*," he explained. "We meditate at the Ko'ehlaeu'at trees and cleanse ourselves before battle."

Aélla added while scrubbing her arms, "The water heals us."

Klaud sat fully clothed by her side. He watched the warriors with sad eyes.

"You aren't joining them?" Neer asked.

"No," he said. "Nesiat are forbidden from partaking in sacred rituals."

Aélla argued, "You are not nesiat!"

Klaud was silent when she glanced back at him with a firm eye. She turned away and dipped her hand into a bowl of wet kohl and dragged her fingers diagonally across her face. She then lathered the kohl into her hair, dying it black. Without her white locks, she was nearly as unrecognizable as her brother.

Neer eyed the warriors surrounding the spring. Her brows knitted, and she asked, "Where's Avelloch?"

Klaud pointed toward the edge of the encampment, where Avelloch sat with Blaid beneath a glowing Tree. His steel sword was leaned against the trunk, and he peered at his reflection, marking his face with black designs.

Neer stepped closer and carefully knelt by his side. He glanced at her before refocusing on his task. She watched silently as he drew a familiar runic symbol across his left temple. Neer held her breath and looked at him, realizing how similar he appeared to the Nasir.

"What are you doing?" she asked, her voice trembling.

He completed the design and leaned back. Their eyes met, and she was shaken by the darkness in his eyes.

"Why do you look like that?" she pressed.

He turned away, reluctant to explain. "The last time I saw the Nasir, he was sliding a dagger down my spine." He paused with fury. "I want him to see that same monster when I drive my sword through his heart."

Neer breathed heavily. She touched the symbol on his face and quickly pulled her hand away, as if grazing the rune would somehow call upon the man himself. "You look just like him."

Avelloch turned away, disturbed. Deciding not to press him further, Neer stared at the design, remembering all the horrors inflicted by the Nasir. She absently touched the branded scar on her arm. Having it etched onto her skin was a permanent reminder of all she had been through. It was a mark tying her forever to those who had caused her such sorrow and pain. She could never escape it. Never be without it. The cloud of despair following her was forever engraved upon her skin.

She knew Avelloch carried that pain, and it now showed in the perfectly drawn runes on his face. Unable to see him in such a way—to brand himself and appear so undeniably similar to the man who had caused him so much agony—Neer grabbed a cleaning rag and dipped it into the bowl of water at Avelloch's side. She gently took his face and looked deep into his eyes. Tenderly, she pressed the rag against his temple and pulled downward, smearing the design. Avelloch stiffened beneath her touch.

"This is not who you are," she said. "He doesn't own you. He didn't make you. And when you kill him, it'll be *you* who breaks the chains."

She paused for a moment, happy to find the anger shielding his eyes was fractured. No longer did he stand beneath the weight of his rage.

"Keep your wit," she continued. "There are more important things than your vengeance."

The abrasive sound of a war horn echoed from the center of camp, and Neer flinched at its sudden noise. One blow was given, calling everyone forward. Humans, dressed in chainmail and gambeson armor, stood around the campfire. To the west, the evaesh warriors gathered together. Though they were allies, their presence alone unsettled the humans, who kept a fair distance and cut them fearful glances.

The avel's leather armor, polished swords, and fierce appearances were a stark contrast to the lesser equipped, trembling humans. They were gods among men. A true testament to their ferocity and strength. Gazing between them, Neer understood the fear they emitted. Had she not known the evae—not been introduced to their customs or trained by their best warriors—she'd find herself quivering too.

Reiman exited his tent, and Neer glanced around, searching for Gil, who was usually at his side.

"The Klaet'il will not take another soul," Reiman said, and the crowds fell silent. "We will march forward and put an end to their tirade. No longer shall the people suffer beneath the hands of the wicked. Today, and all days to come, we will fight. We will conquer. We will prevail!"

Everyone raised their swords with loud cheers. Boots stomped against the ground in a rhythmic chant.

"Let no man die without blood on his steel and strength in his heart!" Reiman called above the chaos. "Walk tall, my brothers! Let us look death in the eye and strike our blades through its heart!"

The forest trembled as they cheered.

Their rallying was interrupted by a deep gasp that came from Morganis, who sat in her meditations. The Tree behind her flickered with the light of her eyes, and she choked on her breath. Soon, the crowd quieted, and everyone turned to her.

"Mor?" Coryn called. He pushed through the crowd and rushed to her side. "Morganis? Snap out of it!"

He tapped her face and shook her shoulders, but her eyes never closed. The flickering never ceased.

Stuck in her meditations, Morganis began to seize. Her body shook, and white foam spilled from her lips. An unsettled murmur moved through the crowd. When Coryn touched her shoulder, Morganis turned to the sky and unleashed an agonized scream. Her back arched and arms curled toward her chest. The Tree brightened. Its light was blinding. Her raw voice penetrated the silence.

Suddenly, she collapsed to the ground. The echo of her screams still rang through everyone's minds. Sunlight replaced the glow of the Tree as it stood dormant and limp, no longer casting its constant stream of light.

No one breathed. They only stared at Morganis, who lay slumped in the dirt. Her head had fallen aside and eyes were dull. Blood trickled from her nose and ears.

"Mor?" Coryn said, his voice becoming frantic. "Morganis!"

He attempted to revive her, breathing into her mouth and thrusting his hands against her chest. Aélla made her way through the crowd. She knelt at Coryn's side, hoping to give her aid, but Coryn shoved her back.

As she tumbled aside, Klaud appeared instantly behind Coryn, pressing the tip of his spear against his back. The avel warriors drew their weapons, and Aélla quickly raised her arm, holding off an attack against the still-frantic human.

Klaud stepped back at Aélla's silent command. His simmering eyes were fixed on Coryn, who hadn't seemed to notice the others as he focused on saving Morganis.

He continued pushing against her chest. "No…" he said through clenched teeth. "Come on! Come on!" He beat his fist against her unmoving chest. "Come on!"

Reiman inhaled a deep breath. He stepped to Coryn's side and gently placed a hand on his shoulder. Coryn shook his head, reluctant to give up. With a deep huff, he slumped forward and rubbed his face.

"Her raven was killed," Reiman explained. With a grave voice, he turned to the crowd and announced with unshakable strength, "They know we're here."

CHAPTER TWENTY-SIX

Taken
Nerana

Neer stood at the war table with Reiman, Wallace, Avelloch, and the evaesh commander, Cael.

"What do we do?" she asked, not caring to translate for the evae to understand. "We have to find him!"

"Our priorities must remain on the mission," Reiman stated, staring at the figurines with distant eyes. "Gilbrich has survived for centuries without—"

"Reiman," Neer demanded. She leaned over, forcing their eyes to meet. There was fear in him—it was heavily guarded, but she felt it. "We. Have. To. Find. Him."

His jaw clenched, not of anger, but concern. He shifted his gaze back to the map, scanning it diligently with his hardened eyes.

Cael spoke quietly, saying, "What does this mean for our people? We can't rush in if they know we're coming."

Avelloch's chest puffed, and he crossed his arms. "We should call off the attack," he said.

"What?" Cael argued. "We can't allow the Klaet'il to get away with this!"

"If we rush in now, they'll be waiting. We can't—"

"What are you saying?" Neer interjected.

They turned to her, taken aback by her anger.

"We aren't abandoning these people! We aren't abandoning Gil!"

Reiman placed his hand on her shoulder. "No one's saying that," he stated. "But we need a plan."

"What plan?" She shook his hand away. "If they know we're coming, they'll take the villagers and leave before we get the chance to do anything. We have to go *now*. Our goal was never to defeat the Klaet'il—it was to protect the villagers, right? To find those that were taken and make this right!"

She glanced between them, suddenly realizing their goals had become personal. They didn't truly wish to save anyone. Their mission was to kill the Nasir and put an end to his massacres.

"You...," she started, pausing to collect her thoughts. "You're disgusting! All of you!"

"Nerana—"

"Don't give me that! You were never going to try to find Thurandír's people, were you?"

Reiman's face hardened with anger. Lines formed between his brows as he stared at Neer, who held a damning glare. She shook her head and paced back and forth, overcome with fury. Her body trembled and chest ached with the icy sting of frost and rage.

"How could you do this?" she said. "How could you lie like this?"

"We hoped to find his people," Reiman said, speaking with authority that demanded respect. "But it was never a guarantee. Our goal was always to stop the Klaet'il. You understand the sacrifices of war, Nerana. You *cannot* save everyone."

"I made a promise, Reiman." Her eyes burned through his, spewing with the fire that simmered deep in her soul. "We aren't letting this happen to anyone else."

"We have to do this rationally. If we storm into Ik'Nharaii, we will—"

"Save a lot more people than if we're standing here, wasting time with senseless battleplans!" She swiped the figurines off the table and glared at her father. "I won't lose him."

His condemning stare was enough to break even the bravest of men, but Neer was strengthened by it. Holding her father's gaze, she felt a swell of energy rising within her, tearing at her soul, begging to be unleashed. She wouldn't allow Gil to be taken. The war and gods and fate be damned, she would find him.

Her chest ached as she fought against the fury festering inside. She lurched forward, gripping her chest. Reiman and Avelloch reached over, lending their hands, but she pushed them away.

"Don't touch me!" she snapped and then marched from the tent.

Outside, she spotted several Brotherhood soldiers placing Morganis's body onto a makeshift pyre of chopped wood and dried leaves. They stared down at her as the tinder was lit, and Neer turned away, tired of so much death and grief.

At the center of camp, Aélla sat with the others. Their downcast eyes were a reminder of the fear and pain they all endured. Neer looked at each of them for a moment longer before shifting her eyes to the firepit where Y'ven stood alone. He stared down at the flames, which had been constantly burning since his arrival. Dru was amid the flames, soaking up as much heat as she could in the cool autumn days.

Neer studied Y'ven's slumped posture, yellowed skin, and bandaged arm. He was growing weaker, and everyone feared the worst. Blinking away the tears that burned her eyes, Neer calmly approached his side. Y'ven glanced at her, then returned his attention to the fire.

"How are you feeling?" she asked.

They were silent as the flames popped and whirred. He held his arms over the heat, careful not to catch the linen bandage ablaze.

Y'ven gave her a tired, grunted response.

Neer closed her eyes. "Y'ven," she started, knowing he would argue, as he had each time it was mentioned. "You need to stay behind."

His lips pursed and eyes narrowed, slightly. In his weakened state, he could hardly muster the chagrin and anger that would typically twist his face.

"Listen to me, please." She touched his arm and looked up at him, but he refused to meet her eyes. "Being a warrior means knowing when to fight and when to flee. If you go out there, you *will* die." Her grip tightened. "If you don't treat this...you will die. Your son will never know his father's name. Dru will lose her truest family."

Neer paused, waiting for him to speak. But Y'ven remained firm in his beliefs, not showing an ounce of consideration to her tearful pleas.

Closing her eyes, she said, "Please, Y'ven...You won't prove anything by going out there and dying. Let us help you...I can't lose anyone else."

He was silent and stiff for a moment. Slowly, he placed his large hand atop her. She looked up at him, expecting to meet his gaze. But his eyes were focused on the fires.

Speaking vax, he said, "I have lived through many terrible things. I've lost my bond mate, my son, my brother, my home...my pride..." He paused. "My son will know his father fought to restore his honor. He will know there is strength in our blood."

Neer was shaken with grief when he turned to meet her eyes.

"I will not cower in defeat," he said. "When I die, it will be by the blade, not the venom coursing through my veins. I will fight, Ürok." His voice was strong. "I will fight."

Neer's lip quivered. She turned away and nodded, accepting his answer.

The flames felt hotter as grief and despair swirled through her, but she held herself together. Sulking wouldn't save them. It wouldn't bring back those who were lost. She had to fight to protect those she loved. Just like Y'ven, she had to fight.

Her thoughts were broken when Altvára flew overhead with a resounding *caw*. Klaud had sent him to search the area for any sign of Gil soon after Morganis's death. The raven dove into Reiman's tent, and Neer watched with a heavy heart as her father exited with the others.

She held her breath, ready to find him.

Ready for war.

A horn blew, and everyone gathered around. There was a blanket of grief and sorrow that fell over their hearts, shrouding the world in layers of irrevocable silence. They'd lost hope, and that was a dangerous thing.

Reiman stood tall with his arms behind his back. He surveyed the group before him with proud, strong eyes. "I know these times are trying for us all," he began, speaking with confidence that caused many to lift their eyes.

The evaesh commander translated for his warriors.

"But we will not falter beneath the hands of the wicked," Reiman continued. "The elves are no different than the Knights we've slain time and time again. These ruthless men with ruthless hearts will show no mercy. They will rip and tear until they have taken all that is ours. But no more!"

He raised his sword, reflecting sunlight against the faces before him.

"We will bring justice to those who have fallen!" he called, and the crowd stood taller.

Purpose filled their defeated eyes. Their shoulders broadened and chins rose as Reiman spoke truthful words laced with undeniable power.

"We will avenge all who have been taken! Every life—every drop of blood will have a name! We will not cower now! Stand with me, brothers! Let us fight for those without voices! Let us fight for those who have fallen! Let us fight for our freedom!"

A roar of cheering erupted through the crowd as the soldiers stomped and raised their swords high.

"Let us ride!" Reiman called. "And take back what is ours!"

The ground trembled as soldiers gathered their weapons and stood in tight formations. Commanders paced at the front lines, shouting orders to their men. Avel warriors stood tall and proud, their dark armor a shadow against the evergreen.

Neer was at her horse, hesitant. Her hands shook as she tightened her saddle. She closed her eyes and exhaled several slow, calming breaths. Gil's face entered her mind, and bile rose in her throat. She shook her head to push the thoughts away.

He would make it. She wouldn't let him die.

The horse whinnied, and she patted its neck. Searching for the source of its sudden fear, she found Blaid sitting at her side. Their eyes met, and she gave him a sad, quivering smile.

"You should stay behind," she said. "I need to know at least one thing I care about will make it through today."

Blaid snorted in response, and Neer exhaled a laugh. She knelt to his side and scratched behind his ears.

"Keep them safe, yeah?" she said. "The *Zaeril* likes to think himself invincible."

Blue eyes met with hers, and Blaid huffed. Neer pulled her hands away and gave him a stern look.

Raising a brow, she said, "I should've known you do too."

As soldiers filtered into the stables to saddle their stallions and mares, Neer mounted her horse and rode to Reiman's side. Her eyes flicked to Avelloch's, who sat atop a large horse with Aélla. He gave her a stiff nod, and she returned the gesture.

Her eyes moved to the others, who were scattered across the formations. Coryn stood in white apothecary robes, while the others wore darker colors suited for the forest. Klaud, Thurandír, and Thallon were grouped with the avel.

The war horn sounded with two quick bursts, and everyone marched forward, heading deep into the forest. Closer to finding the Nasir and saving Gil.

The sun was fading into early evening as Neer rode through the forest with Reiman. Two formations of warriors were behind them, marching toward the village gates, hoping to reach them before the Klaet'il made their attack. But Neer had other plans. While the others would continue toward the village, sealing the gates and protecting the residents, she, Reiman, and Wallace would follow Altvára to Gil.

Horse hooves beat against the soil, disturbing the silence as the trio steered away from the soldiers behind, following an unmarked path into the woods. Birds took flight and animals scurried away, hiding from the noise.

They rode quickly through the forest, and Neer kept her eyes on the raven, being sure to stay on his path. Her face was red and lips were pursed. A hollow pit formed in her chest, growing larger with every stride of her mare.

Teal eyes scanned the forest, searching for any sign of her missing friend. Water splashed against her breeches when the horse trudged through a shallow creak, and low-hanging limbs swept against her face, causing light red lines to form across her cheeks. Her eyes narrowed as she looked ahead, where a faint stream of grey smoke rose from the grass.

Neer leaned forward, and the horse ran faster. Reiman called out to her, demanding that she keep close, but she ignored his commands. Her heart thundered in her chest, matching the beat of the hooves smashing against the ground. Gil was there. She could feel it. He had to be.

Her horse whinnied and came to a halt when Neer pulled back the reins. She breathed heavily, staring at the campsite. A smoldering fire was surrounded by white, blood-spattered feathers. Small chamber pots were overturned, leaking with foul odor and brown liquid. Dozens of impressions were laid upon the grass in the shapes of bedrolls.

The limbs rustled above, and Neer snatched her sword while looking upward. Through the golden leaves, she spotted a white squirrel leaping through the branches.

"Nerana!" Reiman snapped, approaching her side. "Have you lost all wit?"

"They were here," she said.

Reiman exhaled a sharp breath. He focused on the feathers. Without speaking, he dismounted his horse and approached the fire. Neer followed, and Wallace gathered their horses. Reiman knelt to the ground and collected a feather. His eyes narrowed, and he twisted the quill between his fingers.

"What is this?" Neer asked.

"These are Morganis's feathers," he explained. "They belonged to her raven."

Neer scanned the bloody mess beneath her boots. Thin animal bones were scattered throughout the quills. Kneeling by the embering pit, searching for clues, Neer spotted the charred remains of a raven. Its neck was broken, and a deep wound opened its chest.

"Is this how she died?" she asked, her eyes glued to the animal. She gazed for seconds longer, hoping this raven wasn't Gil, who had transformed himself before scouting ahead.

Reiman dropped the feather and wiped his hand on his cloak. His light blue eyes scanned the quiet forest. With a nod, he said, "If the connection is severed before the host rejoins with their companion, their brains will hemorrhage."

Neer turned away and closed her eyes. The raven had been brutally attacked before having its neck snapped. Morganis's scream echoed in Neer's mind. The blood-curdling cries, her eyes flickering and body convulsing. She must've felt everything just before its life was taken, severing their connection and sealing her fate.

Slowly, Neer rose to her feet. She pushed the thoughts of Morganis from her mind. Now wasn't the time for sorrow or guilt. Searching the area, Neer noticed the feathers led north. She tapped Reiman's arm and pointed out the path. He inhaled a deep breath.

"Stay here," he said, unsheathing his sword. "I'll—"

"I'm going with you."

Their eyes met, and he gave her a light nod, knowing she wouldn't back down. He raised his hand to Wallace in a silent command to stay put. The warrior didn't argue. He stood strong and tall in his position by the fire, clutching the giant broadsword in his thick fists.

Neer followed Reiman forward. Their eyes were on the forest, searching the trees and limbs above. Her heart pounded in her throat, and weak knees carried her onward. She wouldn't give up. Gil wouldn't be made a victim of the Klaet'il. She'd burn this forest down before allowing him to suffer.

More rustling came from above. Neer and Reiman turned upward, their swords raised. While she examined the limbs, Reiman scanned the forest floor. His narrowed eyes veered slowly from left to right.

"Come," he said, and Neer trailed behind.

They followed the path of feathers, knowing it was a trap but having no other choice. Altvára had led them here—to this place. They couldn't turn back now.

Reiman said, "Gilbrich could be—" He turned sharply to the left and demanded, "Shield!"

Neer dropped her weapon and raised hands. Energy burned in her chest as she created a dome-shaped barrier around them. Fire ripped through her veins as arrows rained from the sky, smashing against her magic. Sweat rolled down her face, and her throat burned as she released a raw, bloody scream.

Reiman whipped his head from left to right. He breathed heavily, panicked. Suddenly, the assault came to a pause, and the world was deathly silent. White cracks crazed the shimmering barrier like thick webs, making it difficult to see the world around. Raspy breaths escaped Neer's throat as she struggled to maintain her energy. Her arms were weak and chest ached.

Teal eyes veered to Reiman when drew his sword as a shadow lurked nearby.

"Hold," he said to Neer.

She grunted, raising her arms higher, willing herself to keep hold of the barrier. Through tired eyes, she watched a figure in a dark hooded cloak step closer. Sunlight erased the shadow of his hood, revealing the gaunt, lifeless face of the Nasir. Soulless eyes stared at Reiman as they stood face-to-face, separated only by Neer's fragile shield.

Black veins surrounded the Nasir's dark, sunken eyes. He struck his hand forward, and Neer shuddered when his icy touch moved through her barrier.

A sharp wheeze came from Reiman when the Nasir clutched his throat, squeezing tightly.

"No!" Neer screamed.

Her barrier vanished, and she swung her sword. The blade swept through the air, moving closer to the Nasir. Just before it sliced deep into his flesh, he turned, and Neer's fury faded to horror when her blade struck against Reiman's side.

Chapter Twenty-Seven

A Fleeting Dream
Aélla

GOLDEN RAYS OF A FADING sun sprayed across the horizon as Aélla rode with Avelloch through the quiet woods. A sprawling lake was to their left, sparkling with early evening sunlight. Aélla gazed upon its beauty, wishing for peace. Hoping those she loved would make it through this alive.

Since their journey began, she and Avelloch had hardly spoken a word. She knew he was worried, though he'd never speak it aloud. They had few moments together throughout their lives, as time and circumstances had caused their paths to drift apart. But distance couldn't sever the bond they shared. No one understood their struggles, and in many ways, they only had each other.

He turned back to look at her, and she quickly turned away. His eyes lingered on her for a moment longer. "We'll make it," he said.

She nodded. "But will the others?"

"Klaud would never leave you behind. You know that." He refocused on the forest ahead. "Thallon's good at running away, and the others can hold their own."

A sad smile pulled her lips. She wanted his words to help, but the dread of knowing this could all come to an end pressed too heavily on her soul. She gulped down her swelling emotions and crossed her arms, fighting against the pain that begged to release.

Her eyes moved to the horizon, where the sun began its descent. The days were falling shorter, and with each new dawn, Aélla felt the tug of icy energy beckoning her toward its everlasting embrace. It was a struggle to fight against it on the best of days, when the world was at peace and kanavin didn't roam the lands.

But now, it was unbearable.

She exhaled a shallow breath and closed her eyes. "He's going to be there."

She didn't have to say his name. Avelloch understood who she spoke of.

"He was in Aragoth," she continued. "I spoke to him…I…"

Tears spilled from her eyes, and Avelloch pulled the reins, coming to a stop. Her chest heaved, and she sobbed into her hands. Avelloch reached back and clutched her arm. His touch was gentle and strong. But she knew more than anyone how deep this wound festered inside him. What the Nasir had done to them was unforgiveable. And Avelloch carried that rage, allowing it to simmer and grow as he spent his days outcast and alone, haunted by what his life had become.

"I'm sorry," she whispered. "For all he's done to you…for what he's done to us…"

He turned away, staring at the water with a tight jaw. When he cleared his throat, Aélla wiped her tears and grasped at the strands of strength that seemed to wane with each passing day.

"There is something inside of him, Avelloch. Something dark." She paused. "He can't be stopped."

Avelloch inhaled a deep breath. Sunlight reflected against the water and glistened across his painted face. For a moment, he was silent and still, and she hoped he would gift her with words of encouragement. But his eyes seeped with fury and regret. Deep anger silenced any notion of peace that could quell the ache in his soul. But they knew that once the Nasir was gone—once the world was made anew—they could finally embrace the serenity they had searched so long to find.

"Come on," he said, breaking her thoughts. He clicked his tongue, and the horse continued, walking slowly toward the large village walls in the distance.

With every step, they drew closer, and Aélla's heart thundered in her chest. She didn't want to face him. She didn't want to lose anyone she loved.

"Avelloch," she started, struggling to find the words.

He was silent as he waited. Patient, as always.

"I'm very glad you're here with me," she said. "And I'm sorry this is the path I've chosen…The last thing I ever want to do is leave you behind."

She licked her lips and blinked her tears away.

"If we don't make it through today…I just need you to know that I couldn't ask for a better brother. Despite what the world may think of you, I am proud to be your family."

Avelloch didn't breathe as his eyes shifted to the ground. When he blinked, his posture relaxed. Slowly, he turned back and touched Aélla's arm. His grip was heavy, as if he were leaning on her for strength. When their gazes met, she was stricken by the pain in his eyes. For so long, he had been outcast and alone. There weren't many memories they shared since his banishment, and she was glad to have him by her side now.

Looking into his eyes, she knew he felt the same.

Closer to the village, they spotted several large huts gathered amidst the trees. Aélla had never visited Ik'Nharaii, but she knew it was the largest e'liaa settlement in all of Nyn'Dira. Their governments involved a mixture of lanathess and evaesh customs.° Despite the prejudice from the forest clans, the e'liaa were mostly kind and welcoming to all. Aélla had always admired that strength to coexist, even in the face of adversity.

A large wall, surrounded by leaves and tall grass, protected the village. Its only points of entry were the east and western gates, which would soon be occupied by the avel and Brotherhood forces.

° Earl Braskán was a lanathess. His great-great-grandparents helped found the e'liaan communities in an attempt to bridge the gap between evae and lanathess. While it worked to create several prospering villages throughout the forest, it led to indisputable hostility between the natives, particularly the klaet'il, who view e'liaa as dro'famehl, or unworthy.

Aélla stared up at its height as she and her brother dismounted the saddle. She turned to Avelloch and clutched his hand. "Are you ready?" she asked.

He glanced at her before turning back to the wall. With a deep breath, he gave a subtle nod and closed his eyes. Aélla focused on her energy and teleported them to the other side.

They reappeared within the city and stumbled forward. Aélla caught herself on the porch railing of a nearby home. She glanced around, expecting resistance. But there was silence. The dirt roads were empty, and homes were quiet.

Her stomach churned. She glanced at her brother, and the fear in his eyes was more telling than any words he could ever speak. Purple light shimmered against Avelloch's sword, and he held it close. Aélla's heart vibrated her chest. She walked alongside her brother, waiting for someone to emerge. Wondering how the Klaet'il could have attacked such a protected city. There was no bloodshed or evidence of a fight. No disheveled thatching on the roofs from glynfir talons. No markings of the fil'veraal or bodies lying in the streets.

"They must've evacuated," Aélla said. "Surely, they—"

She inhaled a sharp gasp when a loud noise shuffled from inside the Earl's longhouse. Avelloch stood before her. His fists were tight around the hilt of his blades, and he breathed heavily as they slowly, quietly, stepped around the side of the cabin and peered at its front entry. Three Klaet'il warriors stood guard—two on a balcony above the door with longbows, one below with a long sword.

"He's tóavel," Avelloch explained of the lone guard below. "See the markings on his chest?"

Aélla's heart jolted. Tóavel warriors were among the fiercest and most agile fighters of the Klaet'il. They earned their markings for every avel warrior they'd slain. Fifteen were needed to complete the design, and this warrior had two, with a third nearly complete.

"Stay here," Avelloch whispered. "I'll take out the archers and then—"

"You aren't doing this alone."

SHADOWS OF NYN'DIRA

His lips pursed together before he turned away. Whatever waited for them, it wouldn't be met with kindness. The Klaet'il had laid their trap, and it was too late to turn back. They had to know what happened to the missing villagers. Had to put an end to the Klaet'il's madness.

Avelloch turned to her and whispered his plan. Her eyes widened with fear. She started to protest, but he placed his hand to her lips. Their eyes met, and she knew to trust him. She held his gaze for as long as he'd allow, and when he stepped away, she inhaled a quiet gasp.

She turned from left to right, searching for him in the alley or rooftops. But he was gone. A whisper in the wind. Gulping down her fear, Aélla pressed herself against the wall, and slowly, painfully slowly, she inched around to the front of the cabin. Her breathing was ragged and body trembled with fear.

She peered around the porch and then stepped into the open. The chattering sound of Klaet'il voices became silent when she came into view. Her eyes lifted to the warriors. Their looming glares struck her with fear, and her legs quivered, begging to run. But she willed herself to stay put.

Harsh voices broke through the silence, and chills ran down Aélla's arms. An archer nocked his arrow, while the guard below readied his weapon. She glanced at each of them, noticing their sly laughter and cunning grins.

Following Avelloch's plan, Aélla bowed her head and lifted her arms. As she did, an archer drew back his arrow. Just before it was released, a shadow leapt onto the balcony from behind. Avelloch snaked his arm around the guard and pierced a dagger through the back of his neck.

A choked gasp spewed blood into the air. Before the man hit the ground, Avelloch turned sharply, whipping his blade across the second archer's throat. A line of red formed across his skin. Blood drained down his chest, and the man collapsed to his knees, gurgling. Bubbles formed across his throat as he fought for breath.

The guard below turned around with confusion and anger. His eyes widened when he noticed his comrades lying in pools of their own blood. Not a trace of their assailant was left behind. Avelloch had slipped away, disappearing before the second archer's body hit the ground.

The last Klaet'il turned to Aélla, who remained in her deep bow. His furious words carved through the air, and he marched forward. Sunlight glinted against his sword, pointed in her direction.

She breathed heavily, arms still raised, head still bowed. His footsteps drew closer, but she remained intensely still. Silent. Waiting.

Aélla could smell his stench as he stood before her. With a growl, he raised his weapon, and she closed her eyes, trusting her brother. He had told her to remain still. Don't fight back. Save her energy for whoever was inside. And so, she would.

The cold touch of sharp steel embraced her neck, and before it bit into her flesh, slicing her head from her neck, the Klaet'il inhaled a sudden, sharp gasp. Aélla trembled. The blade hovered against her skin before ripping away when the Klaet'il turned around.

He reached back and yanked a dagger from his shoulder. Blood drained down his back, coating his markings and scars in red. A raw, vicious scream vibrated from his throat.

"*Keth'saun* Zaeril *nor'kraa tumavëk*," he growled before spitting on the ground.

Aélla lifted her eyes, searching for Avelloch. The Klaet'il glanced from left to right. He stepped back, bringing himself closer to her, and she leapt back when he stumbled with a pained growl. Landing on his knee, he reached with a shaky hand, clutching the shaft of an arrow lodged in his side.

Breathing heavily, the Klaet'il tore it from his flesh. He stood, chest heaving. Eyes blazing with fury. Another arrow swept from the east, and the warrior spun aside, swiping it with his sword. The arrow snapped in two. Splinters fell to the ground at his feet.

He scanned the roofs and balconies, searching for Avelloch. But there was no one. He was a ghost. A shadow in the sun, unable to be seen.

SHADOWS OF NYN'DIRA

Aélla gasped when the Klaet'il yanked her back and shoved a dagger against her throat. She felt her every heartbeat thump against the blade. Her frantic eyes searched the rooftops. He wouldn't allow her to die.

She had to trust.

The guard shouted wildly to the wind, calling upon the Zaeril. A dark figure emerged from an alley to their left, and the Klaet'il turned to view him. Avelloch stalked forward, twisting his weapons in his hands. Dark eyes set on the man holding Aélla.

Fear trickled down her spine. It wasn't her brother who stood before her. His hair, face, and eyes belonged to another. Someone much worse. Far more vicious and cunning.

Avelloch paced back and forth, the blades still spinning. His eyes flicked to Aélla, and he gave her a subtle nod.

She understood his silent command. And as his fingers wriggled against his weapons, Aélla closed her eyes. Energy culminated in her chest, expanding through her limbs and into her palms. She placed her hands upon the Klaet'il's arm and turned to face him. Their eyes met, and she melded their minds. Her energy wove through his thoughts, securing them to her will.

"Release me," she whispered.

The pressure of his grasp receded when he stepped back, and Avelloch raced forward. Aélla spoke to the Klaet'il through her mind, forcing him to release his weapon. He obeyed, unable to break free from her will, so long as their eyes were connected and her hands were upon his flesh. But her energy was waning. It clawed at her chest and sent ice through her veins.

When she blinked, their connection was severed. She quickly backed away, putting distance between them.

The Klaet'il turned when Avelloch lunged at him from behind. Avelloch leapt into the air, striking his blade at the Klaet'il's back. The Klaet'il flipped aside and grabbed his longsword. When he struck, Avelloch leapt aside, but his skin was split when the blade sliced into his shoulder.

He staggered aside with a hiss. Blood dripped through his fingers when he clutched his arm. The Klaet'il cackled and spoke with sharp, cutting words. Avelloch's lip twitched. Fury displayed in his dark eyes. When the Klaet'il charged, Avelloch raised his weapons.

Steel clashed. Avelloch blocked the attack with his left hand and struck at the Klaet'il's side with his right. The Klaet'il leaned aside and kneed Avelloch in the groin. Avelloch lurched forward with a pained gasp. Bloody fingers grabbed his face, and the hard crack of their skulls resounded as the Klaet'il smashed their foreheads together.

Avelloch dropped his swords and stumbled back. He collapsed to the ground in a daze. Blood drained down his face in lines of red, cascading over his eyes and lips. The Klaet'il marched forward. He stood over Avelloch, looking down with hateful eyes. Aélla stepped closer, but Avelloch lifted his hand, stopping her.

Her jaw dropped. She gazed at her brother, fearful. His breathing was ragged and tired eyes struggled to stay open.

"Zaeril *muiro griva*," the Klaet'il said with pride.

He struck his blade at Avelloch's chest. Aélla lifted her arms, ready to stop him with her magic. But before she could, Avelloch twisted his legs around the Klaet'il's ankle.

He crashed to the ground, and Avelloch knelt over him. The Klaet'il yelped when Avelloch punched his injured side. He struck his face, and the Klaet'il's teeth flung from his lips.

"What are you doing here?" Avelloch shouted. His voice was raw.

He grabbed a handful of the Klaet'il's hair and lifted him up. Their faces were close. Blood trickled from the Klaet'il's parted lips.

"Where are they?"

A sinister smile twisted the Klaet'il's face. Laughter erupted from his throat, and Avelloch snarled.

Aélla reached forward when the Klaet'il snatched a dagger from the sheath on his hip. As he struck upward, the weapon disappeared from his grasp. Avelloch's eyes narrowed when the Klaet'il's empty fist slammed against his side. Their eyes met, and Avelloch pushed him back.

The Klaet'il thrashed beneath him, but Avelloch squeezed his throat. Eyes of pure rage stared down at the man beneath him, watching his life slowly drain. His arms were tight and lips were pursed. Scratches covered his face and neck as the Klaet'il fought against him, attempting to break free.

But Avelloch was built of stone, unflinching. The Klaet'il's eyes became red, and his body fell limp. Blood-coated fingers slowly released their grip on the Klaet'il's bruised throat.

Aélla stood, watching her brother kneel over the man he killed. She had never seen such darkness in anyone. Such ruthless anger. Lost in her misery, she dropped the Klaet'il's dagger.

As it fell to the ground, Avelloch turned to meet her gaze. His expression was deadly, but beneath the fury and hatred, there was sorrow and shame. He could see the fear in her eyes. She couldn't hide it. Slowly, he turned away, staring at the hands that had taken so many lives. His shoulders slouched when he bowed his head.

The sun dipped beneath the edge of the world, and the forest was dark. Clouds blanketed the sky, concealing the glow of the moons. A chill ran down Aélla's arms. She glanced through the village, searching for her people, knowing they should arrive shortly. But there was no one. The streets were empty.

A crash resounded from within the longhouse. It shook the walls and echoed loudly through the quiet village. Aélla stepped back with a gasp. Avelloch was at her side, his swords in hand. Dark eyes fixed on the longhouse.

Another jolt shook the cabin. Aélla lifted her arms, ready to defend. She breathed heavily and winced at the harsh sting of dark energy pricking her skin. It was in the air, all around them. They breathed it in like poison.

"Avelloch," she whispered, her voice thick with terror. He slowly turned to her, and when their eyes met, she was weighted by his fear.

His eyes ripped away when the doors of the longhouse burst open. Splinters rained through the air, landing atop the ground at their feet. A deep, sawing growl vibrated from a shadow stalking through the entry. Its long snout, covered in torn flesh that exposed its teeth, slowly appeared through the darkness.

It took another step closer, and glowing hazel eyes shone through the veil of shadows. A deep scar stretched over the creature's left brow. Its large body was a twisted mixture of different creatures. Four paws, with claws long as a hand, scraped against the wooden entry. Antlers rose from its wide, bear-like head.

Avelloch pulled Aélla back as the creature climbed down the steps. It stood on the street several paces ahead. Aélla flinched when it turned to the sky and exhaled an ear-shattering roar. The sound was a culmination of several different animals calling all at once.

But beneath it all, lingering within the fractured, woven growls, was the voice of a dreled. High-pitched and raspy, it spoke only a single word.

"*Run!*"

And then it charged.

Chapter Twenty-Eight

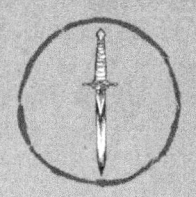

A Touch of Death
Nerana

As the blade split the fibers of Reiman's tunic, Neer's sword vanished and reappeared instantly in her opposite hand. She fell into a defensive posture, glaring into the Nasir's cold, dead eyes.

"Where is he?" she demanded.

He glowered and then shoved Reiman aside. Her father fell to the dirt with a deep grunt. Reiman crawled to his knees, ready to defend his daughter, but a warrior aimed her arrow at his head. Her companion, a man with a scarred lip, stole Reiman's weapons and tossed them into the forest.

Neer tightened her grip on her sword. Anger spewed from her eyes. The Nasir stepped closer, and she stiffened. Fear caught in her throat, and she held her breath, staring into the eyes of death itself. He lifted his hand, and a black ring with pulsing white veins rested on his finger.

Neer drew back her sword, ready to fight, but Reiman's agonized scream held her in place. She turned to him, watching as he leaned forward, writhing. An arrow was lodged in his side. From behind, another was nocked.

"Flee!" Reiman called. "Go!"

A warrior kicked his back and he fell with a pained cry. Neer flinched but held herself back. Her furious eyes set on the Nasir. He was expressionless. Devoid of emotion. Empty.

But she felt something within him. It churned with pain Flashes overtook her vision. Voices ripped through her mind, mixing with a swell of sorrow and agony.

"*You are no father of mine.*"

She gasped when the cold shadow of death washed over, like a cloud of despair and regret. The touch of icy steel tore through her chest, yet no weapon had met her skin. She was overcome with a pain that wasn't her own. The visions were real. They looked her in the eye as the Nasir held her gaze.

He lifted his hand, and Neer watched the ring that inched closer to her skin. Its power was overwhelming. Cold energy swirled through her, reaching out to caress the madness smoldering deep inside her soul, begging to be unleashed. Her body was stiff as darkness clouded her vision. She attempted to fight, tried to flee, but she was frozen. Soon, the ice turned to blistered heat. It sweltered within, burning her lungs and tearing through her veins, but she couldn't scream. Her body was plagued with tormenting, agonizing pain.

Dark energy swept from Neer's forehead, funneling into the ring as it moved closer. Her eyes crossed and body was numb. Nothing but pain. Excruciating pain. It swirled in her chest, ripping and tearing at her soul. Fracturing her mind and splintering her thoughts. She was broken, subjected to the will of her magic as it was twisted with the energy of the ring.

The Nasir reached closer, and she felt the icy touch of his palm hovering over her flesh. Fire erupted through her mind, seizing all thoughts. Washing her in agony.

Reiman's voice was muted as he shouted at the Nasir. His words were cutting. Broken and desperate. With a scream, he leapt to his feet. An arrow grazed his thigh, splitting his skin and drawing thick blood. But his rage overpowered his senses. He released a violent scream and slammed the Nasir to the dirt.

The cold touch gripping Neer's soul was severed, and she collapsed to the ground. Choked breaths escaped her throat as her body convulsed. Solid black eyes rolled back into her head.

SHADOWS OF NYN'DIRA

Reiman's fist struck the Nasir's cheek, and the crunch of broken teeth filled the air. He raised his arm for a second strike, but the sharp sting of an arrow carving into his neck caused him to flinch. Reiman rolled aside, evading a second arrow that drew inches from his skin. Bark cracked when it lodged deep into a tree.

Footfalls raced closer when the Klaet'il warriors charged. Reiman knelt to the ground, breathing heavily. His eyes flashed to Neer, where she lay unconscious on the grass. Her body was motionless, and her chest rose with slow breaths.

Harsh words reined from the Klaet'il, and Reiman cut his gaze to the archers.

"Drimil'Nizotl *reeknorai*! Naik'avel Nasir *trimast*!"

Reiman's eyes narrowed as the warrior spoke with harsh, violent words.

The Klaet'il paced back and forth. He released a vicious growl and said, "*Leithor miget* Nasir *frolok mrollo*!"

Reiman's eyes shifted slowly to the female warrior as she drew back another arrow. Her companion breathed heavily, staring at Reiman with eyes of pure hatred.

The female's voice called through the air when she unleashed a violent war cry and released the string. Reiman rushed forward, bending like grass in the wind as he dodged the arrow hurtling toward his chest. A pained grunt rolled from his throat as he ripped out the arrow still lodged in his side.

Before the Klaet'il had time to release another arrow, Reiman lunged forward. She inhaled a sharp gasp when he lodged his arrow upward through her chin. Blood spilled from her lips as she choked for breath. Reiman watched her without expression. His eyes were hard as stone. Emotionless, as she trembled then slumped forward.

He stepped back, and she fell to the ground, lifeless.

Reiman turned aside, viewing the remaining Klaet'il from the corner of his eye. He was calm, as if the Klaet'il warriors before him were nothing more than unruly children. Blood trickled down Reiman's face, rolling over his lips and into his perfectly manicured beard. His light blue eyes were unwavering, watching the Klaet'il rage.

The archer screamed and ripped a mace from its sheath on his belt. Its spiked head was made of sharpened bones.

Reiman spun aside, feeling the wind from the mace that struck for his arm. He landed with a limp, and blood poured from the wound on his thigh. His face tightened with pain, but he remained steady.

With a scream, the Klaet'il turned back. His weapon ripped through the air. Reiman collided their forearms, blocking the hit. Their faces were close. Fury poured from the Klaet'il's unhinged eyes.

The warrior ripped his arm away, ready to strike, and Reiman glided around him, smooth as water. Reaching around, Reiman grabbed his jaw and swiftly twisted. The crack of broken bones erupted through the air. The Klaet'il fell silent, and Reiman dropped him to the ground.

Reiman stood calm in his place, unaffected by his enemies. His eyes veered to the Nasir who was slowly crawling to his knees. Reiman snatched the mace from the ground. Steady footsteps brought him closer to the Nasir. He raised the weapon and struck downward.

Just as it reached his skull, the Nasir grabbed the wooden handle. His grip was firm, holding off the attack. Reiman's face twisted with anger. His arms were tight as he fought against the Nasir's iron grip.

The white lines crazing the Nasir's ring started to glow. Reiman's eyes widened. He staggered back, releasing the mace. Hard breaths escaped his lungs. The Nasir was motionless, his eyes never shifting from Reiman.

Faint growls and shrill screams rose from the forest in every direction. The ground trembled beneath the sound of quick-moving footsteps. Birds took flight, soaring through the canopy as trees snapped and fell.

Reiman whipped his head from left to right, searching for an escape. His eyes set on the Nasir, and his face paled. The glowing ring still shimmered on his finger, and a sinister smile pulled his lips.

The crash of footfalls reigned closer, and leaves tore from the trees as a horde of vicious creatures of darkness charged from the shadows.

Aélla stared into the eyes of the mangled kanavin. She had never heard a creature of night speak. Its word was foreign, spoken in the human tongue, but she knew it held the familiar tenor and rasp of a dreled.

Its mouth opened, reaching out for Aélla's throat.

"*Run!*" the dreled's voice moaned beneath a heavy growl.

Aélla withheld a scream as she was pulled aside by her cloak, and dirt filled her mouth when she fell to the ground. Avelloch stood over her. He breathed heavily, staring at the kanavin pacing the streets.

Another blood-curdling growl shook the air.

"*Liars!*" the voice said. "*End this…*" His foreign voice became lost within the rumbling growls. "*Find* Nerana!"

Aélla's heart skipped at the mention of Neer's name. She and Avelloch shared a terrified glance.

"*Run!*"

The kanavin ran forward. Aélla clutched Avelloch's leg, and they disappeared.

A rift tore through the air as sizzling magic wove through the night. Aélla and Avelloch fell from its height, landing hard atop the ground. The world was dark and heavy with the stench of blood and death. The clash of steel and shrieking screams echoed all around as they sat on the edge of a vicious attack.

In every direction, kanavin tore through the soldiers. Their flesh was ripped, and innards were flung through the air. Hungry gnarls erupted through the throats of twisted, leathered creatures as they picked through the piles of corpses. Dust coated the mangled bodies. Limbs were strewn throughout the village. Organs, dripping with blood, hung from rafters and roofs. Faces were torn open, and flesh was ripped from bone.

Aélla's eyes swept the streets before falling on white robes that were mixed with the hordes of torn leather armor. Her heart jolted when she recognized it was Neer's friend, Coryn. Blood spattered his mangled body. Tissue and flesh hung from his cheeks, where his lower jaw had been ripped from his face.

She turned away and closed her eyes. Voices of the dead whispered through her mind, tearing into her soul. Clawing at her sanity. She whimpered, struggling against their pain.

Stuck in her torment, she was unaware of the low grunt that echoed from behind. Heavy footsteps dragged across the ground, moving closer. Aélla was pulled from her affliction when the rancid stench of excrement filled the air, and a large figure appeared through the haze, directly behind her.

Holding her breath, Aélla closed her eyes, preparing to flee, but a vibrating screech came from the creature behind. She turned back as the kanavin with sharp claws swiped down at her.

Aélla lurched aside, unable to fully react as its talons swept closer. The odor of its sickly flesh disappeared when a swipe of steel cut through its arm. A pained scream bellowed from its bloated throat. Its severed hand faded to ash as it fell to the ground. Aélla turned, unable to view her savior as quick flashes of steel cut through the surrounding kanavin.

Ash filled the air, and she leaned forward, choking. Her chest ached as she hacked. When the last creature added more thickness to the plume clinging to her throat, a shadow appeared at her side, and Aélla leaned back, horror-stricken by the figure before her.

Moonlight glistened against his too-pale skin, and his golden eyes gazed into hers.

"Azae'l."

Aélla leaned forward, falling into Klaud's arms. He caught her as she sank into his touch. Nearby, Avelloch fought alongside the avel commander, Cael. Thurandír was to the east, perched on a roof behind a chimney.

Avelloch raced forward. He leapt off a fallen soldier and sank his blades deep into the chest of a raging kanavin. As it faded to ash, a scream came from behind. He turned, eyes wide as Cael was grabbed by a creature with four thick arms. Enormous claws sank into Cael's chest, penetrating through his back.

An arrow sank into the side of the kanavin's head, resting with five others that were loosed in quick succession. The crack of bones and deep tearing of flesh whispered beneath Cael's raw, gravelly scream as the kanavin slowly ripped him apart. Blood spilled to the ground like a steaming waterfall of red. Organs and tissue splashed in the growing pool below.

Avelloch stumbled back, watching the scene before him. Blood sprayed through the air, landing like drops of rain across his skin and cloak. The kanavin roared and heaved Cael's body at the rooftops, directly at Thurandír.

"No!" Aélla screamed.

Klaud vanished from her side. He landed on the roof and grabbed Thurandír just as Cael's mangled body crashed into the chimney. Bones snapped, and the thatched roof collapsed beneath them. Aélla leapt to her feet when they fell through the wide opening in the ceiling.

"Go!" Avelloch called to his sister.

Aélla turned to him, watching as he stood with Y'ven and two avel soldiers.

"Get out of here!"

But she was frozen. Her eyes flashed between her brother and the home. When a kanavin struck down, heaving its claws at Y'ven, Aélla lifted her arms in his direction. A fragile, translucent shield appeared before him. Sharp claws dragged against the barrier, and Aélla's chest burned with searing heat.

She released her magic and sank to her knees, screaming.

From above, a glass ball full of white mist was flung from a rooftop. It shattered against the ground at the kanavin's feet, and thick mist clouded the creature in a haze of light. The kanavin shrieked and thrashed, unable to escape the pure energy burning their flesh.

Avelloch rushed toward the haze, leaving his comrades behind. As he neared the kanavin, it leapt from the smoke, dragging black vapor with its shriveling, damaged skin.

Sharp fangs were exposed as its giant maw opened, prepared to devour him.

Avelloch released a furious shout. He dragged the edge of his glowing sword across his arm, drawing blood that caused the weapon to brighten. Purple light shone from the clear veins weaving through the steel, enchanting the blade with ancient magic.

As the kanavin snapped its jaws, Avelloch ducked and spun aside. With a hard swipe, his blade met with the creature's thick skin, and the magic of his sword tore through the air. A shockwave of energy was emitted on impact, ripping through the kanavin. Bones crunched and organs burst beneath the force.

The creature released one last scream before fading to ash. It billowed through the air, clinging to throats and burning eyes. Avelloch dropped his weapons and fell to his knees, choking.

More creatures growled and shrieked all around. Soldiers screamed and flesh was torn as they fled into the safety of nearby homes. Aélla sat perfectly still, watching with horror as the soldiers who remained fell. Their silhouettes were dancing shadows against the hazed darkness of Ik'Nharaii.

Y'ven and five avel raced to Aélla's side, and she was quickly led through the streets. Her eyes were on the home where Klaud and Thurandír had disappeared. Not a sound came from inside.

"No…," she whimpered.

Y'ven yanked Avelloch to his feet, and they followed after Aélla to a nearby home. They stepped to the door, and Thallon leapt onto the porch from the roof. He tossed a ball of mist at the remaining kanavin before slipping inside. The explosion of his orb rattled the walls as everyone sat inside, waiting.

Deep howls and grunts echoed throughout the village as the last of the soldiers were slain.

Avelloch leaned against the back wall, withholding muffled coughs as he struggled to breathe. An avel soldier lay on the floor, moaning, while two others wrapped her side in bandages, securing the gash in her chest.

SHADOWS OF NYN'DIRA

"Drimil," a warrior whispered. "Please...help her."

Aélla didn't hear his pleas as she stared out the window, witnessing the carnage of the Nasir's destruction. Piles of bodies littered the streets, like mounds of waste tossed aside.

Kanavin sniffed through the bodies, tossing aside those they discarded and feasting on others. A woman's moaned cries rose from the north. Her voice was a whisper against the snarls that ravaged the deceased. The sound of tearing flesh filled the air, and the woman shrieked before falling silent.

Crooked, misshapen shadows of the kanavin moved throughout the village before slowly coming to a stop. They stood tall, like strong pillars in a sea of the damned. And Aélla watched as they became incredibly still. Perfectly silent.

Her eyes narrowed. Their attention moved south, away from the cabin where she sat. Before she had time to collect her thoughts, the kanavin fled the streets. Their hooves and claws tore through the bodies as they stampeded south in a vicious, rageful horde. Thallon pulled Aélla away from the window and ducked to the ground when shadows passed them by. The roof trembled when creatures climbed across buildings and leapt over the village walls.

Aélla covered her ears as Thallon knelt over her. The rattling calmed as the creatures descended into the forest, and the world became still. When the echoing snarls faded into silence, the pressure of Thallon's body receded. He peeked out of the window, scanning the streets.

With a gasp, he raced to the door. The others glanced around in a panic, and two avel followed him out. Aélla glanced at her brother, who knelt on his hands and knees, defeated. Her gaze returned to the door as Thallon returned to the home with Klaud leaning on his shoulder.

Behind them came an avel warrior with Thurandír in his arms. Blood covered the archer's hairline, and his armor was split where two large cuts opened his flesh. Klaud stepped away from Thallon's grasp. He stumbled into the table and leaned forward, coughing. Ash coated his body in a layer of black, and lines of dark red outlined his face where his forehead was slashed. He inhaled two ragged breaths and then collapsed to his knees, rolling onto his side.

"Kila!" Thallon exclaimed. He dropped to Klaud's side and felt for a pulse. His shoulders relaxed, and he nodded before turning to Aélla. "Heal him!" He pointed at Thurandír, who lay writhing nearby.

Aélla crawled to Thurandír's side. Tears carved trails through the ash and blood staining his face. Light whimpers and moans wheezed through his throat, and his dark blue eyes shifted to Aélla, pleading.

"You're okay," she cried. "Just rest."

Her hands trembled as she pressed them firmly against his side, and he unleashed a loud cry. Raw, erratic energy sizzled through her veins. She wasn't weak, but her magic was cold and painful. Her teeth clenched, and she fought through the blaze scorching her chest.

A raw, bleeding scream escaped her tightened throat. His flesh had hardly begun to seal together when the agony overwhelmed her, and Aélla fell back, her chest heaving. She leaned against the wall, clutching her heart.

Thallon and Avelloch shared a long, worried glance. Their eyes shifted to Thurandír, and Thallon felt for a pulse in his neck. When he nodded, they exhaled deep sighs of relief.

Aélla inhaled a deep sniff. Her body ached with emptiness and grief. "What's happening?" she asked. "How…"

Thallon sighed. "He's using the ring," he said. "He turned them into kanavin…"

The silence was heavy. Aélla knew the Nasir had the ring, and she knew he intended to use it. But not to this degree. He had slain hundreds of innocents in his pursuit of power. Whole civilizations had disappeared, and now they stood at the threshold of his madness. The monument of his destruction. Beneath their feet were the ashes and blood of all those who had opposed him. Who sought to fight against his will and strength.

He had always been unstoppable, but now, he was invincible. Ice tugged at Aélla's chest, and she crossed her arms. The voices of the dead clawed at her mind. Their pleading, terrified sounds wept for an end. Begged for mercy. Called out for their families.

Aélla wiped her nose and shook her head. "We didn't hear a battle," she said. "What happened?"

Thallon raked his fingers through his hair and closed his eyes. "We arrived at the western gates, and the village was empty. We eventually made it here and met up with the lanathess soldiers." He paused. "As soon as the sun set...they came. Dozens of them."

Avelloch's expression became grim. He glanced through the home, slowly taking in the faces around them. "Why did they flee?" he asked.

Everyone was silent, suddenly aware of the kanavin's strange actions. The creatures weren't known to work together in such a way, and they'd never form armies or follow one another from battle to battle.

As the realization struck him, Avelloch leapt to his feet. He marched to the window, inspecting the village. "Was Neer with you?"

Thallon's face paled. "N-no...why?"

Dark eyes set on the streets before Avelloch snatched his swords and opened the door. "They're going after her."

The Nasir lay still on the ground, smiling at the creatures of darkness racing by. They avoided his body as he commanded them forward. Reiman stood above Neer, who lay on her back, immobilized by the power of the ring. He breathed heavily, watching them close in but unable to flee.

Icy energy wove through the air, and the forest trembled. Leaves rustled above, whispering of chaos and death. Neer lay with her eyes closed. Visions of darkness swept through her mind.

A strike of agony caused her to gasp. She opened her eyes, and all she saw was black.

Neer sat alone in a pit of darkness. Shadows wove through the air, carrying an influx of emotion: anger, sadness, loss, vengeance, regret. But she was empty. Devoid of want or feeling or desire. A vacant soul standing amid thousands of raging, woeful cries.

H.C. NEWELL

She turned from left to right, watching as phantoms swept through the abyss. She felt no pain. No confusion or regret. She was hollow. Death could take her away, and she'd allow it to pull her asunder.

Shadows moved like liquid night, and Neer fell aside when the icy touch of a wraith crashed through her. The heavy emotions it carried struck against her with unrelenting force. Another followed. And another. Over and over, the wraiths swept through her like a cold wind.

She was battered. The emptiness was filled with terror and rage and sorrow. Her eyes darkened, and black veins crawled away from them like bolts of lightning. She choked on her breath. Her heart was cold as stone.

Through the phantoms swarming her, like flies on meat, she saw the figure of a man. He was dark as night, a shadow on shadow. Teal eyes stared back at hers, and frost chilled the air when he reached out his hand.

Her arm trembled. She fought against the torture plaguing her soul. Reaching out, their fingers nearly touched. Rime coiled around her fingertips. But its icy sting was a pleasantry to the agony festering within.

"*Fohl'nok melän...,*" he said, his hand drawing nearer. "Free us."

Unable to feel, unable to care, Neer reached out and placed her hand within his.

The creatures closed in, and Reiman stood above her with the mace raised high. He unleashed a hellish scream, prepared for the end, when suddenly, the creatures halted. They stood in a wide circle, just an arm's reach away.

The world was intensely silent.

Not a whisper drifted through the cold night air before a light tremble rattled the ground. Reiman stepped back, searching for its source. His eyes fell to Neer, and his jaw dropped. Horror-stricken, he watched as she rose from the ground, as if being lifted by the gods themselves. Her body was limp and eyes were closed. Dirty hair waved lightly, hanging in the air.

A shockwave tore through the forest when her black eyes opened. Reiman fell to the ground. Trees were

SHADOWS OF NYN'DIRA

cracked in half beneath the weight of her energy. Dull light emitted from her body, shining like a dying flame.

She lifted her eyes to the sky. A cloud of shadows caressed her body, waving like tendrils of smoke. Dark cracks formed across her skin, bleeding with black mist. The creatures began squealing and smashing their heads in pain. Ash filled the air as mist rose from their bodies, and they slowly faded to dust. Their grunts and screams dwindled into silence as they disappeared.

The forest was still. Soot hovered in the air, staining the grass and trees. Reiman breathed into the crook of his arm and closed his burning eyes.

Suddenly, winds ripped through the trees. Leaves were torn from limbs as a strong gale pushed through the forest. Reiman fell aside, unable to withstand the squall pummeling him. He peered through the swirling ash, finding Neer at its center. A vortex moved around her, growing smaller as it reached her chest.

The energy funneled into her, and pain ignited from deep within. Her soul was shattered as bone-chilling magic ripped through her. The emptiness was replaced with agony. A deep, unending pain that couldn't be quelled. She felt every dark, eviscerating sting as the magic that transformed the creatures of darkness was absorbed into her body.

Neer hovered in the air, paralyzed as the energy swirled into her core. The darkness that overtook her eyes faded. Smoke no longer rose from her cracked, broken skin. She was a child, terrified and alone. Her throat bled as she shrieked, releasing the torment building up inside. Her body hovered in the air, trapped by the energy shackling her in place.

Through the darkness, Avelloch burst through the trees with Blaid at his side. He staggered back, watching as Neer screamed in agony. Reiman sat alone on the ground, frozen with terror. Two dead Klaet'il and Neer, hovering in the air, were his only company.

Moisture rose from Neer's eyes as painful energy pummeled and ripped through her chest. Her eyes flicked to Avelloch's, and she screamed. Too weak to fight against the agony that plagued her, she stretched her fingers in his direction. Her teeth clenched so hard they nearly cracked.

Avelloch breathed heavily. His eyes flashed to Reiman before returning to Neer. Their gazes met before she closed her eyes, consumed with torture. Avelloch rushed forward, fighting against the winds shoving him back. Blaid pushed against his back, and together, they moved through the intense storm. Cold energy sliced his skin, drawing thin lines across his face and arms.

Moving closer, Avelloch lunged forward. His arms wrapped around Neer's side, grabbing her from the air. She inhaled a sharp breath as they fell to the ground. The pain was released, and she was left empty. Immobile. Cold as death itself.

The winds receded, and the forest was still. Lying on her back, Neer exhaled a long, slow breath, and black mist rose from her parted lips.

Chapter Twenty-Nine

Light of the Seven
Nerana

"Extend your heart to the Father, and he shall mend your broken soul."

— Rotharion, *The Book of Light*

Firelight flickered against the walls of a small shack. Sunlight glinted through cracks in the aged walls, casting light against Neer's skin where she lay atop an old cot beneath fur blankets. Her face twitched as she wove in and out of dreams, reliving the nightmares she had faced at the hands of the Nasir. Voices, death, and unrelenting agony sank through her with every icy wind. She couldn't breathe through the frost encasing her lungs, crawling slowly through the fabric of her soul.

The light creak of a wooden stool broke the silence when Avelloch shifted in his seat. He leaned forward with his chin propped onto his folded hands. Distant eyes were fixed on Neer, who rested just beside him. The dark circles around his eyes revealed his lack of sleep since the battle two days past. Bloody bandages wrapped his shoulder beneath his filthy tunic.

Voices murmured from outside, and the leather cot creaked as Neer began to stir. Slowly, she opened her tired eyes and blinked her vision into focus. Chills covered her skin as she sat up. A frigid cloud swelled in her chest, combatting the warmth of the hearth nearby. She looked around with half-opened eyes before fixing her gaze on Avelloch, who sat still and quiet at her side.

Too exhausted to speak, Neer exhaled a light groan and gripped her aching head. A deep pulse throbbed within her skull. "Avelloch?" she asked groggily. "What happened?"

He was quiet, staring at her without expression. But she could see it within him, the confusion and pain.

"Avelloch?" she asked, becoming more alert. "Where are they?"

His jaw clenched before he admitted, "Outside."

"Are they okay?"

He nodded. "They're fine."

She studied him for a moment, finding his demeanor off-putting. Something had happened. Something he was hesitant to explain. Her heart rose to her throat, and she gulped down the lump that had formed. "What aren't you telling me?" she asked.

Avelloch closed his eyes. Through several slow breaths, he explained, "The Nasir got away…Only a handful of our soldiers survived."

"What?" Her heart sank. "But…But I thought the village was safe. They were—"

"They knew we were coming…We were led into a trap."

Tears filled her eyes, and she quickly wiped them away. "The others are okay? They all made it out?"

He nodded.

She sniffed and then bit her quivering lip. "The Brotherhood…" She cleared her throat. "Did anyone…Are they…"

Avelloch slumped forward. Neer stared at him through tear-filled eyes. For several seconds, he was quiet, leaning forward with closed eyes. Pain swelled in Neer's chest, and she waited, fearing the words she didn't want to believe. When their eyes met, she held her breath. He didn't speak, but the silence was enough.

They were gone.

So many she had known for so long—men who had fought and lived beside her—now lay dead. Cut down by the hands of the Nasir. She shook her head to rid it of the intruding thoughts, though they crept back in, reminding her of all the lives that were unfairly taken because of her.

SHADOWS OF NYN'DIRA

Had she not attacked the priest in Ravinshire, the Order would have never slain the village. They'd have never sent so many men into the forest, and the Brotherhood, her family, would have never entered enemy lands in an effort to find and protect her.

Among all the faces entering her mind, there was one who was most pressing. But she was sure he had survived. The Nasir had led her and Reiman into a trap, but he wasn't there. His body wasn't hanging in the trees or torn apart by creatures of darkness. He wasn't used as bait or bargaining.

Gil had to be alive.

Neer's voice cracked as she asked, "Did they find him?"

She choked on her breath, broken by the thought. Tears streamed down her face, and she held Avelloch's woeful gaze.

"Is Gil okay?"

His jaw clenched. Before he could speak, the door opened, and sunlight brightened the dark room. Neer's eyes bore into Avelloch, but he turned away. A shadow stalked through the room, growing larger as Reiman stepped closer.

"Nerana," he said. "How are you, my child?"

Her misty eyes were glued to Avelloch. Through a heavy heart, she ripped her attention away and turned to her father. He passed her a waterskin, but she hadn't the strength to take it. Without speaking, he forced it into her hand and lifted the spout to her lips.

"Drink," he said. "You need to replenish your strength."

Empty, broken eyes stared at him. He gave a firmer, pressing look, one a father gives his stubborn child. But she was frozen in place. Her heart too heavy to care.

"Nerana," Reiman said with a soft voice. "You must—"

"Where is Gil?"

His voice was silenced. Guarded eyes met with hers, and she was silent, expecting the worst. Refusing to believe it was true. Reiman exhaled a deep breath. His eyes fell away, and for a moment, the world was still. Seconds became an eternity as they sat in a heavy silence. He closed his eyes and sighed.

"Gilbrich…did his duty to the Brotherhood. He gave his life in service of our freedom."

A sharp breath caught in Neer's throat, and she sat unblinking, staring into a void as the words repeated in her mind. But they held little meaning. She couldn't grasp the severity of his loss or finality of his death. Gil had survived for too long to perish now, at the hands of the elves.

She sat immobile, hardly breathing. Her wide eyes were unblinking as she drifted into a spiraling abyss of misery and denial.

Avelloch shifted, and his brows knitted with concern when he took in Neer's catatonic state. He glanced at Reiman, who stood without expression, and then returned his gaze to Neer. Carefully, he leaned forward and touched her hand. She blinked her thoughts away. Their eyes met, and she was numb to his concern or affection. There was no sadness or grief or pain. Only emptiness. Bleak, unencumbered emptiness.

"Neer?" Avelloch said.

Her eyes fell away. Ice prickled her chest, and she curled her fist over her heart. "Why don't I feel anything?" she asked. Her jaw clenched. "Why don't I care?"

Reiman said, "There is only so much tragedy a mind can take. Stay here and rest. I'll convene with the others to—"

"No," she said. "I want to see them. I need to…" Her voice faded, and heaviness swelled inside. Riddled with confusion and doubt, she shook her head to refocus her mind. "I need to get out of this room."

Avelloch and Reiman were silent as she slowly stood and made her way to the door. Outside, sunlight warmed her skin, and an internal chill filled her veins with ice. It swept through her, anchoring her heart to the void inside. She felt unsteady, disconnected, as if her mind and soul were two separate entities.

"Nerana?"

Her eyes lifted as Aella's voice filtered through the air. She stood with Thallon and Klaud in a small clearing, where four cabins rested in a semi-circle atop a grassy knoll. Flowerbeds, wooden tables, and a firepit were within the center of the quaint village.

SHADOWS OF NYN'DIRA

Aélla's eye was black, and her left forearm was wrapped in bandages. Thallon and Klaud were littered with bruises and cuts. A deep scratch split Klaud's skin along his jaw, creating a red line through his growing beard. Y'ven stood when Neer stepped toward the group. He leaned aside, clutching his injured arm.

A trail of sparkling orange light whirled through the air as Dru approached Neer. She hovered an arm's reach away, staring with concern.

Aélla stepped closer and asked, "How are you feeling?"

Neer crossed her arms. With a shrug she said, "Okay."

Aélla glanced at her brother, who shared an equally sorrowful look. Neer closed her eyes when Reiman placed his hand on her shoulder. It was firm and heavy, nothing like the gentle, comforting touch she needed.

"She'll be all right," he stated. "Nerana has strength unmatched. We'll see her through this."

Aélla's expression washed with misery. Her voice was timid as she said, "Why don't we go wash up? There's a river nearby."

The vacant expression never lifted from Neer's eyes. Aélla took her arm and led her away. Peaceful winds swept through the air, filling the emptiness inside Neer with the soft sting of calming energy. She closed her eyes and breathed in the scent of fresh air. For a moment, the war and its torments didn't exist. The forest erased her pain, and she felt embraced by its tranquility.

There were no words spoken as she and Aélla wandered through the woods. They stepped across a lonesome wooden bridge stretching over a shallow embankment of boulders and roots. Water trickled through the ditch, splashing against the rocks as it headed further south. Neer came to a stop. She placed her hands atop the railing and stared at the forest.

"It seems so peaceful," she said through a hollow, broken voice. Distant eyes watched the water sweeping away, traveling further into the endless forest. "You'd never know of all the death and sorrow...the massacres taking place all around us."

Aélla leaned against the railing. Her dark blue eyes were guarded as she gazed ahead.

Neer could see the unrest within her. The disturbance that was evident in Avelloch's eyes had come to life in Aélla, and it replaced the emptiness with a tinge of fear.

Swallowing through a dry throat, Neer asked, "What happened during the battle?"

Aélla was hesitant, avoiding Neer's eyes as she became lost in her misery. Blinking her thoughts away, she inhaled a deep breath. "Maybe we should wait until—"

"Tell me."

Aélla licked her lips and exhaled. She slumped forward with her head bowed, portraying the look of a defeated warrior. Loose hair hung across her shoulders, shielding her face.

"The Nasir," she started, her voice shaking, "turned everyone into kanavin…We believe he's building an army." She paused. "We were slaughtered…A few avel made it out…But the rest…"

White hair glistened in the sunlight when she lifted her head. Tears filled her eyes, and she bit her lip, struggling to contain her grief.

Neer watched her, riddled with confusion and guilt. Her people had been torn apart by creatures of darkness, yet still, she felt nothing. No sorrow. No pain. No sense of loss.

Her mind went to Gil, and she asked, "Was he there?"

A tear slid down Aélla's cheek when she closed her eyes. Neer had expected to feel the same deep sense of dread, like a stone pulling her further into an endless abyss. But she was hollow. Entirely broken. Her words were as empty as her soul.

Aélla straightened and wiped her eyes. Stammering over her words, she admitted, "Yes. He was there…in the village…"

Neer watched her for a moment, and the slight sting of fear trickled down her chest. Aélla had never known Gilbrich, aside from their brief interactions at camp. There were few reasons she'd react so deeply to the death of a stranger, especially after witnessing such a vicious attack.

SHADOWS OF NYN'DIRA

The words were acid on her tongue as Neer said, "He was a creature of darkness...wasn't he?"

Aélla's tears dripped down her reddened face. Her dark blue eyes met with Neer's, and the answer was evident in her devastated eyes. Neer turned away. She clenched her jaw, knowing there should be pain. Immeasurable, indescribable pain.

She lifted her hand to her heart, surprised to find it was still beating. The emptiness was akin to the peace of death, and for a moment, she had wondered if she was truly alive.

"What's happening to me?" she asked, her voice as silent as the wind. Eyes, shrouded with pain she couldn't feel, met with Aélla's. "Why am I so...empty?"

Aélla calmly took her hand. She blinked away her tears and leaned her head onto Neer's shoulder. They stood in silence, and the calm breeze was like battering winds against Neer's mind, clashing with the storm brewing deep inside.

Neer washed by the river and returned to the village with Aélla. The aroma of cooking meat filled the air. Smoke rose from a pit in the center of the homes where a boar roasted above the flames. Reiman stood by the fire with Wallace and four evae. They spoke quietly to one another while he turned the spit. Each of the warriors were wrapped in bandages or covered in wounds.

"You haven't healed them?" Neer asked. She turned to Aélla, who kept her eyes on the ground.

Seconds passed, before she explained, "My energy is weakening. I'm not strong enough to heal them all."

Teal eyes flashed to the evae, one of which had two missing fingers on her bandaged hand, while another had a chipped tooth and broken nose. Aélla explained she needed to tend to Thurandír's wounds. She invited Neer inside, but she refused, needing a moment alone.

Aélla reluctantly disappeared into a nearby home, and Neer crossed her arms, eyeing the village. Dense trees surrounded the small settlement, leaving them vulnerable to the creatures that lurked in the night. Thunder rumbled through the sky, bringing with it the scent of rain. While the others quickly moved the spit indoors, Neer stood outside, allowing the sweeping winds to carry her thoughts away.

Voices murmured within the cabins, and shadows passed by the window as the others prepared for the night. But to the left, within the cabin Aélla had entered, there was silence. Firelight brightened the window as dark clouds overtook the sky. The light clink of a pestle and mortar came from the home—Klaud mixed potions by the window.

A calming chime hummed through the forest as leaves rustled in the growing winds. Neer stepped away from the village, needing a moment alone. She collected a longsword from a table before wandering east, far into the forest. Large drops of rain fell from the sky, pattering against the leaves and trickling down to the forest floor.

The soil illuminated beneath her feet as her weight pressed against the grasses. Glowing plants brightened as the storm rolled overhead. Energy swelled through the air, beckoning Neer forward, and she blindly followed, uncaring of her fate. Willing to allow the forest to take her wherever it saw fit.

Further east, she came to a large statue of Kirena, the Divine of compassion and health. Surrounding her aged effigy were hundreds of swords. They spread throughout the forest, growing thicker the closer they came to her statue. Neer stood amongst the monument of the dead, overcome with peace. Her eyes shifted to Kirena, and she wondered if the teachings were true. If being in the presence of a Divine, whether in the flesh or by standing at its shrine, would gift one with their calming embrace.

Standing at the sanctum of the blessed, Neer couldn't understand why the Divine of health was surrounded by a tribute for the fallen, as it was Zynther who was the Divine of life and death. He would lead the departed to the eternal lands of Arcae and in life would carry one's spirit into the womb. Many birth and funeral rites were dedicated to his will, but the Prayer of Pleading, recited just before death, was said to Kirena, who would grace her beloved with peace.

Neer eyed the forest, listening to the rain draw closer before falling upon her skin. She lifted her palms and closed her eyes. Water washed over her, weighing her clothes and hair. Mud splashed when she sank to her knees. Resting amid the cemetery of swords, the emptiness drenching her soul was lifted. And then she felt it. The deep, unrelenting strike of pain. Like the spark of a flame, it flickered inside, growing stronger before burning with inescapable heartache.

Tears mixed with the rain sliding down her face. Her lip quivered and eyes were clenched shut. She breathed in quick bursts. Her loud cries were silenced by the storm.

Mud and grass coated her arms when she leaned forward, bringing her face to the grass. Her body trembled and fists tightened as she wept.

"Please…," she begged. "Make this end…"

Neer lifted her head and stared at the statue.

"What do you want me do!" The storm grew stronger while she spoke to the Divine, begging for answers. "Tell me!"

Desperate for answers, overwhelmed by her grief, Neer straightened on her knees and cupped her hands together in front of her chest. She breathed heavily, fighting against the sob rising in her throat. And then she said the sacred prayer, one spoken to Rothar, the overseer of the immortal plane. The god of gods.

"Divine's grace is fleeting and warm. Whosoever challenge it be warned. The love of the Father carries the many. The souls of the wicked be burned aplenty." She paused, hoping for a break in the storm or a warm hand to touch her back. But when there was nothing, she continued, "Father, hear my prayer. Please… I beg you…" She clenched her teeth, fighting back tears. "Answer me, please. If you're real, please…end this madness. Just let me go."

She waited, but still, there was nothing. Not a shift in the wind or calmness to soothe the ache in her soul. More tears spilled from her eyes.

"What have I done to deserve this hell?"

The storms raged on, spreading rain and lightning throughout the land. Dusk slowly crept over the world, masking the forest with a deep shade of blackness. Glowing plants brightened the woods, their faint colors glistening against the sea of steel.

Neer clutched the stolen sword in her hand. Her fingers ached as she held tightly to the hilt, unable to let go. But time had taught her that all things must come to an end. And through the pain, she would find strength. She would find redemption.

She would find revenge.

A tear slid down her cheek as she pictured Gil's face, and with a pained cry, she shoved the sword in the ground. The blade wavered and stood in place, becoming one with the collection of haunting farewells. Neer gazed at the sword, broken by what it represented. Eviscerated by his cruel, undeserved fate. She ran her fingers down its length and whispered a final goodbye.

Her distorted reflection slowly disappeared as she marched away, leaving a piece of her soul with the monument behind.

Chapter Thirty

Home
Aéllu

"*So long as you are alive, I will always have a home.*"

— Merethyl Liadrinel to her children, Aélla and Avelloch

AÉLLA RESTED AT A TABLE in the small cabin. She watched silently as Klaud sat next to Thurandír on a wooden stool. A thin tube connected their arms, carrying blood into Thurandír's weak body. His dark skin was ashen as he lay on a bed, groaning in agony. The deep gash that had opened his side was sealed, and despite his condition, his health was slowly improving.

Unrest swirled within Aélla's chest, and she crossed her arms, hoping to rid herself of the guilt. Magic sweltered in the air, but it was icy and painful. She couldn't find the strength within her to heal him. Not when the energy that kept everything in balance was so distorted and hollow. The forest which once gifted her with strength and peace now made her feel breathless and weak. The battle to stay pure and undiluted was growing harder with each passing day. She fought and struggled to regain her strength, but the Nasir was winning.

The cycle couldn't be stopped.

Her thoughts shifted to Klaud as he carefully removed the needle from his vein. He did the same for Thurandír, then wrapped their elbows in tight bandages to stop the bleeding. With a sigh, he leaned forward with his head down. Long, dirty hair hung across his shoulders, masking his face in darkness.

"This can't be happening...," he said, speaking his thoughts aloud.

Aélla understood his sorrow. She felt it too. The Nasir had always done unspeakable things, but he had dipped further into madness than she ever thought possible.

"He wants everything to fall," she said. Sadness crashed through her like a cold wind, but her tears had dried long ago.

Too caught in her misery, she didn't notice when Klaud turned to her. Pity seeped from his tired gaze.

"Azae'l," he started, but she lifted her hand to quiet him.

Inhaling a shallow breath, she gathered as much strength as she could and said, "I'll go speak to the Eirean. They can't allow him to get away with this."

"They won't listen to you."

"Then I'll make them listen." Her voice was stern and direct.

Klaud was silenced by her rigid authority, which she didn't display often. His golden eyes fell away. "You know what you'll have to do," he said. "What you'll have to tell them."

She held her breath and her heart skipped. No one else knew the truth of the Nasir—who he was or what he had done. No one but Avelloch and Klaud, who had sworn long ago to keep the burden of his identity silent.

But the time had come to reveal the truth. The Eirean would know who he was, and she could only hope they would choose understanding instead of the branding iron.

She nodded, still stuck in her thoughts. "I know," she said. Closing her eyes, she contained her fear and then looked at Klaud. "Stay here until I return. Make sure the others know where I've gone."

"Make haste, Azae'l." Their eyes met. "We don't have much time."

Her boots tapped against the floor as she moved across the room. Standing before Klaud, she took his face in her hands. His eyes closed as she gently swept her thumbs across his skin. Words weren't enough to express her gratitude for all he had done for her. The sacrifices and pain he endured to keep her safe.

"*Mela'anum,*" she whispered, and his closed eyes twitched, expressing the pain and relief at her words. "We'll make it through this."

He clenched his teeth and then gave a stiff nod. She examined him for a moment longer, taking in the broken man before her. Someone so strong had never looked more defeated. His skin was cold beneath her lips when she tenderly kissed his forehead. Before he had time to speak or offer to accompany her to Navarre, Aélla inhaled a deep breath and disappeared.

The heat of magic was replaced by chilly autumn air when Aélla fell from a magical rift. Searing magic sizzled like translucent flames before closing in on itself, disappearing as if it never existed. Aélla knelt on the ground, clutching her chest where a cold ache settled deep in her soul. Where her magic felt weak and unstable.

"Drimil?"

Aélla lifted her eyes when several strangers hovered around her. She gazed up at them, recognizing many of their faces. Maxis, a baker, knelt beside her. He placed a thin hand on her shoulder and looked into her eyes.

"Aélla?" he asked. "Are you all right?"

"Max," she said, comforted by his warming presence. For a time following her mother's death, Maxis had gifted Aélla and her family a loaf of bread every few days. It wasn't much, but it was enough for her to remember his kindness. "I'm all right."

He gently grasped her arm and helped guide her to her feet. Aélla dusted off her robes and stood tall, portraying a sense of strength. Her gaze moved from the villagers to the cobble courtyard where they all stood.

Tall trees, some thrice as wide as a full-grown man, towered throughout her sprawling hometown of Navarre. Leaves rustled and chimed with a gentle breeze. Aélla closed her eyes, breathing in the scent like perfume. It had been too long since she was home. There was an undeniable sense of peace here, as if the world and its terrors no longer existed. Surrounded by the familiar aroma of cinnamon-berry pies, misting waterfalls, and crisp leaves, she was whole.

She was home.

And there was nowhere in the world she would rather be. The warmth and tenderness of her neighbors filled her with a sense of security and community that couldn't be felt elsewhere.

"Drimil?"

Aélla blinked her tears away.

"Is everything all right?"

"Where are the others?"

"Was Klaud truly banished?"

Her breath caught in her throat as the onlookers asked many questions. Unwilling to give them answers, she said, "We're doing the best that we can."

"Aélla," Krina, a young woman who had grown up in the home next to Aélla's, stepped forward. Beautiful dark hair hung to her mid-back. She carried a smile that could light up even the darkest of rooms. Krina hesitated, not having seen her childhood friend since she embarked on her journey as Drimil'Rothar.

Aélla pulled her into a tight embrace. "How are you, Krina?"

"I'm all right," she said. "It has been so long since you returned home. What has brought you here?"

A knot formed in Aélla's gut. She turned away and took a measured step back, putting distance between them. She regained her composure, and said, "I need to speak with the Eirean."

"Why? Is something wrong?"

Voices overlapped as everyone chimed in, speculating on the cause of her return. Aélla gulped down her growing emotions. She forced a convincing smile, one she had learned to perfect since her mother's death, and explained, "Everything is fine. I just need to convene with them."

Krina's expression faded to sadness. Her dark blue eyes flittered between the others, who stood in silence, waiting for the truth. With a nervous sigh, Krina said, "I don't mean to disrespect you by questioning, Drimil'Rothar…but…we know about the attacks."

"What?" Aélla said, grasping at the strands of her composure.

"There are survivors. They fled and were found by the avel." She paused. "We know the humans are abducting the e'liaa."

Aélla inhaled a deep breath, angered by the lies they'd been told. She pleaded with the Eirean not long ago to aid them in the fight against the Klaet'il, but they wouldn't listen. Now they had begun manipulating the villagers into believing the humans were to blame for these attacks. Surely, the e'liaa would tell the truth, but the Eirean were clever, knowing how to cast doubt into people's hearts. Their word was law, and their position was one of esteemed respect. If they said it was the humans, there would be no question to their claim.

"Where are they?" Aélla asked. "The survivors?"

"The Eirean have them housed in a village nearby. We aren't allowed to visit. Because of all that's happened, the Eirean just want to give them peace."

Aélla nodded. Before she had time to speak, the growing crowd parted, and a man approached. He dropped to his knee before her in a respectful bow. "Drimil'Rothar," he said.

"Aen'mysvaral," she greeted.

He stood, tall and proud. "I'm here to escort you to the Eirean chambers."

Her eyes shifted to the rooftops and trees, searching for the stia'dyr watching the village. She knew the spies must've informed the Eirean of her arrival, as there was no other way for them to know so quickly.

Aélla gave Krina a forced smile, one that drew her lips into a nearly invisible line. "It was good to see you, Krina."

"You too. Stay safe, Aélla."

She nodded and then took a step behind Aen'mysvaral before turning back around. Her eyes shifted to each of the faces staring at her. Memories flooded her mind as she gazed at each of them, and the weight of misery sank into her gut at the thought of never seeing her home again.

Anything could happen, and she wouldn't be there to protect them.

Standing tall, Aélla inhaled a deep breath and lowered into a bow. A hush fell over the village. Sunlight beamed from above, brightening her hair as she stayed in her position, giving her thanks to the people who raised her. Who gave her love, comfort, and protection, even in her darkest times.

She straightened and smiled a genuine, loving grin. "Thank you all"—a tear slid down her cheek—"for everything."

Tears streamed down their faces. Women covered their eyes, while men wiped their noses. The sniffling sounds of a quiet goodbye filled the forest. Aélla's heart was heavy with grief. She knew her journey would take her far from home, and the chance to return anytime soon was very slim. To be there was a privilege she didn't expect, and she now understood the vows she took that swore against ever returning to one's place of comfort.

Everyone stepped forward, and the light scuffle of boots filled the silence. The nearest villagers placed their hands upon Aélla, touching her shoulders, scalp, back, and arms. They bowed their heads as each person behind touched those before them, reaching out to their savior. Their last hope.

Aélla turned toward the sky and closed her eyes. Sunlight glinted against the wetness of her cheeks. This was her home. Her family.

She would never forget them, no matter what may happen.

Everyone stood in a somber silence before slowly backing away, allowing Aélla to depart with Aen'mysvaral. Her fists were balled at her sides when she forced herself away, not daring to look back for fear of breaking down. This was her choice. It was what she had to do to keep them safe. And she would fight until the bitter end to protect them.

Aen'mysvaral was quiet as he led her through the familiar paths to the Eirean chambers. It wasn't necessary for her to be escorted, but she was certain Aen'mysvaral took pride in leading the way.

The sun shifted in the sky as they wandered the woods, trekking higher and moving closer to their destination.

"Elidyr," Aélla said, calling the warrior by his given name.

He looked at her from the corner of his good eye.

"What do you know of the attacks taking place?"

His chest puffed with a deep inhalation. Fixing his eyes ahead, he stated, "The Eirean have informed us that—"

"Elidyr," she said, demanding the truth.

Though he was Thallon's brother, they had never formally met until Aélla had taken her vows and gained the title of Drimil'Rothar. Since then, Elidyr had always shown her the greatest respect. He was a man of few words who would often forgo his own morality to uphold the laws.

But she saw a shift in him when she spoke his name. He held much respect for her position, which many put above the Eirean themselves, though that belief held no truth. Aélla was merely a servant of the people, not an authority. Yet, still, she was viewed as above the laws. Untouchable.

The truest form of power.

Elidyr was silent for a moment, and then he said, "The e'liaa claim it was the Klaet'il. But the Eirean—"

"What do *you* believe?"

He hesitated, unwilling to compromise in his loyalty to the Eirean, who had given him everything.

Aélla came to a stop and grabbed his arm, forcing him to turn to her. She met his gaze, and he was baffled by the coldness of her eyes.

"Do not forsake your honor for their loyalty," she said, cold as ice. "Too many times, they've silenced assaults like this. When will it be enough?" Her words were cutting and direct. "Thurandir lost his family to these attacks. Your own brother is risking his life by fighting in the Nasir's war. Would you truly degrade their sacrifices by siding with those who would rather sit in silence than do what's right?"

Elidyr stared at the ground, disturbed.

Aélla released her grip on his arm. Her eyes were dark and cold as a moonless night as she stared at him. After several seconds, she shook her head. "If you can't decide what's right, then you aren't needed by my side."

Her footsteps were steady when she marched away, following the overgrown trail up the hillside. Minutes passed before the sound of quick footfalls echoed from behind. She glanced back, giving no indication of her relief, when Elidyr stepped to her side. There wasn't a word spoken as they walked toward their destination, finding unity in their silence.

Further up the hill, they approached the Eirean's longhouse. While removing their weapons, Torvála, an eólin with energy that could strengthen or reduce another's magical power, stepped forward. She was the guardian of Aardn, forced from a young age to be the shield of the Eirean. Many eólin, such as Klaud, were cut from the same cloth. Molded by fate to be servants or slaves to those in power.

Luckily, Klaud's mother had swept him away, taking him far from his home in the mountains and finding refuge in Navarre. He was ridiculed throughout his childhood for being different, and while he was once hunted for his blood and power, the trouble his existence caused had faded over time. He had proven himself as a member of their society and was treated as an equal.

Torvála wasn't as fortunate. This fate was all she had ever known. Much like the stia'dyr who resided forever within the confines of the longhouse ahead, they were the unwilling subjects of the Eirean.

Torvála stepped closer, her skin coated in white tempera and red runes. It was the look she had always worn.

"Aélla Líadrinel," she said, lifting her hand for Aélla to take. "The council awaits your arrival."

"Torvála," Aélla replied. Her voice was sharp as fresh steel.

It was customary to kiss Torvála's hand, a gesture meant to show good faith before entering the sacred chambers. But Aélla refused to acknowledge this honor. Instead, she stood firm in her anger. Unchanged in her willful disobedience to their deeply held customs.

Torvála withdrew her hand and shifted her attention to Elidyr. She greeted him by name and extended her hand. The warrior hesitated, glancing warily at Aélla before ultimately giving in to his fear of their leaders. He kissed Torvála's fingers and bowed.

"Torvála," he said.

The guardian stood before them, still and quiet as a statue. Her eyes were shrouded by the thick material hanging over her face. She whispered a chant, and Aélla inhaled a deep breath when the slight churning in her chest became heavy and dense. It was customary for drimil to relinquish their powers before approaching the Eirean, yet Aélla never grew used to the discomfort it brought.

"You may proceed into the chambers," Torvála stated and then stepped aside.

Aélla gathered her strength and then confidently entered the large double doors. Elidyr was a step behind, his shoulders broad and gaze focused.

A stream of grey smoke rose from the firepit where the council gathered. Glisseríel and Falavar, the Eirean of clan Rhyl, sat amidst six empty chairs. This wasn't surprising to Aélla, who had only convened with the full Eirean council twice in her life—once being directly after she had taken her vows of Drimil'Rothar, and second after she was awakened from the Nasir's cursed sleep.

"Aélla," Glisseríel said with all the venom of a rattlesnake. "What has brought you into these chambers?"

"You tell me, Master Eirean," she replied, dwarfing his icy tone with a harsh inflection of her own. "I pled with this council, seeking aid against the Klaet'il, and you have allowed them to continue their assault. Innocent people are dying at the hands of—"

"Silence!" he snapped. The wooden chair creaked as he stood. His face was red, and veins were swollen in his neck. "How dare you enter this hall with such disgrace! Do not mistake your place, Drimil. You may have taken the path of a savior, but you still bow to your rightful leaders."

Her eyes darkened. Without her magic, she felt the tendrils of anger weaving through her mind, gripping her thoughts and pulling at the strands of her fragile emotions.

"We need your help," she said as kindly as she could muster, though her rage seeped through. "The Klaet'il are turning e'liaa and humans into kanavin. The longer you wait, the more innocent blood will be shed."

Glisseríel scoffed with a laugh. "Preposterous!" he exclaimed. "What evidence do you have to support these claims? The Klaet'il have denied any involvement with the Nasir or these attacks against our people!"

"What about the survivors?" Aélla argued. "They know who attacked them."

Falavar, who sat quietly in his chair, said, "The survivors are in shock, Master Drimil. Their accounts cannot be taken as fact, not after the horrors they've witnessed."

"If we don't put an end to this, then more innocent blood will be shed! You have trusted my words time and time again. Why has your loyalty changed?"

"There is nothing disloyal about questioning the judgement of a child, Drimil," Falavar stated. "You have been through many harrowing adventures since you've taken your vows, going so far as to blame the Nasir for the curse placed upon you without a shred of evidence."

Glisseríel added, "And now you walk the path to Tre'lan Rothar with two known nesiat, Drimil'Nizotl, and a vaxros warrior. Forgive me if your decisions have caused us to reconsider the validity of your accusations."

Aélla's anger flared. She clenched her teeth and breathed heavily, fighting to extinguish the flame that stoked the heat of her fury. But it burned too hot to ignore, and she could no longer allow them to disregard the truth before them. Not when so many were dying at the hands of the Nasir.

"You're cowards!" she exclaimed. "You'd rather convince our people that the lanathess are behind these attacks than face the truth you've been so willing to hide behind all this time!"

"If our people are divided in a time of war, the forest will fall!"

"If the Nasir continues on this path, the *world* will fall!"

Her voice echoed through the wide hall, and the Eirean fell silent before her anger. Their eyes were guarded and stunned, never witnessing the depth of her rage. She hid it well, forcing her troubles and woes aside for the good of the world. But there was no redemption in sacrificing the innocent to keep unity among the people. She would fight for them, whether it saw her at the end of a branding iron or not. She would fight for those whose voices had been silenced.

"I won't allow the Nasir to continue this assault," she said. "And should you choose to stand against me, there will be no mercy."

Falavar's lip twitched. "Making threats against us is unwise, even for Drimil'Rothar."

"Making an enemy of me is unwise, even for an Eirean leader."

The Eirean glared at her beneath lowered brows. Their faces were taut with unbridled fury. She felt the heat of their rage drifting through the embers and pricking her skin, like a thousand shards of broken glass. But she never faltered beneath the weight of their gazes. They would believe her. She would make sure of it.

Falavar exhaled a deep breath. He leaned back in his chair and clasped his hands together. "You would have us believe that the Nasir, a man with whom you've had unreasonable hatred against for many summers, has laid siege to several e'liaan villages, transformed hundreds of innocent people into kanavin using the *claviaa muinsii*, and seeks to destroy the forest during a time of war?"

Aélla took several calming breaths, forcing her anger aside. "My hatred is not unreasonable. I *know* the Nasir was behind the curse that nearly took my life. I fought against him and the Klact'il in the desert. I witnessed the kanavin he created using the ring."

Glisseriel added, "The absurdity of your claims cannot be verified. Anyone who uses the ring to such an extent would be reduced to ash! No one could withstand such power."

"*He* can!"

Falavar said, "It seems your abhorrence of the Nasir has clouded your judgement. No man could ever—"

"Listen to me!" She took a step closer, pleading. "The Nasir is not like you or me. He's been changed! Corrupted!"

Glisseríel huffed. "This meeting is getting us nowhere. Until you have proof that the Nasir is—"

"I have proof," she said. Her heart thundered in her chest. A cold sweat dampened her skin as she stared at her leaders, prepared to reveal her most dangerous secret. One that could cause irreversible unrest and distrust between them.

The Eirean looked at her, silently waiting as she stared at the floor, gathering the strength to speak.

Her fists balled and throat was tight.

"Well?" Glisseríel pressed, becoming impatient.

Aélla breathed heavily. She glanced at Elidyr, hoping he would understand. Hoping they would *all* understand. Closing her eyes, she gulped down her fear. "The Nasir was not born Klaet'il. He didn't perform their rituals or take the avour'il to become a proven tóavel warrior." She paused, pushing away the nervous pounding in her chest. "He was one of us."

Falavar's eyes narrowed with suspicion. "Who was he?" he asked.

Her eyes flashed to the Eirean, and she quickly averted their condemning glares. "His name…was Aegrandir Líadrinel."

A silent rift tore through the room when she revealed the true identity of their most vicious enemy. The Eirean were silent, staring at Aélla with wide eyes. Their faces had fallen paler, and their lips were parted.

"Aegrandir?" Glisseríel stated, shock replacing his anger. "But he's—"

"I know," she said, her fists balled at her sides. Eyes burning with tears.

With forced resolve, she lifted her gaze and said aloud her most deadly secret. A secret she had hoped would never be revealed. A secret that could cost her everything.

"The Nasir…"—she closed her eyes in shame—"is my father."

Chapter Thirty-One

Fractured Faith
Aélla

"Any known origins of the Nasir must be brought forth immediately. Perjury of these facts will be met with the swift, unforgiving hand of justice."

— Eirean decree

SILENCE SWEPT ACROSS THE ROOM, draping the hall with heavy tension. It was thick in the air, catching in Aélla's throat as she stared at her leaders, prepared for whatever judgement they sought to pass. Aélla had known keeping this secret could cost her everything. The Nasir had been the cause of trouble for many, many summers, and had they known his true identity—had the Eirean known of his relationship to Aélla—she feared his power may not have grown to what it had become. Ruthless and unhinged.

Unstoppable.

He had led assaults throughout the forest, seeking to gain control of rival clans or to release his anger on e'liaan villages. Due to their deep hatred for humanity, the Klaet'il considered the mixed-blood to be *fisthraa*, or abominations. The peaceful half-race typically kept to themselves, making them an easy target. They wanted no quarrel with anyone and sought only to live in peace.

Aélla understood her father's deep, unending hatred for the humans, who had taken her mother away so long ago. She had left to search for Avelloch, who was playing in the woods, when she vanished. Avelloch didn't speak much after her disappearance, and soon, he was gone too. For a time, her father was all she had.

But after her mother's death, he had changed and become someone entirely different. A once noble warrior and devoted father had fallen into madness. He was lost, and although he was there, watching over her, Aélla had never felt more alone.

She fought back her sorrow, thinking of her family and what could have been. It wasn't until Avelloch's banishment that Aélla understood the truth, and the world crashed around her.

"Aélla," Glisseríel snapped. His voice was sharp and direct, as if he had spoken her name several times.

She lifted her gaze to meet with his and found nothing but fury in his cold eyes.

"Explain yourself."

Her eyes fell away, and she inhaled a deep breath. Emotions roared through her, ripping at her like sharp claws, shredding and beating until there was nothing left. Her jaw clenched and body stiffened. Speaking of him was difficult. After so long, she still couldn't accept who he was or what he had become.

Elidyr leaned close, inspecting her with wide, sorrowful eyes. "Master Drimil…," he whispered. There was no authority in his usually rigid voice. It was softer, as if speaking to a frightened child.

Regaining her strength, Aélla stood tall and clasped her hands behind her back. She glanced between the Eirean, studying their angered expressions. "I was a child when my father died," she explained. "I learned the truth of who he had become long after."

Fil'veraal, the second Eirean, stated, "Aegrandir was dead, yet now he is alive. Did you have anything to do with his saving?"

"He wasn't saved," she said, and her strong voice was outweighed by a sudden wave of sorrow and guilt. Her throat was suddenly dry and chest was heavy. "He's been turned."

Glisseríel's eyes simmered. His red face glowed brighter than the embers in the firepit separating him from

Aélla and Elidyr. Through clenched teeth, he mustered the word, "How?"

"I don't know."

His chiseled voice etched through the thick air. "You don't know?"

"No," she stated. "There is only one other who could have brought him back."

Fil'veraal said, "Even with the power of tre'lan Zynther, Elashor wouldn't have the capability of bringing someone back. Not with the autonomy the Nasir has."

The Eirean placed a finger to his chin in deep thought. His eyes flicked to the left, where the stia'dyr servants were positioned against the wall. "Braithe," he said, and a woman with light brown hair turned to face him.

The others kept their eyes on the floor, unmoving.

"Find the necromancer. We'll keep our eyes on him until our warriors can bring him to our chambers. This will *not* go unpunished."

Elidyr stepped forward. "Elashor couldn't have done this, Master Eirean. Even with the energy of the tre'lan, it's impossible."

"Yet it *is* possible!" Fil'veraal exclaimed, his anger rising alongside his gravelly voice. "He may not have had the strength, but he was part of it."

Angry eyes veered to Aélla, striking through her like daggers.

"As for you," he warned, "this is treason of the highest degree. To withhold such vital knowledge of the Nasir's true identity—to have him linked directly to you and your *filthy* brother. We cannot—"

"Avelloch is *not* filthy!" she exclaimed, and the Eirean fell instantly silent.

His lips pursed and eyes were wide with fury. Before he had the chance to speak, Aélla continued, her own rage dominating his.

"Without him we would *all* be dead! I couldn't have become Drimil'Rothar without him. He went after the Nasir when I was cursed because *you* were too cowardly to fight against him! We now stand at the brink of war, yet you still cower like children."

The room was deathly silent when she paused, soaking in their fury and shock. Allowing it to fuel the unrest brewing deep in her soul. Before meeting Neer, Aélla was a prisoner to her beliefs. An unyielding light in a world cast in darkness. She followed in the path set before her, believing it to be one she had chosen for herself.

But these misguided notions of peace and inner strength had blinded her to the truth that was all around her. She had focused too heavily on her goals and allowed many innocent people to die.

Speaking with irrevocable authority and conviction, she said, "I will not waver under the pressure of defeat. I won't allow innocent people to die while I have the power to help them. They look to *me* as their savior because they know that I will do what's right. You have banished *two* of my guardians for senseless reasonings. Destroyed hundreds of lives to protect your position. But when the drums of war are beating at your doorstep, do not expect anyone to be here for *you*."

There was silence as her voice faded. Deep, unending silence.

Elidyr breathed heavily. He stood strong beside Aélla, his shoulders broad and posture straight—a soldier ready for command. But his eyes were coated in confusion and misery, a stark contrast to the heat emanating from the Eirean's deadly glares.

Glisseríel's voice was sharp as broken glass when he spoke. "How. Dare. You! You come into these sacred chambers, seeking aid in this war against the Klaet'il—a war we cannot afford to fight—in an effort to save the *halfbloods!*" He scoffed with a laugh. "They should be grateful we have allowed them into our lands at all!"

Aélla stiffened, fighting against the anger that threatened to unleash. Beside her, Elidyr's confusion slipped into anger. A deep line formed between his brow, and his eyes narrowed with contempt.

The Eirean's voice shook the air as his fury unleashed. But soon, he was quiet, heaving deep breaths as his wide eyes were set on Aélla, waiting for her response. She knew he wanted an apology, but she refused to give it. Standing in her strength, she knew her choices were right. The world would have never given her a chance had they known of her connection to the Nasir.

The image of her brother, who had been wrongfully accused of treason and murder, would be solidified in their minds. His lineage would be his downfall, thinking he had fallen into the madness, the same as his father.

Aélla broadened her shoulders and lifted her chin, accepting whatever judgement may fall. She would die to protect the innocent from harm. It was the vow she had taken long ago and one she repeated each night before sleep, reminding herself of the hardships and struggles to come.

Staring into the eyes of her leaders, she understood the weight of that decision.

Glisseríel's lip twitched. His eyes were unhinged and face was blood red. He took several deep breaths. "Had you not taken the vows…," he started, "had you not become the world's savior…I would hang you in the streets for the dishonor you have avowed."

Elidyr glared at the Eirean, and his fists tightened at his sides.

"This war will be won without you," the Eirean continued. "The Nasir is not our concern. These tales you have spoken of kanavin and necromancy are a clear manipulation." His eyes narrowed. "I am ashamed to have bestowed the title of Drimil'Rothar to a child so weak and sheltered."

Aélla didn't speak. She knew her words would fall on deaf ears, so she stood in her confidence, not allowing his painful words to fracture her strength.

Glisseríel continued, "You will leave the forest, immediately. The world will not know of this most disturbing secret, lest it tarnish the integrity of the very council who gave you your name. But make no mistake, Aélla Líadrinel…you are no longer part of our people. The evae will know who you are once you've completed your journey. The world will know the truth of your lies and tainted blood." His eyes simmered. "You are no hero. You are a *disgrace.*"

His words ripped through her, slicing her flesh and soul. The strength she conveyed was slipping. A knot formed in her throat as emotions rose to the surface. She fought to contain them, to convey the sense of confidence a savior should. But she was weakened by their words, which had been harsher than she could have ever imagined.

"Leave this council chamber at once," Glisseríel continued. "And do not come back."

Fil'veraal turned to Elidyr. "See to it that the Drimil and her company are escorted to the borders immediately," the Eirean said. "If any of them see to fight against this judgement, kill them."

Aélla inhaled a shallow breath, shaken by the severity of his words. Elidyr lowered into a stiff bow. His posture was rigid and brows were pulled together with rage. He stood and placed a hand on the small of Aélla's back, guiding her out of the chambers.

They walked together in silence, unable to speak. The burden of the Eirean's ruling weighed them with sorrow and anger. Aélla knew she couldn't abandon her home—not when the people needed her. The Nasir wouldn't stop his pursuits, and she wouldn't allow the e'liaa to fall victim to his reign.

The forest became sparse as they headed west, away from the center of Navarre. Following narrow foot trails, they marched quietly through the evergreen. A calming scent of jasmine filled Aélla's nose, and tears flooded her eyes. Through the woods, she could spot the white fields, which were tended to by Bek'il and Deelah, two florists she had come to know throughout her childhood.

The scent filled Aélla with memories of a time when she and Klaud would spend their nights lying in the flowers, staring up at the sky and imagining their lives.

They would never see or smell those flowers again. Her home would soon fade into the shadows of a life she used to know. Everything she held close was slipping away, and soon, the world would know the truth. That she was part of the Nasir. That all of the actions and cruelty he inflicted

SHADOWS OF NYN'DIRA

were connected to her and Avelloch. Every step they took would be viewed with condemnation.

As they moved closer to the fields, Aélla stepped away from the path. Elidyr turned, watching her with a curious eye, as she strode away. Her misty eyes were fixed on the flowers while she waded through the petals. Coming to a stop in the center of the meadow, she closed her eyes and brought her hands to her chest. Her chin lifted, and she embraced the warmth of sunshine beaming against her tear-stained cheeks.

A light breeze lifted the quiet that had weighed the land in misery. Flower petals broke away to wisp happily through the air, drenching the forest with a sweet and rich aroma. Ensnared by memories, Aélla sank to her knees. She lay back with her arms wide, just as she used to, and looked up at the sky.

Flowers danced around her as the forest gifted her with its warming presence. She smiled, knowing that while the Eirean may not accept her, Nyn'Dira did. The people she fought for wouldn't betray her. The forest would always know the truth.

She closed her eyes and breathed in the scent of home. It was one she never wanted to forget and vowed to always carry with her.

The sounds of birds whistling in the sky caught her attention, and her eyes snapped open. She watched a flock of azae'l songbirds fly past, dancing in beautiful, weaving patterns. A smile pulled the edge of her lips, and her chin quivered. Klaud had always said Aélla was as peaceful and strong as an azae'l, which appeared innocent but fought for their flocks with a vengeance.

The azae'ls would often swarm the fields, searching the flowers for meals. Oftentimes, the birds would hop over Aélla and Klaud as they lay in the dirt, becoming one with the nature surrounding them.

A blue feather drifted down from the sky, landing softly in the dirt by Aélla's hand. It was a parting gift from the world she used to know. She gripped the feather and held it close to her chest. Her cries were silent as she lay alone, embraced by sunlight. The forest never settled, sending a light breeze her way from every direction. The flowers danced toward her, and branches swayed overhead. Shadows blocked out the sun as the azae'ls circled the sky before landing in the field. Their soft chirps echoed noisily around Aélla, filling her dread with peace.

She opened her eyes, watching as the world wept alongside her with a final goodbye, sensing the tides of change. Another tear slipped from her eye, and she held the feather tighter, becoming one with the forest and sky.

"Thank you," she whispered, and the forest responded with a deep, calming wind.

Once her tears had dried, Aélla rose to her feet. The azae'ls took flight, soaring high above in various formations before disappearing into the sky.

Aélla wiped her face and inhaled a deep breath. She dusted the grass from her robes and slipped the feather into her pocket. Her eyes met with Elidyr's, who was waiting at the edge of the field. The strong soldier she had always known held a look of sorrow and guilt. She studied him for a moment, before carefully approaching his side.

He stood two hands taller, and his muscular build made her appear childlike as she stared up at him, holding his gaze.

"Your brother is in my company," she said. "Will you force him away too?"

Elidyr's jaw clenched. Slowly, he turned away, eying the flowers. "The Eirean have betrayed us."

Aélla's hair swept across her face from the gentle breeze. "You'll be called a traitor for saying such things."

He was silent, staring absently at the forest. "My loyalty is to my home," he said, and then his eyes shifted to hers. "I will fight to defend it."

Aélla reached out and grasped his arm. Their eyes met, and she felt the swell of trust forming between them. Being one of their commanding officers, Elidyr had seen firsthand what the Eirean were capable of.

His voice was strong as he said, "The world will know you as a hero, Master Drimil." He paused with intent. "We will never forget who you are."

She smiled and gave him a thankful nod. "Come on," Aélla said, stepping away from him and continuing on their original path. "It's a long journey back to the others."

He walked alongside her, his posture strong and determined. His dark blue eyes scanned the forest, and when he was sure they were alone, Elidyr said, "I won't be escorting you back."

Aélla glanced at him, hiding her shock and elation.

"I'll gather my men, and we'll fight alongside you. We won't allow the Klaet'il to get away with this."

She stood taller, with pride. "You'll go against the Eirean to fight with me?"

He nodded. "The people fear the Eirean, but they respect you. We won't be swayed so easily."

There was a break in his words when he helped Aélla climb over a large fallen tree. He followed behind, leaping over its height and landing beside her with a thud.

Continuing on, he said, "The forest will be divided over torn loyalties. Many believe the lanathess are to blame for these attacks against the e'liaa. They won't fight against the Klaet'il if the Eirean are pushing them toward the invasion."

"I have enough strength on my side to fight the Nasir."

Elidyr slowed to a stop, and Aélla turned to him, watching him tighten his fists and stare at the ground. His eyes shifted from left to right as he sifted through his thoughts. "I understand the dishonor that comes from familial treason."

He exhaled a slow breath, clearly disturbed. Aélla knew he was referring to his brother, N'iossca, who had defected from their clan long ago after the Eirean executed his partner, Caline.

Elidyr continued, "Who else knows about your father?"

Aélla paused and explained, "Avelloch and Klaud."

He swallowed. "Does Thallon..." His words disappeared, and he closed his eyes, fearing the worst. Whoever else kept this secret would surely be hanged.

"No," she reassured him, and his shoulders slumped with relief. "Only the three of us know the truth."

Eased by her words, Elidyr regained his strength and marched forward. Aélla followed, walking alongside him.

The path disappeared as they headed further into the forest. A sawmill could be heard through the thicket of trees, erasing the scent of grass and leaves with that of freshly cut wood. Aélla knew they were toeing the boundary line of Navarre, and soon, they'd be embraced by the quiet expanse of the forest.

"What are your plans?" Elidyr asked. "Where should I bring my warriors?"

"I'm going to Galiendör to approach Galdir. With any luck, I'll be able to restore strength to the forest. It may not be much, but it can buy us more time."

He nodded. "I'll send as many as I can to your aid."

"We don't know the Nasir's next moves. He'll most likely continue targeting the e'liaan settlements."

He gave another nod.

They passed by Sh'Ansal, an expansive lake bordering Navarre territory. Many dock houses and rowboats were sprawled across its shores. People swam in the deep waters, splashing and laughing as if the forest was a calm and beautiful place. As if two days north there weren't fires and death sweeping the lands.

"Drimil." Elidyr grasped her arm and came to a stop. She turned to face him as he said, "Get back to your people. Make haste. I'll send others as quickly as I'm able."

"Don't get yourself or your family persecuted for my crimes, Elidyr. Stay true to your vows and keep your loved ones safe."

He eyed the lake, watching children play in the water. "My family will never be safe. Not until we put an end to this madness." His attention returned to her, and he dug through his pocket. "There is something else."

He passed her a rolled parchment and said, "His family's alive."

Aélla's brows furrowed, then realization struck her. She glanced up at Elidyr with parted lips. He lowered into a respectful bow.

"Be well, Master Drimil. When you make the call...the avel will listen."

Aélla bowed and watched with pride as Elidyr strongly marched away.

Chapter Thirty-Two

Of Axe and Flame
Nerana

"Grömek vortuuk sakala torvein."
We are none without honor and strength

– Sayings of the Vaxros

WINDS PRESSED AGAINST THE WALLS of a cabin, and the shelter groaned in protest. Its constant creaks and moans lifted the harrowing silence as everyone sat inside with not a word spoken. Neer lay on a cot, staring at the ceiling. Her mind wandered from one thing to the next, trying desperately to forget her sorrow and grief.

She thought of the evaesh warriors and how they had departed long ago, seeking to gather more avel in the impending battle to come. They'd never allow the Klaet'il to get away with this, and while there was little hope of gaining help from the Eirean, Neer still clung to whatever sliver of it was left, praying Aélla could convince them to see reason.

But those in power wished to stay in power, and they'd never risk their position by admitting their mistake in ignoring Aélla's initial pleas for help. Neer knew by how easily they had banished Klaud, who was an esteemed member of their advising council, that the Eirean were far less honorable than the evae seemed to believe.

SHADOWS OF NYN'DIRA

A shadow stalked the room, and Neer's thoughts were broken when Avelloch stepped away from the hearth. Her cot shifted when he sat along its edge. He turned to her with pity in his eyes, and her stomach churned. She kept her focus on the ceiling, not accepting his sympathy.

Across the room, Thurandír lay on a second cot. It was much larger than the one Neer rested on, with a feather mattress and thick furs. His chest rose and fell as he lay in a deep sleep. Y'ven sat before the flames, gripping his arm in agony. His large shadow engulfed Thurandír in darkness, undoubtedly easing him into his restful slumber.

A low growl rumbled from Y'ven's throat, mixing with the sounds of the creaking hut. His skin had faded from its natural crimson to dark yellow as his infection spread. Bright orange veins crawled across his skin from beneath the blood-soaked bandages.

Dru stood on the floor in front of him. She rubbed her tiny hands together in deep concern. Her tinkling voice was lost to the overpowering sounds of the creaking cabin as she spoke to Y'ven. But he never responded. His shoulders broadened with every deep, exhausted breath, and he wove in and out of consciousness. Yellow eyes would slide closed, only to reopen quickly with a sudden jerk of his head, fighting to stay awake.

Steady footsteps tapped against the floor as Reiman approached his side. He knelt beside the warrior and placed his hand upon Y'ven's slumped shoulder. "Y'ven," he said, his voice rising just above a whisper.

The vaxros turned to him with dreary eyes.

"You know what we must do."

Neer turned to them, her attention shifting to their conversation as her father's words laced the air. Thallon, who sat beside Klaud scribbling in a notebook, was broken from his concentration. He and Klaud shared a glance before lifting their eyes to the vaxros.

"Cannot," Y'ven said through a slurred voice. "Disgraced…"

"There is no honor in a senseless death." Reiman tightened his grip on Y'ven's shoulder. "You are a warrior. A brother. The guardian of Drimil'Rothar."

Y'ven exhaled a gruff sigh somewhere between reluctance and relief. He was torn between his pride as a vaxros warrior and his honor in being Drimil'Rothar's guardian. He had vowed to protect her, and he couldn't forsake her now.

Reiman continued, "I will gather some potions to numb the pain, and we'll—"

"No." His angered voice shook the air.

Everyone was silent, expecting him to unleash the rage sawing through his voice, revealing his pain.

"I am a warrior. I will not be disgraced."

Dru shook her head in deep worry as Y'ven rose to his feet. He caught himself on the wall and leaned forward, taking heaved breaths. The anger thickening the air subsided while he stood by the fire, understanding his fate. Realizing a choice had to be made.

The walls trembled when he unleashed a chiseled, angry growl. He snatched an axe from the floor by the hearth and then marched outside. A heavy silence fell through the room before everyone quickly followed behind, hoping to stop him before he attempted to remove his arm himself.

Thallon raced to his side, his panicked voice ringing through the air like chiming bells while he begged Y'ven to reconsider. "You can't do this on your own!" he exclaimed. "Let us help you!"

A vicious growl tore from Y'ven's throat, resounding through the woods. He turned and snatched Thallon by the collar. He clawed against Y'ven's thick forearm as he was pulled close. His dark blue eyes were wide as the vaxros glared at him.

Neer rushed over and placed her hands on each of their shoulders, nudging them slightly apart. "Y'ven," she started, "you aren't alone. Whatever struggles you face, we face them together."

"It is not our way." He spoke through bared teeth in his native tongue.

"You're one of *us* now."

His dull yellow eyes flashed to hers, and she held his gaze, showing no sign of weakness as his lip snarled.

"*We* are your people. Let us help you."

SHADOWS OF NYN'DIRA

"I cannot. I will dishonor my name. My family."

"There is no shame in accepting help when you need it." She paused, noticing the hint of relief in his tired eyes. "If you do this alone…you could die." Tears welled in her eyes. She clenched her teeth, fighting against the agony rising in her chest. "I'm not losing anyone else."

His anger softened, and his eyes slowly fell away. Thallon shifted before touching his chest when Y'ven released his grasp. The vaxros exhaled a deep breath. With his eyes closed, he gave a subtle nod. Neer's shoulders dropped with relief.

Reiman approached his side and reached for the axe. Y'ven stared at his leader's outstretched hand, reluctant to hand over his control and allow another to desecrate his body. His jaw tightened, and he stood in silence. Slowly, he passed the weapon to Reiman, and a wave of relief swept through the air.

Sunlight glinted through the trees, casting streams of golden light through the forest that glimmered against the scars tracing his chest. He was immobile, gripping his injured arm as his body trembled with agony.

Klaud stepped forward and placed a long, flat board on the grass. He swept it of any debris before slowly turning to Y'ven. The vaxros stared down at the cutting board, too stiff in his reluctance to move.

"Come," Reiman said, nudging him forward.

Y'ven closed his eyes and slowly lay on his back. Klaud gently pulled his injured arm outward, positioning it across the length of the wood. Avelloch stepped from the cabin with two axes in his hands. His jaw was clenched as he approached, gazing with hard eyes as Reiman and Klaud held Y'ven's arms into place. Filthy bandages were thrown into a pile, leaving Y'ven's deep, pus-ridden wound exposed. Necrosis had eaten away most of the flesh on his inner forearm. Bright veins crawled away from the wound like webs, traveling upward to his inner elbow and down across his palm.

"Isn't there another way?" Thallon asked.

Reiman said, "There is no cure for a wisper's venom. If we don't remove his arm, he will die." He turned to Y'ven, who lay with his eyes closed, anticipating the pain. "Are you sure you want no relief from the pain, brother?"

Y'ven remained still, giving his response with the sound of silence. Seconds passed before Reiman glanced at Avelloch and gave him a stiff nod. Avelloch inhaled a timid breath and then knelt by Y'ven's side.

Neer stood with Dru on her shoulder, unable to breathe as they watched the horror before them. Knowing this was what he needed but hating it all the same.

The sharp blade of the axe hovered above Y'ven's skin. "Are you ready?" Avelloch asked.

With his eyes firmly shut, Y'ven turned toward the sky. He wriggled into the grass while Reiman and Klaud pressed down on his arms, pinning them in place. Seconds passed, and they waited, watching him breathe heavily. Riddled with pain and fear.

A low growl rumbled from Y'ven's throat, and when he gave a quick nod, Avelloch placed the blade to his skin, inches above his elbow. He hesitated for a moment, staring at the scalding blade that didn't so much as hiss against Y'ven's thick flesh.

Not a second passed before Avelloch lifted the second axe and smashed its blunt end against the weapon touching Y'ven's arm. His skin split, and the loud sizzle of burning muscle filled the air. Y'ven gritted his teeth. The loud clink of the axes smacked together twice more, and tremors erupted through Y'ven's body. His face was taut and teeth were bared, but he withheld his agony.

Reiman and Klaud held him down when his shoulders began to quiver, reacting to the pain. He jerked away from the blade chiseling further through his muscle, and a deep roar echoed through the forest, causing birds to take flight.

"Thallon!" Klaud called.

Thallon flinched and then rushed forward. He fell to his knees and pressed firmly against Y'ven's shoulders.

The rhythmic clink of the axes created a deadly tempo as Avelloch hammered against the weapon, crunching through bone. Flesh squelched as he pulled Y'ven's arm away, tossing it into the grass. The severed limb drained with thick, poisoned blood.

Y'ven's fingers were still curled into a tight fist.

The sizzle of raw muscle crawled beneath the sound of another quaking growl. Avelloch held the burning axe against Y'ven's stump, sealing his wound. His jaw clenched and lips were pursed as he held firm to the weapon.

Neer's stomach churned when the smell of blood and burnt flesh swept through the air. She turned away, holding her breath and clutching her stomach. Her eyes flicked to her shoulder to check on Dru, and Neer was shocked to find she was no longer there.

She had no time to search for the distraught faeth when the echoing sounds of Y'ven's tortured growls came to a sudden halt. The forest fell intensely silent. A sullen hush blanketed the darkening land. It was a quiet both unnerving and welcome.

Y'ven sank into the grass, breathing deeply through a raw throat. The others slowly released their grasps on his arms, and a silent wave of relief eased the burden of guilt.

The sounds of rustling grass injected life back into the quiet forest when Avelloch leaned back. He dropped the axes to the ground and rubbed his face. A calming breeze brought a faint swell of magic, and Neer inhaled a deep breath, calmed by its ever-present sting. The warmth of energy connecting all living things moved through her, touching the very fabric of her soul. Weaving through the holes of loneliness and guilt as she stared at Y'ven's severed arm.

Klaud gently lifted it from the ground. He held it like a wounded dove, careful not to further tarnish Y'ven's sacrifice by showing any signs of disrespect. Without speaking, he departed the group and entered the cabin. The door was left ajar, leaving just enough space for Neer to witness him place Y'ven's limb into the hearth. An orange glow brightened from within the home as it caught fire.

Thallon's voice pulled Neer's attention back to the group.

"We have to give him *aithmir*," he said to Reiman "It will prevent an infection."

Reiman spoke quietly to him, while Y'ven lay with his eyes closed. His chest rose and fell, gifting Neer with relief.

She watched him breathe, thankful he was still alive. That he would *remain* alive.

With another look around, Neer rose to her feet and retreated to the cabin. Her eyes shifted to the hearth, and she was eased to find Dru hovering within the flames. Thurandír rested peacefully on the bed.

Wooden legs grated against the floor when Neer dragged a chair to the cot and waited for him to wake.

Moonlight caressed the world with a gentle glow, and night overtook the quiet forest. Flames popped and whirred within the hearth, spraying embers and smoke into the chimney. Dru hovered within the firelight, never leaving, even as Y'ven had returned and taken his place by the glowing warmth.

He lay asleep beside the roaring heat, keeping his stump close to the flames, allowing its energy to heal him as he slept. A deep, gravely saw tore from his throat when he fell into a deep slumber. The sound was heavier than it had ever been, chiseling through the cool night air and fracturing any hope of sleep Neer may have had.

Unable to ignore his constant snoring, she sat at the table with Avelloch, Thallon, and Klaud. Reiman and Wallace had chosen long ago to reside in a neighboring hut for the night.

Neer leaned forward with her head in her hands. Dirty hair draped across her face like shredded curtains, hiding the exhaustion that showed itself in the dark circles beneath her eyes.

Her eyes flicked to Thallon, who sat in deep silence to her right. His face was washed of its color and eyes were wide. Neer straightened, causing her chair to creak, and Thallon blinked his heavy thoughts away. He glanced through the room, as if he had forgotten where he was.

"Are you all right?" Neer asked.

He gave an uneven nod. "Yeah," he said.

She placed her hand on his arm, and he exhaled a deep breath.

"This is so fucked up," Thallon said. "It's so fucking…"

He shook his head and then wiped his face. Gazing through the room, his eyes paused on Thurandír. Thallon breathed heavily with sorrow before returning his attention to the others at the table.

"How can you three sit here like this? As if this is fucking normal?"

Klaud said, "This isn't normal. Not for any of us."

"I feel like I'm losing my mind! The world is going to shit, and you're just—" He made an inarticulate gesture with his arm. Shaking his head, he fell silent, though the discontent flared in his eyes.

Avelloch leaned forward, resting his chin on his folded hands. His posture was relaxed, though his eyes were sorrowful. Neer's attention drifted to Y'ven, and she glanced at his wrapped arm. The sound of his bones cracking and flesh tearing were seared into her mind, and she was thankful for his sawing snore. It muted the echoes of his bloodcurdling growls repeating through her mind.

"What do we do now?" she asked. "How can we stop this?"

"What do you mean?" Thallon remarked. "We can't stop it! We're all fucked!"

"Thallon," Klaud said sternly, like a father scolding his child.

"He turned them all to kanavin, Klaud! People were ripped apart." He clutched his messy hair. "I can still hear it! Their screams and bones and the fucking smell!"

Neer stared at the table, washed with guilt. She was the reason for all of this chaos. Deep in her soul, she knew it. There was unrest around her, and everyone—humans, elves, vaxros, dreleds—they all viewed her as a demon. The Child of Skye.

A monster to be purged.

And though she didn't want to admit it, she was starting to believe it herself.

Neer was jolted from her thoughts when the sudden sound of crackling magic echoed from outside. Everyone stood when Klaud moved to the window. He peered outside and then stepped to the door.

"She's back," he said.

The others trailed close behind. The night air was made colder when Neer stepped outside, deprived of the hearth's warm embrace. She crossed her arms and breathed through chattering teeth. Avelloch rushed forward, huddling around his sister with Klaud.

Neer and Thallon joined them as Aélla rose to her feet. "What happened?" Klaud asked. "Did you tell them?"

Aélla's eyes hardened. She stared at the ground, stiff with sorrow. With a timid gulp, she gave them a nod almost too subtle to see. Avelloch became intensely quiet, and his jaw tensed.

"And?" Klaud pressed.

Aélla hesitated. Her lips pursed together and eyes shifted from left to right, never settling on anything as she gathered her thoughts. "They…They *want* the Nasir to continue his assault."

Anger flared through Avelloch. "What? Why the fuck would they—"

"They want to blame the lanathess," she said, her voice a gentle breeze beneath the weight of his rage. "We have to get to Galdir. Soon. Elidyr will gather as many avel as he can. They'll come to defend us should the Nasir see to attack us again."

"Elidyr?" Thallon asked, his eyes lifting to hers with a bit of hope. "He's going to help us?"

Aélla nodded with a light smile. "Thurandír is his warrior, and you are his brother." She paused. "He won't leave you behind."

Thallon's jaw tightened. He inhaled a deep breath and turned away.

Avelloch asked, "So we just move on? Get to the tree and strengthen its energy…for what? The Klaet'il are still killing our people. The lanathess are still invading!"

"It can buy us time," Klaud said, answering for Aélla.

"For what?" Avelloch retorted. "Our focus should be on the Nasir! If he isn't stopped, he will have an army powerful enough to kill the entire fucking continent!"

"Please," Aélla begged.

Avelloch shook his head, spewing with rage.

"This is all that I know to do, Avelloch. I can't fight every battle. If we don't continue toward tre'lan Rothar, then all of this will be for nothing."

Neer glanced between them, her heart thrumming in her chest. She pushed through her fear and said, "The Nasir is after me."

Everyone turned to her, their expressions a mixture of confusion and shock.

"He didn't go after Aélla in the village. He led Reiman and me away from everyone, and he…He tried to…." Her thoughts were muddled, and she fought to remember what had happened that night. But the images moved too quickly to pin down with words. "I don't know what he did, but he did it to *me*."

She lifted her eyes to the others.

"If we go to Galdir, he will follow us. We can lay a trap for him there and use this to our advantage."

Everyone was silent, contemplating her words.

They turned to Klaud as he said, "The ydris are incredible warriors, and they have full faith in Drimil'Rothar. I believe they will fight alongside us."

Thallon argued, "We can't pull more innocent people into another battle like this!"

"We have to get to Galdir, Thallon," Aélla said, her voice frail. Her posture still slouched and weak. "I'll speak to Eirean Calasiem when we arrive at ydris territory. She can decide if her people will help us against the Nasir."

Her eyes shifted to each person before her, studying the anguish and unrest in their tired, battle-worn eyes.

"There has been more than enough heartache and war," she said. "We should rest for now and regain our strength. Once the others are able, we'll make our way to Galiendör."

Everyone agreed, and the conversations soon fell silent. The night air coiled around them, gripping with a frigid sting. Thallon took his leave, escaping the cold for the warmth of the cabin. The quick stream of flickering light faded as the door closed behind him, concealing the heat of the roaring fire inside.

Neer lifted her eyes to the others, who stood in solemn silence. Aélla's posture was slouched and weak. She breathed heavily, as if fighting back deep, heavy emotions.

Closing her eyes, she said, "Nerana, I need to speak with my brother and Klaud."

Avelloch's jaw tensed, and his gaze hardened, while Klaud stood motionless, his sullen eyes fixed on Aélla, who refused to meet their stares. Neer glanced between them, hoping for an answer, but when they had none to give, she walked silently to the cabin.

As the opened the door, her eyes flicked to the trio standing beneath the moonlight. A tear slid down Aélla's cheek, and she took Avelloch and Klaud's hands. Neer turned away and slipped into the cabin, closing the door behind.

Chapter Thirty-Three

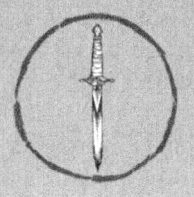

A Father's Love
Nerana

"Weep not, my dear child, for you have found a place to call home."

— Reiman to his daughter, Nerana

Neer sat in the forest, alone, deep in her meditations. Sweat glistened down her temples, and visions flashed through her mind. She thought of Gil and the terrible fate he had endured. All of the moments they shared were now hers to remember, alone. There was no one else to reminisce stories of a life she would never see again.

She thought of Coryn and all the others who had been by her side, had fought to protect her, who were now gone. Mangled and torn apart. Before the thoughts could solidify into grief, she pushed them away, as she always had, and focused on every slow, intentional breath. But the flashes never stopped:

Thallon's home after she had choked him in a fit of rage...Klaud's skull being compressed beneath the weight of her magic...Loryk's body lying limp beneath the glow of a shimmering Tree...His weight as she carried him home, bloated and rotting...

The look of fear in everyone's eyes...

She felt lost, like a rat in a maze, searching for a way out, only to find another wall blocking her path. Her breathing quickened. Sweat formed across her brow. The raw sting of ice and steel dragged against her flesh, sinking into her bones where it fizzled and burned. Her teeth were clenched and eyes were closed tight.

A voice, cold as a winter's breeze, crept through her mind, weaving the pieces of her broken, battered thoughts. Like shards of glass being fused together, the images became clear. His voice whispered from deep inside, sending chills down her spine.

"*Free us…*"

The mist shrouding her thoughts cleared, revealing the face of another. His skin was pale as death and closed eyes were painted with veins crawling across his skin like thick, overlapping webs. Shadows grew from his body, snaking through the void as they extended far beyond his reach.

Neer breathed heavily. Her fists were pressed together and arms were tight. Sunlight cast through the swaying branches, gleaming against her damp skin.

In her mind, she saw the man, standing alone, whispering through closed lips. Suddenly, his eyes opened, and solid black irises flashed with a hint of teal.

Neer inhaled a deep breath and fell back. The crisp air was cold against her sweat-laden skin. A deep pain settled in her chest, and she curled inward, fighting against its affliction. The air was heavier, wrought with emptiness and pain. So much pain.

She felt the tides shifting, dragging her sanity further from the shore, forever lost to the abyss. No amount of strength or perseverance could change her fate. The winds of change would carry her to the end, and while she fought against its pull, she knew it was near. Every day dragging her closer to a cold and empty death. Hollow. Broken. Filled with inescapable rage.

Grass rustled behind, and Neer exhaled a slow breath, relinquished of her thoughts. She glanced back at Wallace, who, at Reiman's command, stood as her protective sword and shield. Thick hands were folded over the large handle of his great sword. Neer examined the blade, which was twice the width of her arm and nearly half the length of her body. She had never seen a weapon so massive and thought

SHADOWS OF NYN'DIRA

it may have belonged to a Knight of the Order, whom Wallace nearly matched in size and strength.

A calming breeze swept by, and Neer closed her eyes. She inhaled the woodsy aroma and sank into its embrace, feeling the life of the world moving through her. Leaning forward, she ran her fingers through the grass and slowly lay on her stomach. Energy culminated in her chest, expanding outward to grasp the spirit of the forest around her. Every swaying limb and gust of wind coalesced with the magic simmering in her soul, forcing it to calm. She felt the patter of feet, paws, and hooves as animals roamed the understory.

Neer buried her face in the grass and inhaled a deep breath. The forest pulled toward her, bending every blade of grass and sway of the wind in her direction. She exhaled, and the forest relaxed.

"Help me...," she whispered, speaking directly to fate and the world itself.

Wallace lifted his eyes, watching as the leaves danced and swayed. Sunrays beamed through the rustling canopy, gliding warm light against Neer's broken, defeated body. A figure approached from the left, and Wallace turned. The tight muscles in his arms relaxed when his eyes met with Reiman's.

The evae lifted his hand in a silent signal for the warrior to retreat. Without pause, Wallace trudged through the forest, disappearing in the direction of the village.

Neer was motionless on the ground, feeling every impression of his boots against the soil while he walked away. Reiman's steps were lighter but heavy with confidence as he strode to her side. Realizing her moment of solitude had slipped away, Neer crawled back and sat on her knees.

Reiman stood tall and strong at her side, a true pillar of strength. He looked down at Neer, who kept her eyes on the grass. His light blue eyes scanned the forest, before he said, "Are you all right?"

Her hand curled over her chest, feeling for a heartbeat she wasn't sure was there. With every thrum against her ribs, she was reminded she was alive. This was her life, and she had to go on. "Do you think the Divines are real?"

Reiman took pause at her question, his brows furrowing, ever so slightly. "There is no reason to question such futile things. Whether the Divines exist or whether they do not, it doesn't change the truth of our circumstances."

Neer shook her head. "It could change everything."

He raised a brow. "Is that what you believe?"

"I don't know what I believe anymore." She lifted her eyes to the forest, still holding on to the connection tying her life to everything around her. "All that I know is that the world views me as a monster…and lately…I've started to feel like one."

Reiman sat by her side. He placed his hand on her shoulder, and the connection she felt to the world was severed. A heavy void replaced the peace, and her heart ached.

"You are no monster," he reassured, speaking with a tone both strong and kind. "The world wishes to make you into something you were never meant to be. Do not allow their lies to tarnish your soul."

"Things are happening to me, Reiman. Things I can't explain." She closed her eyes and sank forward. "I feel…different."

"You've been through many great perils, my child. Too much loss and grief can stain your soul with sorrow. It can make you feel as though the world is devoid of its color or light."

Her chin quivered, but she pushed the sadness aside. "I can't take this anymore. Everyone I love is fading…*I* am fading."

His arm slid around her shoulders, and she was pulled into a strong embrace. His touch was cold and stiff, but it was one Neer had longed for since her family was taken and the world she knew was shattered. Sitting beneath the sun, wrapped in his arms, she felt the comfort that came from a father's embrace. It was a strong, immovable force that would protect her from the world and its cruelty.

"In life, you will have tribulation," he started, "but you have overcome the worst odds." He turned and wiped the tears escaping her woeful eyes. "Do not be frightened or dismayed by your circumstances. There is no time for mourning, or crying, or pain. If you want to survive, you must fight. Find your strength, my child. You have more than you know."

She inhaled a deep breath, absorbing his words as they sank deep into her soul, soothing the storm within. "Will you stay with us?" she asked.

He gave a subtle nod. "We'll see this to the end. I won't let you fall."

Neer wrapped around his waist and leaned into his touch. With the comfort of solitude and silence, they sat together, unbothered by the world and its woes as she accepted the protection of his embrace.

Aélla sat on a stool by Thurandír's side, watching him sleep. Her body was weak as she had spent the better part of the morning gifting him with healing energy. The warm bite of magic felt cold and heavy as the days carried on, becoming shorter with every rise of the moon.

Her eyes shifted to Klaud when he took his place by her side and leaned against the back of his wooden chair. He passed Aélla a waterskin, and she accepted, relishing in the wetness that soothed her parched tongue. Half the pouch had been drunk before the spout left her lips.

The stool creaked when she leaned forward. White locks fell across her shoulders, shrouding her face from view.

"You should rest," Klaud said. "He's healing."

Through several deep breaths, Aélla nodded and swiped her hair away from her face. A rolled parchment crinkled in her hand.

"What's this?" Klaud asked.

Aélla pulled the note closer, though he hadn't reached for it. Her eyes were fixed on Thurandír, watching him breathe slow, steady breaths. The gash in his side had sealed into a pink scar, and his coloring had returned.

"It's a note from his family," she said, her gaze shifting to Klaud. "They're alive."

His golden eyes widened, and his attention darted to Thurandír. "How?"

"I don't know, but Elidyr promised they're safe...He gave this to me." Her fingers coiled gently around the note. She was silent for a moment, thinking of her time back home, when she spoke to the avel commander after lying in the fields of jasmine.

Klaud turned when Aélla stood. She trifled through her belongings and retrieved a blue azae'l feather. Holding it close, she returned to Klaud's side and passed it to him. Confusion pulled his brow, only briefly, before relief and sorrow washed his expression.

He carefully took the feather, twisting it between two fingers.

"I went back to the gardens," Aélla explained, and Klaud's lips pursed. "I just had to see it one last time."

His golden eyes glistened with fresh tears he wouldn't allow to fall. So much of their life had been spent together, and while Aélla had fond memories of her family, it was Klaud's face she pictured when she thought of home. After her mother's death, when she was only a child, her father had changed. Become ruthless and angered. He was violent, blaming Avelloch for their mother's death.

Aélla had pushed away the guilt and terror that once sealed her heart with grief. After Avelloch left, Klaud promised to watch over her. Her father was an esteemed and respected leader of the avel, and she was always too frightened to tell of the horrors he inflicted upon her and her brother. A brother everyone viewed as unruly and wild.

The nights when her father would fall into another rage, Aélla found safety with Klaud and his mother. She had always looked up to him, and eventually, as life and time passed, their bond deepened into something more.

Aélla raked her fingers through his hair, reminiscing over memories long past. She kissed his head and held him close, feeling his warmth and inhaling his scent. "We will get through this," she whispered. "*You* will get through this."

He breathed heavily, understanding the outcome of this journey. Knowing where fate would lead them.

"Aélla...I—"

His timid, broken voice was interrupted when the door behind opened. His head sank further, and Aélla turned to find Neer entering the hut. She glanced at the others, and then came to a stop.

"Sorry, I'll—"

"It's fine," Klaud said. The chair squealed against a wooden floor when he quickly stood and fled the room.

Neer stepped aside, watching with a curious eye as the door shut behind him. She turned to Aélla with a questioning look. "Is he okay?" she asked.

Aélla nodded unconvincingly. "He will be all right."

Neer stepped closer, studying Aélla's dejected expression. "Will you?"

Forcing a smile, Aélla met her eyes. "I am fine, Nerana."

Neer crossed her arms. She scanned the room, searching for the right words to say. They were silent for a while, too riddled with sorrow and pain to speak. Aélla's gaze fell to the deep scar across Neer's cheek. It was a mark given by Thorne during an attack that had taken nearly all of their lives.

She turned away, realizing how difficult this journey had become. There was more pain and devastation than she could have ever imagined. And she knew as things fell further into madness—as chaos strengthened and overtook the land—their path would see more bloodshed and heartache.

While the others had lived through grief, no one seemed to carry it more than Neer, who stood with a weight against her back, unable to fight against the crushing force of her power. Aélla understood her torment. Had she never been given the proper training, she would have fallen into madness. The pull of dark energy—to give oneself to anger and sadness and deceit—was far easier than forgiveness and peace. It was a struggle to keep herself pure, but she did so, not for herself, but for the fate of everyone else.

The light tapping of boots fractured the intense silence as Aélla moved to Neer's side. She gripped Neer's hand

and closed her eyes. Energy poured through her, soaking into Neer's flesh and converging with the raging emotions that flared within her unsettled soul. The tendrils of Aélla's magic were prickled with ice as they wove through Neer's core, masking her ache with tranquility.

Neer stared at their hands. Her brows were knitted in confusion, and she glanced at Aélla. "How can you do this?" she asked.

Aélla clutched her hand, not daring to let go and allow Neer's pain to circumvent the easement she had been given. "Tre'lan Udur," Aélla explained. "I can—*we*—can manipulate emotions and thoughts.°"

Neer's cold hand was pulled from Aélla's grasp, and a look of disgust filled her eyes. She stared at Aélla with condemnation. "Why would you do that?" she remarked.

"It's a form of dark energy," Aélla explained. She withdrew her hands, clutching them against her chest. "I only use it if absolutely necessary."

"Have you been using it on me?"

"No."

"Is that why I'm so willing to follow you instead of taking my own path?"

"No!" Aélla stood taller, though her eyes were pleading. "I would never do that. Your choices have always been your own. We're friends, Nerana."

She stepped closer, reaching for Neer's hand, and was saddened when Neer backed away. Her eyes were still guarded, and a look of uncertainty stained her face. Aélla's lips parted, and she felt the weight of distrust forming

---

* Tre'lan Udur, or the Realm of illusion, grants one the ability of empathic manipulation and telekinesis.

With the full strength of Udur, a sorcerer shall possess the ability to alter emotions so long as there is skin-to-skin contact between the user and their subject.

Should the magic bearer place both hands upon their subject's flesh, and retain eye contact, the sorcerer may telekinetically share their own thoughts, memories, or emotions, or alter those of their subjects. The duration of this mind altering capability has been debated since the time of the First Blood, with those claiming that anyone with such a power may use it to alter the minds of their subjects without their knowledge, leading to unintentional control that cannot be justly accounted for.

SHADOWS OF NYN'DIRA

between them, building a wedge she feared may never be repaired.

Neer closed her eyes and gripped her forehead, as if cradling a sudden ache. "I'm sorry. I know you wouldn't do that," she said. "In my head, I know it...but my soul says something different. I can't stop it."

Fear trickled down Aélla's spine. She inhaled several deep breaths and took a timid step closer. Neer became tense but never moved away. Aélla was patient, carefully grasping her hand and allowing the swell of energy to ease the burden of Neer's mind.

"We're in this together," Aélla said, her voice strong with promise.

Neer turned to her, and Aélla was crushed by the pain in her eyes. Unyielding pain that begged for relief Aélla couldn't give.

As Neer started to speak, a noise came from behind. It was a light groan, followed by the faint shuffle of linens atop a creaking leather cot. Aélla turned around, her heart jolting as Thurandír began to stir. She released her grip on Neer's hand, and they rushed to his side.

Slowly, his eyes slid open, and he gripped his side with a groan.

"Thurandír?" Aélla said.

He blinked several times before staring up at the ceiling. His dreary eyes met with hers, and his brows pulled together. "Drimil—"

His voice faded into a slew of deep, raspy coughs. Neer passed him a waterskin, and he quickly drank its contents. Liquid spilled from the edges of his lips before he yanked the spout away with a deep sigh. Breathing deeply, he turned to the others at his bedside.

"Drimil?" He strained to speak. "Neer?"

"Hey kid," Neer teased with a smile that didn't reach her eyes. "How are you feeling?"

"I'm no kid," he said, causing Neer to chuckle. Thurandír looked around, disoriented. "What happened?"

Aélla stated, "You were injured in the battle of Ik'Navhaa." She paused. "The Nasir defeated us...Our group is all that is left."

His eyes widened with pain. They quickly flashed to Neer, who shared in his grief.

"What about my people?" He started to sit, and a sharp wince contorted his face.

Aélla guided him back to the bed with a gentle touch.

"We have to find them! We can't—"

"Thurandír…," she said, speaking with the affection of an apologetic mother.

His face twisted with anguish. He shook his head and covered his face, overcome with sorrow.

Aélla collected the rolled parchment from the table and passed it to him. She touched his arm, and he turned to her before eying the note.

"What is this?" he asked.

"It's a note, from your family." Their eyes met. "They're alive."

His jaw dropped. He glanced between Aélla and Neer, grappled by disbelief. The bed creaked when he sat up, ignoring the pain as he hurriedly unrolled the note, nearly ripping the page in half in his haste. His watery eyes scanned the words, and a wave of relief slumped his shoulders forward. A vibrant smile stretched his lips, and he erupted with laughter.

"They're alive!" he exclaimed, tears streaming down his cheeks. "They're alive!"

Aélla pulled him into a tight embrace, and he held her close.

"Thank you, Master Drimil!" he said. "Thank you!"

She rubbed his back before pulling away. The sorrow that weighed her chest was lifted at the sight of his beaming grin. He trembled with happiness. Light shone from his eyes as he spoke of his family, explaining they had left for Navarre just before the invasion.

"Rylyn wanted to have her baby at home, in Navarre," he said, speaking of his brother's partner. "It's a boy! They named him Thurnin, just like Ianae said they would!"

Thurandír forgot his injuries and sorrow as he basked in his joy. While his voice laced the cabin with an endless stream of gleeful words, Aélla glanced at Neer, who stood silently by their side. A light smile graced her lips, but her eyes were saturated in grief.

Aélla took Neer's hand and squeezed her palm, a silent promise to always be together. They were family, and no matter the cost, Aélla would see her through this. The path they took wasn't meant for the weak, and they would prevail.

Together.

Chapter Thirty-Four

Purpose and Prayers
Avelloch

> "The world is our god, noble and proud, and it speaks to all living things. Magic's a gift for only the blessed, those who can hear as it sings."
>
> – Kellyna, First Blood Poet and Bard

QUIET FOOTSTEPS RUSTLED THE GRASS as Avelloch moved through the forest, stalking his prey. The sun had risen for the third time since the attack on Ik'Navhaa, and he knew they were coming closer to another battle. Closer to facing the Nasir and ending this massacre. Fear settled in his gut, churning his stomach, but he pushed it aside. There was no room for fear in his heart. What was left of his soul had been stripped away by years of torture and isolation.

All he had was hatred, and he would drive it through his father's chest with the sharp edge of his blade.

Avelloch ducked behind a tree, pressing himself against the uneven bark when the elk he had been pursuing halted. Its ears twitched, and it scanned the forest, searching for its intruder. Avelloch peeked around his cover, watching the animal look around before dipping its head to eat.

Thurandír's bow was light in his hands as he drew back an arrow. With his eyes set on the elk, he prepared to release, but the sweltering thoughts of the Nasir and what he had done to Neer flashed through his mind. Her body hovering midair, dark energy funneling into her core. The tears in her eyes and her heart-shattering screams.

Reiman sitting on the ground, too paralyzed to save her.

Anger flourished from deep within, drawing beads of sweat across Avelloch's brow. His arm shook, holding the drawn arrow for too long. The elk snapped its head upward. Its ears twitched before it turned in Avelloch's direction. Their eyes met, and the elk dashed away, disappearing into the underbrush.

"*Kila!*" Avelloch exclaimed, then dropped his arms. He took several deep breaths, quelling the rage that spewed from his dark eyes. As the thoughts consumed him, Avelloch stepped away, no longer interested in the hunt.

He wandered far into the woods, accepting the forest's tranquility. Animals skittered through the grasses and leapt across the limbs, filling the silence with simple melodies only sung by nature. Following the sound of lapping water, Avelloch made his way to a quick-flowing stream. He knelt at the bank and removed his gloves.

Autumn air cooled his clammy skin as he extended his fingers, glancing between his healthy and shriveled flesh. His right hand was shrouded in darkness, and while the pain had become manageable over time, it still pulsed with a constant ache, reminding him of what she was capable of.

Reminding him of what she could become.

He shook his head, ridding himself of the intrusive thoughts. With a deep sigh, Avelloch leaned forward and dipped his hands beneath the water. He drank from the stream before splashing his face.

Sitting alone, he stared up at the trees, watching them dance in the breeze. While the others had a place to call home, a community with people to share stories, Avelloch had the forest. The trees and streams and animals were his community. The quiet whisper of the wind, his only companion.

Each day, he felt the life of his home receding. The warmth and peace were dwindling, and soon, they would cease forever.

He thought of Neer and the stories her existence held. The power and rage within her were as true as the sun and sky, but he knew it wasn't born with her. Fate was merciless and cruel, and it lay a blanket of frost over her soul.

He could see the fear and conflict in her eyes. She didn't want this, and he would find a way to save her.

If there could be one survivor in this war, it would be Neer. She would find the peace she deserved. The peace they *all* deserved.

Energy swept through Avelloch, dragging his thoughts southward with the wind. He eyed the forest, hearing its call. The energy was peaceful and calm, yet it held an edge of sorrow. Avelloch gathered the bow and followed the wind. His steps were quick and silent, weaving through the forest.

The winds calmed, and the forest was silent. He came to a stop, listening. Waiting for direction. As he scanned the empty woods, a low voice perked his ears. It was spoken in a soft whisper.

His eyes narrowed, and he followed the sound. With the bow strapped to his back, Avelloch retrieved his swords. A deep line formed between his brows, and he inched closer. He passed by several swords staked into the ground and soon realized he was approaching *Casthyl*.

Weaving through the thickening monuments, he spotted a figure crouched along the scattered weapons. She leaned forward on her knees with her hands cupped together in front of her chest. Her eyes were closed, and her words were pleading as she spoke in the human tongue.

Avelloch sheathed his swords. He watched her with a careful eye, noticing the brokenness of her posture and the weeping of her voice. In front of her, standing tall, was the evaesh sword of an avel warrior.

He stepped away to give her privacy, but her voice stayed his feet.

"Avelloch?" she said. "What are you doing out here?"

Their eyes met, and he explained, "Hunting."

She turned away, gazing at the sword. Her fingers slid down its length. "I was just talking to Gil. And Loryk."

Avelloch trailed through the swords and approached her side. He knelt beside her, watching the light in her eyes fade to sorrow. His looked at the sword. "Why?"

"It just helps. If there's an *afterlife*, maybe they can hear me." She paused. "Maybe they're still by my side."

His face twisted at the unfamiliar word, *afterlife*, but he wouldn't question her. Not now, while she was grieving. Instead, he asked, "What are you saying to them?"

A light smile pulled her lips, though it was broken and sad. She touched the sword again, as if feeling it could somehow connect her to those who were gone. "Just that I love them," she said. "And I hope they're together...wherever they are." A tear slid down her cheek, and she quickly wiped it away.

Avelloch nodded. "I'm sure Loryk's songs are really making the *aft-loff* a pleasant place to be."

Neer's laughter ignited a spark in her sullen eyes. "*Afterlife*," she corrected. "It's where your soul goes once you die."

His brows pulled together in confusion, and Neer followed his expression.

"You've never heard of the afterlife?"

He shook his head, curiosity filling his mind. "When you die, your bones turn to dust," he said. "Your energy is released back into the world."

"What about your soul? You know, what makes you...*you*?" Their eyes met, and she smiled at his bewilderment. She pressed a finger against his heart. "*This* is your soul. It lives on even after your body dies. At least, that's what the humans believe."

"Does the soul die?"

She shook her head. "The world is a cruel place, but the afterlife is meant to be beautiful. Full of peace and happiness."

His eyes shifted to the monument of swords. "Why would anyone choose to live through this then?"

"Because there's still a chance this all ends when we die. Existence may not extend beyond our lives."

Her words sank deep into his soul, rattling his mind with questions that didn't seem to have answers. He thought about the humans and of their devotion to the *Divines*. They persecuted and butchered and enslaved in the name of their gods. Yet they still devoted their lives to such vicious beings, who would cast aside the pure for the power of the wicked.

"How do you know the *Divines* are real?"

Neer didn't choose to correct his horrible mispronunciation. Instead, she explained, "We don't. Not entirely. It just gives people hope that there is something more. When we're lost or alone, it's nice to think there is someone else out there, looking over our shoulders. Something bigger than we are."

He gave a slow, thoughtful nod. Thinking back to the humans he had slain, before finding Neer and reuniting with the others, Avelloch cupped his hands in front of his chest, just as the human had done when Avelloch threatened to end his life.

Just as Neer had done when she spoke to Loryk and Gil.

Neer watched him with a curious eye as he struggled to remember the stance they held. With a smile, she moved his hands into position.

"Now close your eyes," she explained. "And say the sacred prayer."

"Why?"

"It's just what you do," she said. "It's how we begin our prayers."

"What's *prayer*?" His eyes flashed to hers, and he was allayed by the peace in her eyes.

"It's how we communicate with the Divines. Now, close your eyes."

Avelloch repeated the sacred prayer as she recited it to him. "Divine's grace is fleeting and warm. Whosoever challenge it be warned. The love of the Father carries the many. The souls of the wicked be burned aplenty."

"Now," she said, "you just speak to them."

He peeked at her through a half-opened eye and raised his brow.

Her hidden smile diluted the confusion in her eyes when she asked, "What?"

"*That* is your sacred prayer?" he retorted. "'Whosoever challenge it be warned?'"

Neer shook with laughter. "No one said the Divines had to be peaceful, did they?"

"You follow them," he countered.

"*I* don't," she argued. "It's just—I...It's all I've got left, I guess. One last hope that if they're real, maybe they'll hear my pleas and end this madness."

Neer slouched forward, her posture sinking as she was weighted by dread.

The limbs rustled above before the shrieking sound of a raven's *caw* shattered the silence. Neer flinched, and Avelloch set his focus above. His eyes fell on Altvára, who stared down at them before ruffling his feathers and soaring through the trees.

Avelloch exhaled a despondent sigh. His eyes scanned over the haunting graveyard before him. "They're calling us back," he explained.

Neer blinked away her tears and touched the sword. "He deserved so much better than this. They both did." She paused, clenching her teeth and fighting through her misery. "Thank you for everything, Gil...I'll never forget you."

Her lip quivered, and as more tears spilled from her eyes, Neer ripped her hand away. She marched into the forest, back in the direction of the cabins. Avelloch watched her disappear. He turned to face the sword and gently touched its smooth surface, wondering if what she said was true and if they could hear her cries.

Avelloch spent several minutes alone before trailing behind Neer. Sunlight burned his eyes when he broke through the dense trees and into the small clearing where the cabins stood. Neer waited outside before entering the cabin together with him.

The home was warm with firelight as they stepped inside. Y'ven sat on his knees at the hearth. Thick bandages wrapped the stump of his right arm. Avelloch clenched his hands into fists, still feeling the vibrations of the clinking axes carving through muscle and bone.

"I thought you were hunting," Thallon sneered.

Avelloch's expression was one of boredom. He had grown increasingly tired of Thallon's constant griping.

"He was with me," Neer explained.

Thallon scoffed. "Of course, he was. If you're going to run off into the sunset together, at least let someone know. We've been waiting for you to get back."

As Neer began to argue in his defense, Avelloch placed his hand on her shoulder. She fell silent, and he left the cabin with the bow in hand.

Late into the evening, everyone sat on benches around a roaring fire in the center of the homes. A cauldron of stew boiled above the flames, filling their noses with the aroma of fresh boar and spices.

Reiman sat across the fire with Wallace. He leaned forward with his hands clasped together. Avelloch watched him, studying his posture and the calmness of his light blue eyes. His stomach churned, wondering about his motives and why he had defected to the human lands. Why he had chosen to take in a drimil'lana instead of casting her aside like all the others.

When Reiman's eyes lifted, Avelloch held his gaze, unwilling to compromise his strength. While others shuttered in Reiman's presence, Avelloch saw him as a threat. Someone not to be trusted. While Neer had attempted to forge an alliance between them, there was heavy doubt from both sides.

Avelloch turned away, breaking their long, silent glare, when Klaud bumped his shoulder. He passed a waterskin, and Avelloch took a drink, happy to taste the floral tang of m'yashk. Through several more gulps, he wiped his lips and leaned forward, clutching the pouch in his hands.

While the others played games and roared with laughter, Avelloch was quiet with contempt. Klaud matched his posture, and they stared into the flames.

"That wasn't for you to keep, you know," Klaud remarked.

Avelloch laughed through his nose. "Hope you've got more, brenavae." He took another long sip before passing the drink back to Klaud, who finished it off. The warmth of spirits rose to Avelloch's face, flushing his cheeks with redness as the strong drink took hold of his senses. He relished in its numbness, wishing it could erase the unrest brewing inside.

"We'll leave for Galiendör at first light," Klaud explained.

"Are you going with Aélla? To Galdir."

Klaud's eyes were distant, and he slowly nodded.

Avelloch was silent, understanding the path to Galdir was dangerous. Extremely dangerous. To obtain the energy from the mother of all Ko'ehlaeu'at trees, one must enter the forbidden gates of the avour'il.

He tensed at the thought, knowing their survival was slim. Throughout its history, the avour'il had been known for its mystery and unrivaled terror. Many who survived were left with horrible nightmares and anguish. Even with the shame of being banished, those who received the *fil'veraal* chose the noose or seclusion over any potential freedom the avour'il could provide—those branded were permitted to enter its depths to absolve their punishment and reenter society as an equal.

Avelloch glanced at Klaud's right hand, where the branding scar raised his flesh. "You'll no longer be nesiat," he said.

Klaud tilted his hand to examine the scar. "My place in the forest doesn't concern me."

Avelloch fixed his attention on his own twisting hands. Firelight brightened against his left hand, while the blackened skin of his right absorbed its orange glow. The mark of the nesiat, or *soulless*, was no longer present atop his flesh after Neer had stripped his skin bare in Nhamashel. But he still held the title and shame of being branded a traitor.

His thoughts were shattered when Thurandír leapt into the air, cheering. Aélla, Neer, Y'ven, and Thallon were huddled close, griping and staring at a pair of dice on the bench. Blaid was curled by Neer's feet. His eyes opened narrowly before he closed them with a disgruntled huff.

"That's four in a row!" Thurandír cheered with a smile.

"You're cheating," Thallon remarked.

"No way! How can I cheat at rolling dice?"

As they argued, Dru fluttered from Y'ven's shoulder. She landed gracefully atop the bench and picked up a wooden dice. The small object appeared large in her hands as she turned it over. Her large eyes lifted to Y'ven, and he spoke to her in his native tongue, undoubtedly explaining the rules.

"Go on, Dru!" Aélla said with a smile.

The faeth bounced with glee and then dropped the dice. She did the same for the second, and everyone huddled around.

"Aw," Thurandír said with a grin. "Better luck next time, little thing."

Dru's orange aura turned bright red. She wriggled with fury before lifting her arms outward. Two small flames blasted the game pieces, engulfing them with blazing heat. Everyone lurched back when she angrily fled into the night, leaving a trail of orange light in her wake.

Everyone turned to one another with wide eyes and stifled smiles. Soon, laughter erupted from their throats, and the forest was alive with merriment. Aélla's smile was bright as she eyed those around her, taking in their comfort and joy.

"Wait," Thurandír exclaimed. "I think I saw more dice in the cabin."

He raced to the nearest home, eager to continue their games. Neer turned to Thallon, laughing as he spoke to her with a wry smile.

Avelloch's gaze was ripped away when an arm wrapped around his shoulders, and he was pulled toward Klaud. Aélla's bright hair separated them when she hugged them from behind.

"Smile," she said, before stretching Klaud's lips into a grin. "That's better."

"You've had too much m'yashk, Drimil," Avelloch teased.

She gave him a daring look and then stole the waterskin from Klaud's hands. Avelloch chuckled when she shook it in front of his face.

"*I* am not the one who's had too much to drink, brother."

"Is that m'yashk?" Neer asked.

Aélla tossed her the pouch and Thallon playfully snatched it from the air. Neer laughed when he popped the spout into his lips and then quickly pulled it away.

"It's empty!"

Klaud teased, "Should have sat on this side of the fire."

"That side has the spirits; this side has the women." Thallon cocked his head aside and raised his brows. "I think I'll keep my place."

"In your dreams," Neer remarked.

"Every night."

She playfully shoved his head aside, and Thallon burst with laughter. Aélla kissed Avelloch and Klaud's heads before returning to her place at Neer's side. They fell into different conversations, full of laughter and smiles. A stream of orange light crawled from the open door of the cabin, and Thurandír raced toward the group. His arm was raised high as he cheerfully exclaimed he had found more dice.

The fires burned late into the night. Everyone sat in its warm glow, embraced by laughter, knowing that tomorrow, their journey would start again.

Chapter Thirty-Five

Galiendör
Nerana

"Indigenous to the land of Nyn'Dira, the ydris hold the closest ties to Galdir and its undiluted energy, giving them the deepest connection to nature of any living being."

— *Sikvana Runeth*, A First Blood tome of ancient races

MORNING CAME, BRINGING A CHILL that settled deep in Neer's bones. She lay on the floor of the cabin, curled into Blaid's warmth. He had moved to her side during the night, helping her ward off the cold as she shivered in her sleep.

Her dreams were interrupted when someone lightly shook her shoulder. She opened her dreary eyes and turned to Thurandír, who stood overhead, extending a hand. Neer groaned with a stretch. She took his hand and was lifted to her feet.

"Ready to go?" he asked.

She gave him a sleepy glare, and he chuckled.

"Must be a human thing. My mother is also a grump in the morning."

Her glare deepened, and he stepped away with a smile.

Aélla passed Neer her belongings, and she nodded in silent appreciation. The evae gifted her a well-meaning smile before exiting the cabin. Riddled with exhaustion, Neer rubbed her face and sighed. She got herself dressed, laced up her boots, and stepped outside. Cold morning air clung to her skin, sending chills down her arms.

Reiman and Wallace exited their cabin, and everyone set off into the forest, toward Galiendör.

Days passed as they moved closer toward their destination. Neer walked alongside Blaid and Y'ven. She studied at his unwrapped arm, which slowly healed into uneven, lumpy scars.

"Dishonored," he remarked, and Neer quickly turned away, cursing herself for staring.

"I'm sorry," she said. "I didn't mean to—"

"Is all right, ürok. Will fight again. Stronger than before." He clenched his left hand into a tight fist, determined.

"There's a story of a one-armed warrior," she said, remembering the tales from her childhood. "His name was Sirion Boe. He fought in the Great War and lost his arm to an evaesh soldier. Afterward, everyone convinced him to lay down his arms and take up the life of a commoner. But Sirion refused. He wouldn't allow it to define his worth or dictate his life."

Y'ven was silent, listening as Neer continued.

"So he trained day and night, and eventually, he became known as one of the greatest warriors of our time. He's a legend, Y'ven. There are monuments in his honor and texts taught in school of his heroism and perseverance." Their eyes met, and she said, "And he wasn't half the warrior you are."

Y'ven smiled and raised his head with renewed purpose. Dru perched herself on Neer's shoulder, and they walked in a comfortable silence.

As the sun lowered in the sky, they came to the edge of a sprawling lakeside village. Dozens of round homes made of light-colored wood were connected by bridges stretching over the grasses and water. Sunlight glistened against the lake, sending waves of sparkling light dancing against the trees. Neer breathed in the smell of fresh wood and moisture. It reminded her much of Llyne, in the logging districts.

People with antlers and animalistic legs wandered the many bridges, reeling in nets from the water and carrying woven baskets of wares. They wore clothes of leather and hide.

"This is Galiendör," Aélla explained. "One of the villages bordering Rhyl and ydris territory."

"Why are we here?" Thurandír asked.

Aélla inhaled a timid breath. Her eyes shifted to two guards who walked toward the group with wary eyes and sturdy spears. They were tall, standing mere inches shy of Y'ven's enormous height, with thick antlers adorned with colorful ropes, feathers, and beads.

"This is one of the entries into their lands."

Neer asked. "Can't we just walk through the woods?"

Thallon explained, "They have magic protecting their lands. It keeps them hidden and safe from outsiders."

Before they could continue, the guards approached. They spoke their common language, and Aélla bowed. As they exchanged words, Neer stared for far too long, noticing the guardsman's near-perfect physique and strong, deer-like legs. She'd never seen anyone like them before, other than the ydris Eirean. Blue war paint covered their chests, arms, and faces in beautiful, strong patterns. Their faces were chiseled and strong, with thin lips and large brown eyes.

She had heard of the half-evaesh, half-animal race from texts when she was younger, during her schooling in Styyr. Back then, she had learned from the humans that the ydris—or *half-bred beasts*, as the general populace preferred to call them—were said to have been killed off centuries ago. Tales told of the King of the Beasts waging a senseless and aggressive battle against humanity during the time of the Great War, and that in his ignorant "animal mind," he hadn't considered the strength or scale of the human legions.

Rumors were spread throughout Laeroth of the mounted head of the King being displayed in High Priest Beinon's meeting room, as a way to show his dominance over the now-extinct race. The stories of the ydris depicted them as vicious, primal beings, with their intelligence matching the animals for which they resembled.

Neer was both surprised and humbled to find these stories to be untrue. The ydris, as far as she knew them, with what little she had seen of the Eirean, weren't beast-like or monstrous at all. Much like the deer and elk, they were peaceful and calm, yet they held the same wisdom and strength as their evaesh cousins.

Neer shifted her gaze when one of the two guards stepped away. He walked briskly across the wide, sturdy bridges, disappearing into a sea of nameless faces. The other guard remained in his place, watching the group with narrowed eyes.

"Well?" Thallon pressed when Aélla turned to face them.

"They are offended that we don't speak the common tongue but are willing to allow us entry if their leader approves." Aélla glanced aside as the others spoke of the possibility of being turned away.

Klaud watched her for a moment, noticing the distant look in her eye that went unnoticed by the others. "What is it?" he asked.

The group fell silent at the sound of his careful words. Her hands fidgeted at her waist, and she turned away, suddenly unsure of herself.

"Azae'l," he pressed.

She released a deep breath, though her eyes remained focused on her hands. "They said the Klaet'il have been attacking. Their borders are sealed, but they're still getting in."

Thurandír asked, "Why are the Klaet'il attacking ydris territory?"

Reiman added, "They could be preparing a pre-emptive attack. Drimil, does anyone else know of your plans to approach Galdir?"

Aélla thought for a moment and then shook her head. "Only us."

Klaud crossed his arms. "Ydris lands are protected," he said. "How are they getting in?"

Everyone fell silent, trying to find the answer. They knew the Klaet'il would follow them to Galiendör as they had spies of their own lurking through the woods. Neer examined the trees, searching for the white fur or feathers of a stia'dyr's animal companion. But the branches were bare.

The silence was lifted when Thallon exhaled with a defeated sigh. "Kila…"

"What?" Aélla asked.

He shook his head. "N'iossea is with the Klaet'il…He knows where to get in."

"How?" Avelloch asked, fury edging his voice.

Thallon paced around, wiping his face with his hands. "Shit! Shit! Shit!"

"What's happening?" Thurandír asked. "Who is N'iossea?"

Thallon turned to the sky, exhaling a deep, exasperated breath. With a slight shake of his head, he closed his eyes, and admitted, "He is my brother."

Avelloch demanded, "How does he know where to get in?"

Thallon turned to him with shame in his eyes and reluctantly admitted, "Because I told him."

A silent tension rose within the group. It thickened the air and sent a wave of discontent through the unblinking eyes staring at Thallon. His hands were buried in messy hair, clutching his scalp in shame. While the others were more damning in their approach, Neer found herself pitying him. She could see the anguish and remorse in his deeply disturbed expression. A man of constant words suddenly couldn't speak, and it troubled her more than she was willing to admit.

"Explain yourself," Klaud demanded, a quiver of fury evident in his usually calm voice.

Thallon's shoulders slumped, and he exhaled a shaky breath. "He's my brother," he started. "I didn't think—"

"No," Avelloch snapped. "You *never* think, do you?"

"Avelloch…," Aélla calmly warned.

Klaud added, "He is right, Azae'l. N'iossea has always been unstable. Trusting him with this was foolish."

SHADOWS OF NYN'DIRA

"He's my brother!" Thallon exclaimed.

"You had no right—" Avelloch's words overlapped with Thallon's, and they fell into a volatile argument.

"Oh, that's perfect, coming from a *nesiat* like you—!"

"I'd *never* betray innocent people—!"

"Just your own family, right?"

Avelloch inhaled a sharp, angry breath. Strong fists were clutched at his sides. Neer could see the contempt in his eyes. The hatred and regret. Thallon held the same expression, though it wasn't nearly as pained or shadowed in grief. Instead, his was spewing from the surface, more evident in his wide eyes and quick breaths.

The residents had taken notice of the group's sudden squabble, with many stealing cautious glances as they walked by. Several ydris warriors had appeared throughout the wood, keeping a close eye on the outsiders. Thick spears and bows were held tight in their hands.

"We need to stay calm," Aélla warned. "If we can't control our anger, then we will upset the balance *and* be viewed as hostile to the ydris."

Thallon's lip twitched, and he held Avelloch's dark gaze. Thurandír stepped closer.

"Come on," he said, lightly tugging Thallon's arm. "Let's take a walk."

Thallon angrily swatted him away and marched into the forest. Thurandír lifted his arms in an exasperated shrug before following after him.

Everyone released deep breaths as the tension melted away. Avelloch and Klaud shared a glance, while the others closed their eyes, thankful to have a moment of peace.

"We cannot have this infighting," Aélla said, her strong voice coated in authority. "I mean it, Avelloch. You are much stronger than he is. Much more capable of staying quiet and letting go of your anger."

"Fight," Y'ven suggested. "Resolve with strength."

Avelloch pointed at the vaxros. "I like that plan," he said.

Y'ven proudly nodded in approval. Klaud chuckled, while Aélla softly glared at her brother's pathetic attempt at humor. Though everyone knew, if she allowed it, he and

Thallon wouldn't shy away from a ruthless fight to unleash the hatred brewing between them.

"Leave noisy evae to trees," Y'ven said. "Too much anger. He disturbs Master Drimil."

"We aren't leaving him," Neer argued. "Thallon's a lot to handle, but he's part of our family, right? He deserves the right to be heard. Just as we all do."

Aélla nodded in agreement. The conversations died, and everyone stood in silence. The weight of their argument slowly crushed their souls. Each day, that weight grew stronger, and the days—however long they once seemed—were slowly dying. Fading into darkness much sooner, leaving the world vulnerable to the creatures that rose in the night.

Shadows crawled across the forest floor as the amber glow of a lowering sun sent waves of heat throughout the trees. Neer watched as long streams of darkness were cast by towering trunks, consuming all in their path.

Avelloch turned to her, drawing his brows at the sight of her distant eyes. She was deep in thought, absently rubbing her fingers against the branded scar hidden beneath her sleeve.

Dru stood on Y'ven's shoulder, her large eyes scanning their surroundings. She flinched and then excitedly tugged his hair. He turned to her, curious as she pointed to the village. Her tinkering voice broke everyone of their dazes.

Neer blinked her thoughts away and focused on the ydris approaching. The leader stepped closer, and Neer recognized her as the member of the Eirean council. Aélla took notice and leaned forward in a respectful bow. The others quickly followed.

The Eirean stood before them, her brown eyes peering beneath a mask of bone. She stood tall and appeared even stronger than the warriors meant to protect the village.

"Drimil," the Eirean said, bowing slightly toward Aélla. "My warriors counted nine in your company, but my eyes see fewer."

"Two of our men stepped away, Lady Calasiem," Aélla said, her voice soft and pure. "I will have Klaud retrieve them."

SHADOWS OF NYN'DIRA

Without speaking, Klaud brisked away, following in Thallon and Thurandír's path. Calasiem eyed the faces of each remaining person. She stepped casually to Y'ven, inspecting his height and stature with curious eyes.

"What do they call you?" she asked.

He stood taller, never breaking her gaze. "Y'ven."

She placed her palm against his cheek and closed her eyes. With a deep inhale, she slid her fingers down to his jaw. "Your songs are angry and distorted. Colors washed in crimson and grey." Her eyes opened. "What is your race, Y'ven?"

"Vaxros."

"I would be proud to stand against you in battle someday."

She glanced at Dru, who stood atop Y'ven's shoulder. Calasiem smiled and reached out her hand, beckoning the faeth into her palm. Dru inched closer, staring curiously at her empty hand. She glanced at Y'ven, unsure, and he nodded toward Calasiem, urging Dru forward.

Dru shifted her attention back to Calasiem's hand, then puffed her chest in anger. She turned away, arms crossed and nose high in the air. Calasiem's smile widened. Without speaking, she retracted her hand and stepped to Avelloch. She drew in a quick, shallow breath and muttered in her language.

Avelloch stiffened at her reaction, and he glanced at Aélla, whose horrified eyes were now fixed on her brother. Avelloch's jaw tightened, and he swallowed the lump in his throat.

Calasiem inched closer, cupping his face in her hands. She closed her eyes, inhaling a slow breath. Her foreign words whispered through the air, like leaves rustling in the wind. Calasiem leaned forward, pressing their foreheads together. Her eyes were closed, and she spoke softly in her native language.

"*Grö mc'lok fortuu* afahél *y'sparda.*"

Their eyes met when she backed away, keeping her hands on his face.

"Your songs are angry and colors dark. But it is not too late to change your melody." She placed her hands on his shoulders, and he stiffened, staring deep into her eyes. "You are not yet abandoned, *Zaeril'Nesiat*. The forest weeps for you…Allow the spirits to set you free."

Neer tensed when the Eirean turned to her. As she stepped closer, staring cautiously into her teal eyes, footsteps shuffled in the grass behind. Calasiem's attention turned to Thallon and Thurandír as they stood beside Neer and lowered into perfect bows.

"Lady Calasiem," Thallon said. "It's an honor to be in your presence again."

Calasiem nodded at them, glanced at Neer, and then stepped back to eye the group. Klaud took his place next to Aélla, completing the half-circle. Calasiem held her hands together at her waist.

"This is your company, Master Drimil?" She eyed each person, starting with Y'ven, and said, "Echoes of anger…violence…rage…deceit…vengeance…pride…scorn…regret…and power." Her eyes met with Aélla's, completing the formation. "Six of your companions are not permitted within these lands. Is this the fellowship you seek?"

Aélla stood taller, with pride. "I trust them all with my life."

"But should we trust them with ours?"

A hint of anger flashed in Aélla's calm eyes. With a slow exhale, the flicker of rage was snuffed out.

Calasiem continued, "Your journey is one of great sacrifice and honor, but do not dilute your colors with shades of black."

Aélla said, "Thank you for your wisdom. I trust you know why we're here?"

Calasiem straightened, bringing herself to Y'ven's height. She stood with her arms behind her back. "The forest weeps. The winds sing a fading tune of sorrow and loss." Her eyes met with Aélla's. "You are here to approach Galdir."

Aélla nodded. "Yes."

Calasiem's shoulders broadened with a deep inhale. "We will accept you, Master Drimil. But be warned…the path to Galdir's energy has been tainted with chaos. The avour'il that once brought honor and strength is now haunted by shadow and rot."

No one spoke as her words rang through the air. A cold wind swept past, swirling with fear and sadness.

"Dusk is upon us," Calasiem explained, "and the gates to Galdir seal at night. Until then, you will all be welcome here with respect and honor. Maeve, my daughter, will oversee your stay." Her eyes flicked to Aélla. "You will be escorted to the avour'il at first light."

The Eirean turned away, studying the bandages on Klaud's hand before averting her attention to Avelloch's blackened arm. "The avour'il is open to those who seek its path. Should either of you wish to enter its perils, you are welcome to do so."

With a smile, she bowed and turned away, taking several strides toward the village.

"Lady Calasiem!" Aélla called. Her words steadied the Eirean's pace, and she veered back to the evae, waiting patiently for her to continue. "Your warriors informed us of the Klaet'il invaders." She paused, waiting for Calasiem to respond. But she remained silent, and Aélla continued, "If there is anything we can do to help…"

"Thank you, Master Drimil. The ydris are strong in numbers but not in pride. We will accept any help you are willing to give."

The Eirean stepped away, and everyone exhaled a sigh of relief. They eyed an ydris woman who approached from the forest. She carried a basket of large yellow fruits[*] and wore red warpaint across her exposed chest, arms, and face. Colorful flowers were woven into her hair and hung from the scapular at her waist. She had an innocent face, with large eyes, a pointed chin, and softly rounded cheeks.

"Good evening," she greeted with a smile. "My name is Maeve. It's a pleasure to meet you." With a soft smile, she

---

[*] Quay fruit (pronounced KEE fruit) grow exclusively within the protected borders of ydris lands.

The lumpy, yellow fruits contain enough nourishing supplements that no other provisions are needed throughout the day.

Because of their natural abundance and nutrients, the ydris consume the quay fruit as their primary source of nourishment.

tilted the basket toward everyone. They each picked a fruit as she moved through the semi-circle. "You are a diverse bunch."

"One of each is our goal," Thallon joked, taking a bite of his meal. "Want to join us? We're still missing a few to complete the set."

She giggled without response. Thallon smiled and shared a glance with Thurandír, who playfully bumped his arm. Maeve's cheeks were still tinged with pink as she stepped to Neer, as her wide eyes grew larger.

"You are the *ruanafeil*,°" Maeve stated. "The one they are searching for."

"She is my guardian," Aélla announced. "And is to be treated as such."

"O-of course," Maeve said, suddenly flustered. "I did not mean to offend, Master Drimil. It's just…I have never met one of her kind before." Her eyes flashed between Neer and Wallace, who stood behind with his arms crossed. "You do not have leathered skin or horns, like the stories say."

Thurandír admitted, "I thought Drimil'Nizotl would have fangs and a barbed tail."

Neer gave him a disapproving glare. Maeve smiled.

"Well, I'm glad to meet you. The spirits would not have granted you such safe passage had they not wished for you to be here."

Neer twisted the large fruit in her hands as Maeve stepped to Avelloch and Y'ven. The ydris spoke briefly to the vaxros, admiring his large physique and "curious" red skin, before heading toward the village. "If you'll follow me," she called.

Maeve led them across many bridges, speaking candidly of her home and pointing to the various shops, armories, and taverns. Neer walked alongside Avelloch, while Thurandír and Thallon were ahead. She could hear their conversation as Thallon spoke of the beautiful women.

° Pronunciation: roo-ah-nah-fail

In the language of the humans, ruanafeil translates to mean *magic bearing human*

SHADOWS OF NYN'DIRA

"Think I have a chance with her?" Thallon asked.

"Maeve?" Thurandír bit into his fruit, spilling juice down his chin. "No way. The ydris are too pure for a *f'yet* like you."

Thallon playfully shoved him aside, and Thurandír gripped his healing side, chuckling. Neer set her eyes on the village, watching several locals wander the bridges, their hooves tapping against sturdy wooden planks. The smell of fish and boiled cabbage stung her nose as they passed by a long row of barrels and boiling cauldrons. Enormous trees towered throughout the forest and rose from the lake. Streams of smoke plumed from arched doorways carved into the trunks. Two men stepped out of one of the trees, stumbling as they laughed and smiled.

"That is *tredek ylorniimok*," Thallon explained. "The smoke comes from star weed. You inhale it, and it alters your mind."

"Sounds like you could use some of that," Neer teased with a smile. "Maybe then we'd all want to be around you."

He flicked her nose, and she laughed while pushing him away.

Klaud added with a wry smile, "I recall Avelloch trying star weed once."

Avelloch covered his face with his hand.

"I remember that!" Thallon said with a laugh. "He wanted us to try it, but we were too scared, so he just did it on his own."

Neer smiled. "Guess you really *did* have a wild side, huh?"

Avelloch glanced at her with a smile not well hidden. She admired his playful grin, happy to see him in such comfort and ease.

Thallon continued, "He was talking to the walls and then vomited all over my mother's freshly woven rug."

Neer and Thurandír's faces twisted in disgust. They turned to Avelloch, laughing as he exhaled a deep sigh. Neer looked at him, a smile still lingering on her lips, when suddenly, a flash of darkness overtook her vision. As soon as it came, it disappeared, bringing a wave of ice moving through her like a slow cloud.

Her breath caught in her throat, and she gripped her head, reeling from the experience. No one but Avelloch had seemed to notice as they walked ahead, carrying vibrant conversations of their pasts and admiring the village. Teal eyes met with his dark blue orbs, and another flash seized her mind...

She stood alone in a pit of darkness. Devoid of want or feeling. Empty and hollow as death itself. Wraiths flew around her, creating an endless void of darkness as they wove through the air, moving closer before crashing through her chest.

The vision disappeared, and Neer inhaled a sharp gasp. She stood on the bridge, confused and disoriented. Beads of sweat formed along her brow, and her heart rattled her ribcage.

"Neer?" Avelloch asked.

Reiman approached her side, his eyes glazed with concern. When he touched her arm, she leapt back with a gasp. He withdrew his hand, and Neer turned away, glancing quickly at her surroundings. Nothing had changed. The village was still at peace. Not a whisper of her vision had been made real. But she felt it, deep in her soul...a void that left her hollow and numb.

Still gazing through the village, her eyes set upon Calasiem, who stood nearby, staring back at her. The Eirean marched forward, her large eyes never shifting from Neer's as she brushed past several villagers.

Avelloch stepped before Neer, guarding her from the approaching Eirean. Calasiem didn't seem to notice his presence as she held Neer's gaze. The calmness she once displayed had turned to stone, and her voice was grim.

She reached out her hand and demanded, "Come with me."

Chapter Thirty-Six

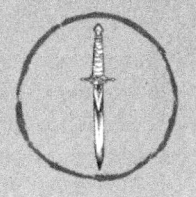

All shall Fade
Nerana

"Give in to the power that has graced your soul. Untether, and be set free."

— Nizotl, *The Book of Deceit*

Reiman stood tall, displaying his power and authority, even in the face of an Eirean leader. "What's the meaning of this?" he remarked.

Calasiem's soft voice dulled the sharpness of his demanding tone. "She must divert the course of annihilation."

Avelloch stiffened. "Where are you taking her?"

"Come," she said to him, reaching out her hand. "You, too, shall be the catalyst of change."

Neer shared a timid glance with Avelloch before turning her attention to Reiman, who looked upon the Eirean with deadly eyes.

"It's fine, Reiman," she reassured. "We'll meet up with you all later."

"I'll accompany you. We can—"

Calasiem raised her hand to him. Softly, she said, "The world has seen too many shades of grey. You must stay behind."

Neer touched his arm and gave a calm nod, but he never fell from his defensive posture. The haunting look in his eyes never faded.

Feeling as though she had somehow betrayed him, Neer regretfully forced herself away. She walked alongside Avelloch, following Calasiem across the bridges. Fresh darkness had taken over the land after the sun made its descent, leaving the glowing forest to reflect beautiful light across the vast, quiet lake. Torches were lit along the bridges, and the villagers wore glowing vines and flowers across their antlers. Neer wanted to admire the beauty surrounding her—to be lost in such serenity—but the visions she had seen still gripped her mind, however distant they had become.

Their walk was quick, taking them to a large tree within the lake. It was surrounded by dozens of small huts, with a web of narrow bridges connecting each home to the next. Firelight glowed within the windows, dancing to the sound of laughter and soft words.

They approached a moss-covered tree before stepping through an arched doorway in its trunk. Spiral stairs were carved into the hollowed center, leading downward beneath the surface of the water. Glowing moss and overlapping vines clung to the tree, lighting their path. Cool, humid air pricked Neer's skin and caused her to shiver. She crossed her arms over her chest, hoping to quell the discomfort.

Further down, the air was murky and smelled of fish. Soon, they came to the base of the trunk and stepped through a doorway leading to the bottom of the lake. Moonlight cast through the waters surrounding them, creating a beautiful lightshow across the moss-covered dirt at their feet. Neer approached the glistening water, which towered over them in a wide dome. Looking closer, she realized their haven was created by an invisible barrier.

Throughout the lake were the sunken ruins of an ancient civilization. Large pillars without roofs, crumbled walls, and half-buried homes were nothing more than ghosts forgotten with time. Calasiem led them to the center of the barrier, where the skeleton of a Tree stood alone. Its limbs were limp, and flower petals were scattered across the ground, crunching beneath their feet.

SHADOWS OF NYN'DIRA

Neer and Avelloch followed Calasiem, who sat by the tree, gazing up with sad eyes. "The time has come," she said, prompting Neer and Avelloch to share a wary glance. "Our ancestors have foretold of this day. When a great darkness would devour the world."

She reached out and placed her palm against the cracked bark.

"The songs of this tree stopped many moons ago, and so the forest, it weeps. Soon, the world will lose its melodies to chaos. And then there will be silence."

Neer and Avelloch were quiet, listening to her haunting words.

Calasiem drew back her hand, and asked, "What do you know of the Ko'ehlaeu'at?"

They were silent before Avelloch stated, "They're the birth of all magic. Its original creators."

"Yes. Galdir is the largest Ko'ehlaeu'at in the world—its roots span from the southern coasts of Nyn'Dira to deep beneath the mines of Uadin. Within them is life and power."

She returned her attention to the tree, dragging her fingertips down its trunk.

"They have the purest form of energy. And when they are gone...the world will fall."

Neer clenched her jaw. She breathed heavily, overcome with remorse. "Am I doing this?" she asked. Calasiem turned to her, but Neer's focus was on the dry, cracked limbs. "Is my magic destroying everything?"

The seconds felt like an eternity before Calasiem calmly responded with a confident, "No." Their eyes met, and she continued, "But it will."

Avelloch asked, "Is there a way we can stop it?"

"The evae believe that naik'avel, a cycle of darkness and chaos, looms overhead. But the ydris have faith in the spirits. We believe that all energy is absorbed into the Ko'ehlaeu'at and cleansed before being released back into our world." She paused, her deer-like ears tilting downward with sorrow. "But the balance has shifted, and our land is teeming with shadows. We cannot stop the anger and hatred that is set upon us. These wars will bring death, and death has many colors, most of them dark and opaque."

"I can stop the war," Neer said. "If the Order has me, they'll cease this attack."

"Foolish words ring from a clever mind. The *ruana*° have sought war with the evae for centuries. But they have never had just cause. Your capture will do nothing but lay shadow over a bleak and cold world."

"What can I do?" she asked in a near shout. "I can't just let them destroy everything! If my magic is causing this, then—"

"Energy," Calasiem calmly explained, "is an expression of will, and everyone determines its color. Songs of war, vengeance, death, and despair give rise to anger and sorrow that outweigh the light. Those who wield magic hold greater influence over these colors and songs. Your anger disturbs the balance, but it alone does not disrupt the harmony."

Neer stared at the Tree, taking in its dull, lifeless appearance. Even in death, it wept. Its songs were silent, yet its voice was clear. She felt the ripple that pulled at the seams of the world, separating the balance maintaining order and peace.

"Why did you bring us here?" she asked. "What do you want me to do?"

Calasiem said, "Galdir's magic is strained, and the shadow it leaks can be felt throughout the world. It's stronger the closer you come to its center. This is why you have visions. It is why you are here." She paused. "Should Drimil'Rothar enter the sacred lands, the madness will consume her. But your strength can see you through."

Stepping forward, Calasiem pressed her palms over their hearts.

"Your souls are not stained with black. The avour'il will take you to dark places. You will have no magic." She eyed Neer and then Avelloch. "Only your strength shall see you

---

° Pronunciation: roo-ah-nah

In the language of the humans, ruana translates to mean *human*

through. Galdir still sings, and until it is silenced, it will see you to your fate."

As she withdrew her hands, Avelloch asked, "You're asking Neer to approach Galdir?"

Calasiem paced around. A troubled look pulled her brow, and she exhaled a deep breath, fixing her gaze on the tree. "Long ago, there was another. A ruanafeil with songs of rage and madness. He entered the sacred realm, joined his energy with Galdir...and the world was washed in misery."

Neer held her breath. She knew of these stories. They were well known throughout Laeroth, though any mention of such blasphemy from anyone other than the priests was met with the severest of punishments. It was the story of Ateus, the Man-God who nearly destroyed the world. The teachings told of his power and rage, using the magic of the gods to enslave the population to his will. The Child of Skye was often mentioned alongside his stories. Tales of her lineage tracing back to his reign were known throughout the country.

Neer had always feared they were true. That somehow Nizotl, the Divine of darkness and deceit, had gifted her with magic, just as he had given it to Ateus so long ago. She wondered if the Divines were real and if they had truly chosen her for this fate, or if it had been no more than bad luck that saw her with such a rare and dangerous gift.

Neer's thoughts were broken when Avelloch asked, "You believe this will happen with Neer?"

Calasiem straightened with a deep inhale. "Not if we can cleanse her energy before it's too late. Allow Galdir to wash you of the anger and shade that twists your soul."

Neer stiffened when Calasiem placed a hand on her shoulder.

The ydris said, "The choice is yours, ruanafeil. Just remember that no matter which path you take, the beat of your drums will ring throughout the world."

With one last glance at the tree, Calasiem stepped to the doorway, prepared to leave.

"Before dawn, you will be gathered for the *Saearatal*. It is a ceremony for those who wish to enter the sacred lands.

We offer this in hopes that your songs will bring peace back to a world teeming with sorrow."

Calasiem tipped her head and then quietly exited the underwater dome.

Neer and Avelloch were silent. She stared at the tree, contemplating her fate. Trying to find a way out of this. But she knew there was none. Aélla would never survive through a realm of darkness. Her soul couldn't withstand such rage or fear…She would be corrupted by it.

"I don't want to do this," Neer admitted. She wanted Avelloch to convince her to turn away. To say that she truly did have a choice in this…but that was a fleeting dream.

There was no one else. It had to be her.

"I'm going with you," he said.

She turned to him, her eyes wide with fear.

He continued, "If you go alone, you could die."

"I don't want you risking your life for me. Not again."

"Going alone won't change what happened in Nhamashel. It won't prove anything if you die."

"This has nothing to do with Nhamashel," she snapped, her emotions pouring like a river. "I just…I can't lose you too!"

She turned away, unable to face him. Before he could speak, she marched away, disappearing through the doorway.

At the village, Aélla sat at the Inn with the others, glancing at the door every few seconds. Thallon and Thurandír sat on a large, cushioned bench, drinking cider and watching beautiful women flock to Y'ven's side, entranced by his exotic appearance. Dru stood on the table before him, flames wisping in her anger as she shook her fist at his admirers. Reiman sat in the corner, surveying the room. His brooding eyes watched the patrons wander by, while Wallace stood at his side, a strong and protective guard.

"Where are they?" Aélla asked, still scanning the room, searching for Avelloch and Neer.

"They are fine," Klaud said. "We need to speak to Thallon about what he knows."

She leaned forward with her head in her hands. Platinum hair splayed across the table's grain, like rivers of white. The Klaet'il were invading ydris territory, a land sacred, pure, and protected. Each day, the balance shifted, and now as the tides of war were turning, the disturbance she felt with every shift of the wind became stronger. A weight pulling her into a dark and lonely abyss. She fought against it—against the anchor dragging her further toward chaos—and her soul was tired. So achingly tired.

When she took the vow and proudly became Drimil'Rothar, the whispers of darkness and chaos had been nothing more than rumors. She knew it would come, but even then, with her visions and prophecies and ancient blood, the threat seemed too far off to be of grave concern. In her young mind, she believed naik'avel could be warded off before it ever truly started.

What foolish, ignorant dreams. Aélla had seen the fires and destruction...She knew the downfall they were to face. Yet still, she had chosen this path. A path of terror and anguish and pain. The elders had warned her of the suffering she would endure, the heartache and loneliness. Sometimes, she wished she could go back and undo her promise. Take back the vow and live a normal, comfortable life for as long as she could.

But that was not her way. She couldn't allow the world to fall while she had the power to stop it. Fate was not determined by the stars or spirits or magic. Her path was hers to choose, and she had to see it through.

Her shoulders slumped forward when Klaud softly rubbed her back. When he pulled his hand away and cleared his throat, Aélla lifted her eyes to find Maeve approaching their table. She carried three wooden mugs of steaming cider.

"I thought you may be parched from your travels," she said, placing the beverages on the table. Aella wrapped her fingers around the warm cup.

"Thank you," Klaud said.

Maeve sat across from them and sipped her own drink. "I want to thank you, Master Drimil, for seeing the ruanafeil to—"

"Her name is Nerana," Aélla said, a bit harsher than intended.

Closing her eyes, Aélla exhaled a soft breath. She could feel their eyes on her but didn't have the patience to apologize. Not when the subtle pull of madness had a grip on her soul, forcing her to fight against it without rest.

Aélla asked, "The avour'il is very dangerous. Is there no other way to commune with Galdir?"

There was answer in the silence. She bowed her head, still hoping for things to change. She knew Avelloch and Klaud would follow her into the avour'il—the only true passage to Galdir—and the chances of them all surviving were nonexistent.

As if reading her mind, Klaud said, "We survived the Trials, and they're far more dangerous."

"Someone died, Klaud."

Guilt flashed in his eyes before he turned away. "Yes...but we're strong, Azae'l. We'll survive."

Maeve glanced between them, taking in their sorrowful expressions. "Do you know the story of the avour'il?" she asked.

Aélla shook her head, her eyes glued to her mug.

Thurandír approached the table with Thallon and said, "It's a tale of two brothers, right?" They got comfortable at the table with fresh mugs in hand. "One gave up his soul for the magic within the trees."

"Not quite." Maeve smiled. "Our version is a little different. They say that long ago, when—"

A sudden hush quieted the room, and the group glanced around. The low voices slowly rose to a light chatter when Lady Calasiem entered the room. She glanced at her daughter with a smile before approaching the table.

"Master Drimil," she greeted. "I see you are in low spirits. Have my people not treated you well?"

Aélla sat straighter. "Your people have been most gracious, Lady Calasiem. I am only worried about tomorrow. The avour'il is a dangerous test."

Her dull eyes brightened when Avelloch and Neer entered the room moments later. Reiman approached his daughter, while Avelloch looked around before spotting Aélla. He waited for Neer, and they made their way across the room. Reiman and Wallace trailed behind.

They gathered around the table and were quickly handed mugs of cider by a passing ydris. The steaming drinks were set before them, though neither seemed to have an appetite.

Calasiem placed her hand on Neer's shoulder. She smiled before averting her attention to the far side of the room when several women giggled. She eyed Y'ven, who was perched in the center of the crowd. With a curious eye, she casually approached him. They spoke briefly before Calasiem took his hand and led him from the Inn.

"No way!" Thallon griped, watching them leave.

Thurandír rubbed his shoulder when Thallon leaned forward in a defeated slump, clearly upset by the lack of attention from the locals. Dru's bright red aura glowed, and she fled the room in a rage, disappearing into the night.

Aélla eyed Avelloch, concerned by the grave look in his eyes. "Are you all right?" she asked.

He blinked his thoughts away and glanced at her. With a nod, he inhaled a deep breath and sipped his drink. Aélla watched him for a moment longer before returning her focus to Maeve.

"Maybe we should save the stories for another time."

Thurandír whined in protest, and Neer asked, "What stories?"

Thurandír stated, "The avour'il."

"I want to hear it."

When no one protested, Maeve began, "Long ago, before the time of the ahn'clave, there was a great darkness that swept across the land. The people were divided, and misery painted the world. Two brothers, Jorod and Roswyn, were rivals. Always striving to be the better warrior and man, they fought each other at every turn.

"Roswyn, the cleverer of the two, understood that magic flowed within the Ko'ehlaeu'at. Determined to defeat his brother and become leader of their clan, Roswyn traveled to the forest and approached Galdir, the largest and most powerful Ko'ehlaeu'at tree, and drank its mystical sap.

"The tree responded by converging their energies and gifting him with magic of his own. Confident with power, Roswyn returned home and placed his hand upon his brother's shoulder, turning him to ash.

"Roswyn ruled over his people for decades, slipping slowly into madness. Desperate for power, he moved his people to the forest and forced them to drink from the tree. Few sought to defeat him with their newfound strength, but his magic had grown, and he was unstoppable.

"Together with his people, they created a new realm, one that could not be seen but exists alongside ours. This was the only true path to Galdir's magic, and Roswyn ruled over this secret kingdom for centuries.

"But he did not know that his people had been escaping. Throughout the years, these magical evae had been living in our world, creating children of their own."

"The First Blood," Thurandír stated.

Maeve nodded. "It is said the existence of magic within us was a mistake. We were never meant to hold such power."

"What happened next?" Thallon asked, engrossed in the tale.

The others listened intently, not realizing how quiet or empty the inn had become since the story began.

Maeve continued, "When Roswyn heard of this treachery, he knew it was only a matter of time before they would come for him. Consumed with madness, he sealed the gates to his realm, trapping everyone inside. Once you enter, there is only one way out."

"What's that?" Neer asked.

Avelloch answered before Maeve had the chance. "You have to make it to Galdir and drink the sap. If your spirit is pure, it will place you back in Nyn'Dira."

Neer's jaw clenched. "And if it isn't?"

He hesitated, staring at his blackened fingers, curling them inward. "Then you are trapped there…forever."

SHADOWS OF NYN'DIRA

Silence fell over them like a blanket of frost. Aélla crossed her arms, unable to push away the fear rising to her throat. She couldn't allow her brother or Klaud to enter such a dangerous and unpredictable place.

But she knew they wouldn't allow her to enter this realm alone. For a moment, she considered subduing them with her magic, putting them to sleep or altering their mentality to agree to stay behind, but those thoughts were swept away the moment they entered her mind. She wouldn't be that person, no matter how painful their choices were.

No matter how destroyed she would be at their loss.

"It's really dangerous?" Neer asked, her voice timid. "The avour'il?"

"Yes," Maeve answered. "The realm isn't meant for mortals like us. Especially those without magic. And now that Galdir is weakening, the avour'il—or *Sacred Lands*— is diluted in darkness. It's full of kanavin and shadows."

Neer clenched her jaw. A deep unrest settled in her eyes. Folding her hands into fists atop the table, she said, "I'll do it." Her eyes lifted, gazing at everyone. "I'll go to Galdir."

"What?" Aélla said. "Nerana, you can't—"

"It has to be, Aélla. You know that." She stared into her eyes, lips pursed. Regret and sorrow heavy in her voice. "Maybe...it can fix me."

Aélla shook her head, unable to speak beneath the weight of Neer's request. Unable to push away the harrowing thoughts and unease, she politely excused herself from the table. Stepping outside, she inhaled a breath of fresh air. The moons had risen, casting purple light across a quiet world. Torchlight and glowing flora reflected against the lake, and for a moment, Aélla felt at peace.

Her eyes shifted to a soft orange glow hovering by a large tree. Realizing it was Dru, Aélla made her way over. The faeth was alone, pressing her ear against the bark.

"I'm not here to cause trouble," Aélla said when Dru noticed her.

She floated to Aélla and perched defeatedly atop her shoulder. With her legs crossed, she leaned forward with her head in her hands.

"What's wrong?" Aélla asked.

Dru's tinkling voice filled the air. She pointed to the tree, and fire spewed from her body.

"Y'ven and Calasiem are there?"

Dru nodded feverishly. Aélla exhaled a deep breath.

"It's hard to let go sometimes," she said, "when the people we care about do things we wish they wouldn't…"

Her eyes met with Dru's, and she smiled.

"But it's important to remember that these are their choices. There were many who didn't want me to follow in this path and take the vow of Drimil'Rothar, but I did…and I'm grateful to have been given the honor to make that choice on my own."

With a sad smile, she stepped away from the tree and wandered the bridges, with Dru still perched on her shoulder. Tears filled her eyes as she admired the beauty of the forest. A place she loved more than anywhere in the world. But pain wasn't a luxury she was able to feel. As her vows promised, she would forego her worldly tethers and be free in the way of the Light.

Stepping to the edge of a pier, she sat on her knees, overlooking the lake and glowing forest. Closing her eyes, she forced the tears away and spent her time alone in deep, undisturbed meditations.

Chapter Thirty-Seven

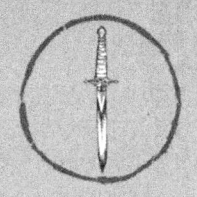

Echo in the Void
Nerana

"The avour'il is a dangerous, deadly feat, forbidden from most. Those who wish to enter its perils must be willing to face their death in a most gruesome and undeserving fate. Any who survive shall be recompensed for their lifetime of isolation, as the forest will have deemed you worthy, and so, too, shall we."

— Eirean declaration of the avour'il

Neer sat in the inn, staring at the table. Conversations flittered through the air around her, creating chaos in her unsettled mind. Closing her eyes, she leaned forward and held her head in her hands.

"Neer," Thallon started, his voice guarded. "You can't do this. Your energy is too unstable. If you converge with Galdir...it could be catastrophic."

"You don't think I know that?"

"You just need to consider the implication of what you're doing! The last time a drimil'lana converged with the tree, it nearly destroyed the world!"

"I'm not a monster, Thallon!" Neer's voice silenced the stream of conversations flowing from nearby tables. Everyone turned as she spoke, unleashing the torment and regret pinned to her chest. "I know what this can do! I know what just being *alive* can do! But I'm not Ateus! I'm not a spawn of darkness that wants to rid the world of light, so you can all stop looking at me like I am!"

Reiman spoke up, stating, "Was this the Eirean's idea?"

Neer turned away, crushed by the weight of his condemnation. "She only gave me the option. Aélla's too weak to survive." She closed her eyes, forcing herself to believe the words she felt were untrue. "She said that it isn't too late for me to change things."

Reiman said, "Calasiem does not care for your safety. She has not witnessed the rage that arises within you." He paused. "We just believe that your instability is a risk. The infrastructure that keeps the world in balance is a fragile thing. If your energy is too diluted, then—"

"What's made it diluted?" she remarked, slamming her palms against the table. "Since birth, my life has been one cruelty after another! How am I supposed to fix this if all my options are shut down?" She glanced to each person at the table.

Their downcast eyes revealed their conviction. They were afraid of her, afraid of what she could do.

Afraid that she would destroy everything.

"So, that's it then?" Neer remarked. "I just keep meditating and shoving everything aside while all that I know crumbles before my eyes! Well, what if I can't do it anymore, Reiman?"

His light blue eyes flashed to hers.

"What if I'm not strong enough to do this on my own?"

His jaw clenched and eyes steeped with anger. "You carried yourself into the Trials of Blood against all better judgement and caused a senseless, avoidable death. You drove your blade through the chest of a priest and sent the countries into war. You've latched yourself to the evae and have neglected your duties to the people who raised you! The Brotherhood was decimated in a war that *you* began!

"Do not believe yourself a victim in this, Nerana. You continue to deviate from the paths set before you, and you have, once again, failed to take responsibility! Entering the avour'il will be a grave mistake. Your energy is too unstable. If you fail—and I have full belief that you will—then this will be the *end*."

Sorrow consumed her anger, bringing tears to her glaring eyes as his words stung the deepest parts of her soul.

Her face was red and lips were pursed as she stared at him, unable to speak through the pain tightening her throat.

Everyone was silent, looking at her father with wide, angry eyes. Avelloch breathed heavily, simmering with deep, unsullied rage.

Reiman kept his gaze locked with Neer's, beating her down with his disappointed eyes. "For once," he started, "just do what others far wiser tell you."

Avelloch's lip twitched. When Reiman stood, Avelloch followed, snatching his sword from its sheath. His chair crashed to the ground, causing everyone to flinch. Reiman turned to him, unperturbed by the raw fury emanating from Avelloch's deadly eyes. Standing taller, Reiman straightened his cloak and stepped away from the table.

Wallace dutifully followed, and the group watched them march across the Inn, disappearing behind a door leading to the guest rooms.

Neer stared at the table, unable to speak. Unable to face the others as her father's words repeated in her mind, reminding her of all the grief and sorrow she had caused, lacing her thoughts with doubt. She struggled to find a solution for the pain and destruction she had caused.

"Don't listen to him," Thallon said, his voice strained with anger. "He's just—"

"He's right," Neer said. Her chin quivered, and she clenched her teeth, forcing the pain aside. "He's right…I've caused this. All of it."

"That isn't true!" Thurandír argued. He rushed to her side and leaned forward against the table, attempting to meet her eyes. "You are good, Neer. *You* were the one that risked everything to come with me when my village was attacked. We knew it was foolish. We knew it would probably see us dead, but you did it anyway."

Neer shook her head, unable to hear him through her father's repeated words. "What should I do?" she asked, her eyes shifting to each of the faces staring back at her. "Just tell me what to do…"

Avelloch took several deep breaths. He placed his sword back into the sheath on his back and slowly sat. His hands curled in and out of tight fists. "Aélla won't survive to Galdir," he said, still staring at his hands. "And Calasiem believes that you can be healed if you cleanse your energy at the tree."

"She said that?" Thallon asked.

Avelloch gave a stiff nod, nearly too subtle to see. "This choice is yours, Neer. No one knows what will happen, but it's a risk we have to take. Just as the Trials were a risk. Just as *everything* we do is a risk."

Klaud nodded. "No one can predict the outcome of their choices."

Thurandír asked, "You're doing what you think is right, aren't you?"

Neer wiped her tears with a nod.

He touched her shoulder and said, "Then it doesn't sound like a mistake to me."

The table fell intensely silent. Neer bowed her head and closed her eyes, feeling the warmth of their words and acceptance. Wishing that her father could show her that same encouragement. While the others were angry at his harshness, Neer understood his frustration. He had always steered her toward a clear and stable path, one that would keep her energy contained and secure. But time after time, she had chosen to forge her own way, and now that they stood at the edge of change, she feared he may be right once again.

Neer clutched her chest, feeling the slow rhythm of her beating heart. She knew this path was far too steep for her to take alone, and with her magic pulling her further into an endless, vicious abyss, she had to accept that some choices were out of her control.

"Aélla won't survive," she said, curling her fist over her heart. "I'm not strong enough to fight this on my own…" Through several deep breaths, she made her decision, one she feared she may come to regret. "I'll go to Galdir." Her eyes lifted to the others. "I'll make this right."

Avelloch turned away and closed his eyes. Thurandír pulled her into a tight hug.

"You will make it," he whispered. "No way will the avour'il be your downfall."

She hugged him back, accepting his strong, brotherly embrace. "Thank you for seeing me," she said.

He pulled away with a sniff. "Us lanathess have to stick together, right?"

Neer chuckled while wiping her eyes. "You're a good friend, Thurandír. Whatever happens, just always know that, okay? Don't ever change."

"You got it, Drimil."

Klaud leaned forward with his hands clasped together. He stared at the table and said, "I will join you."

Neer stiffened, surprised by his offer.

"You won't make it alone."

She considered his words and the selfless vow to see her through such a perilous journey. But rage boiled inside at his attempt at redemption. Neer bit her lip and shook her head, fighting against the hatred slowly rising to the surface. "No," she said. "Thank you, but I can't."

"Neer," Thallon started, "if you go alone, you'll—"

"I'm not taking anyone else with me," she said. "If I go in there with Klaud, I don't know what will happen. I don't know how the forest will judge me if the hatred I feel transcends through my magic."

Klaud gave a slow, sorrowful nod. He sat for several seconds before quietly leaving the table. Neer watched him leave, happy he hadn't argued. Her eyes shifted to Thallon, who sat across the table, staring at her with deep anguish.

"Are you sure this is what you want to do, Neer?" he asked. "If this doesn't work...if the forest doesn't accept you..." He rubbed his forehead. "You could be trapped forever. You could cause this all to end."

"That won't be her fault!" Thurandír argued.

Thallon lifted his fingers in defense, too heavy with grief to raise his arms. His defeated expression deepened, and he deflated with a slow exhale. "I just...I don't want you to die." Their eyes met, and she was shattered by his devastation. "Just, make it out of there, all right?"

She nodded and quickly wiped her tears. As moisture filled Thallon's eyes, he shook his head and swiftly left the table. Thurandír patted Neer's shoulder before following him outside.

The Inn had fallen quiet as the night grew later. With no more than a handful of patrons at the various tables, Neer and Avelloch were alone. Their eyes were fixed on the table, never veering toward each other as they sat in deep, numbing misery.

"You don't have to do this," Avelloch said. His strained voice cracked, and he cleared his throat. Through clenched teeth, he added, "We can find another way."

"There is no other way," Neer said. "I can feel this growing inside me. Every day, it gets stronger, and I lose another piece of myself."

Avelloch covered his lips and shook his head. A tear glided down his cheek, and he swiped it away. Leaning back, he wiped his face with a deep sigh. His jaw clenched several times as more tears threatened to fall from his hardened eyes.

"Avelloch," Neer said, and he shuddered when she cupped his cheek in her hand.

Her thumb rubbed softly against his smooth skin, and she examined the face she met so long ago. A strong, deadly warrior who had held his blade to her throat was now reduced to tears at the thought of her demise. Her throat tightened and chest ached, watching him fight against the agony gripping his soul. He was just as broken and misunderstood as her, and the thought of leaving him alone fractured what was left of her heart.

She wanted to speak, to admit how she felt and bridge the gap between them, but words weren't enough. Neer couldn't express how painfully long she had waited for someone to see so deep into her soul. And for her to see so deep into his.

Their eyes were locked as they sat together, washed in grief as they shared what could be their final goodbye. But she wouldn't give up. No matter what it would take, he would survive. If she had to crawl through hell itself to get back to him, she would do it.

Unable to say aloud what her magic had repressed, she closed her eyes and leaned forward. His hands slid across her waist when their lips came together, and the world faded into shades of darkness and silence.

Tears fell from her eyes when his lips moved against hers, sending waves of emotion crashing through her soul. The silence of their affection rang clear as he pulled her close, their lips never parting, the force drawing them together holding strong and secure. She could have stayed there forever, wrapped in his arms, forgetting the world and its sorrows. In that moment, she was whole.

In that moment, she was home.

Cold bit her skin when his warmth receded. She breathed heavily, closing her eyes while his forehead rested against hers. He slid his hand to her heart, feeling its quick thrum against her chest.

"Nerana *mëvek*," he said. *"Vas neemo see'nah, vakaal."*

His words touched the core of her soul, melting the ice that froze her heart. With a nod, she placed her lips to his and sank into his touch, vowing to never leave him behind.

Early in the morning, before dawn had swept the world with light, Neer awoke to the sound of a light tapping at the door. She stirred before opening her eyes. Calasiem's voice echoed through the doorway, beckoning them to wake. The room was dark, with only the glow of firelight streaming through the bottom of the door frame.

With a slow exhale, Neer sank into Avelloch's chest. His skin was warm as he lay beneath her, staring at the ceiling with tired eyes. Strong arms had held her secure throughout the night, and she wished to lay there forever, but as familiar voices echoed through the hall, she knew their time had come to an end.

They regretfully climbed out of bed and slipped into their clothes. Once dressed, she and Avelloch stepped into the hall to meet with the others. Aélla quickly approached, wrapping her arms around Neer's back.

"You do not have to do this," she said. "We can find another way! I will go and—"

"It's fine," Neer explained with a forced smile. "You've done enough for me. Let me do this for you."

Aélla shook her head. "But you could die…"

"All this ends with me, right?"

Through heavy tears, Aélla wrapped around her once again, and Neer hugged her back, thankful to have found such a loyal, honest friend. A sister.

Her family.

As Aélla pulled away, Neer gazed at everyone around her. Their eyes were tearful and faces were long.

"I'll make it," she promised. "But if I don't…if this fails and I never see you again…or if things fall into madness…just know that I love you. All of you." She inhaled a deep breath, fighting back the tears. "You'll never know just how important you are to me."

Everyone stepped forward, gifting her with tight, loving embraces. Klaud reached forward to take her hand. She looked into his eyes and gripped his arm. As he stepped away, Y'ven took his place. Dru lunged for Neer, smacking hard against her cheek with a wail. Neer rubbed her back with a fingertip, and Y'ven carefully pulled the faeth away.

"Be strong, ürok," he said, extending his hand, and she gripped his forearm in a strong shake. "This will not defeat you," he spoke in his native tongue. "You are more than this."

She smiled as he repeated the words she had said to him so long ago, when he lost all confidence after sparring with Thurandír.

Neer glanced through the crowd before spotting Reiman standing outside his door. His mournful eyes were set on his daughter as he stood alone. The others followed Calasiem through the hall, while Neer made her way to his side.

"You're still taking your own path, I see," he remarked.

She turned away with a nod. "I don't know what else to do."

His cold glare softened when he exhaled a deep breath and pulled her into a gentle embrace. She rested against his chest, listening to the slow beat of his heart.

"No matter the path you choose," he said, "you will always be my daughter."

Neer squeezed her eyes shut, not daring to allow her tears to fall. "I love you," she whispered. "Thank you for everything."

Reiman rubbed her back and kissed her head. "Make it through this," he said, pulling away and looking into her eyes. "Do not let this be your end."

She nodded and wiped her tears.

"Go on," he said. "The others are waiting."

"You aren't coming?"

"I won't see my child off to what could be her death. I'll meet you at the gates once you've returned."

Neer nodded and pulled him into another quick embrace. She kissed his cheek and regretfully stepped away.

Across the Inn, Neer spotted the others through the opened entry. She stepped outside, where the world was bright with torchlight and song. A soft, melodic voice, pure as the finest silk, rang through the air, singing words in the ydris tongue.

Villagers lined the pathway far into the trees. Bone masks smeared with blue warpaint covered their faces. Their antlers, now painted in black, were absent of their glowing vines or flowers. They stood several paces apart, each of them holding a flickering torch in their right hands and large twigs in their left.

"What is this?" Neer asked.

"This is *Saearatal*," Calasiem explained. "Those who wish to enter the sacred lands, please, step forward."

Neer glanced at Aélla. Their eyes met briefly before Neer stepped forward, standing tall beside Calasiem. Avelloch took several deep breaths and trailed after her.

"Wait—" Aélla started, reaching out for her brother before stopping herself.

Avelloch's dark blue eyes met with hers in a long, silent farewell.

Although Neer was angry he had chosen to ignore her pleas to stay behind, part of her admired his devotion. There were many who had fought alongside her, but only one who had fought *for* her. She was glad to have someone who cared so deeply.

The other part—the part brimming beneath the surface with fire—was angry he had ignored her wishes. Angry he would risk himself for someone like her. If she were to die during the avour'il, it would be a blessing for the world. Maybe then the devastation following her would cease.

But if *he* died, especially if she lived, it would only further pull at the raveled and frayed edges of her soul. Darkening whatever sickness boiled within her.

Calasiem stared at Klaud, awaiting his approach, but he stayed his feet.

The Eirean accepted a large bowl of black liquid from a nearby ydris, and the ceremony began. "We will guide you to the gates of the avour'il," she explained. "Allow the spirits to guide you toward Galdir. End this cycle of madness that's been cast upon us...Bring peace back to our thunderous melodies."

Calasiem walked ahead, guiding Neer and Avelloch forward. Each villager dipped their twigs into the bowl of black liquid. Neer flinched when the moisture was flicked across her face. They did the same to Avelloch, spattering his hair and cheeks.

"This is sap from Galdir," Calasiem explained. "It is stained with black, just as the colors of your spirit."

As they walked past, each person flicked them with sap and then extinguished their torches. They then knelt to the ground, bowing their heads. Neer and Avelloch followed Calasiem to a dirt path in the woods, lined with ydris villagers. The beautiful, haunting song grew louder with each step.

The forest was quiet, partaking in the ritual with obedient silence, carrying the woman's soft melodies far through the trees and into the village, where it wouldn't naturally be heard. At the end of the long trail, the sun sprayed rays of golden light from beyond the hillside, illuminating a beautiful clearing. Tall grass lay a blanket of green atop the flat canvas.

The woman who sang, an ydris with white antlers and unmasked face, stood at the edge of the clearing. She held her hands together at her waist and wore a loose white gown that gathered at her hooves.

The last torch was extinguished, and the woman's angelic voice faded to silence with one final, ringing note.

SHADOWS OF NYN'DIRA

Calasiem stood beside the singing woman and turned to Avelloch and Neer.

She closed her eyes and raised her arms high into the air. Facing the sky, she opened her now-solid white eyes. Speaking in the language of the ydris, she said a slow chant. Her words strung together like iron chains, linking herself, the trees, the sky—all that surrounded her—to the forest.

Neer looked at Avelloch. He was a piece of black marble melting in the morning sunlight. Sap trickled down his face like dark tempera. Their eyes locked when he turned to meet her gaze. Neer was afraid, though she didn't show it. She wouldn't, not now. This was what she had to do. All roads led here. Surely, this wouldn't be their end.

And while he masked it well, she could see that same fear within Avelloch, clinging to the edge of his pulled lip and the pinch in his brow.

An abrupt crack in the trees pulled their attention to the forest. Calasiem remained in her chants, her words still lacing the fabric of life and energy. And the forest responded.

Slowly, the trees uprooted themselves. Pieces of bark fell to the grass as the trunks twisted and bent. Sticks and leaves molded together when half a dozen trees levitated toward the center of the meadow.

The sun revealed itself from beyond the far side of the hill, sending streams of light to cast through the broken, twisting pieces of wood. The light danced across Neer's painted skin, and she watched in silence as the trees wove together, creating a large open doorway. Golden light from the rising sun cast around its arch, but inside was shadowed.

Calasiem's voice faded, and she lowered her head. Her eyes now held their natural color.

"It is time," she said. "Enter the void and accept your fate."

Avelloch and Neer glanced at one another. Her heart was in her throat, and she couldn't bring herself forward. Visions of the Trials and Nhamashel flashed through her mind. She thought of Avelloch lying face down in the mud, unbreathing...unable to be saved.

Her thoughts were interrupted when he slid his hand into hers. Their eyes met, and the hint of fear he once displayed had disappeared. Now, there was only strength.

She clutched his hand, mimicking his resolve, and together, they stepped to the gates of the avour'il. Peering through the opening, they saw the forest exactly as it appeared around them. But there was no sun. No life or promise.

There was nothing but shadow and silence.

"Let the spirits guide you," Calasiem said from behind.

With one final look into Avelloch's eyes, Neer held tighter to his hand, and they stepped through the doorway...into the land of eternal darkness.

Chapter Thirty-Eight

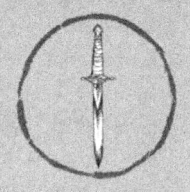

First Breath
Nerana

Neer stepped through the gateway of the avour'il, and she stumbled forward, feeling too light to stand. Each breath was full and easy. Kneeling in the dirt, she felt different. Empty yet alive. Anger and pain no longer burned inside her. She was free of the shackles binding her soul to the ever-growing darkness and agony.

She was free of her magic.

Neer studied the silhouette of her hands through the darkness. Touching her chest, she realized in the emptiness, there was peace. The tormenting thoughts and feelings that plagued her mind were absent. The sweltering pulse of energy was gone, and she now understood what it was like to be without it. Warm, relaxed, and free.

Her eyes shifted to Avelloch when he knelt beside her. He placed his hand on her back and leaned close to view her face. "Are you all right?" he asked.

She smiled. It was the first genuine smile that she had in many years. So long, in fact, she couldn't recall the last time she grinned out of pure happiness and ease.

"Neer?" he asked, his voice coated with concern.

"I'm good," she said, still chuckling. "Great, actually."

His confusion worsened. She knew he thought her mad, and maybe she was, but she didn't care. For now, she relished in the absence of her magic. Of the tearing and twisting and pain that ripped her soul apart. Some part of her wished to stay there forever, the peace she felt outweighing any fear she once had.

With a deep exhale, she closed her eyes. Avelloch was beside her, his hand still on her back.

"Is this what it's like?" she asked. "To live without it?"

"Without what?"

Her smile widened, and she turned to him, eyes burning with fresh tears. "Magic."

He was quiet for a moment, admiring the unbridled happiness in her eyes. She knew he didn't want to take that away, but beneath the softness of his eyes was darkness and pain. They needed to move. She knew that, and if not for Avelloch being there, she may have sat much longer. But she couldn't risk his safety, not after he came here for her.

Neer eyed the forest veiled in black. There were no moons to offset the darkness shrouding the world in frost. The sap clinging to her face and arms grew colder, and the weight of her reality quickly sank in. "Where do we go?" she asked.

He looked around. "I don't know. The energy connecting me to the trees is blocked too. I can't hear them."

"You don't know where the Tree is? Galdir?"

"No. Without the moons it's impossible to know which direction to go."

"How big is this place?"

His jaw clenched. "Big. I've heard it spans across all of Nyn'Dira."

Fear trickled down her spine, wiping what was left of her smile from her lips. "And it's full of creatures of darkness?"

Their eyes met, and his fear was her answer. They sat in silence for a moment longer before he said, "The sun was rising through the doorway." He pointed straight ahead, toward the direction of the shrouded sunlight. "That's east. We came from the southwest, so the center of the forest would be…" He rotated his arm to the right. "This way."

"What's in the center of the forest?"

"Galdir. But it'll be easy to lose our way."

"We should—"

Her voice was silenced by a low deep growl coming from the void. Avelloch quickly turned around. Neer was behind him, her heart racing. Footsteps shuffled closer, followed by deep, rattling clicks. Neer was frozen, listening while the sounds moved from left to right, as if the creature was searching for them.

Her voice was a muted whisper, nearly too low for her to hear, when she asked, "What is—"

The creature shrieked at the sound of her voice. Neer gasped, and the screaming ceased. The silence was heavy. Every vein throbbed with her fast-beating heart. She was immobile, gazing into the darkness, waiting for what lurked beyond to leap from the shadows.

Suddenly, the silence was broken by quick, sprinting steps coming right at them. Neer started to run, but Avelloch gripped her arm, keeping her still. She turned to him, stricken by the darkness in his eyes. He stood calm and ready, watching as the silhouette of a twisted, misshapen man charged.

It closed in, and Neer breathed heavily, fighting the urge to run. Her muscles ached, but she stood her ground, waiting for Avelloch's signal. Trusting he was making the right call.

The putrid odor of rotten flesh filled her nose when the creature came closer. Within seconds, it was upon them, shrieking with loud clicks.

Flailing arms reached out for Neer. She lurched back, and Avelloch plunged his blade through its skull. Its body fell limp, and its noises were silenced. Neer held her breath, staring into empty, bleeding eye sockets. Its black, shriveled skin was nearly invisible in the darkness.

The squelch of tearing flesh filled the silence when Avelloch ripped his sword away. Neer stepped back when the lifeless body faded to ash at her feet. Their eyes were glued to the creature, too petrified to move.

Neer lifted her eyes to the forest when the sounds of distant, overlapping clicks echoed all around. Dozens of creatures stalked the darkness, drawing closer with every slow step.

Avelloch breathed heavily. Without making a sound, he leaned close and whispered, "We need to move."

Neer's wide eyes met with his. She wanted to argue, but the fear kept her silent. Whatever dread he felt was masked with strength, and it gave her confidence. Their eyes shifted to the right, in the direction they were meant to go, where the echoing and footsteps were most dense.

They walked together through the void, searching for shadows or creatures in the dark. The clicking and whistles echoed all around. Avelloch grabbed her arm, and they halted.

His grip was tight on her forearm, and they stood silently, watching a shadow lurk nearby. Its body twitched as it stalked closer, clicking through its throat and sniffing the air. Neer held her breath when it stepped beside her. She wanted to run, but any movement would alert the creature of her presence.

It leaned closer, bringing its rotten face inches from her own. Sharp teeth grazed her ear. Its throat rumbled with overlapping clicks and whistles. A twitching, contorted body leaned in, pinning her between its stench and Avelloch. Neer clenched her teeth, fighting the urge to drive her sword through its chest. But its body was too close. If she moved, it would notice, and she couldn't risk it calling the others closer.

Her heart raced when Avelloch slowly, carefully, raised his weapon. Cold breath swept across Neer's face as the creature's open mouth lingered inches away. A thick, icy tongue slid across her cheek, and she shuddered.

The creature lurched back. An ear-shattering screech vibrated from its throat. Neer screamed, and Avelloch yanked her aside. He swiped his blade through its neck, and the forest was silent. A deep thud pounded against the soil when its head fell to the ground. The haunting silence transformed into loud, echoing growls. Heavy footfalls charged at them from every direction.

Avelloch glanced from left to right. Neer was at his side, waiting. She breathed heavily, her body quivering with terror. They couldn't fight so many creatures. Not without magic. There must have been hundreds of them, all trampling closer.

The ground trembled beneath the horde. And then shadows emerged through the trees. Misshapen, limping creatures, in the shapes of evae, raced closer. Their screeching and clicks rang loudly through the empty woods.

SHADOWS OF NYN'DIRA

Her heart stopped when Avelloch's strong voice resounded over the chaos as he demanded, "Run!"

Klaud stood next to Aélla in the doorway of the inn, watching the ydris depart from their ceremonial tasks. The beautiful songs that came from deep within the forest were silent, and Aélla held her breath.

Klaud placed his hand on her shoulder, and she blinked her thoughts away. "They'll be fine, Azae'l," he said, his voice carrying the strength he knew she needed, though he was just as worried as her.

Aélla exhaled a soft breath. "We need to talk to Thallon about the Klaet'il."

His grip tightened when she attempted to step away. "Wait," he said. "You can talk to me. Even Drimil'Rothar is still evae. You can't ignore that you have emotions."

"You know that isn't true."

"Azae'l"—he tilted her head, a finger under her chin—"talk to me."

She struggled before explaining, "I'm just afraid, Klaud. When I took the vow, I understood my fate and the path laid before me...but if I lose everyone that I love...was it all worth saving in the end?" She quickly wiped her tears away. "That was selfish. I shouldn't have—"

"It's all right. You aren't selfish."

"This is much harder than I thought it would be...If I wouldn't have become Drimil'Rothar, they wouldn't be in the avour'il right now."

Klaud pulled her into a tight embrace. "Their choices are their own, Azae'l. Even if you hadn't become what are you, the Nasir would still be out there." He paused when she sniffed.

"There are many things we wish we could change," he said, "but these are the choices we made. We have to carry on and see them through."

She wiped her eyes and carefully pushed away. "We really need to focus," she said. "Thallon knows where—"

"I'll speak to Thallon. You should rest until they return."

She gave a halfhearted nod, and he watched with sadness as she sat at an empty table with her head down. Since taking the vow, she had become someone he didn't recognize. Before, in her youth, Aella was always happy and free, like an azae'l songbird soaring through the skies.

Klaud's attention broke from Aélla when Thallon walked by. He tapped his arm and said, "We need to talk."

"About?"

Klaud's eyes narrowed with heavy disapproval.

"The sun has barely risen," Thallon argued. "You can't possibly be wound this tight."

Klaud was silent, and Thallon huffed. He then motioned to the door with a slow, reluctant wave of his arm.

"You're a lot scarier than you used to be," Thallon said to Klaud. "Got the look of a killer."

Klaud gave him another empty, unfavorable glare. It seemed time had done little to change Thallon, who still acted in the ways of his youth. Always spouting off witty remarks or yielding to his emotions. It had been many summers since the two of them had been together, and while it was a comfort to have his childhood friends at his side, there was an irreparable rift between them. One that was always looming, no matter the stories or smiles or peace.

Once outside, they walked across a nearby bridge. Morning sunlight glistened against the lapping water, creating a golden lightshow. Klaud shoved his hands into his pockets, while Thallon sipped his drink.

They came to the end of a short bridge and stood together, quietly admiring the view.

Thallon held the mug in his hands, sunlight dancing across his face, and asked, "What's this about?"

Klaud surveyed the lake and surrounding forest. "The Klaet'il." Their eyes met. "What do you know?"

"It was a long time ago. Elidyr took me out to teach me to hunt. We tracked a doe through the forest and saw it disappear"—he snapped his fingers—"just like that. So, we followed it and found that it came here, to ydris territory."

"What does this have to do with N'iossea?"

Thallon sighed. "Caline was ydris. She and N'iossea were inseparable."

Klaud thought for a moment, vaguely remembering as he hadn't been especially close to Thallon's brothers. "Ydris and evae are forbade from intimate relations," he said, reciting the laws which prevented ydris and evae from having children, who hardly survived past birth.

"I know," Thallon said. "They knew, but they didn't care." With another sigh, he pinched the bridge of his nose. "I told him where he could get through and be with her. I didn't know he would eventually defect and join the Klaet'il! I was just trying to help my brother!"

Klaud closed his eyes. He wanted to be angry, but he understood Thallon's reasonings. Loyalty was everything, and he'd never turn his back on family. Now that N'iossea had turned his back on them, he could see the confliction and regret in Thallon's eyes.

Brushing the thoughts away, Klaud said, "We have to tell them."

Thallon's sorrowful eyes were focused on his feet. "Yeah…I know."

Klaud studied his expression, which was washed in guilt. "I won't tell them it was N'iossea."

Thallon turned to Klaud with knitted brows. "He betrayed them. He betrayed everyone."

"You're brothers." Their eyes met. "We are brothers."

Thallon smiled. They stood in silence for several minutes, watching the sun slowly rise. "Do you think they'll make it?" Thallon asked.

Klaud tilted his head aside, silently asking Thallon to follow as he walked toward the inn. "I don't know."

Thallon placed his hand on Klaud's shoulder. "I know it's been a long time, but I'm glad you're here. Avelloch too. Feels like we're kids again sometimes."

"If only."

They wandered closer to the inn, watching villagers prepare for the day.

"Guess those dreams of fighting off the lanathess together and saving the world are finally coming true, huh?"

Klaud was silent.

Thallon continued, "I guess if this is the end...I'm glad to have my true brothers at my side."

He and Klaud shared a smile. As they stepped away from the water, a harsh voice cut through the silence, shattering the stillness of morning. Through the trees, several ydris warriors marched closer. Their faces were taut with anger. Behind them, tied at the wrists with thick ropes, were six evaesh prisoners. Two of which were raging in an attempt to break free.

Thallon's jaw dropped. He stepped closer with wide eyes. Klaud followed his gaze and inhaled a pained breath. Among the six bloody warriors was N'iossea. His arms and chest were marked in the way of the Klaet'il, and fresh blood was painted across his skin.

Klaud pulled Thallon aside when the group walked by, following a path that took them back into the woods. Thallon gasped when he met N'iossea's gaze. His brother's anger faltered slightly as their eyes lingered. With a vicious growl, he turned away, yanking at the binds that detained him.

Four Klaet'il walked behind him. The last prisoner was a woman—an eólin, like Klaud. Their features were nearly identical, with pale skin, long faces, and distinctly colored eyes. Where his were golden, hers were green. Her dark eyes stared ahead as she walked among men she clearly didn't belong with.

"Kila...," Thallon gasped, his voice so quiet Klaud hardly heard it.

Klaud didn't speak. He knew this woman, who had been born of the same fate as him. Fear jolted his heart when she strode by, her hands tied with her palms pressed together, subduing her magic.

Her elemental magic.

Glowing green eyes met with Klaud's, and he held his breath. Ithronél smiled a sly grin and then refocused her attention on the path ahead.

Chapter Thirty-Nine

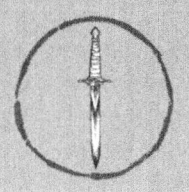

Blood and Fear
Nerana

Neer raced through the forest with Avelloch, dodging low-hanging limbs and twisted roots. The pattering of quick footfalls was silent against the pounding in her ears. She breathed heavily, unable to mask her terror. There were too many of them. Without her magic, she felt lost. Too encumbered by fear to think.

She knew there was something more out there. Something dark. Its presence loomed over the shadowed land, like a blanket of cold, rotten death. She felt the sting of its energy the further they moved into the forest, away from the entrance that had sealed itself upon their arrival.

The growling and clicks grew louder as more creatures closed in. They came from everywhere all at once, running through the dark, unseen. Neer attempted to use her magic. She fought to muster any spark of energy. But it was gone.

Avelloch was a step behind. When a creature leapt from the shadows, he turned back. Its sharp nails swiped at Neer's arm. An icy, putrid limb scratched through her sleeve.

Avelloch yanked her back and jabbed his sword into the creature's side. He slammed it to the ground. Blood-curdling screams vibrated from its throat, calling the others closer. Their footsteps were quick. Overlapping clicks transformed into furious growls.

Neer held her sword in a trembling hand. Her eyes shifted to Avelloch. He snatched his weapon from the creature's flesh and drove his blade through its skull. The silence of its screams gave rise to the snarls and footfalls drawing nearer. Dozens of creatures closed in, moving too quick to detect. Avelloch stepped to Neer's side. They stood with their backs together, waiting. Watching the shadows move through the trees.

"Your sword absorbs their energy," Avelloch said. "When I tell you to fall, you fall."

She nodded, though he couldn't see. Her heart was in her throat. Dark figures moved like wraiths, disappearing behind trees and leaping down from the limbs.

Rancid odor filled the air when a shadow leapt from the darkness. Razor-sharp nails dragged across Neer's chest piece. She slashed its face and kicked it back. A graveled scream rang in her ears, and she leaned forward with a cry, the sound rattling her brain.

Hunched over, Neer didn't notice when another creature sprang from the shadows. Its jaw was open as it dove for her neck. Avelloch shifted, and Neer followed his movement. She ducked to the right, and he struck through the chest of the creature lunging at her. He yanked the sword away and turned around, standing back-to-back with Neer as more figures approached.

Ash coated their faces as they slashed through leathered flesh. The creatures squealed and shrieked, falling to the ground, twitching before fading. Neer sliced through the jaw of another and then smashed its head with her boot.

With every swipe against decaying skin, her weapon glowed brighter. She glanced at Avelloch, realizing his sword was shining in tandem with hers. Neer lurched right while he struck left, splitting open the chests of two approaching figures. In the same motion, Neer drove her weapon into the side of another creature, blade to hilt.

Thick mucus sprayed from its cracked lips, spattering her face with wetness and stench. Its arms flailed, and Neer pulled her sword from its gut, dragging steaming entrails from its serrated flesh. A quick hand struck for Neer's chest. Sharp nails inched closer, splitting the fibers of her sleeve. Avelloch slashed through the creature's wrist, severing its hand from limb.

Its shriek was silenced when Neer struck her blade upward beneath its chin. The creature faded to ash, coating her in another layer of black dust.

For a moment, there was a pause in the attack. Neer breathed heavily, feeling Avelloch's shoulders rise and fall. He stood behind her, his arms tight and breathing steady.

The ground trembled beneath another approaching horde. Avelloch stood taller.

"What do we do?" Neer asked. Her eyes darted from left to right, and she heard only the echoing clicks and shrieks closing in.

Shadowy figures dashed through the underbrush.

Her throat tightened when they came into view. Dozens of shrieking figures charged, their contorted bodies weaving from left to right as they ran on twisted feet and curved spines.

Avelloch breathed quicker. His eyes narrowed, and he tightened his grip on his sword. Neer matched his stance, masking her terror with confidence and strength. They had to focus. She wouldn't let him die here.

The creatures burst through the darkness, screeching and clawing. Avelloch raised his sword.

"Now!" he screamed, and sliced across his forearm.

They sank to their knees, and Avelloch shoved his blade deep into the soil. He pulled Neer close when the sword brightened. The world shook when a shockwave of light expanded from the weapon, moving in a wide circle. Branches tore from trees, while decayed flesh and bloody innards rained from the sky.

Neer collapsed into Avelloch's arms, cradling her pounding head. They knelt on a patch of grass surrounded by fresh dirt where the ground had been stripped bare. The world spun, and Neer blinked her vision into focus. Shadows that had once stalked the land were absent. Their noises silent. Piles of flesh and severed limbs lay in the dirt, steaming as they faded to dust.

"Come on," Avelloch said, stumbling to his feet before catching himself on a tree. He took several deep breaths.

Ash hazed the air, clinging to his throat, causing him to hack and cough.

Neer sat on her knees, too disoriented to focus. Avelloch's rumbled coughs were muted in her ears as she surveyed the land through distorted, swaying vision. Her eyes shifted to her weapon, which had lost its glow after Avelloch's attack.

She looked from east to west, listening to the quiet and searching for intruders. Slowly, Avelloch turned to meet Neer's gaze. His eyes fell away, and he covered his lips, coughing. Neer took a moment to gather herself and then rose to her feet. She pulled Avelloch's sword from the dirt and approached his side. He cleared his throat while accepting the weapon.

"We have to keep moving," he said through a hoarse voice.

He staggered forward with a wince, and Neer helped steady him. Warm blood seeped from the cut on his arm and coated her fingers in red. When he gripped his side with a groan, Neer lifted the bottom of his tunic, stricken to find deep scratches on his side.

Her heart sank when she reached for the small pouch on her belt and found it wasn't there. She stepped away, desperate to find it. Searching through the grass, her fingers grazed over broken vials, dirty bandages, and crushed hardtack strewn beneath layers of ash.

"Shit…," she griped, staring at the dirty remnants of her belongings. "Have you got anything? …Avelloch?"

Neer turned to find him leaning against a tree, swaying from vertigo. Rushing to his side, she dug through the small pack on his belt, thankful to find a vial of healing potion tucked inside.

"No," he growled. "Save it. There are…needles…and gut."

"You want me to…to stitch you up?" There was a heavy tremor to her voice. She had never sutured anyone's wounds. Her hands were more adept at striking through her enemies, not bandaging them up.

"I can do it," he said.

"What? No, you can't—"

"We need to hurry!"

Neer held his stare for a moment longer before glancing around. The forest was too dark, and ash hovered in the air, making it impossible to clean his wound. They were also too exposed, standing amid sparse trees and shallow underbrush.

Every direction was bleak, with no shred of distant light or sound to help guide their path. They were entirely abandoned by nature, left to scour the dark in hopes that fate — and a bit of luck — would lead them to safety. Neer returned her attention to Avelloch. She knew they had to go southeast, but the threat of danger would be denser near the apex of the forest.

Guiding his arm around her shoulders, she led them west, further away from their destination. It was a foolish decision to veer from their path, but they couldn't risk another encounter.

Time passed slowly. Its only sign being the increasing ache in Neer's back from carrying Avelloch's growing weight on her shoulders. His feet dragged the ground, and his breathing was heavy. Too heavy. He needed to rest. They needed water and a safe place to hide.

But there was nowhere to go. Nowhere to seek shelter or aid. They were lost, and Neer knew that if she veered off of her path, which had been as straight a line as she could go, they would never find their way out.

Traveling further, on the verge of collapse from exhaustion and dehydration, the faint glow of water appeared through the haze. With a spark of excitement, Neer trudged forward, keeping her eyes on their surroundings, thankful no creatures had spawned from the darkness to attack.

She sighed with relief when they stepped to a shallow creek. The water was illuminated with streams of light reflecting against the trees and grass. Avelloch held his breath as Neer guided him to the ground. He leaned against a tree with his head back and eyes closed.

Neer felt his sweltering face before rushing to the water with her canteen. Once filled, she returned to Avelloch's side and placed the spout to his lips. He calmly took it and drank half the contents. With a sigh, he returned the canteen to her and weakly removed his chest piece.

Neer drank the rest of the water and then refilled it before moving back to his side. He was motionless as she cleaned his wounds and then retrieved the needle and gut from his pack. Her hands trembled when she pressed the hooked needle against his torn flesh. She held her breath and wiped her sweat away with her dirty sleeve.

Fear wasn't an option. She knew this. But it was easier said than done. Closing her eyes, she counted to five—as she was taught long ago—and reopened them with fresh confidence. Avelloch lay still, slumped against the tree. She hoped he was unconscious and wouldn't feel the pain of her ill-equipped hands.

Blood coated her fingers, piercing the needle into his skin. He didn't react. Didn't so much as flinch or twitch his eye as he lay motionless. Unconscious. This settled her fear, and she continued with steadier hands.

Once finished, she tied off the gut, cleaned his awfully sutured wounds, and then wrapped his abdomen in thick bandages. While lifting his shirt to better place the dressing, she noticed black markings on his chest. Unveiling his skin, she was stricken by the black designs, similar to those worn by the Klaet'il, etched onto his shoulder and upper chest.

She ran her fingers across the markings, curious to know why he had them. They hadn't been there when she first met him long ago. Her hand trailed across his skin, now following a map of scars to the center of his chest. Through the soft glow of water light, Neer touched the faint blemish over his heart.

Her mind spun, remembering how she had saved him and his words when he wished that she hadn't. She quickly pushed the thoughts away, becoming too overwhelmed to think clearly.

The forest was calm, though the faint whispers of growling, hungry creatures echoed through the air like a dying wind. Carefully, Neer lay Avelloch on the grass, watching as he slept. She couldn't block the thoughts creeping into her mind, giving rise to the fear as she wondered if he would ever wake, or if his soul would be lost to this plane forever.

Aélla stood outside with the others. Her arms were crossed over her chest as she listened to Thallon speak of the prisoners. She couldn't imagine why Ithronél would be in ydris territory and not at the Nasir's side.

"We have to do something," Thallon said. "If we tell them N'iossea is my brother, they'll—"

"Lose faith in us," Thurandír explained. "Your brother is invading with the Klaet'il. If we tell them of your connection to him, they could see us all as a threat."

Klaud added. "I agree. We must tread lightly."

"We can't let him die!" Thallon exclaimed. "He isn't like them! He's just—"

"He is Klaet'il, Thallon."

Rage reddened Thallon's face. He pulled Klaud by the collar and glared hatefully into his eyes. "He is my *brother*!"

Aélla placed her hand on Thallon's arm. "Please. Let us consider this without violence."

"I won't let him die!" He shoved Klaud back. "We have to save him!"

She nodded. "Okay. Just allow us to think this through. We can't resolve this with anger."

Thallon breathed deeply, overcome with heavy grief. He shook his head and paced back and forth, gripping his head. "What the hell is he doing?" he muttered. "Why is he such a fucking fool?"

Thurandír watched him with worried eyes. He glanced at Aélla and said, "There must be some way you can speak to the prisoners."

"Elidyr is coming, right?" Thallon stated. "They'll listen to him! He's a respected leader!"

Aélla twisted her hands together in deep thought. So much could go wrong should she say the wrong thing, and with her mind filled with the dread of losing her brother, she worried of making a mistake. Should she find herself as the cause of N'iossea's execution, Thallon would never forgive her. They'd lose a trusted friend and sink further into the chaos threatening to pull them apart.

But Aélla had to try, not only for Thallon, but herself as well. She needed answers. If the Klaet'il were in ydris lands, she had to know why.

With a slight nod, she lifted her eyes to the others. "Stay here," she said. "I will speak with Calasiem and see if I can meet with N'iossea and the others."

"I want to come with you," Thallon said.

"No," she kindly rejected. "I think it is best if I do this alone."

"But, he's—"

She took his hand. "I will try to save him for you. But you must realize that he is our enemy, Thallon. If he has come here to wage war against the ydris…there is nothing I can do."

His jaw clenched. With a stiff nod, he turned away. She could see the fear in his eyes. It was a hard thing to have a brother so misguided and scorned, and she wished they didn't share in that pain. Thallon gave no further response, and Aélla stepped away.

She walked tall, displaying strength amid those much more seasoned in prowess and battle. Though she was smaller, she wouldn't allow the ydris to intimidate her. Just as she had held her strength against the vaxros, so too would she display her authority here. The ydris were kind and reasonable, but they still carried their faults. Dishonor and malice were met with unforgiving justice.

The village was alive with quiet chatter below and soft melodies above. Aélla listened to the humming of the wind, feeling it guide her toward a vacant area of the village. Past a cluster of homes and into the trees, she heard angry evaesh voices. They were speaking evaesh'Klaet'il, though N'iossea carried a Rhyl accent.

Stepping closer, Aélla came to find six men and one woman kneeling on the ground. Their arms were pinned to the soil by tree roots twisted to their elbows. To the right was Ithronél, the Nasir's second-in-command. Drimil'Aenwyn, the sorceress of elemental energy. While the others bowed in defeat, she retained her dignity, keeping her head high and mouth closed. Her green eyes met with Aélla's, and not a flash of surprise or relief moved through Ithronél's cold eyes. It was as if they didn't know each other at all.

"You," a voice hissed from her left.

Aélla turned, staring at the man she believed to be N'iossea. He shared similar features to Thallon, just enough for her to conclude they were brothers. His hair was shaven on both sides, and a thick braid traveled down the center of his scalp, hanging to his mid-back.

"Drimil'Rothar." His heavily accented voice made him hard to understand as he spoke the native tongue of the Klaet'il. "Why have you come here? The lanathess attack us, yet you escort them through our lands!"

Aélla stood taller. "Why are you here, N'iossea?"

He spat in her direction. "Do not call me that."

Her eyes veered back to Ithronél, wanting to speak to her, but N'iossea continued snapping spiteful remarks in an attempt to rile her.

With a deep exhale, Aélla stepped to his side. She ignored his hateful words and placed her hand on his bare shoulder, looking into his eyes. Energy swirled within her, culminating in her chest, before unleashing through her palm and into his flesh. "You will be calm and not speak until you are spoken to."

His body relaxed, and he slowly closed his lips. The anger fumed within his eyes, but he remained silent, unable to fight against the will of her magic. It was unjust to use her energy in such a way—to quiet those who had words to speak, no matter their ferocity or tone. But the pull of dark energy was too great for her to bear, and without his words, her battle softened.

She stepped to Ithronél, staring down at the woman below. "Why are you here?" Aélla asked.

A sinister smile pulled Ithronél's lips, and she began to laugh. It was a wicked, vile noise that echoed far into the forest, resounding against trees.

Aélla held firm to her strength. Though, being in her presence sent a chill down her spine.

"Why. Are. You. Here?" Aélla asked.

Ithronél's chest trembled with dying laughter. Her glowing green eyes met with Aélla's. "What do you hope to gain, Drimil?" Ithronél said, the words sliding from her tongue. "You hold the most powerful energy known to man, yet you refuse to wield it. Refuse to fight and protect those who fight and bleed for you."

Aélla's eyes narrowed.

Ithronél continued, "We outwitted you at Ik'Navhaa, and now you stand here, believing yourself the victor."

Aélla remained calm and poised in her response. "I'm not the one in chains."

"Yet you were born with shackles and strings."

Aélla's jaw tensed. "My decisions have always been mine to make."

"Oh yes, just like your mother. She chose a life of simplicity and look where that has brought us. Her bones have faded to dust, and our only savior refuses to acknowledge the truth."

"And what truth is that?"

A menacing grin stretched her lips, and Aélla's strength fractured. She inhaled a deep breath, feigning courage as Ithronél explained, "Naik'avel is a lie."

Aélla's heart thrummed. She knew Ithronél was speaking falsities. The Nasir wouldn't have sent her into these lands alone if not to cast doubt into the hearts and minds of those who opposed him.

Noticing her uncertainty, Ithronél continued, "Your title is nothing more than a distraction, a symbol of peace as the world drags itself into chaos, time and time again. There is no pre-destined cycle. No light or dark. There is only the strong and weak."

Aélla gulped down the lump in her throat. Her voice was strong as she said, "What are you doing here? What does the Klaet'il want?"

The darkness weighing her features gave Ithronél a menacing appearance. Ice moved through Aélla's veins as she said, "To take back what is ours."

The fear was prominent in Aélla's eyes. Before she had time to speak, a familiar voice came from behind. It was strong and deep, spoken from a man in charge. Aélla turned around to find Elidyr standing behind her.

"Drimil," he said with a slight bow. "It's an honor to be in your presence, again."

"Elidyr," she greeted.

He glanced at each of the prisoners, and when his eyes fell to his brother, he clenched his jaw. Hatred spewed from N'iossea's rageful glare.

"Where is Thallon?" Elidyr asked Aélla, still staring at his brother.

"He's safe," Aélla promised.

Elidyr stepped closer to N'iossea and shook his head in disgust. "What have you become, brother?"

Having been spoken to, N'iossea was released from Aélla's magic. Spit flung from his lips as he cackled like a madman. His face turned red and eyes were wide. "I am what you made me, brother!" Anger quickly replaced his hysteria, and he growled. "You are lucky it was only your eye that I clawed out after you butchered Caline!"

"You understood the laws when you lay with her, N'iossea. Evae and ydris—"

"An innocent woman is dead because you chose to protect your laws."

"I saved you! Had I not stepped in, the Eirean would've condemned you too."

Another maniacal laugh. "Oh, thank you! Thank you, dear sweet Aen'mysvaral, for saving a poor, defenseless, ignorant soul such as mine!" The laughter faded with his words, replaced by something dark Menacing. He breathed heavily, unhinged. "You chose your path, Elidyr...and I've chosen mine."

Elidyr glanced at Aélla and then the prisoners. There was a deep, heavy silence between them. "Why are you here?" Elidyr asked his brother.

"You know what we want."

Elidyr glowered. "Enough with your games, N'iossea. Have you come here to seek Drimil'Rothar?"

A cunning smile twisted his face with a look of madness. "No. Her life is as useless as yours, *brother*." His eyes met with Aélla's, and he said, "We aren't here for you…We're here for *her*."

Chapter Forty

Desperation
Nerana

Neer sat by the stream, tending to her shallow cuts and deep bruises. The water was clouded with muck as she washed her face and arms. She then sat alone, leaning against the tree next to Avelloch, her eyes scanning the forest with purposeful intent.

"Feels like the first time we met…when I saved you from those dogs in Vleland," she said, still studying the forest.

Avelloch slept beside her, unable to hear her words.

"Funny how things turn out, isn't it? I was a farmer's daughter before I became this. Cooking meals and raising children…That would've been my future."

She smiled in recollection.

"I would've married young, probably to another farmer. We would've stayed in our village and lived a normal, boring life." She paused, imagining what could've been. "I would still hate it, but I suppose it's better than this."

Her eyes veered to Avelloch.

"You're a lot different too. All that happiness and spirit is just a ghost of who you used to be…a cruel reminder that life goes on."

She drew up her knees and wrapped her arms around them. Staring into the distance, she thought of her past and the life she used to have. Neer wondered where her path would've taken her had she been born without magic. The thought used to keep her awake at night, along with the guilt of wanting a life so far from the people she loved—

Reiman, Gil…Loryk…She would've never wished to be without them, yet now she longed to go back. To whisk herself away into the faded dreams of a life she'd never have. Her mother's gentle smile, the laughter of her childhood friends, the warmth of a familiar embrace. These were all distant memories slipping through the cracks of her muddled, fractured mind.

Wrapped in her thoughts, she was stunned to find peace where there was once anger and sorrow. The pain gripping her was absent, and for the first time in distant memory, she could piece together her thoughts without the intrusion of her crippling rage.

"All my life, I've never felt like I belonged," she said, her quiet voice laced with sadness. "I've never had anyone that truly understood…"

Her eyes shifted to Avelloch, and she tenderly clutched his arm, needing to feel him. Needing him to hear the words her fury had quieted long ago. With too many thoughts sweeping her mind, she spent the rest of her time in hushed solitude, basking in the peace she knew wouldn't last.

Fading between consciousness and sleep, Neer felt a cold presence hovering nearby. Its stench pulled her awake, and she opened her eyes, finding a crooked figure leaning overhead. Hot breath plumed across her face, like a cloud of rancid death. Her eyes watered and lungs burned. She held her breath, too fearful to move or breathe.

The creature was grotesque, with a heavily arched spine, four misshapen arms, and a head that appeared to melt into its torso. It inched closer, and Neer closed her eyes. Slowly—carefully—she wrapped her fingers around the hilt of her dagger. The leather was cold beneath her heated flesh. She drew the weapon halfway from its sheath, and the creature grumbled in protest. Its sound was akin to that of an angry hog.

Neer froze. Her body trembled when the creature sniffed her hair. She was hopeless, unable to move beneath its presence. A deep pit formed in her gut. She struggled to find a way out of this. A way to survive.

Her eyes shifted to the world around. The creature inched closer. It dragged a sharp finger down Neer's arm, cutting her skin. Her teeth clenched, and she withheld a scream. Sweat dripped down her face. She breathed too quick; her heart raced too fast. She was going to die. There was no way to escape. The creature was too close.

It leaned closer.

Several rows of sharp fangs hovered above her cheek. Neer backed away, pressing into the tree. Its jaws lurched forward, snapping at her face, and she leaned aside, evading its fangs.

Bark cracked when its teeth sank into the tree. The creature ripped away and shrieked. Neer crawled aside. Her dagger dropped to the ground, disappearing in the grass as she fled. Heavy footsteps shook the ground. The beast followed, its talons swiping at her legs.

A strong grip took hold of her ankle. She fought against it, screaming as she was dragged backward. Blood rushed to her head when she was hoisted into the air. Her sword fell from its sheath, crashing to the ground. Still clutching her ankle, the creature grabbed her opposite wrist and slowly began to pull.

Neer's scream echoed through the quiet wood. Her skin burned as her limbs were tugged further apart.

"Avelloch!" she shrieked, hoping he'd wake and hear her cries. His name slipped from her lips twice more until the pain erased all words from her tongue.

The creature leaned in. Putrid breath and rows of teeth were inches from her face. Hot saliva flung across her cheeks as it released an ear-shattering screech.

Neer's heart raced. She kicked and clawed its hands, hoping to free herself. But its skin was too thick. Her nails cracked and bled against its flesh.

Suddenly, Neer fell to the ground. Lying in the grass, she watched the creature stumble. Its thick claws moved to its chest, where a stream of slime poured from a fresh incision.

Neer backed away when it crashed to the ground, bursting into ash. Particles clung to her throat, and she turned aside, coughing. Avelloch stood ahead with thick slime spattered across his arms and face. The green goo coated his sword. He breathed heavily, hesitant to move and alert anything nearby. He glanced around before his eyes fell to Neer. She lay writhing in the dirt; muffled whimpers escaped her clenched teeth.

He fell to her side, grimacing at the pain of his injuries. "Neer?"

She clutched her aching shoulder and slowly sat up with a grunt. They checked her injuries, being sure her shoulder and hip weren't misaligned or broken. When she found herself aching but without serious injury, she exhaled a deep breath.

Avelloch eyed their surroundings. "Where are we?" he asked.

"I don't know." Her voice was shaky. "West." She winced. "I ran as straight as I could."

With a heavy sigh, Avelloch led Neer back to camp. He gathered his belongings and refilled his canteen. Neer sat beside him, noticing his pursed lips. Though he withheld the pain of his injuries, blood stained his bandages, and she feared his stitching may have come loose. The self-inflicted slice to his right arm had scabbed over, leaving a thin line across his blackened skin.

"I should check your side. It could be infected," she said. "I need to use the potion to—"

"I'm fine," he said, the quiver in his voice betraying his sense of strength.

He drank from his canteen, and Neer watched him for a moment longer.

"We're going to die here, aren't we?" she asked.

With another sigh, he leaned forward, closing his eyes. "No. We can make it."

Tears filled her eyes. She had never felt such fear or hopelessness. The forest was unforgiving in its darkness. And the monsters stalking this plane made it all the more terrifying. They could be anywhere, lurking within the shadows, waiting to attack. Neer crossed her arms, ignoring the pain in her shoulder as she fought for an inkling of protection.

"We have to keep our heads," Avelloch said, gathering his weapons. "We're smarter than the kanavin. So long as we remember that, we should be okay."

Neer scoffed, her eyes veering through the endless shadows. "There you go again...keeping *me* positive in these damned tests and trials."

His smile faded into a sharp groan. He leaned aside, grasping his injured side. Neer checked his wounds, glad to find they weren't infected, and used the remaining bandages to rewrap them. As she helped him slip into his top, Neer ran her fingers across his shoulder. He became tense beneath her touch, not daring to look in her direction.

She examined the black markings on his skin. "Why do you have these?" she asked.

His jaw clenched, and for a moment, he was silent. Too silent. She glanced at his face, realizing how stiff he had become. Seconds passed, and he released a shallow breath.

"They were given to me. It..." He struggled to find the right word. "I had no choice."

"Who did this to you? Why would they—"

"It's done, Neer." Soft eyes met with hers. "Talking about it won't change what happened."

"Are you safe?" she asked, her fear rising with every syllable. "Are they going to do this to you again?"

There was silence. A deep, unending silence that formed a pit in her gut. Avelloch closed his eyes, unwilling to answer. When their eyes met, she was gripped by his sorrow and guilt. Somehow, it was worse than the anger he once held. Deeper and more cutting.

He struggled for a moment before whispering, "I'm sorry."

Her thoughts raged, twisting her emotions into a vortex of confusion and pain. She shook her head to clear her mind. "You have nothing to apologize for," she said. "You've done nothing wrong."

His face paled. He turned away and inhaled a deep breath, the darkness returning to his eyes. His gaze set on the woods, where faint rustling echoed in the distance. "Come on," he whispered. "We can't stay here."

Neer opened her mouth to speak, but the words never came. Instead, she helped tie his chest armor together and slid her sword into its sheath.

Hours into their journey felt more like days, leaving them disoriented and sluggish. Avelloch had slowed his pace, walking with a crouched limp while gripping his side. Neer matched his pace, keeping her sword in hand and eyes on the forest. Her hip throbbed with every step, and she silently begged whatever gods were out there to see them quickly to the end of this wretched place.

They walked together in silence, being mindful of their steps to not draw any attention to themselves. Soon, the far-off whispers grew into loud shrieks and pained cries. Voices of men and women shouted from the distance, begging for mercy.

"This place is a nightmare," Neer whispered.

"We need to—"

At that moment, a voice called out from the distance. "You there!"

The voice was exuberant, edging on friendly.

Avelloch reached for his second sword as the figure of a man stepped forward. The stranger waved politely, and Neer inhaled a quiet breath. His entire head, from his nose to nape, was nothing more than flesh. Only his ears and lips made up his features, and when he spoke, Neer felt as if she recognized his voice. But she couldn't place who it belonged to. The face in her mind was blurred.

The stranger wore overalls coated in dirt and sweat. His skin was fair, and his hands portrayed the calluses of a farmer. "You don't look like you belong here," the man said with a hint of laughter.

Neer glanced at Avelloch, and her fear worsened. His wide eyes displayed a horror she had never seen, and it haunted her more than the creature before them.

She started to speak, but Avelloch quickly covered her mouth. He stared into her eyes and carefully shook his head. She took heed of his warning, not daring to make another sound. The stranger stood ahead, patiently awaiting their response.

Avelloch waved Neer forward, and together, they walked carefully by the man who stood perfectly still. His eyeless face stared at the tree where they once stood.

Avelloch circled behind him and then lunged forward, striking at his back. The man stepped aside as if gliding on air. His movement was fluid and quick. He turned around to face his attacker, and Avelloch was frozen once more. His shoulders rose and fell as he stared at the faceless man.

The man's head tilted aside, ever so slightly, portraying a sense of curiosity. Avelloch pursed his lips and stepped back.

"That wasn't very nice," the man said.

Neer grabbed her sword, and as if able to see it, the man focused his attention on her weapon. A twisted smile transformed his flesh-ridden face into a sinister mask of darkness.

Neer choked on her breath, fighting the urge to flee. Every vein pulsed through her body; she felt every thrum ringing loudly in her ears. Beads of sweat formed across her temple, dripping down her face and burning her eyes. The darkness of this plane seemed to deepen as she stared at the man whose phantom eyes were upon her.

His posture straightened, and he began to sing. It was a soft melody every human child knew. Their mothers would hum it while cradling their babes. Fathers would sing before kissing their children goodnight. Neer had heard it often in her younger childhood, before flames forever silenced the solaced tunes.

Avelloch inhaled a deep breath. His eyes narrowed as the man's soft, elegant voice rang through the cold night air.

> *Rise with the dawn, sweet child of mine...*
> *Rise with the dawn and sing...*
> *For your smile is the sun, and laughter's so sweet...*
> *For always my baby you'll be...*
>
> *Sleep with the moon, sweet child of mine...*
> *Sleep with the moon and dream...*
> *For the night is dark, but don't worry, my sweet...*
> *For always my baby you'll be...*

His voice was smooth as silk and sweet as the purest honey. Neer could listen to him sing for an eternity and never grow tired of his melodies. They were comforting, like a warm embrace. She felt his words in her soul, easing the ache that filled her heart.

For a moment, the world stood still, and Neer hadn't a care as she wrapped herself in his voice, accepting its peace. Neer searched desperately through her mind, weaving through every memory, but his face was never there. His warmth and comfort were familiar, yet they didn't exist, even in the deepest parts of her most faded memories.

He repeated the song for the third time, and a sinking feeling tugged at Neer's gut. She lifted her eyes to the faceless man, whose voice was pure and protective, cradling her with a father's touch.

Father.

The word held little meaning, but somewhere in her mind, it fit. No longer did she have to search as its presence stood before her, unrecognizable and blurred.

Still, he sang, his voice remaining as calm and nurturing as it always had, never missing a note as he crooned:

> *For the night is dark, but don't worry, my sweet...*
> *For always my Vaeda you'll be...*

Her blood ran cold as ice, freezing her in place. Before she had time to draw another horrified breath, sharp claws sank into her shoulders, and she was pulled into the shadows.

Chapter Forty-One

Unforgiven
Thallon

Beautiful music flowed through the inn as a harpist played soft melodies by the hearth. Her notes were pure and unbroken, weaving together the many quiet conversations buzzing throughout the room. Thallon sat at a table with his hands folded together atop its wooden surface. He bowed his head in deep contemplation, his mind racing through every possibility, but each thought led to the same result: N'iossea was going to die.

With the thoughts of losing his brother looming in his mind, he didn't notice when Klaud stepped to his side. His golden eyes peered at Thallon for a moment before he settled into the chair next to him.

"Thallon. How are you?"

Thallon scoffed. "How do you think? My brother is going to be executed." The chair creaked when he leaned back and rubbed his face in frustration. "He's attacking them...The laws are clear," he continued. "I know you think he deserves it. Maybe he does...but N'iossea wasn't always like this. He was driven to madness by Elidyr and our people."

His dark blue eyes cut to Klaud.

"You should understand that. When the Nasir cursed Aélla, you would have sacrificed everything to keep her alive."

Klaud turned away, and Thallon continued.

"I remember what you said back then."

"Thallon—"

"That you would burn this world living if she didn't make it. You would flay every person that followed the Nasir and then rip him apart from the inside out." He paused as Klaud faced him. "I can't let him die because he was pushed into this."

"He's our enemy, Thallon! He's killing innocent people."

"We don't know that! N'iossea isn't evil, Klaud. He's just lost his way!" He calmed himself as others began to stare.

Klaud's golden eyes veered from left to right as he became lost in thought. "What do you suggest we do?"

Surprised, Thallon glanced around and then leaned closer. "We should—"

At that moment, a figure appeared behind them, and Klaud leaned away—a quiet signal for Thallon to stop speaking. He understood, sealing his lips and turning around to view their intruder. When his eyes set upon his brother, Thallon glared.

"Elidyr."

Elidyr stood tall, staring down at him with eyes masked in authority. "Thallon. We need to talk."

Thallon leaned forward with his hands folded together. "Then let's talk."

"Alone."

Thallon matched his gaze, but he knew his brother wouldn't back down. It wasn't his way. With a heavy sigh, Thallon stood, grabbed a small pack by his side, and stepped outside. Six avel warriors were huddled together nearby. Thurandír had joined them, though no one seemed to notice his presence as they spoke to the more seasoned, vetted warriors among their group.

Thallon slid his hands into his pockets as he and Elidyr stalked away from the inn. Locals wandered the bridges, paying no mind to the evaesh warrior in their midst. Far from the bustle of town, Thallon broke the long, insufferable silence.

"What do you want?" he asked.

Elidyr puffed his chest. His focus remained on the trail ahead. "I want to know of your position with N'iossea."

"My position?" he repeated. "What the hell does that mean?"

Elidyr glowered, disturbed by Thallon's lack of respect. But unlike most who had stood beneath his brother's oppressive glare, Thallon wasn't intimidated. Being one of the most famed and fiercest warriors within the avel, Elidyr had always stood by the laws—no matter the consequences or reasonings.

Elidyr continued, speaking with rigid authority, "He's going to be tried and executed."

Thallon shook his head and spoke words he knew his brother wanted to hear. "So what? He's a screw-up anyway. Best to rid the world of his madness before he shames our family any further."

"Is that truly how you feel?"

"What does it matter? What's done is done. You, mother, and father washed your hands of him long ago."

"He left us, Thallon."

"Because *you* murdered Caline!" Thallon's voice was sharp with hatred. He turned to Elidyr, standing face-to-face, blocking the path. "Are you truly so callous that you would see your own brother to his death for the madness that *you* set upon him?"

"Thallon—"

"N'iossea didn't deserve that! He shouldn't be executed for—"

"Thallon!" His voice shook with power, silencing his brother's rage.

Their eyes met, and for the first time since childhood, Thallon detected a hint of compassion beneath Elidyr's cold glare.

"I don't want him to die…," Elidyr started, "but he is not who he once was. You must understand this. He has taken the vow of the Klaet'il and is a promised member of their society."

Thallon stepped aside, rubbing the back of his neck. "I can't let him die, Elidyr. I know who he is…I know what he has done…But maybe if we show him some compassion, he could change his mind! Maybe if—"

"He won't."

Thallon clenched his jaw, struggling to contain the misery swelling inside. "I don't care what he's done. I won't turn my back on him. He won't lose the only family he has left."

With one last lingering glare, Thallon marched away.

Through the forest, Thallon came to the edge of the prison encampment. An ydris warrior walked by each of his captives, giving them water and a ripe quay fruit. Thallon's eyes were glued to N'iossea, who appeared sickly with pale skin and a thin frame. Black markings and thin scars were scattered across his face, arms, and chest, displaying his loyalty to the Klaet'il.

Thallon's eyes shifted to the ydris warrior placing the quay fruit to N'iossea's lips, and N'iossea lurched forward, attempting to bite his captor. In one quick movement, the ydris pulled back the fruit and spun his wooden staff. The crack of solid wood smacked against N'iossea's head. Thallon flinched at the sound, hating to see what had become of his brother.

The ydris sneered at his prisoner before marching away. Thallon waited in the shadows until the warrior was out of sight, and then he leapt from the tree line. The prisoners turned to him as he approached, but he paid them no mind. He had hardly noticed their presence at all, studying the roots and vines restraining his brother.

Thallon fell to his knees before N'iossea, and for the first time in many summers, they were together. A flood of emotion crashed through Thallon, but he held himself together, not entirely sure how he should feel. Staring into his brother's eyes, he was brought back to his childhood and reminisced over the days long gone.

"Thallon," N'iossea sneered with a hint of sarcasm. "Come to rescue me, have you?"

"Shut up," Thallon hissed, his voice barely above a whisper. "Do you want to live or not?"

N'iossea was silent while Thallon tugged against the roots. He attempted to carve through them with his dagger, but the blade dulled before he made any real progress.

"The forest will decide his fate," a voice called from behind.

Thallon whipped around and stared at Ithronél, who he had forgotten was there.

She spoke smoothly, with patience. "We cannot escape."

Thallon refocused on N'iossea, ignoring Ithronél's obvious guise. She was up to something, and he wouldn't fall for it.

"Kill him," Ithronél said. "Any Klaet'il who cannot save themselves is unworthy."

"Free him!" Thallon remarked. "You're an elemental! Why have you allowed yourself to be captured?"

Ithronél's only response was a twisted smile.

Thallon glanced at his brother. His heart sank when their eyes met, and he saw the madness brewing inside. It was a deep, unsettled rage that couldn't be quelled. What happened so long ago had broken him. He was changed—lost. But still, Thallon couldn't give up on him. He couldn't allow him to die like this, defenseless and chained.

"Do it, baby brother," N'iossea taunted. "Drive that blade through my heart and prove what a brave warrior you are."

"Stop it," Thallon demanded.

"You were always *weak*. Stuck with your head in books. Have you ever been inside of a woman? Have you felt the cold steel of your sword slicing through the heart of your enemies?" He spat on the ground at Thallon's knees. "Will this make you worthy to them? If you want to prove something, then prove it. Go on!"

"I'm trying to help you!"

"The day that I accept help from a feeble little fawn like you is the day that I—"

"Avoid execution?"

Their eyes met, and Thallon held on to his anger as his brother, the most foolish and quick with his tongue, stoked the flames of his pride.

"I am on your side, you idiot!"

N'iossea bit his tongue, though Thallon could see he was withholding many other spiteful words. With a growl, Thallon continued cutting at the roots, hardly making progress. Beads of sweat formed across his brow, and as the night grew colder, the moons displayed their colors.

Thallon had switched his dagger for an axe, hacking carefully at the roots before cutting them away with his knife. The anger slowly melted from N'iossea's eyes, and by the time his left hand was pulled free, he had a look more humbled than vicious. Thallon paid him no mind, focusing on freeing him before any guards returned.

"Why are you doing this?" N'iossea asked in evaesh'Rhyl. He spoke softly, sounding more like the person Thallon knew than the man he had become.

"Going to talk me out of it?" Thallon said gruffly. He struck the roots twice more before N'iossea responded.

"You are a loyal brother."

Thallon paused. He wiped his brow and turned to N'iossea. "You should try it sometime."

A twisted smile erased all sense of the man Thallon knew. "If I wasn't loyal, I would snatch that axe from your hand and sink it into your neck."

Thallon glared. "I understand your hatred for the others, but you have no reason to hate *me*. I looked up to you! I fought for you when Caline—"

N'iossea snatched a dagger hidden beneath his belt and shoved it against Thallon's throat. "Do *not* speak her name." His sharp voice cut through the air as he spoke in evaesh'Klaet'il.

Thallon exhaled a deep, saddened breath, as if it were one of the last he would ever make. The sting of the blade pulsed through him, and he pulled away from his brother's rage.

"You've always been an idiot," Thallon remarked. "Doing things without a thought of the consequences. Look at yourself. Look at what you've become—threatening your own brother! When I'm trying to help you!"

He shoved N'iossea back.

"Fuck you," Thallon snapped. "I'm risking *my* life to save you! For what? So, you can go and kill more innocent people? You're insane!"

N'iossea chuckled darkly. "You think me mad, do you?"

SHADOWS OF NYN'DIRA

A shade of darkness cast across his eyes, and he lifted his dagger. Thallon leaned back, a quiver of fear striking his heart. Moonlight glimmered against N'iossea's blade as he held Thallon's gaze, and then struck it downward.

Thallon lurched back, evading the attack that missed his thigh by mere inches. N'iossea's dark eyes peered at him beneath his lowered brow. His lips were pursed and hatred was pure.

The chipped roots restraining N'iossea's arm began to creak as he fought to break free. Thallon leaned aside, horrified by N'iossea's cracking bones and tearing flesh as he ripped his arm from the roots.

N'iossea's companions called to him, begging for freedom. He marched to the first of his men, who knelt to the ground just like the others, and a look of disgust painted his face.

"Come on, *lat'Runa*,°" the kneeling man hissed in his native tongue. "What are you waiting for?"

N'iossea released a growl and slashed his blade across the man's throat. The others shouted in protest while the man gurgled on his blood. They fought against their restraints, displaying nothing but rage as N'iossea stepped to each of them and dragged his dagger across their necks, slicing to the bone.

Thallon watched, addled with shock as his brother mercilessly killed his own comrades. Their gargled breaths fell silent, and the deranged warrior approached Ithronél. He pressed his dagger to her throat and stared into her cold eyes. N'iossea hesitated before removing the weapon from her throat. He then rushed to Thallon's side and stole his pack.

N'iossea shoved his bloody dagger in Thallon's face, his unhinged eyes wide with insanity.

"You risked your life to save a man like me," N'iossea said, "yet I'm the one who's mad?"

---

* Upon N'iossea's acceptance into Clan Klaet'il, he was given a new name, *Runa*.

° The prefix *lat* is given to those who are not born to the Clan but have chosen to take their vows. While it is meant to signify their newfound loyalty, many natural born Klaet'il see it as a disgrace, viewing those who aren't born of their blood to be lesser.

Chills ran down Thallon's spine when N'iossea smiled, and with a chilling laugh, he stood.

"Until we meet again, *brother*."

Thallon couldn't breathe as N'iossea turned away and fled.

Neer was dragged into the forest. Talons sharp as freshly smithed blades tore into her flesh. She fought against the agony, clawing at the creature behind. Her fingers bled, scratching with ripped nails against rough flesh the texture of tree bark.

She was thrown to the ground and exhaled a deep breath. Scrambling to her feet, she reached for her sword and found her scabbard empty. Her bloody hands snatched her dagger from the sheath on her hip. Neer glanced around, searching for whatever had pulled her out there.

But she was alone.

There were no monsters or ghouls or faceless men. Just darkness. Deep, undisturbed darkness. Her breaths were ragged, and she peered from left to right. Nothing was familiar. Wherever she had been taken didn't feel far, maybe a few meters at most, yet she stood someplace different. The forest was now full of thin trees and dead pine straw. The smell of fresh water wafted across her nose, as if a lake was nearby. It reminded her of home.

Tears burned her tired eyes. She would never find her way back. And worse, she was alone. Stuck in this dangerous place of madness and despair. But her thoughts weren't on her own survival, and through the terror fusing her feet to the ground, she shouted for the one whose fate truly mattered.

"Avelloch!"

Her voice was more a squeal than words. She called for him again, but there was no response. Not even the echo of her own voice slid through the cold, dark air. Her legs were heavy, like aged stone, but she forced herself forward. All thought of proper technique and stance were swept from her mind as she inched ahead, holding the weapon in front of her chest with both hands.

Suddenly, an influx of voices echoed from all around. They rattled her mind, nearly drawing a shriek from her tightened throat. She came to a halt, closing her eyes as the onslaught of voices raged through the air. Some vicious, others quiet with cowardice.

As soon as they came, they disappeared. And the silence was deafening. Sweat dripped down her face like fresh rain. She lifted her eyes and was immobilized by terror. Standing before her, staring with a furrowed brow, was Avelloch. His glowing sword was held in a blood-spattered hand.

Neer turned her shaky head from left to right. She released a timid exhale, her eyes veering back to him. He was silent and still, as if made of stone. Her heart skipped, and she wondered if this was another foul creature of darkness, one that had taken his form.

She stepped forward, inspecting his posture and expression. And then she halted.

This wasn't him. It couldn't be.

He was too stiff, too frozen. Her fingers tightened on her dagger. She parted her lips to speak and quickly sealed them, remembering their encounter with the faceless man.

"Are you all right?" he asked with a step forward. "Neer?"

Her lungs froze. It was his voice. His words. She stared at him, fearful. Panicked. Unsure of what to do. Thoughts raged through her mind, pulling at the strands of her sanity. She was lost, uncertain of what was truth or fiction. Uncertain the man before her was the one she fought and cried and lay with, or if he was something else entirely.

"Neer," he said, still clutching his sword. "We have to go!"

She wanted to speak, but fear had sliced her tongue and made her mute.

"What are you doing?" he asked.

Tears stung her eyes. She inched closer, holding her breath. Choking on withheld sobs.

Avelloch glanced at her, and his eyes were washed with concern. "Neer?" he asked.

She shook her head, and a loud cry escaped her throat. This wasn't Avelloch. She repeated it in her mind until the words lost their meaning. She bit her lip to withhold her grief.

A slow step brought her closer.

She wanted to run and strike her blade through his chest. Quick and easy. But she couldn't. Her legs could hardly lift from the ground as the weight of what she had to do pressed against her.

Avelloch didn't move. He never raised his weapon or shifted his stance as Neer approached him. Standing close, she saw he was exactly the same. Every scar, every mark. A perfect replica of the man she knew.

But this wasn't him. She had to believe it. Whatever this was, it wouldn't stop chasing her. The voices and memories and impossibly different forest weren't real. They were conjured by something else, something that needed her voice to attack, but she wouldn't give it.

Slowly, she lifted her blade to his chest, its edge trembling in her unsteady hand.

"What are you doing?" he snapped, causing her to flinch. "Neer!"

Tears streamed down her face, and spit flung through her pursed lips. He could be there, standing before her, trapped in visions just like herself. Her strength faltered, and she pulled the dagger away. Still, he didn't move. Never pushed her away or reached for his weapon. There was no sigh of relief or comforting embrace to reassure her of his truth. Only silence and a cold, dark stare from unflinching eyes.

She stared into those eyes, hopelessly lost. This wasn't Avelloch.

It wasn't Avelloch.

It wasn't him.

With a deep breath, Neer closed her eyes and plunged her dagger through his chest. She felt his muscles rip, the blade sinking through his flesh. He gasped, and she opened her eyes, petrified. She stumbled back, crashing to the ground as he fell into her.

Crimson bubbled in his lips, draining down his chin. Her body shook, and she stared at him, their faces close enough to smell his blood. And then the cold, hard truth was made all too real as she looked into his fearful, confused eyes.

He wasn't fading to ash.

She was wrong.

This was Avelloch…and she had killed him.

Chapter Forty-Two

Last Breath
Avelloch

AVELLOCH STARED AT THE IMAGE of his father. Blood soaked through his armor, drenching it in red. The worn and unraveled hilt of a dagger stood proudly in his chest. Its blade plunged through his heart, exactly where it was struck so long ago.

Avelloch knew Neer was seeing a different image of someone she recognized. It was the way of the tova, creatures that took the image of someone familiar to its prey. Using memories to communicate, the tova were only able to speak in words or phrases the person had said to its victim, in the way they said them, making it easy to identify as a kanavin.

"You are my son," Avelloch's father said, his voice genuine and soft. Unrecognizable after so many years of torture and pain.

Avelloch balled his fists, unwilling to be trapped by his memories. His nightmares.

"You can always come to me," his father continued, "and I will be there."

Neer's shrieks filled the silence, and Avelloch turned as she was dragged into the forest. He ran after her, tripping over roots and rocks. The world became darker as she was pulled further into the abyss, too quick for him to keep up. But he had to keep going. If she was swept away, he'd never find her again. She'd be lost in this realm, forced to fight and survive alone.

"No!" he screamed when she faded into the shadows. "Neer!"

He pushed forward, ignoring the burning in his thighs and ache in his lungs. Faster still, he ran, until the world gave out beneath his feet, and he collapsed into a pit of thick, warm

SHADOWS OF NYN'DIRA

liquid. The tang of blood filled his mouth and nose, and he struggled to resurface.

There was nothing beneath him but hot, sticky blood. It was all around, seeping through his clothes and into his pores. He swam higher but never reached the surface. His lungs burned, begging for another breath. Striking him with pain as his life drew closer to an end.

"You did this!" his father's voice hissed through his mind, and the deep throb of a phantom boot smashed against Avelloch's ribs.

Blood filled his mouth, and he closed his lips, determined to survive.

"It should have been you!"

Another kick, this time to his gut. He gritted his teeth, withholding a life-ending gasp.

"If I ever see you again...if I hear your name whispered through the wind..." His father's haunting voice rang loudly in Avelloch's mind, as if he was shouting in his ear, replaying the worst moments of his life. "She'll be next."

Avelloch broke free from the lake of crimson and inhaled a deep breath. Blood coated his skin like liquid armor, painting his body from scalp to heel in dark red. He wiped his eyes, smearing more stinging blood beneath his lids as he searched for the shore. His body was tired, and he knew he wouldn't last much longer.

Steam rose from the lake, obscuring his vision. He swam straight, hoping to find land. Blood dripped down his face, seeping through his lips and burning his tongue with the taste of copper. He took another stroke forward, and his palm pressed against thick grass. Burning eyes lifted to the bank, and he exhaled a relieved sigh. Footsteps drew closer, and Neer knelt before him.

He breathed a sigh of relief, thankful she was alive.

"Avelloch...," she said. "You're alive. Thank the gods, you're alive!"

"Neer—"

As the word slipped from his tongue, he realized his mistake. Before he could react, she grabbed his head and thrust him beneath the surface. Sharp talons sank into his scalp, holding him in place. Blood splashed as he fought to free himself, unable to remove its iron grip.

Kicking against the edge of the pit, he thrust himself back, pulling the tova into its depths. Its grip released, and Avelloch heaved himself out of the blood. The sutures on his side tore, sending a strike of burning pain through his body. Weak arms gave out when he crawled across the grass, hacking and gasping for breath.

"Avelloch!" Neer's voice rang through the forest, the tova holding on to her image. It thrashed in the pool, unable to save itself. "Avelloch!"

He covered his ears, sickened by her voice and desperate pleas.

"Please don't leave me…," she begged, and he sucked in a sharp breath, pained by her words. "Don't let me die alone."

He sat up, watching her reach out for him, her eyes pleading. And for a moment, he doubted himself. The magic and pain had pulled at the strands of his sanity, but he had to keep his wit. This wasn't Neer. Ten throbbing puncture wounds across his scalp reminded him of that, and so he remained motionless, watching her sink beneath the surface, her fingers twitching as she was dragged under. Bubbles broke the surface when she exhaled a final breath.

Avelloch leaned forward and closed his eyes. The tova was dead, and he had to move. But his body surged with agony. Bleeding cuts tore with his every movement. His head throbbed and throat was raw.

His spirit was weak. This place was far worse than he ever imagined. The tales of its horrors were nothing in comparison to the mind-numbing effect it had on his body and soul.

He inhaled a deep breath, clutched his poorly sutured side, and forced himself to stand. His muscles ached in protest, and a deep groan slipped from his throat. Blood dripped from his forehead into his eyes and mouth. He breathed heavily, taking ragged, tired steps.

This place wouldn't conquer him. He could still fight. So long as he was breathing, he would fight. And he would find her.

Tired feet dragged across the ground as he pressed on, walking for what felt like hours, surrounded by darkness. His eyes struggled to stay open, and he stumbled as he dozed off. He quickly caught himself, and pain radiated from his side as it split further open.

Avelloch collapsed to his knees. Uneven breaths burst from his lungs, and he curled inward, gripping his side. Warm blood seeped through his fingers, dripping to the ground.

"Fuck...," he groaned through clenched teeth.

"Sleep...," a voice whispered through the air, hollow as a void. Empty and weightless.

Avelloch's body trembled, and he fought to stay conscious. But his body was tired, and his eyes begged to close. Just for a moment, he could rest and then start again.

His head bobbed, and his eyes slowly shut. He felt the warmth of sleep take over and allowed its gentle embrace to soothe the discomfort that had stricken him. The deep, pulsating throb of every muscle, the sting of his injuries and weariness of his mind. It could all end. All he had to do...was sleep.

"No!" Neer's voice broke the silence.

Avelloch was jolted awake. He lifted his head, listening as she spoke through choked sobs.

"Please...please...Avelloch!"

He couldn't leave her out there, alone. Weak and delirious. If he faded now, he'd never wake. The creatures would feast on his defenseless body. He had to keep going. There was no other way.

Gritting his teeth so hard they nearly cracked, he pushed forward, following the sound of her cries. It could be a trick, he knew that. But it had been so long—too long—that they'd been separated. He had to take a chance.

Any chance.

Neer sat alone, staring at the blood bubbling from Avelloch's lips. When he drew his last breath, the weight of his body pressed into her. Stifled cries escaped from her throat, and she collapsed into him, wailing. The weight of his body became lighter as he slumped to the ground.

He fell from her trembling hands and burst into a cloud of ash. The particles clung to her wet face and dirty clothes. She stared at the remnants of his body floating through the air, realizing he was a creature of darkness. Realizing it was all an illusion.

A jolt struck her chest, and she leaned forward, gasping for breath. Tears streamed down her face, carving trails through the filth staining her cheeks. She couldn't understand what had just happened. This place—its illusions and mysteries—were overbearing. And without her magic, she felt too much. Her heart beat too fast.

She breathed heavily, hunched forward in pain.

When footsteps shuffled from behind, she leapt to her feet and brought her blade to the throat of her enemy.

A quick hand gripped her wrist when her weapon tugged against flesh, and her eyes met with Avelloch's. Confusion and fear fell through her. He was drenched in dried blood. No part of him had been spared. Too terrified to speak, Neer stood motionless before him.

His eyes were wide with uncertainty. She could see the fear in him, and it haunted her.

"Neer…," he started, and she was shattered by the tremble in his voice.

She parted her lips, but no words could form.

"It's me. I…" Avelloch paused with thought. "That kanavin can only replicate memories. It can't speak anything you haven't heard me say." Another pause, this time with anticipation. He was waiting for a response. "Please, Neer," he said. "Speak to me…"

Neer shook her head and stepped away. She pressed her sword firmer against his chest, when he dug through his pouch and retrieved a small item. He stepped closer and placed it into her hand.

"It's me, Neer," he said, blue eyes seeping with worry.

She glanced at the item in her hand, and her jaw clenched. It was her tiaavan. The one he had taken from her room so long ago. Their eyes met, and she breathed heavily, still unsure. But she couldn't get through this without him. She had to know and was prepared to fight if he was another monster.

Her voice trembled as she spoke. "Avelloch?"

He exhaled a deep breath and bowed his head. Stepping forward, he wrapped her in his arms, and she leaned into his chest. They stood together, held in a tight embrace, too fearful of letting go. She needed his presence and strength, more than she ever thought she could. His grip tightened before he stepped back and looked at her with bloodshot, tired eyes.

"Are you hurt?" he asked.

"A-are you?"

He shook his head and then turned away. Glancing through the forest, he clutched her hand and headed southeast. "We have to keep moving."

A pained groan escaped his throat when he stumbled forward.

"Avelloch!" she exclaimed, grasping his arm.

He grunted while hunching over. Fresh blood coated his fingers when he touched his side.

"Gods!" Neer gasped. "We have to do something!"

"We can't…" His words were slurred. "The kanavin—"

"You will die! Do you understand? If we don't fix this…if we can't stop the bleeding, then—"

Tears flooded her eyes, and the words caught in her throat. She turned away, choking on her breath.

"Dammit!" she snapped.

Her hands trembled when she wiped the moisture from her eyes and stepped forward, gazing at their surroundings.

"Which way do we go? Where the hells are we?"

Her heartrate quickened and vision blurred. They were stuck here, forced to travel and fight until finding their way. She gulped down the lump in her throat, trying hard not to panic. But in her delirium, she couldn't contain her emotions. She couldn't stop the dread that infiltrated her mind, sinking her further into madness and despair.

"Avelloch, we—"

He exhaled a shallow breath, and the deep thump of his body crashed against the ground. Neer turned around, stricken by the sight of him lying in the dirt. His breathing was raw, and his body quivered.

"Avelloch!" she wailed, falling to his side. "Come on," she cried. "We have to keep going…please! Just get up…please…Avelloch…"

She shook his shoulders, feverishly trying to wake him. Tears spilled from her eyes as she called his name, shrieking with panic. They were going to die. If he didn't wake, they would never leave this place.

"Avelloch, please! Please, wake up…" Neer wiped the blood from his face and pulled his eyes open. "Please…"

His eyes rolled back before he slowly blinked. Neer gasped with relief. Her cries echoed through the woods as Avelloch began to stir. With a deep groan, he attempted to push himself up. Neer gripped his shoulders, helping him to his knees, but his head fell aside, and he collapsed to the dirt.

"Come on," Neer demanded, forcing him to sit, his eyes struggling to stay open. "You aren't dying here."

Neer ignored the agony of her wounds and pulled Avelloch to his feet. She draped his arm over her shoulders, and together, they walked through the harrowing darkness, hoping to find the right path.

Her legs grew tired as they walked endlessly through the forest, ducking behind trees when creatures stalked the woods. Large roots wove through the soil, causing them to stumble and trip. A gentle dome-shaped glow brightened the distance, bringing the first sign of light since their venture into this realm.

Tears filled her eyes as she gaped at its luminance, which seemed so far away. "Is that it?"

Avelloch lifted his dreary eyes and gave a silent nod.

She groaned while straightening, heaving his weight as he fell weaker. "Come on," she said through deep breaths. "We have to keep going."

"I can't..."

"Avelloch!"

He collapsed forward, causing them both to fall. The scratches on her back tore, and she lay in the dirt, writhing. Every breath brought another wave of agony. She crawled closer to him.

"Avelloch...," she whimpered. "Come on...we have to go."

He breathed heavily, unable to speak.

Neer brought herself to her knees, heaving, and looked around. The sound of trickling water broke through the silence, and the weight of hopelessness lifted from her shoulders.

"Avelloch...," she said, tapping his face.

He lay still with his eyes closed. Tears filled her eyes, and she shook his shoulders, panicked.

"Don't give up!" she cried. "Please! Come on! We've nearly made it, Avelloch. Please..."

Her eyes flashed to the light in the distance, and she knew they were running out of time. Desperate to end this and return home, she pressed her palms against his chest, fighting for a shred of energy that could heal him. Her throat tightened and arms trembled as she searched every ounce of her soul, but it wasn't there. She was entirely void of her magic.

She was unable to save him.

The world was dark with sorrow. Neer leaned over him, examining the infected wounds across his body. Several stitches had popped from the swollen cut on his side, oozing with pus. Neer dug through his pouch before pouring its contents on the ground in her haste. She searched through his blood-crusted things and found the healing potion.

Her relief faded to misery when she realized the top had come loose and the jar was filled with blood. With another glance at the Tree, she inhaled a deep breath and forced herself to stand.

"Avelloch." She pulled his arm, ignoring the searing pain in her shoulders and back. "Come on!"

He exhaled a slurred groan. Neer pulled harder, drawing sweat across her brow, before he was forced into a sitting position. She slung his arm around her shoulder, relieved when he used what little strength he had to stand.

Neer held him close, the distant light burning in her bloodshot eyes as she moved toward the Tree. With every step, the roots twisting through the ground became larger. Some were twice as wide as normal tree trunks and curved high above the ground, creating a web of bridges.

Shallow streams carved through the ground, trickling beneath the roots and crashing against rocks. Their streams of light danced against the trees, creating a lightshow that brought life to the thick darkness.

"We'll be safe here," she said while they climbed down to the water. "The light should keep the creatures away."

Neer lowered Avelloch to the ground beneath a large arched root. He collapsed into the grass, his eyes closed and breathing heavy. Neer watched him with silent grief. She hadn't realized before just how much she needed him. How regretful she was that he had met her and was thrown into this path of sorrow and destruction. If they had never met, he wouldn't be lying here, fighting through this hell. He wouldn't be fighting against the infection threatening to kill him.

"The potion's gone…," she said, tears flooding her eyes. "If you go to sleep, you may not wake…and I don't have the strength to carry you."

"We can rest…," he said, his voice so tired and slurred she could hardly understand it. "We'll make it…"

Neer blinked her tears away, not willing to give in to her grief. She leaned forward and dipped her hands beneath the glowing water to wash away the blood and filth from her skin. Water dripped from her arms when she pulled away from the stream.

Her tired eyes gazed at the beauty around her, wishing for things to be as peaceful as they seemed. But for now, she knew they were safe, and without rest, they'd never make it to the end. A deep groan escaped her throat when she crawled back to rest beside Avelloch. Her body throbbed with every pulse of her heart, sending shockwaves of agony through her broken, tired body.

"We're almost there," she said, her voice slurring and eyes growing heavy. "Please…just make it to the end…"

She gently clutched his hand, and the darkness carried her into a deep, unintentional sleep.

Chapter Forty-Three

Fading Light
Thallon

THE FOREST WAS SILENT as Thallon knelt on the ground, staring at his blistered hands. The tang of copper burned his tongue as blood dripped from his parted lips like melted wax.

Not a whisper of hope or weep of sadness rang from the trees. They were as silent as a void was dark. The heavy stench of blood caused his stomach to twist, and his dark blue eyes flashed to the klaet'il warriors. Their bodies were limp, lying slumped in the grass, their faces buried in thick pools of blood.

To the right, Ithronél knelt with her hands woven securely in place. She stared at Thallon with a look of sheer boredom. As if her own people weren't bleeding out at her side. As if a massacre hadn't taken place just moments before.

Footsteps raced closer, and Thallon bowed his head, uncaring of his punishment. Numb to anything but confusion and guilt. When a figure appeared through the brush, Thallon closed his eyes, awaiting his judgement.

But standing at the edge of the prison was Elidyr. His chest puffed and chin lifted, though his focus remained on N'iossea's shackles, which had yet to disappear back into the soil.

Thallon was silent as footsteps drew closer. When a hand was placed on his shoulder, he opened his eyes, and the color washed from his face when he met his brother's gaze.

"Leave," Elidyr warned, his strong voice coated with worry. "Now."

Thallon trembled, his lips parting as if to speak, but the words never slithered from his tongue. Elidyr knelt before him and gripped his shoulders.

"Thallon!" he remarked, gaining his attention. "Go."

"H-he just…I didn't know!" Thallon said, his words spilling from his lips in a rush of panic. "He killed them! All of them!"

Elidyr turned when ydris voices echoed through the woods. His eyes shifted back to Thallon, and he demanded, "Go…go!"

Before Thallon could rise to his feet, Calasiem burst through the overgrown grass barricading the prison. Three male warriors stood alongside her, each of their eyes scanning the massacre before them.

Thallon shook his head with a gasp. Elidyr stood before him, protective and strong.

Calasiem's eyes veered to Ithronél, who sat bound and disinterested. The Eirean then turned to Thallon. Her glare simmered as she looked upon him with wrath unmatched. "What happened?" her soft voice chiseled through the air, trembling with authority.

Elidyr inhaled a deep breath. His shoulders broadened, and he said, "A prisoner escaped."

"Escaped?" The word lingered in the air, demanding explanation.

"Thallon came to speak to N'iossea. He was—"

"Silence." Her voice was pure and calm, contrasting the fury blazing in her eyes. Her attention shifted to Thallon, and she said, "Tell me what happened."

Thallon gulped through his dry throat. He rubbed his clammy palms against his trousers and closed his eyes. Through several shaky breaths, he explained, "I came to speak to N'iossea. I—He…" Words fumbled in his mind as he fought for a lie that would see him to freedom. But his thoughts were diluted. He clenched his teeth and shook his head. "He killed them."

"How did he escape?"

Thallon became tense. His fists pressed against his thighs as he knelt on the ground, defeated and betrayed. Stripped bare of the loyalty that had always been so closely tied to a brother he had always fought to defend. He was broken. The deep bond he thought they had always shared was severed, and he was faced with the truth.

N'iossea died a long time ago, murdered by the vicious man he had become.

"Tell me what you know of this tragedy," Calasiem said, breaking Thallon's intense, painful thoughts, "and I will show you mercy."

His heart stopped. There would be no mercy. Not if he spoke the truth and told her of what he had done. No matter his reasons, he would be executed. There was no justifiable means for one to supersede the judgement of the forest and free a captive in its grasp. Galdir would have released the prisoners it deemed worthy, while the others would be left to starve, their arms bound and knees bent until they exhaled their final breaths.

Thallon knew N'iossea would have never been freed, not after all the things he had done. And while Thallon regretted his actions, after seeing the twisted look in his brother's eyes, he could never allow either of his brothers to perish in such a way.

"I-I'm sorry...," Thallon whispered. "He is my brother..."

Elidyr stiffened as Calasiem's face tightened with rage. Her jaw clenched and eyes were wide. She glared down at Thallon, who refused to meet her gaze.

Thallon gasped as roots broke through the ground at his sides. They extended upward, slithering around his hands and wrists. He fought against them, struggling to break free. They climbed to his elbow before hardening around his flesh, shackling him in place.

The Eirean shifted her focus to Elidyr when he grabbed his spear, prepared to fight.

"Release him," he said with a growl.

Calasiem's scorn never lifted as she glared into the warrior's eyes. The ground softly trembled from behind, and she casually turned her attention to the righ when the roots

SHADOWS OF NYN'DIRA

once binding the dead prisoners receded into the ground. Scanning the carnage of N'iossea's attack, the Eirean's attention fell to Ithronél. Her eyes narrowed, ever so slightly, and she approached the klaet'il still shackled in place.

She lifted her chin, peering down at Ithronél with a look of condemnation. "You are with the *y'lo khada*.° A follower of the Dark One."

Ithronél held her glare, portraying a sense of strength that outmatched the Eirean's. But Calasiem didn't back down, reflecting her glare with one of equal vigor.

"I am," Ithronél said slowly, holding on to her confidence.

She wasn't afraid of death or pain, and Thallon could tell, by the quiet reservation in Calasiem's eyes, that she knew it too. No amount of intimidation or torture would unbind Ithronél's tongue.

Calasiem searched her eyes for a moment longer and then turned away, peering at the bodies. "The forest sings of deceit," she said. "Colors of red and black and blue."

Ithronél was silent. She eyed the ydris warriors guarding their leader, focusing on their strong posture and sharp spears. Thallon followed her gaze, taking in the strength and ferocity of the men who could easily cut him down.

Calasiem turned and pressed the sharp edge of her spear to Ithronél's throat. Ithronél craned her neck slightly to avoid an irreparable wound.

"Tell me why you've come here," Calasiem said.

Ithronél smiled, and ice wove through Thallon's veins. Calasiem stiffened. "Are there others in our lands?"

Ithronél was silent, staring up at the ydris with eyes of glistening excitement. She was enjoying this. Every moment was going exactly as she had prepared. Calasiem drew her blade against Ithronél's skin, creating a thin red line oozing with fresh blood. The klaet'il hissed before pulling away.

"Speak," Calasiem demanded, her patience wearing thin. "Why have you come here? How did you breach our borders?"

° In the language of the ydris, y'lo khada translates to mean *klaet'il*

Ithronél's smile had vanished. She now glared into Calasiem's eyes with deep, unhinged fury. But still, she did not speak.

Calasiem's words were interrupted when the guards turned on their heels. They lifted their weapons toward the forest, waiting. Elidyr stepped in front of Thallon, shielding him from the advancing threat. No one breathed as the intruders marched forward. Thallon stared unblinking at the forest, and he slumped forward when Aélla's white mane appeared through the shadows. Marching beside her, like a bodyguard from hell, was Y'ven, who appeared monstrous next to the much smaller evae.

The guards fell into a defensive stance, raising their spears as Aella and Y'ven approached. Without a skip in her stride, Aella clutched Y'ven's hand, and they disappeared. Before the guards could react, the duo reappeared behind them, standing before the Eirean.

"What is the meaning of this?" Aélla said, her voice holding an air of authority that nearly outmatched Calasiem's.

The Eirean glowered. "This does not concern you, Master Drimil."

"Matters of this magnitude are precisely my concern, Master Eirean." Fire spewed from Aélla's eyes. "Thallon is my guardian, and I won't have him condemned for saving his brother's life."

"The forest shall decide his fate."

"It isn't our energies that should determine our fate!" Her face was red. "I will not allow anyone else to fall victim to Galdir's sense of justice. Release him, or you will find just how dark this world can truly be."

Calasiem stood taller, displaying strength in her stance. For a moment, the Eirean was at a loss for words, her cautious glare fracturing beneath the icy stare of Drimil'Rothar. Thallon knew Aella wouldn't turn her back on her vows and was surprised Calasiem couldn't see through her cleverly worded lies.

The Eirean's eyes shifted to her men, who stood stiff as stone, their sharp spears pointed at the evae before them. She gave a slight nod, and they stepped closer to Aélla, prepared to apprehend her. Aélla lifted her arms, ready to wield her magic, while Y'ven reached for the axe on his hip.

A rumble shook the world, and everyone stumbled aside. Calasiem caught herself with her spear and glanced toward the west, in the direction of Galdir. Her eyes were wide with terror. Thallon turned to Elidyr, but his attention was on the trees. They watched the limbs sway in the gentle breeze, devoid of their songs. Empty as the wind was free.

The roots twisting Ithronél's arms became dry and brittle before splintering with cracks. Soon, they crumbled, falling to the ground as dry tinder. She lifted her eyes to the others, who were stuck in a solemn trance as the forest fell silent.

A malicious smile twisted her lips. Waves of heat rose from her palms, and before Thallon could speak, a wall of flames swept in their direction.

"Drimil!" Y'ven exclaimed, yanking Aélla into his arms.

Thallon pressed himself into the ground, lying next to Elidyr. The wave of heat washed over them and disappeared into the forest behind.

The world appeared darker when the fire's light vanished. Everyone was silent, glancing at one another and searching for any injured. Realizing he had escaped unscathed, Thallon rose to his knees. The others slowly followed. The ydris warriors leapt to their feet, speaking hurriedly in their native language before darting into the forest.

Calasiem remained on the ground, leaning forward as she gaped at the forest in the direction of Galdir. In the direction of the silence. Thallon followed her focus, and the world felt emptier as the weight of magic that once held the land was lifted. No longer did they wade through the tides of energy keeping the forest in place, binding all those who dwelled within to its power and will.

"What's happening?" Elidyr asked, his worried eyes darting between Calasiem and Aélla.

Thallon's heart twisted when Calasiem's hollow voice rang through the air.

"Galdir…," she said, tears falling from her unblinking eyes, "is dead."

The forest was aglow with dancing lights as Neer woke from her slumber. Her body ached, and she released a whimpered cry when she sat up, tugging her swollen wounds.

Avelloch lay next to her, his eyes closed and breathing steady. His coloring had returned overnight, though his wounds still oozed with pus. Neer lightly shook his shoulders. Three times she said his name before his dreary eyes opened and he sat up, groaning.

He sighed when she led him to the water and helped him drink from the stream. She cupped the water into her hands and lifted it to his face, but he guided her arms away. He leaned forward, wincing, and dipped his hands beneath the water.

Clouds of black filled the stream as he drowsily cleaned himself of the blood coating his skin. Once it ran clear, he gulped several handfuls before leaning back against a large tree root. His breathing was heavy, constrained by his blood-soaked armor.

Neer pulled him forward and helped ease him out of his chest piece and tunic. She dropped the filthy clothes to the ground before inspecting his cuts and bruises.

"What happened to you?" she asked.

Avelloch shook his head, as if to get rid of his thoughts, and closed his eyes without a word spoken.

Neer watched him with silent grief. Her attention fell to his blackened arm, and he became still when she tenderly clutched it in her hands. Dirty fingers trailed across his wet skin, examining the damage. He was silent, watching her with sorrowful eyes, but she didn't notice as she looked at his arm, turning it over to view it in full. His skin was still warm and alive, but it was shriveled and dark, appearing necrotic.

SHADOWS OF NYN'DIRA

She brought his hand to her heart. "I'm going to get you out of here," she promised. "I don't care what it takes. You aren't dying on me."

He weakly clutched her hand in a silent promise of his own.

A sharp pain struck Neer's back, causing her to wince. She pulled away and rubbed the ache. "Gods...," she griped. "I never thought I'd miss my magic. At least it numbed most of the pain. And the feelings. I don't think I've ever felt this much in my entire life."

Avelloch watched her with careful eyes. "What do you feel?"

Her gaze drifted to the trees, and she contemplated her answer. There was peace, even with the tormenting pain. The cloud of anger that drenched her with madness had vaporized, and she felt free. The dancing lights glimmered in her eyes, and she watched them wave against the trees.

"Alive." She paused. "It's odd, don't you think? That a place like this would bring me so much inner peace?"

The lights glistened against the water dripping down Avelloch's face. His eyes were distant, disturbed.

"Avelloch?" she asked.

He blinked and then repositioned himself to get comfortable. "If you could choose to live without your magic and always have this peace...would you do it?"

She knew the answer but was too afraid to say it aloud. Something about her magic troubled him, and she wasn't sure she wanted to know why. Emotions once diluted by anger swelled in her chest, rising to her throat. "Why?" she asked.

"I just...I want you to have peace."

She clenched her jaw. "You're afraid of me—"

"No!" The words erupted from his throat before Neer had time to finish. He looked into her eyes, pleading. "I'm not afraid of you."

"You're afraid of my magic. You think that I'm—"

"I don't think anything, Neer. I just understand what a life of isolation can do to you. I know what it's like to be viewed as a monster."

He turned away, his eyes moving from left to right.

437

"You said that your magic is a curse and if you could take it away you would." He paused. "I just wanted to know if you had changed your mind."

Neer thought for a moment, her hands instinctively going to her chest, where the tearing and pain of her energy always festered and burned. "Magic has made my life a living hell…It's caused me more pain than anyone should ever have to go through…If I could take it away right now and be free of its agony and rage, I'd do it."

Avelloch nodded, returning his focus to the trees. There was a certain calmness that seemed to wash over him, as if this answer had erased any doubt he may have had. They sat together in a comfortable silence, watching the glistening lights and relishing in the safety they brought.

Sitting more comfortably in the grass, Neer leaned against a large root and closed her eyes. The sound of trickling water was as beautiful as a finely tuned lute. She didn't know how long they had been in the avour'il, though it felt like days, and the soft melodies of the forest were nearly lost to her after so long in this haunted realm.

Avelloch washed his things in the water before turning back to Neer. Her stomach growled when she eyed the freshly cleaned quay fruit in his hand. Its yellow skin was ripe and soft with fuzz. With a smile, she accepted the meal. Juice spilled down her chin when she took a large bite. It felt like a lifetime since she had eaten anything.

Leaning forward to quell the pain in her back, she watched Avelloch get comfortable next to her, eating his own fruit dinner.

Neer finished her meal and sucked the juice from her fingers. With a deep exhale, she lay on her side, ignoring her injuries and nuzzling into the soft grass.

"You know," she started, her face half buried in the thick green. "If it weren't for the darkness and constant fear of death, this place wouldn't be half bad."

She sighed.

"I've been to so many places. Seen so many things…beautiful things. It almost makes me think there *are* Divines out there. How else could this world be so full of wonder and beauty and magic?"

Avelloch took his last bite, wiped his hands on his trousers, and then lay next to her. On his back, he looked up at the roots and lights. "Who knows?" he said.

"Well, *someone* knows."

He softly smiled. "Not us."

She chuckled. "Haven't you heard? I know everything."

"You ask a lot of questions for someone who knows everything."

"Just trying to keep you on your toes."

His quiet laughter filled the air, and Neer's smile widened. She edged closer, and he turned to view her. Their faces were close. She licked her thumb and scrubbed a small spatter of blood from his temple.

"If you weren't a warrior," she started, "what would you be?"

"A warrior," he answered flatly.

She playfully glowered. "You had no other ambitions?"

Disgust washed the easement from his eyes, and he reluctantly explained, "My ambitions didn't matter. My father was one of the best warriors of our time. He wouldn't have allowed his only son to veer from that same path."

"That's awful. What happened to him?"

He swallowed his emotions and turned away, staring intently at the roots above. "He's dead."

Her heart sank. She suddenly remembered the vision she had of him as a child, when his father had struck a blade through his chest. A hollow pit formed in her gut, and memories of that night flooded her mind. Neer touched the faded scar above his heart, and chills crawled across Avelloch's skin.

"He tried to kill you…"

His wide eyes flashed to her, but she was lost in the nightmare. The blemish was hardly noticeable as time had left it nearly flat against his skin.

"Why would he do that?" She glanced at him. "You were just a child."

He never blinked. Didn't seem to breathe, staring at her in a state of utter disbelief. "How do you know that?" he asked, his voice hollow.

Her eyes fell away, no longer able to withstand the weight of his gaze. "I was there. Somehow, in my dreams…I saw you."

She pulled her hand away and sat up. He followed, his eyes never shifting from her face, which was haunted and pale. A sharp pain in her shoulder caused her to wince. She rubbed the hurt, though her mind was heavy with memories.

"I heard you arguing," she explained. "He said 'you're no son of mine,' and then he…" Her words faded, and she closed her eyes, unable to say aloud the horrors of that night. "I hit him with my magic, and he smashed his head against a rock…"

A rush of guilt crashed through her. She turned to him, eyes wide.

"I didn't— You don't think that I…killed him?"

Her last words were nothing more than a whisper, a haunting reminder of the power and destruction she held. It was instinct that had attacked his father—pure adrenaline and fear. She had never meant to hurt him…never intended to cause his death.

"No," Avelloch said, his stiff voice interrupting her thoughts. He was tense, wriggling his hand in and out of a tight fist.

Seconds passed before he pushed the words out.

"I did."

Neer's jaw dropped. Confliction coursed through her. He had murdered his father, a man who had maliciously struck a dagger through his heart.

"My mother was taken by the lanathess," Avelloch explained, his voice as cold and sharp as steel. "They had captured me, and she traded her life for mine."

He closed his eyes and clenched his teeth.

"My father blamed me for her death." He shook his head. "That wasn't the first time he had tried to kill me…When I returned home four summers later, he was staring at a ghost."

His fingers clenched into a tight fist.

"We fought, and I drove my dagger through his heart and watched as he died." He closed his eyes. "I was banished soon after."

"What?" she remarked. "But you were a child! He tried to kill you first!"

Avelloch scoffed and shook his head. "My father was the most respected and esteemed warrior of our clan. I was his dishonored son."

"But that isn't true! He was beating you! You were—"

"Not everyone has the gift of magic, Neer," he snapped.

She was taken aback by his harsh words, and the sting of his angry eyes sealed her lips.

"It didn't matter what I said. I knew my fate was sealed the moment I drove that blade through his chest."

Neer blinked her tears away, not daring to show any sign of weakness beneath his unbroken strength. Carefully, she wrapped her arm around his and leaned onto his shoulder. He was tense, never turning in her direction as he relived the horrors of his past. Horrors she had witnessed firsthand.

She pictured the moment his father stood over him with a blade in his hand, promising death. The fear in Avelloch's young, innocent eyes tore at her soul, fracturing every piece of her heart.

A stray tear fell from her eye, and she inhaled a quiet sniff. "I believe you," she whispered.

Though she had seen a glimpse of his past and knew the wrath and intentions of his father, Avelloch still needed to hear it. He had to know she was on his side. It's a terrible thing to take a life, especially one of your family, but he had no other choice. There was no life for him had his father continued to live. Neer understood that rage and vengeance. She lived it every day.

Avelloch shifted, and Neer breathed a sigh of relief when he lifted his hand to hers, wrapping his fingers around her own. She closed her eyes, accepting his silent gesture of trust and gratitude.

"We should keep going," he said. "Get the hell out of here."

Neer agreed, and they rose to their feet, eager to return home.

Hours felt like days as they headed further toward Galdir, where wide roots and branches created a maze of tunnels and bridges. They trekked over the stream, finding the world brighter than a clear summer's day the closer they edged toward the Tree. Lifting her eyes, Neer could see its enormous trunk and long branches towering over the forest. She would normally have been in awe, staring up at such a majestic, otherworldly sight, but her exhaustion and pain had left her depleted of such admiration.

"It's almost over," she said, keeping her eyes on her feet to avoid tripping. "What do you think will be at the end? More monsters? A demon?"

"Nothing," he said.

She laughed through her nose. "If only we were so lucky. Maybe a Divine will show up and grant us passage to eternity. Free from this shithole of a life."

He was silent, and she glanced at him, noticing the somber expression he carried. His eyes were on the ground, distant.

"Avelloch?" she asked.

He blinked and refocused his attention ahead, gazing at the trees and limbs. "What I told you before about my father, only Aélla and Klaud know what happened." His voice trailed away, becoming quiet in his despair. "No one else knows anything."

They came to a slow stop, and he cast his eyes downward, ashamed. Slow-moving lights danced across his body and face.

"I know what I've done can never be taken back...I can never be free from the things I've done or the people I've hurt. If I don't make it out of here...if the forest judges me for my actions and not who I truly am, then—"

"Stop," she said, stepping close. "We're both making it out of here!"

He gazed at her with sorrowful, desperate eyes and tenderly stroked her cheek with his thumb. Tears burned her eyes, and she looked at him, watching as he struggled with his own grief and despair. He truly believed he would die here—that the forest would see him as a monster, just as everyone else had.

"*Vas neemo see'nah, vakaal,*" she said, repeating the words he had spoken to her the night before they entered this realm. She was unsure of its meaning but felt the depth of every word.

His jaw clenched, and Neer closed her eyes when he tenderly kissed her forehead. "No matter what happens," he said, his lips a whisper against her skin, "no matter where this journey takes us...I am always on your side."

Her lip quivered, and hot tears spilled down her cheeks. Avelloch carefully wiped them away and then took her hand, leading them onward.

They walked together in silence, heading closer to the enormous Tree. Large roots, bigger than modest homesteads, towered over them, weaving through the soil and producing glowing trees of their own. Flowers and vines clung to the twisted roots, while slow-moving streams babbled below.

Avelloch moved slowly. His face was gaunt, and sweat poured down his cheeks. They needed to move, but he wasn't able. The infection coursing through him was taking its toll. Neer shook her head to rid herself of the harrowing thoughts. He would survive. He had to.

"Is this what it looks like?" Neer asked, stepping beneath a low-arched root, hoping to keep him alert. "Outside of this place, I mean."

The distant look in Avelloch's eyes become heavier the closer they came to their destination. He was so weak. So tired.

"Yes."

His voice was broken and quiet. Neer gritted her teeth, withholding the sorrow swelling inside. The silence was deafening as they climbed up the enormous roots and arrived at the base of Galdir.

Standing in its presence, Neer was shaken by its infinite size. Glowing limbs hovered above, extending higher than the tallest tree ten times over. Wide limbs, thick with shimmering flowers, masked the sky with its eternal glow.

Galdir's wide trunk stretched for nearly as far as Neer could see. Glimmering sap, as thick as a waterfall, trickled down the bark.

"Is this it?" Neer asked, gazing up at the wonderous Tree.

Avelloch collapsed to his knees. His arms trembled, and he inhaled ragged breaths.

"Avelloch!"

He gripped his side and leaned forward, wincing. "Drink it," he muttered. "The sap...drink it."

Sweat dripped from his face, and he clenched his teeth, breathing too heavily. His face was too taut. Neer sat next to him and gently took his hand. He turned to her, and she was stricken by his fear. Her grip tightened, and she gave him a stiff nod, ignoring her own worries as they sat on the edge of fate, ready to accept whatever path it chose to give.

"Together," she said.

His eyes widened, and he turned away. "No," he said, his jaw tensing as the words slid from his tongue. "You go first."

"What? But—"

"I won't leave while you're stuck here!" He groaned in pain. "You go first...and if you return to Nyn'Dira...I'll drink it too."

Tears filled her eyes. She shook her head. "I'm not leaving you here—"

"This isn't a debate!" he snapped. "You go first, or we never leave."

With a sniff, she set her gaze on the sap. Her hands trembled as they dipped within the liquid, and she was surprised at how warm and smooth it was. She gulped down her emotions and brought her hands to her lips. Avelloch watched her, his breathing deep and eyes unblinking.

She turned to him, peering deep into his soul. "I'll come back for you," she promised. "If you don't return...I'm coming back for you."

"Neer, don't—"

Before he could finish, she tilted her head back and drank the sap. Warmth moved through her, stinging her skin from the inside and bringing chills that raised her hair on end. She leaned back, overcome with power, her soul connecting to the energy of the Tree.

She felt as if she was floating through the air. Her mouth was open and eyes were wide as magic coursed through her. Galdir glowed brighter, blinding with its light.

And then a flash of pain tore through her. Ripping and tearing its way through her soul, shredding her mind with pain. Unable to move, she was stuck in her agony, screaming inside, wishing for an end.

Avelloch was at her side, waiting for the forest to make its judgement. Seconds passed, but Neer remained frozen in place. Soon, Galdir's bright glow began to flicker. Songs of rage and terror tore through the trees, and he fell aside, groaning in pain.

His jaw agape, he watched the glow flicker before dying out, and the world was cast in deep, unrelenting darkness.

Neer inhaled a deep breath as the force burning her soul was lifted. She closed her eyes and leaned forward, gasping for air.

"Avelloch?"

Her voice was a whisper, carried endlessly through the wind. Numbness replaced all sensation, and she was no longer tethered by pain. Peering through the darkness, she realized her surroundings were different. The large roots no longer rested beneath her feet. Instead, they were now far away, standing alone amidst the void.

And nestled atop the roots, nearly invisible against the shadows, were two figures. Peering closer, straining so hard her eyes began to throb, Neer noticed Avelloch's platinum hair. And sitting next to him... was her.

Unable to make sense of what she was seeing, she shouted for him, calling out into an endless void, but her voice was nothing more than an echo in the wind.

"He can't hear you."

With a gasp, Neer turned around. She stiffened at the sight of a stranger standing behind her. Her eyes widened, realizing he wasn't evaesh, but human. His dark metal armor made him nearly invisible in the darkness. Three scars stretched across his face from scalp to jaw.

A tattered black cape hung from his shoulders, waving softly in the wind. He appeared no older than forty, with dark stubble caressing his jaw.

Slowly, Neer stood, staring at him as if he were a ghost.

"Who are you?" she asked, her voice sliding through the air.

"I'm not here," he said, still gazing at the tree. "But you are."

Their eyes met, and Neer took half a step back. She reached for her sword, never veering from his gaze.

From his haunting eyes of teal.

"This is our journey," he said, breaking her trance. "Our paths are in sync. Our destinies the culmination of a thousand years of hatred and deceit."

Slowly, his attention returned to Galdir.

"We are prisoners, catalysts tempered in fire and forged for war. Only you have the power to break the cycle."

Neer stiffened when he turned and gripped her shoulders. Staring into his eyes, she was immobile, frozen by fear and confusion.

His voice was strong and deadly as he warned, "Do not follow in the path laid out for you. Find your way to the Temple of Skye…to the Realm of Darkness…and free us from this hell."

He paused, and for a moment, she felt a spark of hope, as if he understood her pain and could see into her very soul.

"You are not yet the monster they claim you to be," he continued. "Fight for your life, Nerana. Fight for your destiny." His grip tightened on her shoulders. "Fight for your freedom."

CHAPTER FORTY-FOUR

SURVIVAL
Avelloch

THE WORLD WAS DARK with shadows of woe as Avelloch knelt alone, struggling to see through the void surrounding him. Not a whisper of life moved through the air. Galdir was silent, its lights no longer pulsing with energy. And then he felt it—the shift of fate and the dread of what was to come.

Galdir was dead...and Neer had killed it.

His heart sank, and he shook his head, refusing to believe it. This had to be part of the ritual. Surely, Neer couldn't cause this, not when her magic had been stripped away. Not when others far worse had entered this realm and survived without harming the energy or sacred tree.

"Neer." Avelloch's voice was crisp in the cold, dead air. It never echoed or moved beyond his ears as he spoke into a void. Leaning closer, he reached out to touch her shoulder and was stricken by how cold she had become. "Neer!"

He pulled her close, and she collapsed into his arms, unmoving. Panicked, he pressed his fingers against her throat. The gentle thrum of her pulse tapped against his fingers, and he exhaled a deep breath.

"Kila...," he griped. "Fuck!"

His eyes scoured the forest, searching for any sign of light. This couldn't be their end. They couldn't be trapped in this hell forever. He turned back to Neer and tapped her face, trying anything to wake her. But she was unresponsive, frozen in her sleep.

With another glance around, he carefully lay her aside and then rose to his feet. The bright shimmer of his weapon illuminated the air around him, casting light against his filthy skin. He looked at Galdir, standing tall and proud, and then limped toward its trunk, hoping to find answers.

Another step and a soft breeze rang with the songs of promise and life. Avelloch halted, gazing upward as the limbs and leaves hummed a gentle tune. Slowly, as if on command, Galdir began to glow. It was softer and less pure than before, as if illuminated through murky waters.

Avelloch moved back to Neer's side and touched her shoulder, but his hand sank through her skin. His breath caught in his throat, and he watched her slowly fade away before disappearing. His eyes were fixed on the root, now devoid of her existence, and relief washed through him.

She made it out.

She survived.

He turned toward the limbs, gazing at their subtle glow, and a strike of panic jolted through him. Galdir may not glow for much longer. He had to return to Nyn'Dira before it was too late.

He knelt by the glowing sap and dipped his hands within the surface, quickly drinking his fill. A tightness clenched his chest, and he leaned forward, gasping for breath. The tree brightened, blinding him with its light, and then he was weightless.

The brightness faded, and the weight of the world pressed against his shoulders, forcing him into the dirt. He inhaled a deep breath, taking in the scent of grass and fresh, clean air. Slowly, he opened his eyes and found himself lying at the entrance of the avour'il. The twisted root doorway was dry and cracked. And its interior, which once opened to the darkness of the realm, was empty. Nothing but the forest, pure and bright with moonlight, rested on the other side.

A light groan came from behind, and his heart skipped when he turned to find Neer lying next to him. She was on her side, facing the opposite direction.

"Neer," he said, reaching out to her. When he touched her shoulder, the sound of a howling wolf pierced the silence. Avelloch turned and reached for his weapon.

SHADOWS OF NYN'DIRA

His eyes fell to a shadow stalking the woods, and he watched, waiting. Cursing fate for thrusting him into another fight so soon after his escape. His body quaked with agony, begging for a rest. Tired eyes began to blur as infection lulled him toward sleep.

He held his breath, forcing himself to stay alert as the creature stepped closer. When sapphire eyes and coarse, black fur revealed its identity, Avelloch released a deep sigh.

"Blaid...," he said.

The direwolf carefully approached, first peering into Avelloch's dreary, reddened eyes before making his way to Neer. She stirred when Blaid nudged her head, forcing her to wake. He lay next to her, curling around to conceal her in his warmth.

Avelloch leaned forward, the pang of his wounds slamming against him like a harsh gale, thrusting him aside, stricken with agony. He lay on the ground, immobile. The heavy sound of footsteps echoed from all around. Blaid crouched beside Neer, the hair on his back standing tall as he waited, teeth bared. Eyes focused.

Avelloch peered through tired eyes at the half-dozen ydris warriors who encircled them, pointing their spears and swords at Avelloch and Neer. He grunted and winced, forcing himself to his knees. Staring at the soldiers, he grabbed his sword with a quivering hand. He was tired, so damn tired, but he would fight.

Calasiem stepped forward, and Avelloch tightened his grip on his weapon. His hand ached and body was sore. But he held on to his waning strength. They survived. The forest had deemed them worthy, and no one would take that from them.

The Eirean paid him no mind as she approached the cracked, empty doorway.

"No...," she said, sliding her hand against the dry roots crumbling beneath her touch. She leaned forward with her forehead against the archway. Speaking in her native language, she said, *"How could this have happened? What have we done to deserve this injustice?"*

Silent tears slid down her face. Slowly, she stepped away and turned to the others.

"The gate to the sacred lands has been destroyed," she said. "No one may ever again walk in its path."

A heavy silence fell over them, drenching the world with sorrow. Calasiem shifted her attention to Avelloch, and the sadness in her eyes hardened into anger.

"Explain yourself," she demanded, the power of her voice shaking Avelloch to his core.

He straightened on his knees, never veering from her eyes. "We survived."

"Galdir is weak! Its life flickers like a dying flame, whispering of darkness and dread."

His eyes darkened. He could see she wouldn't back down, and his arm tightened, preparing to fight. Blaid stood at his side, crouched and snarling.

From behind, Neer slowly lifted from the ground. She winced and moaned in pain. Her head hung low, causing her filthy hair to mask her face.

"No...," she whimpered, clutching her chest. "No..."

Avelloch's jaw tightened as he listened to her weep. He knew she wasn't concerned with the fate of the avour'il or trees. Her cries were too desperate, too broken. She hated being back here, at the mercy of her magic. Forced to fight against its rage and pain.

Calasiem shifted her focus to Neer. She stepped forward, and Avelloch lifted his swords.

Their eyes met, and he warned, "We survived."

Her body trembled with fury. Before she could speak, Aélla broke through the wall of warriors with Reiman at her side. She inhaled a sharp gasp at the sight of her brother kneeling on the ground. Turning to Calasiem, she demanded, "What are you doing?"

The Eirean breathed heavily, fuming with pain and rage. "They have disturbed the balance. *Ruanafeil* has sealed our fates."

"Have you lost all honor? Have you—"

"Do not speak another syllable, Master Drimil." Calasiem's deadly voice trembled through the cold air. She glared into Aélla's eyes, demanding obedience. But

SHADOWS OF NYN'DIRA

beneath her anger was sorrow. Deep, unsettled sorrow that manifested into anger. She was suffering, just as the forest had suffered.

But Aélla stood tall beneath the weight of her fury, holding a sense of authority that opposed the Eirean's. Reiman's voice hailed over Aélla's as he said, "The forest has deemed her worthy. Had she been the cause of Galdir's weakened strength, it would not have seen fit to return her to Nyn'Dira." His cold eyes narrowed. "Release her."

Calasiem's shoulders lifted when she inhaled a deep breath. Her glare alone was enough to shatter the world and all who inhabited it. She held Reiman's unwavering gaze for several seconds before reluctantly turning away. Calasiem scanned the forest, searching for answers. Her jaw clenched as she struggled over her decision.

When a soft breeze passed, carrying songs of forgiveness and peace, Avelloch closed his eyes, thankful the forest was on their side. He leaned forward with his head down, relieved. He knew Calasiem would listen to its melodies. She would let them go.

"You have brought doom upon us all," Calasiem said, the tears welling once again in her strong eyes.

Avelloch tensed beneath the force of her heavy words.

"The world will be washed in black, and your souls will weep with sorrow and pain."

Calasiem cast her a hateful glare, and Aélla held her breath. The Eirean then glanced at Reiman, who stood proudly by Aélla's side. The Eirean's lip twitched, as if she had wanted to speak, but instead, she turned away and disappeared into the forest with her men.

The tension melted away when they were left alone, no longer under the pressing authority of the Eirean and her warriors. Avelloch turned to Neer as she clutched her chest and groaned.

"We're back...," she said. Her tearful eyes met with his. "You're back..."

He nodded, and Blaid stepped closer, nuzzling himself into Neer's arms.

From behind, Aella lifted her eyes to the trees, which hummed a somber, desperate tune. Without speaking, she stepped to her brother's side and kindly touched his shoulder. He turned to face her and was quickly pulled into a tight embrace. Her grip pulled at his bleeding wounds, sending fire through his veins.

"I was so worried about you," Aélla said before turning to Neer. "Both of you."

Avelloch exhaled a pained grunt, and cold air stung his skin when Aélla pulled back his tattered armor. Her lips parted at the sight of his pus-filled wound. He groaned when she placed her hands gently over his skin and closed her eyes. Magic surged through him, warming his flesh and healing his shallow injuries. The agony pulsing through him was dulled, and he released a deep breath of relief. But the deep cut on his side never healed, and his muscles still ached. He fought against the heaviness pulling his eyes, beckoning him to sleep.

Aélla removed her hands, wiping the blood and pus on her cloak before she turned to Neer. She touched her shoulder, fusing shallow cuts into thick scars. Neer winced while touching her back, and Aélla pulled away with an exhausted breath. Avelloch watched his sister with worried eyes. She breathed heavily—too exhausted for such menial magic use.

"I can't heal your deeper injuries or infections." Her sorrowful eyes shifted from Neer to Avelloch. "I'm sorry…"

Before he could speak, the shadow of a man stood overhead. Blaid tensed, and a low growl sawed from his throat as Reiman said, "Come, my child."

Neer gasped, and her expression was washed with relief when she lifted her eyes. "Reiman…"

Avelloch watched them, guarded, noticing the shift in her father's compassion as Reiman extended his hand. Neer eagerly took it, rising to her feet and wrapping her arms tightly around his waist. He rubbed her hair, and she held him close.

"I'm so relieved that you're alive," he said. "You need proper care. Both of you."

Avelloch withheld a deep groan when he rose to his feet and leaned onto Aélla, struggling to stay awake as his vision blurred.

Neer broke away from her father and limped to Avelloch's side. "Are you okay?" she asked, her tired voice seeping with worry.

He breathed heavily, forcing himself to stay alert, and gave her a silent nod.

"I can put you to sleep," Aélla suggested. "A few days of rest should help heal your injuries."

"There's no time to waste," Reiman explained, gently guiding Neer away. "The Klaet'il have begun their invasions. We must—"

"Wait!" Neer ripped herself away as Reiman urged her forward.

Her eyes met with Avelloch's, and he watched her hobble back to his side. She carefully took his arm and draped it over her shoulders. They both winced and groaned, their injuries pulled and torn. Neer exhaled a laugh.

"We make quite the team, yeah?"

He glanced at her with tired, dreary eyes.

"Don't go dying on me now, *Zaeril*," she said, her voice strained as she carried his burgeoning weight. "I didn't drag you through hell just for you to leave me now."

Avelloch's body ached, and his feet scraped the ground as Aélla and Neer guided him forward. Reiman soon approached, offering his help, but Neer quickly cut him off.

"We've got him," she said, her voice protective and strong.

"But your injuries—"

"I've got him, Reiman." Her grip tightened on Avelloch's back, sending waves of fire coursing through his veins. Neer didn't seem to notice his slight wince when she looked at her father. "Let me do this."

Reiman stared at her with a look of deep concern. He gave a silent nod and stepped aside, allowing them to pass.

Moonlight cast through the dark woods, creating columns of purple light that brightened the path. Avelloch breathed heavily, too weak to lift his feet from the ground. But as they trekked forward, an orange glow of firelight lifted the darkness. They approached the quiet village, and his exhaustion, for a moment, turned to peace. Their boots clunked against planks as they moved from dirt trails to wooden bridges, heading toward the inn. Voices murmured from nearby homes, injecting life into the silent night.

Avelloch's body became heavy, and his eyes were too weighted to keep open. Neer straightened her back with a groan, and Avelloch opened his eyes, realizing how much pressure he was putting on her shoulders. He held himself up to give her relief, and she glanced at him, the strain of carrying his weight evident in the sweat dripping down her face.

"I can walk—"

"Don't be foolish," Neer interrupted. "We're almost there."

Thurandír's voice rang clearer with every step across the bridge, and their eyes lifted. Relief washed over Avelloch, giving a bit of hope and energy as they re-entered civilization. His eyes fell to the archer, who stood with Thallon and several avel armed to the teeth with bows, swords, and armor. Elidyr stood on the docks alone, staring over the water. His large elk was nearby, guarding the group with strength and poise.

An archer lightly tapped Thurandír's arm and then pointed at Avelloch and the others. Thurandír whipped around, his eyes scanning the darkness before falling on his friends.

A bright smile stretched his lips, and with a wave, he called, "Neer! Avelloch!"

He and Thallon rushed to their sides, their heavy footfalls clunking against the wooden bridge. Avelloch groaned when Thurandír pulled him and Neer into a strong embrace.

"Careful," Reiman reprimanded.

Thurandír quickly stepped away, his smile beaming as he glanced between them. "So, you made it!"

"Hardly," Neer said with a groan, and Avelloch attempted to lift himself from her shoulders.

"I've got him," Thallon said, quickly nudging Neer aside before taking her place beneath Avelloch's arm.

Thallon's strength and height released the pressure on Avelloch's back, and he exhaled a light sigh. Heavy eyes met with Thallon's, and he thought himself mad as Thallon looked back at him, not with disgust or anger, but relief.

"It's good to have you back, Av."

Avelloch's brows pulled inward, slightly.

His attention moved to Thurandír. "So, what happened? You look like you've been through it."

Neer's smile slowly faded. Her eyes drifted to her feet, and sorrow weighed her expression. Avelloch watched her, unable to ease the dread as she relived the horrors they had faced. She blinked her thoughts away when a wave of orange light brightened the path, and Klaud exited the inn with Y'ven and Dru.

Klaud's eyes lifted to Neer, and she quickly turned away, still unable to face him. Her brows pulled together, and she clutched her chest, lost in misery. Avelloch knew she was resenting her magic now more than ever. Being without it, even for a short time, had given her a glimpse of the peace she longed for. Now that it was stripped away, the burden of her anger seemed to press heavier against her soul.

Dru slowly came to her side, hovering before her with a tilted head. She inspected the blood and bruises covering Neer's clothes and body.

"I'm okay, Dru," Neer said, forcing a smile.

The faeth's voice tinkled, and embers rose from her body. She then lurched forward, hugging Neer's cheek. Y'ven gripped her arm with an approving nod.

A shadow enveloped Avelloch's vision when Klaud stepped before him, blocking Neer from view. He firmly gripped Avelloch's face with a bright smile. "You look well, brenavae," he said.

Avelloch weakly pulled away from his grasp. "Don't lie, you *drëma 'torvee*," he retorted breathlessly.

Klaud chuckled. "All right, you look like shit."

Aélla smacked Klaud's arm, prompting another laugh. "Do not insult him!"

"What is there to insult?" Klaud said, meeting Avelloch's gaze with a soft smile. "He is free."

For a moment, the pain drenching Avelloch's soul was lifted. Shackles once tethering him to a life of seclusion and exile had been unchained. Surviving the avour'il was the only true means of reclaiming one's place within the forest, and he had made it.

His attention fell to the ground, and he stood in disbelief. The burden weighing his soul with so much misery was suddenly lifted. The darkness cast from being labeled an outsider, a nesiat…a murderer…was gone. The forest had accepted him, just as it had accepted Neer. They could now live among his people as equals.

Klaud took Aélla's place beneath Avelloch's arm, further easing the pressure on his back. A smile touched Aélla's eyes as she celebrated Avelloch's victory. She bounced on her toes before kissing his cheek. Klaud and Thallon spoke cheerfully, carrying his weight and leading him into the warmth of the Inn.

Their overlapping voices became static in Avelloch's ears, and his vision began to fade. He stumbled forward, being quickly caught as he tripped over his dragging feet. Unable to muster the strength to open his eyes, Avelloch exhaled a shallow breath and collapsed to the floor.

Chapter Forty-Five

A Shift of Fate
Aélla

Birds chirped overhead, singing their daily tunes as Aélla sat beneath the trees in deep meditations. A soft wind swept by, cooling her sweaty skin. But she didn't notice. Her mind was trapped in an endless cycle of anger and pain. She struggled against it, using every technique she had learned throughout her lessons and studies...but there was no escape.

Still, she fought, willing herself to embrace calmness and peace. Searching for a way to end the horrors inflicting her mind. Memories she had pushed away long ago flashed before her eyes, reminding her of all she'd been through and warning of what was to come.

Her teeth gritted and lips pursed. A beam of sunlight cast through the trees, as if the heavens had opened and displayed her upon a pedestal of failure and strife. The warm glow heated her skin further, and she opened her eyes with a huff, no longer able to calm her mind or the energy sweltering within.

Breathing heavily with exhaustion, Aélla leaned forward with her head bowed and eyes closed. She sat alone, basking in the solitude. Being so close to Galdir, the forest was more beautiful than any place she had ever seen. Towering trees with wide trunks stood all around her, thick vines crawling up their lengths and disappearing within leaves of red and gold.

Glowing Ko'ehlaeu'at trees brightened the understory with their now-faint glow and floating petals. Aélla rose to her feet and walked back to the village. Days had passed since Neer and Avelloch returned from the avour'il, and he remained in an herb-induced sleep, fighting against the infections and wounds that kept him weak.

Several times she had attempted to heal him, but her magic was falling weaker. She felt the cold chill of night reaching out to her, sliding its icy tendrils down her soul, grasping at her strength. But she wouldn't falter beneath such despair. Her vows were clear: she would fight until the end. This journey wouldn't be easy, and she knew that. But she would prevail. She had to. There was no one else.

It had to be her.

Ydris soldiers guarded the village and scoured the forests, searching for any signs of the Klaet'il. With the strength of Galdir waning, Aélla felt the chill of fear that settled across the village. It was a heavy and inescapable dread laying a blanket of frost over the once peaceful world as the winds of change brought sorrow and rage. The Klaet'il were coming, and so, too, were the humans.

Aélla kept her eyes on the ground and stalked through the village, moving toward the Inn, where she stepped inside to check on her brother. As she entered his room, she was stunned to find Neer was no longer sitting at his bedside.

Her eyes shifted to Avelloch, watching as he slept undisturbed in his bed, just as he had for the last several days. Two nes'seil were checking his healing injuries and re-wrapping his bandages.

His face was gaunt, with dark circles surrounding his eyes. She had never seen him so weak. The poison had festered for too long in his veins, and the ydris had done everything they could to save him, but it didn't seem to be enough. He wasn't healing the way he should, and she worried if he would ever wake again.

Wiping away her tears, Aélla grasped at the broken and frayed strands of her strength and gently kissed his head. "Stay strong, brother," she whispered. "We need you more than you know."

With a heavy heart, she left the room. A light chatter filled the main hall of the inn, and Aélla lifted her eyes, scanning the full tables before spotting Thallon near the back of the room. He was hunched over piles of disheveled parchment, scrawling in a notebook. His hair was just as displaced as his mess of items, falling in front of his face in unkempt patches.

He didn't notice when she stood over him, peering at his notebook with a keen eye. But the words were too scrambled and hastily written for her to properly read.

"Hey, Thallon," she said, her voice somber and deflated.

Thallon inhaled a sharp gasp and leaned back with his hand on his chest. "Kila!" he exclaimed. "Don't sneak up on people like that!"

"I'm sorry."

His brows pulled together. "What's wrong?"

She exhaled a deep breath, nearly deciding to spill her woes, but instead, she bit her tongue. It wasn't the way of Drimil'Rothar to lean on others. She had to be strong and push her worries or doubts aside. "It's nothing," she finally said. "Have you seen the others?"

"No, I haven't—"

His voice was interrupted by another, and they turned as his brother, Elidyr, approached.

"Thallon," the avel leader said. He stood tall and proud, walking alongside Calasiem and Reiman.

Aella stood, staring at them with as much strength as she could muster, though she still appeared weak and tired.

"What's going on?" she asked.

Elidyr glanced at her, and his posture softened. "Apologies, Master Drimil," he started, "but we need to discuss N'iossea and Ithronél's disappearance."

Thallon stood, and Aélla lifted her hand to him, her eyes still focused on Elidyr. "Thallon will not be persecuted for N'iossea's crimes. He acted with impulsivity, not malice." She paused. "I will take full responsibility for the actions of my guardians."

Calasiem's eyes narrowed. "The tides of fate have fallen out of place. Songs of sorrow and clouds of grey seep from Galdir." The Eirean stood taller, bringing herself to nearly twice Aélla's height. "And now you stand before us," she continued, "dishonoring your vows."

"I've dishonored *nothing!*" Her anger cut through the air like a sharp knife, and everyone took half a step back.

Thallon placed his hand on Aélla's shoulder, and she released a deep breath, ashamed of her outburst. Her head fell, and she closed her eyes, struggling to ward off the anger and discontent pulling at her soul.

Reiman's words were thick with intent as he kept his eyes on Aélla. "We should tread carefully, Master Eirean. The balance has surely been disturbed, and its weight will be shouldered by those most sensitive to its will."

Aélla took several deep breaths, not wanting to be viewed as a threat. She straightened and lifted her eyes to those around her, feigning confidence and strength. "We need to speak about Galdir and the future of our people." Her gaze shifted to Elidyr. "What have you learned about the Klaet'il's intentions? How many have breached this territory?"

As he started to speak, Calasiem politely raised her hand to quiet him. "Let us discuss this in a more private setting."

Before they could object, Calasiem strode across the room. The others followed, with Thallon keeping close to Aélla. Outside, they walked through the village, where Calasiem led them to a nearby building. It was long, with a tall gabled roof displaying two enormous antlers at its apex. Through the wooden double doors, they were ushered into an open room with wooden walls and flooring. Hanging braziers were alight with flames, keeping the spacious area warm with amber light. A wooden table stretched through the center of the room, with cushioned chairs on either side. Dinnerware had been placed beautifully atop woven placemats. Bowls of fresh fruit lined the center of the table, offset by decanters of wine and shallow dishes piled with dried herbs.

Calasiem motioned toward the chairs with a wave of her arm. "Please," she said. "Make yourselves comfortable."

Thallon sat beside Aélla, while the others gathered around them. Calasiem took her place at the head of the table, perched in a high-backed chair adorned with vines, flowers, and leaves. She placed her palms against the grain of the table and peered at each of the warriors in her presence.

Soon, the front doors opened, and half a dozen ydris soldiers stepped inside. They took up the empty chairs, leaving only a few vacant seats. Calasiem waved a warrior forward, and he approached her chair.

"Where is my daughter?" she whispered in her native language.

The warrior replied, "She should arrive soon, my lady. We're having trouble finding her."

Calasiem simmered. "There are enemies in our lands, T'kyrus. Find her."

The warrior bowed and then swiftly exited the building.

The room fell silent when Calasiem shifted in her seat. Everyone turned to her, and she inhaled a deep breath, squaring her shoulders.

"War is coming," she remarked. "The Klaet'il attack during the brink of a foreign invasion. They seek to disrupt the balance and wash our colors in black." Her pause was long and thoughtful as she eyed each person in the room. "The ydris have sworn neutrality. We will not take up arms in your conflicts. Our lives are sworn to the sacred Ko'ehlaeu'at."

"Master Eirean, if I may," Reiman started. "The Klaet'il have come to do what everyone in this forest has conspired to achieve." He paused with intent. "They seek to capture Drimil'Nizotl...They seek to harm Nerana."

A heavy tension fell through the large chamber. Aélla held her breath, ready to defend her companion should the Eirean see to hand Neer over to the Klaet'il or humans.

"N'iossea and the others will return to this village," Elidyr explained. "If he's here for Drimil'Nizotl—"

"Then his pursuits are in vain, Commander," Reiman said.

Elidyr glared at him, a heavy suspicion lingering in his deep blue eyes. "Should we sacrifice our people for this drimil'lana? A *human* sorceress?"

"Hey!" Thallon pointed a finger in his brother's face. "The forest has decided her fate. Neer is one of us now, and

I'll be damned if any of you are going to go against that judgement!"

An ydris soldier spoke from across the table. His strong voice rattled through the air, using foreign words most of the outsiders couldn't understand. But Aélla could, and she allowed him to speak as he taunted the evae and called for Neer's execution.

When his voice fell silent, Aélla said in his native tongue, "You may think us weak, but unless we put an end to this chaos, you won't stand a chance."

His wide eyes fixed on her, and he said, "The evae are prideful and full of scorn. The ruana are wicked beyond reason. These have washed our colors. These have *killed* the sacred trees!"

"They aren't dead yet," Aélla proclaimed before speaking evaesh for all to hear. "We can end this. Nerana has proven her worth—she is *not* like the others!"

"That is a foolish wish, Master Drimil," another ydris said. "Ruanafeil will bring songs of sorrow and wrath. The world's melodies will be diluted. Everything will fall, as it has done before."

Thallon leaned close to Aélla and asked, "What are they saying?"

Aélla exhaled an exasperated sigh. She closed her eyes, gathering her thoughts. Fighting against the strands of anger and strife pulling at her heart, causing her to reflect on all that had and could go wrong. Releasing the tension built in her chest, she explained, "They believe Nerana is responsible for this…I think they want to hand her over to the Klaet'il or Ianathess and end the war."

Thallon scoffed while shaking his head. He leaned forward, burying his face in his hands.

Reiman spoke up, laying a blanket of dread over Aélla as he said, "I have an alternative suggestion."

Everyone turned to him, and the room fell deathly silent. Aélla's fists clutched atop her thighs, and she waited, knowing what he would say. Fearing that the others might agree…that *Neer* might agree.

"Hand her to the Brotherhood," he said. "She belongs with us. We still have many soldiers back home. She can return and train with our most esteemed scholars and finally put an end to this war."

Everyone looked at one another, and the easement of their expressions told of their approval. Their *relief*. Neer was nothing more than a tool for them—a pawn to toss away or use to strengthen and fight. But Aélla understood the cost of such oppression. She knew the weight it put on Neer's shoulders—to be pushed aside or viewed as anything less than human.

"No," Aélla said when the others murmured their agreement. The quiet chatter fell silent, and she stood, her dark eyes seething with power and control. "Nerana is my guardian. She has agreed to see me to Tre'lan Rothar, and I have accepted her with honor."

Her eyes narrowed with contempt.

"If you want her to be placed in the protection of the Brotherhood, then you will give that choice to *her*."

"Master Drimil," Calasiem started, "you would truly see Drimil'Nizotl on your quest to—"

"Her name is Nerana." The Eirean was silenced by Aélla's daring eyes. "And she is not evil. She is not full of madness or hatred. She's the result of the malice that *you* have all set upon her!" She paused, taking in the defeat and shame in their eyes. "I won't see her fall. I won't allow this world to crumble."

"Forgive me, Master Drimil," Reiman started, stoking the flames of Aélla's growing rage.

She pushed them away as best she could, but they rose to the surface, bringing sweat to her brow and redness to her cheeks.

"But where are the rest of your guardians? Surely, you have more than Y'ven and this scholar, whom, might I add, allowed the Nasir to take hold of one of the most deadly, dangerous weapons known to man."

Aélla's eyes narrowed and fury sweltered.

Reiman continued, "Aside from Nerana and your brother—who we all know murdered your father in cold blood— there are two others...but they aren't here in this council chamber. Why is that?"

Aélla swallowed her anger, fighting harder than she ever had. Thallon's chair squealed when he stood, ready to defend her, but Aélla lifted her hand, and he fell silent. All eyes were set upon her. Their cold, conflicted gazes tore through her body and mind. She closed her eyes and willed her emotions away, just as she was taught long ago.

"Thurandír is young," she admitted. "This is no place for a newly vetted warrior. And as for Klaud…" Her eyes shifted to Reiman, and for a moment, she held the look of her brother: cold and daring. Powerful. "He was exiled for escorting *your* daughter to the Trials of Blood."

Her eyes shifted to each of the warriors at the table.

"I have taken the vows of Drimil'Rothar, and you have all entrusted this journey to me. I will not fail you." She paused, finding her resolve. "And I trust that you won't fail me."

Chapter Forty-Six

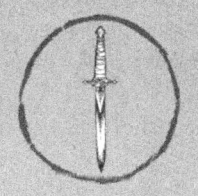

The Power of Rage
Nerana

Neer leaned over Avelloch with her hands on his chest, pushing strong magic into him. The tendrils of ice cut like razors as energy spiraled down her arms and through her palms. She felt every slow beat of his heart throbbing through her veins. The poison coursing through him lay a thick, cold blanket against her flesh. For hours every day, she had him given her energy, keeping him alive as the venom ran its course.

Blaid stood at her side, his fur brushing against her arm and breaking her concentration. She exhaled a deep breath and slowly pulled away. Her eyes shifted to the open window, where the sun rose higher in the cloudless afternoon sky. Neer glanced at her arms, noticing how strong and healthy she appeared. Her complexion never faded as she expelled her energy. Black lines didn't craze her eyes.

She felt powerful. Strong.

Unstoppable.

Neer met Blaid's eyes, and he turned to Avelloch. She followed his gaze. Her fingers trailed along the four black markings, like thick scratches, that etched his skin from his upper chest to his shoulder blade. Dark lines crawled away from the marks, giving his skin the appearance of being cracked and broken.

"He'll make it," she said to Blaid, though the words were meant for herself. She had to believe he would survive. There had been too much loss in her life. Too much pain for him to die. The Divines were cruel and merciless, but even they wouldn't lay so much grief and despair upon one soul. She had to believe that; otherwise, the void she stepped closer toward would swallow her whole.

Heavy paws padded against the wooden floor as Blaid stepped away, finding a spot to lay across the room. Neer watched him, thankful for his protection and company. Should anything happen to Avelloch, at least she'd hold a piece of him with their shared companion.

Sunlight brightened the room, crawling with orange light across the walls before touching Neer's cold skin. She inhaled a breath, feeling its power and warmth. Energy sizzled deep inside, culminating with the warmth of her flesh.

She glanced at Avelloch and turned her palm upward. Concentrating on the heat simmering inside, roiling through her veins like a hot cauldron, she ignited a small flame atop her palm. Sweat glistened against her skin, and she focused heavily on her energy, keeping control of the small, lapping fire.

Her skin flushed as heat radiated from deep within. The flame grew hotter, and she carefully held her arm over Avelloch's head. Orange light danced across his skin, drawing sweat that pulled the poison from his body. Keeping focus on her left hand, she lifted her right and fought to grasp the liquid seeping from his pores. But the energy of two opposing elements was unstable. She couldn't willfully control both.

With a light exhale, she kept the flame alight and wiped his forehead with a cloth.

After several minutes, the heat became unbearable. She closed her fist, extinguishing the flame into a stream of smoke. With a deep exhale, she leaned forward, pressing her fists against the edge of the mattress. Sweat dripped from her face, landing with the stained droplets from her previous attempts at performing the same cleansing ritual.

She drank from a waterskin and turned when a yellow bird flew in through the window. Neer stared at the creature, and her heart was numb, wishing for it to be someone she knew. Someone she would never see again. The bird brought itself to the edge of the dresser, and Neer took several deep breaths, unable to quell the emotions rising in her throat.

Through a trembling lip, she said, "Gil...?"

The bird tilted its head aside and then soared out of the window. A crushing blow hit her chest, and she leaned forward, gasping for air. He was gone. Truly gone. Turned by the Nasir into a horrid creature of darkness. A fate worse than death itself. But the weight of sorrow was numb, and it sank deep into her soul, anchoring her to the cold truth of reality.

Blaid moved to her side and nudged his head into her hip. She sank to her knees and held him close, accepting his comfort.

Feeling as though the room was closing in, Neer stood, took a long glance at Avelloch, and then left. As she opened the door, Thurandír, who had been preparing to knock, stepped back.

"Neer!" he exclaimed. "We're about to go training with the vaxros! Want to come?"

"His name is Y'ven," she said, attempting to appear happy. But the sorrow clung to her eyes like a magnet, revealing the truth of her pain.

Thurandír chuckled. "Saying *vaxros* is much more triumphant, don't you think? No one will mess with us if they know we've got a desert beast on our side."

Neer glowered at his use of such horrid slang. With no energy for an argument, she gave him a nod, agreeing to train. Thurandír raised a fist into the air in his excitement. He took Neer's arm and led her through the crowded inn. Blaid sat in the doorway of Avelloch's room, guarding him from potential intruders.

Neer trailed behind Thurandír, politely stepping past patrons as she headed for the door. Stepping outside, she was met with droves of ydris and avel wandering the bridges and trails. The ydris wore thick armor made of leaves and vines, prepared for battle should the hammer of war strike upon them.

The air was heavy and cold without the warm flow of magic drifting through the air. Neer crossed her arms over her chest, fighting against late autumn's chill. Her eyes were glued to the forest, searching for the Klaet'il and gazing at the softly glowing Trees sprawled throughout the forest.

Wandering down the bridges and paths, Thurandír led her to the center of town. A metropolis of huts, shops, armories, and inns, the large area was full of villagers and soft murmuring voices. Moving to the left, Thurandír opened the door to a large building and ushered Neer inside.

The scent of cinnamon and apples filled her nose. Wooden chairs and tables were spread throughout the crowded room. A square bar rested in its center, where two bakers had pies, bread, and pastries set out for anyone to take. Pitchers of water and wine were among them, and Neer wasted no time filling a glass. She drank her fill before wiping her lips.

"This way," Thurandír called. He snatched half a loaf of cinnamon bread from the bar and tossed it back to Neer, claiming she needed the meal.

She caught it and followed him down a narrow hall, then out of the backdoor and into the forest.

Neer lifted her eyes to the trees. They danced and swayed, but their songs were hollow. Another breeze shifted the air, carrying the weeping sounds of a faint cry. Villagers walked the bridges and trails, speaking with quiet conversations, appearing as if they hadn't heard the wailing or felt its sorrow.

Neer returned her attention to the forest, searching for the source of the cries. Another whisper flowed through the air, coming from the east.

"You coming?" Thurandír called. "We're almost there!"

She stepped closer, ignoring the whispers and trailing after Thurandír, but something caught her eye. Turning to the east, she noticed a figure lying in the woods. Her evergreen robes were stained with dirt, and platinum hair fell from its braid, tumbling across the grass like liquid white.

"Aélla!" Neer exclaimed, then rushed to her side. Moving closer, the pang of hopelessness and dread moved through her, crashing against her soul as pain that wasn't her own sweltered within. She felt the sorrow and confusion of a life fading into the abyss. With every cry, it grew dimmer, yet its pain raged on.

Thurandír fell to Aélla's side, while Neer scanned the forest, searching for the source of the painful cries that brought Aélla to her knees.

"Drimil!" Thurandír pulled Aélla's hair back, revealing her face, which was twisted in agony.

She clutched her hands to her chest and groaned. Neer winced as the voice ripped through her, screaming.

Pleading.

"What's happening?" Thurandír asked, glancing at Neer "Do something!"

Neer stared down at Aélla, trying to make sense of the pain she felt. While its harsh sting was hardly a scratch against Neer's mind, it immobilized Aélla, shackling her to the ground with tormenting pain. The shadow of a raven swept overhead, and Neer lifted her eyes to Altvára perched atop a branch nearby.

Thurandír said, "What's happening to her? What's—"

"Move!"

Klaud's voice rose from the soft murmuring of the crowd. He pushed through with Calasiem and Thallon. His jaw clenched when he noticed Aélla curled on the ground, writhing in agony.

Neer stepped closer to Aélla, reaching out for her, but Calasiem stopped her.

"Don't," she said. "Do not touch her."

"What do you—"

"Your magic is unstable, Drimil. If you touch her, your energies could collide." The Eirean's eyes bore into hers. "She could die."

Neer's eyes widened with fear. Klaud knelt to the ground and brought his face close to Aélla's. His voice was a soft whisper, and he tenderly stroked her back. Unable to speak, Aélla merely shook her head. Redness stained her face and veins swelled in her neck.

"What's happening?" Thurandír asked, his voice panicked.

"It's the imbalance," Calasiem suggested. "Galdir is weak. Any sense of dark energy will drench her soul in pain."

"What can we do?" Neer asked. "There must be something!"

"We must—"

"*Ikala...*," Aélla wheezed, repeating the words filtering through her and Neer's minds. They were spoken in a language Neer didn't know.

The others fell silent, listening to her strained voice.

"*Nourami...ikala de...*"

Calasiem knelt beside her, and her eyes filled with tears. "Why are you saying this?" she asked. "How do you—"

"She's repeating it," Neer explained.

Everyone turned to her, their brows knitted.

"The voice."

Calasiem gritted her teeth. She stood tall and whipped her head from left to right. "T'Kyrus!" she called, and a warrior stepped forward. "Where is my daughter?"

His eyes widened with terror, and Calasiem's rage strengthened.

Neer lifted her eyes, searching the forest. She didn't know whose voice spoke to her. She didn't know what the words repeating in her mind meant, but she knew where they were coming from.

Before Neer had the chance to explain, Aélla pushed herself up on weak arms. She whimpered while clutching her chest. Klaud spoke to her, but she remained silent. Fighting through the agony, Aélla pointed to the east, where the echoes were strongest.

Calasiem marched away, calling a group of nearby guards forward to accompany her. Neer followed behind with Thallon. With every step, the pain of death sliced through her mind. She winced and gritted her teeth, fighting against its iron grip.

"Neer?" Thallon asked, keeping his voice low. He touched her arm and slowed his pace, putting distance between them and the others who marched ahead. "What's going on?" Thallon asked. "This is what happened in the desert, isn't it? Before Y'ven was attacked by the wisper."

SHADOWS OF NYN'DIRA

Neer shook her head, breathing heavy. The weight of sorrow crushed her soul. "No," she said. "This is different...It isn't a creature of darkness."

"What is it?" Thallon pulled her shoulder and came to a stop.

She avoided his gaze, not wanting to say aloud what she feared to be truth.

"What are you talking about? Why was Aélla—"

"I don't know, Thallon!" she snapped. Turning away, she crossed her arms, upset by her outburst. "We have to hurry."

As she stepped away, Thallon gripped his hair. His worried eyes glanced through the forest. With a huff, he raced after Neer, quickly matching her pace as they walked together. "What did Aélla say?" he asked. "Was she speaking *Iana'Igril*?"

The warriors ahead came to a halt, and Neer was overcome by the swell of cold, icy energy. She inhaled a deep breath, fighting against its ache and pain. Feeling its power and rage.

A hard lump formed in her throat as they approached the line of warriors. Calasiem stood several paces ahead. Her eyes were unblinking and body was stiff. Maeve's sobbing voice whispered through Neer's mind, battering her with misery and fear.

The forest was silent in its sorrow. Not a weep of regret or song of peace rang through the air as they stood in the presence of such devastation.

Blood puddled in the grass, dripping from Maeve's hoofed feet. She was strung up between two trees by her arms. Her antlers and face were painted in dark red. The skin of her back was cut and stretched outward, displaying wings like an angel of death.

Carved into her stomach, weeping in the dying sunlight, were the markings of Klaet'il symbols.

"What does that say?" Neer asked, her voice hollow with fear.

Thallon was stiff as he stared at the symbols. Slowly, he pushed the words out, saying, "*Tromala ytekk*...Blood for blood."

Maeve's voice continued whispering through Neer's mind, sinking her to her knees. She clutched her ears, fighting against the weight of her affliction.

"*Ikala... Nouramí...ikala de...,*" Maeve's fading voice wept. "Help...Mother...help me..."

Neer whimpered as icy energy tore at her soul, fizzling through her veins. While the others were entranced by their sorrow and grief, Neer felt the swell of betrayal and anger that rose from the trees. They clung to her sensitive magic, tearing at the strands of her sanity. The icy sting vibrated through her core like footsteps on the ground, charging forward. Beating faster until all she felt were the cold, ruthless tremors of war.

"We have to go," she said, reaching for Thallon's hand.

But he didn't notice. His wide eyes were fixed on the words cut into Maeve's flesh.

"Thallon?"

A shift in the wind tore through the forest, bringing songs of rage and dread. Neer lifted her eyes and fought to stand against the onslaught of agony smashing against her with every gale.

Light expanded from the north before a wave of heat tore through the forest. Everyone staggered back as Maeve's body ignited with flame. The orange glow of a setting sun sprayed across the horizon from behind her, and the world, for a moment, appeared as if it was set ablaze.

Neer gazed at the image, realizing she had seen it before, somewhere deep in her mind. The fires and rage that engulfed everything. It was familiar, but she didn't know how.

Calasiem stared up at her daughter. Glistening tears streamed down her face as she stared upon her scorching, bubbled flesh.

Her sorrow ceased when the crunch of bone pulled a choked breath from her lungs, and Calasiem collapsed to the ground. Blood splashed through the air, and she lay in the puddle gathering beneath her daughter's hooved feet. She was motionless, the sorrow still heavy in her unblinking, lifeless eyes. Maeve's blood dripped from her legs, landing softly atop her mother's face, coating the shaft of an arrow lodged in her skull.

A rush of panic and sorrow burned through Neer as a cold wind swept by. The ydris gasped, their eyes darting to the forest where nature wept.

The pop and crack of burning wood resounded through the empty lands where an orange glow strengthened from the east, in the direction of Galdir. Neer's heart turned to ice when tendrils of heat wisped through the forest as the trees were set ablaze.

And the rhythm of war crashed through their souls as the Klaet'il charged from the haze.

EPILOGUE

The Drums of War

THE FOREST WEPT WITH SONGS OF GRIEF as the sun tucked itself beyond the horizon. Darkening shades of amber lit up the sky, creating a haze of firelight across the quiet world. Voices echoed like the sound of crashing waves as steel clashed and flesh was torn. Light glistened against the blades, and bodies collapsed to the ground, trampled or gashed. Horse hooves beat against the soil, trembling with the deadly tempo of war. Evae charged in formation, striking down the Klaet'il who screamed wildly into the night.

Fires raged, engulfing every tree, burning every blade of grass as it tore through the forest, crawling closer toward Galdir. Animals scurried, fleeing the smoke and ash. Trees cracked and collapsed to dust, spraying embers through the blackened air.

Orange heat crawled across the floating petals of the Ko'ehlaeu'at trees, quickly evaporating them into ash. The forest wailed as each glowing tree was scorched. Its fire burned blue as pure, unadulterated magic was released into the air.

With each dying light, Galdir's magic grew dim. Its glow softened.

Cold winds swept westward, sending waves of sadness and pain that could be felt across the world. The light stings of magic prickled the face of a man in white. His robes rustled in the cool breeze where he stood atop a cliffside along the Whispering Mountains. From this vantage, he could see far across the forest to the white luminance of the largest Tree. A glowing speck above the sea of darkness.

A soft orange glow crawled across the horizon, surrounding the towering light. The magic that sizzled in the air dwindled as the light of the Tree began to fade.

The man inhaled a deep breath, tasting the winds of change.

Moonlight shone from the night sky, reflecting against his pristine beard and dark brown hair. White robes hemmed in gold appeared purple beneath the brightness from above.

Green eyes tore away from the Tree as a figure approached the man's side. He glanced at the curate, whose robes were embroidered with the Sigil of the Order along the upper right breast.

"Grace," Mauro, a man no older than twenty, started with a bow. "It's time."

The man stood taller, breathing in a slow, satisfied drawl. His eyes returned to the Tree, and he watched the light slowly fade, becoming nearly invisible against the horizon. He gave a slight nod, and Mauro quickly stepped away.

Another wind swept past, this time, silent. Empty of its ubiquitous sting.

A low rumble undulated the ground as hundreds of soldiers marched below. Their steel plated armor and iron swords rattled through the silence.

High Priest Beinon watched from his perch, his eyes never veering from the Tree, as his Knights stepped through the weakened magic and into the forest.

The story continues…

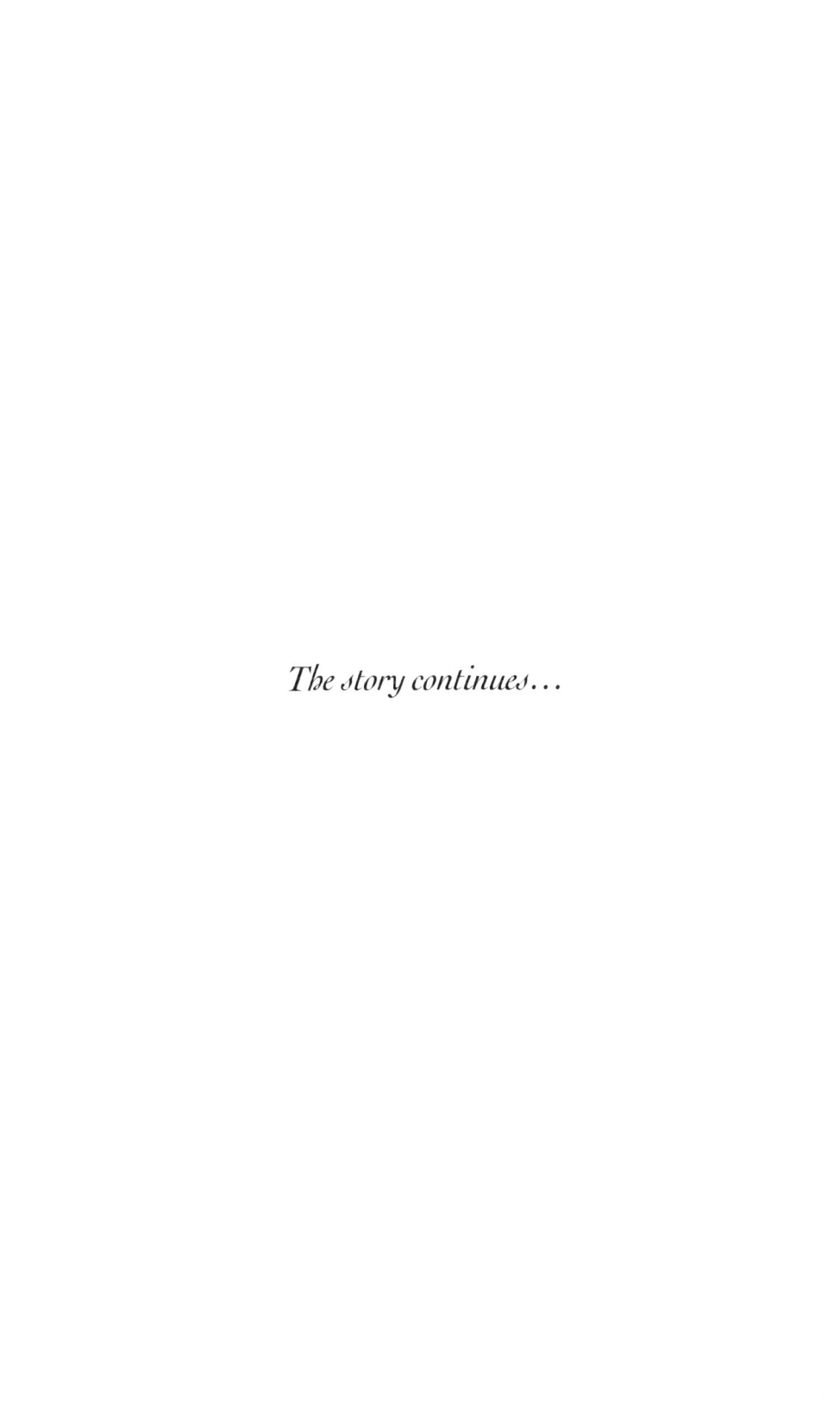

About the Author

H.C. Newell is a Nashville based #1 best-selling epic fantasy author. She started writing screenplays as a child, and that passion for creating stories grew into a love of fiction. In 2014 she started her novel series, and quickly realized that the adventures and lore of an epic fantasy world was her calling. It was then that she devoted all her time, passion, and love into creating the world and characters of *Fallen Light*.

When not writing, H.C. enjoys hiking, photography, playing video games, and spending time with her niece and nephews.

For more information about H.C. Newell and the *Fallen Light* series, please visit:
www.hcnewell.com

THANK YOU

Thank you so much for reading Shadows of Nyn'Dıra (and, well, *all* of my series thus far! That's a huge commitment, and I can't even begin to tell you what it means to me)

I sincerely hope that you enjoyed it! If so, **please consider leaving a review.** As you know, reviews are the lifeblood of all authors, and while you may not feel that your opinion matters - it does!

It isn't the content of the reviews but the quantity. **Whether you leave a detailed analysis, a single sentence, or just a star rating - it all matters.**

So, if you enjoyed the story, I'd love for you to continue to support me by leaving a review on GoodReads and Amazon!

You can also follow me on Twitter or Instagram! I love to meet new readers and talk about my books! Don't be shy, come say hi! I don't bite (hard).

A Storm of Sorrows, book four in the Fallen Light series, is expected to release no later than 2025.

hcnewell.com

Acknowledgements

In addition to those mentioned at the beginning of the novel, I would like to say a special thank you to each person listed below.

<u>Authors:</u>
Sadir S. Samir
Angela Knotts Morse
Daniel T. Jackson
Joshua S. Edwards
Kian Ardalan
Thiago Abdalla

<u>Readers and reviewers:</u>
Dublin Book Reviews
David & Jeeves
Butters
QUINN
Enigmasedge
Bobo
JAMEDI MAH BOYYY
D&J's Epic quest
Charlie from down undaa
Gluteus Maximus and WINI! (Fantasy Fellowship)
Fantasy Book Critic
Craig Bookwyrm
Dominish Books
Andrew Wizardly Reads (my #1 fan)
FanFiAddict
The Broken Binding

To my followers and friends who support this series and encourage me to keep going… *thank you.*

Glossary

Glossary

This glossary is meant to be read <u>after</u> completion of the novel. It contains all characters, references, and places visited throughout the novel

Evaesh Name Translations

Aélla (AYLA) *Joyous spirit*
Aen'mysvaral (ain-MISS-varr-all) *One with a mark upon his face.* Aen'mysvaral received his *sitria* due to the deep scar across his face that blinded his left eye.
Aegrandír (ay-gran-deer) *Man of strength*
Avelloch (av-uh-lock) *Protector of the many*
Azae'l (ah-zayl) *Songbirds;* Childhood nickname for Aélla, given by Klaud
Ithronél (ee-throw-nell) *Fierce warrior*
Klaud (cloud) *Kindness*
Morganis (morr-gone-iss) *Moon and stars*
Nasir (nah-seer) *Bringer of death*
Thallon (talon) *Predator; bird of prey*
Thurandír (thur-an-deer) *Man of compassion*
Zaeril (zay-rill) *Wolf, Lone Wolf*

Magical Realms and Terms

Drimil (drem-ell) *Magic bearer.* This title is generally given to those who are born with the power of all seven realms of magic, though it can be used to describe anyone holding magical energy
Drimil'lana (drem-ell lahn-ah) *Magic bearing human.* To both the humans and non-humans, a drimil'lana is considered an abomination that must be destroyed
Drimil'Rothar (drem-ell row-THARR) *Sorcerer of Light.* This title is given to those who take the vows of Drimil'Rothar and seek guidance from the Light

Drimil'Nizotl (drem-ell nih-ZOLT) *Sorcerer of Chaos*. This title is given to those who are strong in dark energy

Eólin (ee-o-lin) *Unknown; mystery*. This title is given to those who were born without magical energy, yet they possess its power. These individuals are not First Blood and typically wield energy from one of the seven realms of magic

Creatures of Darkness Monsters manifested from the energy of the dead

Kanavin (kahn-ah-veen) *Creatures of the night*

Ko'ehlacu'at (koh-ay-lay-oo-aht) *Giver of purity and peace*. Magically enhanced trees that cleanse the world's energy, keeping in balance

Haeth'r (hay-thurr) *Reanimated corpse*

Tre'lan (tray-lahn) *Magical Realm*. This term is used in conjunction with its corresponding energy

Aenwyn (on-win) *Elements*. This energy allows its user to produce, manipulate, and cast elemental energy, including fire, water, wind, and rock

Leirin (lye-reen) *Restoration*. This energy allows its user to produce, manipulate, and cast restorative spells, including minor healing, advanced healing, and wound transference

Nizotl (niz-olt) *Darkness and chaos*. This energy allows its user to absorb, manipulate, and cast dark energy

Rothar (Row-THARR) *Light*. This energy allows its user to absorb, manipulate, and cast Light energy

Udur (oo-durr) *Illusion*. This energy allows its user to produce, manipulate, and cast illusionary spells, including empathic manipulation, thought transference, and limited mind control

Vethar (veth-urr) *Time*. This energy allows its user to produce, manipulate, and cast teleportative spells, including long and short-range teleportation, apportion, and transtemporal travel

Zynther (zin-thurr) *Mortality*. This energy allows its user to produce, manipulate, and cast necromancy spells. This includes death prevention, reanimation, and mediumship

Human Organizations and Religion

Broken Order Brotherhood A rebel faction that seeks to dismantle the Order of Saro
Order of Saro A religious regime that oversees the human led country of Laeroth
Knights of the Order Genetically modified soldiers
Shadow Blades A mercenary band that follows heavily in the ways of Nizotl, the Divine of darkness, deceit, and trickery
Thorne A bounty hunter with the Shadows Blades
Gaelthral Thorne's Creature of Darkness
The Circle of Six Six Divines worshipped by the Order of Saro
The Circle of Seven Seven Divines worshipped by the Order Saro, former
Rothar (row-THARR) Overseer of the immortal plane
Numera (new-MARE-ah) Divine of nature and elements
Kirena (keer-ee-nah) Divine of purity, compassion, and health
Udur (OO-dur) Divine of wisdom and knowledge
Zynther (zin-thurr) Divine of life and death
Nizotl (nih-ZOLT) Divine of trickery, deceit, and darkness
Vethar (veth-urr) Divine of history and prophecy, former
Ateus (Aye-tee-us) Man-God of chaos and destruction, former
The Old Ways Outdated belief in the Circle of Seven
The New Ways Current belief in the Circle of Six, which excludes the Divine Vethar

Forest Races and Clans

Ahn'clave (on-clave) *First Blood*. A race of evae who vanished without a trace centuries ago
Avel (ah-vell) *Protector of the Realm* Warrior pact of clan Rhyl
Evae A humanoid race native to Nyn'Dira, Vleland, Aragoth, and the Whispering Mountains
Tóavel (tow-ah-vell) *Protector of power* Warrior pact of clan Klaet'il
E'liaa (ee-lee-ah) *Mixed blood* Used in reference to those with human-evaesh blood and the humans or evae they coexist with
Gorn (GORN) A goblin-like race indigenous to Nyn'Dira, allies of clan Klaet'il
Klaet'il (klee-ah-till) *One with nature*. The largest evaesh clan, native to Nyn'Dira
Rhyl (rill) *Dawn of peace*. The second largest evaesh clan, native to Nyn'Dira

Saevrala (save-rah-lah) *Seekers of truth*. The third largest evaesh, natives to the Whispering Mountains
Ydris (EE-driss) Half-evae, half-deer race. The original inhabitants of Nyn'Dira.

Evaesh Words and Phrases

Aardn (are-din) Meeting place of the Eirean
Aeroniat (air-on-ee-ot) *First Light*. The first season of the year; spring
Aithmir (ay-th-meer) Herbal remedy to reduce infection
Alveryan (al-vair-EE-an) First Blood term used in reference to their artifacts, language, or existence
Arnemaeus (arr-nah-may-iss) *Somber Stone*. A stone with the unique ability to absorb and store dark energy
Arnikvia (arr-neek-vee-ah) *A gathering of peace*. An annual ceremony celebrating the life and passing of loved ones
Arun (ah-roon) *Magical artifact*. Describes any object that is magically enhanced
Avour'il (ow-vor-ill) *Sacred Lands*. A dangerous rite of passage banished by many clans
Brenavae (bree-nah-vay) *Brother*. Used in reference to those who share no blood relation
Brenavath (bree-nah-vath) *Band of Brothers; Brotherhood*
Brenavas (bree-nah-vass) *Brothers*
Clavia Muinsii (clay-vee-ah m-yoo-in-see) *Shadow and night*. A weapon with the ability to transform any living being into a Creature of Darkness
Dira (deer-ah) *A gathering of trees*
Dren'seol (dren-see-ole) *One with my soul*. Used in reference to animal companions
Dro'fahmel (drow fah-mell) *Soul of the damned*. A crude term meant for the unworthy or monstrous
Ean'tretaas (ane tray-tahs) *Improving in skill*. Said by Avelloch to Loryk in the Trials of Blood
Élet'atla (Ee-let aht-lah) *Blood for salvation*. A Klaet'il cleansing ritual that includes opening ones back and separating their ribs from their spine. This form of death is meant to cleanse their victim's soul
Fil'veraal (fill-verr-all) *Unworthy, unwashed, unclean*. A branded symbol to mark one's banishment

Fisonaar (fee-s-oh-narr) *First Leaf.* The third season of the year; autumn
Fisthraa (fiss-th-raa) *Abomination.* A crude term meant for the unworthy or monstrous
F'yet (fee-yet) *Fool or incompetent.*
Grenör toveii (gree-norr tow-vee) *What have you done?*
Ik (eek) *Unworthy.* Used in reference to the e'liaan villages
Ilitran (ill-ah-trahn) *A place of power.* Ancient monoliths containing magical energy of powerful drimil
I'Sylyasar (ee-sill-i-ah-sarr) *Sun's Flame.* The second season of the year; summer
Kanavin (kahn-ah-veen) *Creatures of the night.* Monsters manifested from the energy of the dead
Kila (kee-lah) *Shit;fuck.* Crude term of aggravation
Kila grot fiin (kee-lah groht feen) *Pathetic piece of shit.* Spoken to Avelloch by Aegrandír
Lana'igrit (lahn-ah ee-grit) *Human language*
Lanathess (lahn-ah-thess) *Humankind*
Lana'thoviin (lahn-ah tow-veen) *Human territory.* Used in reference to the human country of Laeroth
Lyansthaa (lye-an-s-thaa) Gemstones that are reactive to magical energy
Lyena faa (lye-en-ah fah) *One without respect.* Used in reference to unruly children
Malvainha (mall-vain-ah) *Frost Fall.* Fourth season of the year, winter
Mela'anum (me-lah ah-num) *I love you.* A term of affection said by those in love
Meena'fromein (me-nah frow-me-in) *An unwanted disgrace*
Meena'keen (me-nah keen) *Unwanted; outsider*
M'yashk (me-yash-k) *Evaesh wine*
N'aeth (nay-th) *Traveling stone.* Black transporting stones used to teleport its user from one place to another. May only be used once before its energy is depleted
Naik'avel (nigh-kah-vell) *The end.* A cycle that will consume the world with chaos
Nesiat (ness-ee-aht) *Soulless wanderer.* Title given to those who are banished
Nes'seil (ness-ee-ell) *Person of healing*
Nes'rávei (ness-rah-vee) *Place of healing*
Nyn (nin) *A place of beauty.* Nyn'Dira translates to mean *beautiful forest*
Rad'fyir (rad-f-year) *Cleansing of the spirit.* A ritualistic cleansing performed before battle

Revalor *The unseen.* A clear stone which allows its user to see that which cannot be seen. Used in Curse of the Fallen to reveal the entrance to the Trials of Blood.
See'nah (see-nah) *One who sees my soul*
Senavae (see-nah-vay) *Sister.* Used in reference to those who share no blood relation
Sitria (sih-tree-ah) *Second name.* Nicknames given to those who have proven themselves as warriors
Stia'dyr (stee-ah-deer) *Eyes of another.* Title given to those who can see through the eyes of animals
Spira'veil (spear-ah vale) *Survive.* Said by Avelloch to Loryk in the Trials of Blood
Tek'Brenavath (tech bree-nah-vath) *The Brotherhood*
Tiaavan (tee-ah-valm) Woven trinket meant to attract peace
Tyluaa (tie-lew-ah) *Food; a meal.* Said by Avelloch to Loryk in the Trials of Blood.
Tyluear (tie-lew-air) *Thank you.* Said by Avelloch to Loryk in the Trials of Blood.
Valaforael (val-ah-for-ale) *Unknown; unwelcome*
Zy'mashik (zye mah-sheek) *Ancient rune.* Said by Avelloch in the Trials of Blood

Printed in Great Britain
by Amazon